Marrakech Noir

Marrakech Noir

EDITED BY YASSIN ADNAN

BROOKLYN, NEW YORK, USA
BALLYDEHOB, CO. CORK, IRELAND

This collection comprises works of fiction. All names, characters, places, and incidents are the product of the authors' imaginations. Any resemblance to real events or persons, living or dead, is entirely coincidental.

Published by Akashic Books

Series concept by Tim McLoughlin and Johnny Temple
Marrakech map by Sohrab Habibion

ISBN: 978-1-61775-473-9
Library of Congress Control Number: 2017956561

First printing

Akashic Books
Brooklyn, New York, USA
Ballydehob, Co. Cork, Ireland
Twitter: @AkashicBooks
Facebook: AkashicBooks
E-mail: info@akashicbooks.com
Website: www.akashicbooks.com

ALSO IN THE AKASHIC NOIR SERIES

ATLANTA NOIR, edited by TAYARI JONES
BALTIMORE NOIR, edited by LAURA LIPPMAN
BARCELONA NOIR (SPAIN), edited by ADRIANA V. LÓPEZ & CARMEN OSPINA
BEIRUT NOIR (LEBANON), edited by IMAN HUMAYDAN
BELFAST NOIR (NORTHERN IRELAND), edited by ADRIAN McKINTY & STUART NEVILLE
BOSTON NOIR, edited by DENNIS LEHANE
BOSTON NOIR 2: THE CLASSICS, edited by DENNIS LEHANE, MARY COTTON & JAIME CLARKE
BRONX NOIR, edited by S.J. ROZAN
BROOKLYN NOIR, edited by TIM McLOUGHLIN
BROOKLYN NOIR 2: THE CLASSICS, edited by TIM McLOUGHLIN
BROOKLYN NOIR 3: NOTHING BUT THE TRUTH, edited by TIM McLOUGHLIN & THOMAS ADCOCK
BRUSSELS NOIR (BELGIUM), edited by MICHEL DUFRANNE
BUENOS AIRES NOIR (ARGENTINA), edited by ERNESTO MALLO
BUFFALO NOIR, edited by ED PARK & BRIGID HUGHES
CAPE COD NOIR, edited by DAVID L. ULIN
CHICAGO NOIR, edited by NEAL POLLACK
CHICAGO NOIR: THE CLASSICS, edited by JOE MENO
COPENHAGEN NOIR (DENMARK), edited by BO TAO MICHAËLIS
DALLAS NOIR, edited by DAVID HALE SMITH
D.C. NOIR, edited by GEORGE PELECANOS
D.C. NOIR 2: THE CLASSICS, edited by GEORGE PELECANOS
DELHI NOIR (INDIA), edited by HIRSH SAWHNEY
DETROIT NOIR, edited by E.J. OLSEN & JOHN C. HOCKING
DUBLIN NOIR (IRELAND), edited by KEN BRUEN
HAITI NOIR, edited by EDWIDGE DANTICAT
HAITI NOIR 2: THE CLASSICS, edited by EDWIDGE DANTICAT
HAVANA NOIR (CUBA), edited by ACHY OBEJAS
HELSINKI NOIR (FINLAND), edited by JAMES THOMPSON
INDIAN COUNTRY NOIR, edited by SARAH CORTEZ & LIZ MARTÍNEZ
ISTANBUL NOIR (TURKEY), edited by MUSTAFA ZIYALAN & AMY SPANGLER
KANSAS CITY NOIR, edited by STEVE PAUL
KINGSTON NOIR (JAMAICA), edited by COLIN CHANNER
LAGOS NOIR (NIGERIA), edited by CHRIS ABANI
LAS VEGAS NOIR, edited by JARRET KEENE & TODD JAMES PIERCE
LONDON NOIR (ENGLAND), edited by CATHI UNSWORTH
LONE STAR NOIR, edited by BOBBY BYRD & JOHNNY BYRD
LONG ISLAND NOIR, edited by KAYLIE JONES
LOS ANGELES NOIR, edited by DENISE HAMILTON
LOS ANGELES NOIR 2: THE CLASSICS, edited by DENISE HAMILTON
MANHATTAN NOIR, edited by LAWRENCE BLOCK
MANHATTAN NOIR 2: THE CLASSICS, edited by LAWRENCE BLOCK
MANILA NOIR (PHILIPPINES), edited by JESSICA HAGEDORN
MARSEILLE NOIR (FRANCE), edited by CÉDRIC FABRE
MEMPHIS NOIR, edited by LAUREEN P. CANTWELL & LEONARD GILL
MEXICO CITY NOIR (MEXICO), edited by PACO I. TAIBO II
MIAMI NOIR, edited by LES STANDIFORD
MISSISSIPPI NOIR, edited by TOM FRANKLIN
MONTANA NOIR, edited by JAMES GRADY & KEIR GRAFF
MONTREAL NOIR (CANADA), edited by JOHN McFETRIDGE & JACQUES FILIPPI
MOSCOW NOIR (RUSSIA), edited by NATALIA SMIRNOVA & JULIA GOUMEN
MUMBAI NOIR (INDIA), edited by ALTAF TYREWALA
NEW HAVEN NOIR, edited by AMY BLOOM
NEW JERSEY NOIR, edited by JOYCE CAROL OATES

NEW ORLEANS NOIR, edited by JULIE SMITH
NEW ORLEANS NOIR: THE CLASSICS, edited by JULIE SMITH
OAKLAND NOIR, edited by JERRY THOMPSON & EDDIE MULLER
ORANGE COUNTY NOIR, edited by GARY PHILLIPS
PARIS NOIR (FRANCE), edited by AURÉLIEN MASSON
PHILADELPHIA NOIR, edited by CARLIN ROMANO
PHOENIX NOIR, edited by PATRICK MILLIKIN
PITTSBURGH NOIR, edited by KATHLEEN GEORGE
PORTLAND NOIR, edited by KEVIN SAMPSELL
PRAGUE NOIR (CZECH REPUBLIC), edited by PAVEL MANDYS
PRISON NOIR, edited by JOYCE CAROL OATES
PROVIDENCE NOIR, edited by ANN HOOD
QUEENS NOIR, edited by ROBERT KNIGHTLY
RICHMOND NOIR, edited by ANDREW BLOSSOM, BRIAN CASTLEBERRY & TOM DE HAVEN
RIO NOIR (BRAZIL), edited by TONY BELLOTTO
ROME NOIR (ITALY), edited by CHIARA STANGALINO & MAXIM JAKUBOWSKI
SAN DIEGO NOIR, edited by MARYELIZABETH HART
SAN FRANCISCO NOIR, edited by PETER MARAVELIS
SAN FRANCISCO NOIR 2: THE CLASSICS, edited by PETER MARAVELIS
SAN JUAN NOIR (PUERTO RICO), edited by MAYRA SANTOS-FEBRES
SANTA CRUZ NOIR, edited by SUSIE BRIGHT
SÃO PAULO NOIR (BRAZIL), edited by TONY BELLOTTO
SEATTLE NOIR, edited by CURT COLBERT
SINGAPORE NOIR, edited by CHERYL LU-LIEN TAN
STATEN ISLAND NOIR, edited by PATRICIA SMITH
ST. LOUIS NOIR, edited by SCOTT PHILLIPS
STOCKHOLM NOIR (SWEDEN), edited by NATHAN LARSON & CARL-MICHAEL EDENBORG
ST. PETERSBURG NOIR (RUSSIA), edited by NATALIA SMIRNOVA & JULIA GOUMEN
TEHRAN NOIR (IRAN), edited by SALAR ABDOH
TEL AVIV NOIR (ISRAEL), edited by ETGAR KERET & ASSAF GAVRON
TORONTO NOIR (CANADA), edited by JANINE ARMIN & NATHANIEL G. MOORE
TRINIDAD NOIR (TRINIDAD & TOBAGO), edited by LISA ALLEN-AGOSTINI & JEANNE MASON
TRINIDAD NOIR: THE CLASSICS (TRINIDAD & TOBAGO), edited by EARL LOVELACE & ROBERT ANTONI
TWIN CITIES NOIR, edited by JULIE SCHAPER & STEVEN HORWITZ
USA NOIR, edited by JOHNNY TEMPLE
VENICE NOIR (ITALY), edited by MAXIM JAKUBOWSKI
WALL STREET NOIR, edited by PETER SPIEGELMAN
ZAGREB NOIR (CROATIA), edited by IVAN SRŠEN

FORTHCOMING

ACCRA NOIR (GHANA), edited by NANA-AMA DANQUAH
ADDIS ABABA NOIR (ETHIOPIA), edited by MAAZA MENGISTE
AMSTERDAM NOIR (NETHERLANDS), edited by RENÉ APPEL & JOSH PACHTER
BERKELEY NOIR, edited by JERRY THOMPSON & OWEN HILL
BERLIN NOIR (GERMANY), edited by THOMAS WÖRTCHE
BOGOTÁ NOIR (COLOMBIA), edited by ANDREA MONTEJO
COLUMBUS NOIR, edited by ANDREW WELSH-HUGGINS
HONG KONG NOIR, edited by JASON Y. NG & SUSAN BLUMBERG-KASON
HOUSTON NOIR, edited by GWENDOLYN ZEPEDA
JERUSALEM NOIR, edited by DROR MISHANI
MILWAUKEE NOIR, edited by TIM HENNESSY
NAIROBI NOIR (KENYA), edited by PETER KIMANI
SANTA FE NOIR, edited by ARIEL GORE
SYDNEY NOIR (AUSTRALIA), edited by JOHN DALE
VANCOUVER NOIR (CANADA), edited by SAM WIEBE

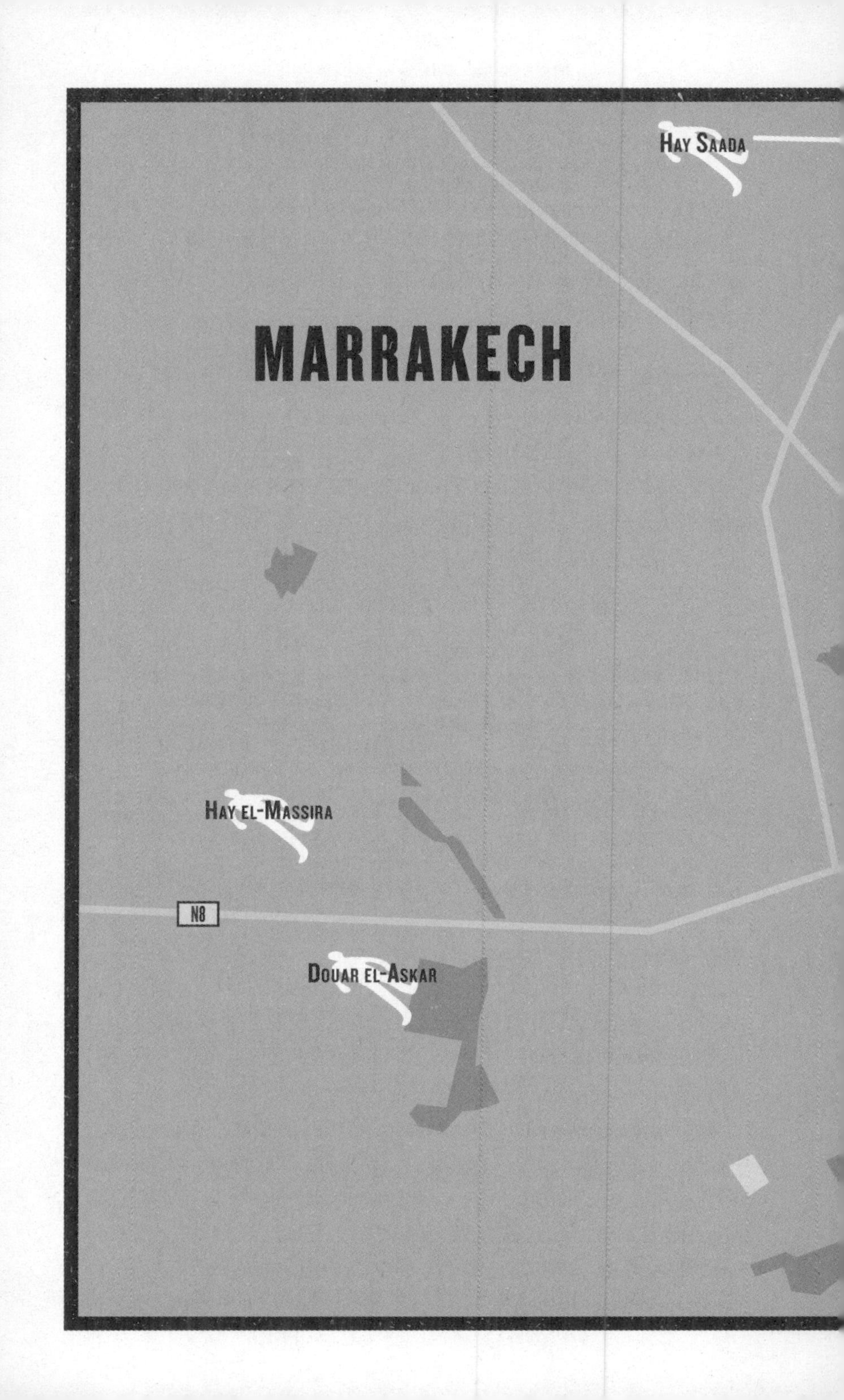
MARRAKECH
Hay Saada
Hay el-Massira
N8
Douar el-Askar

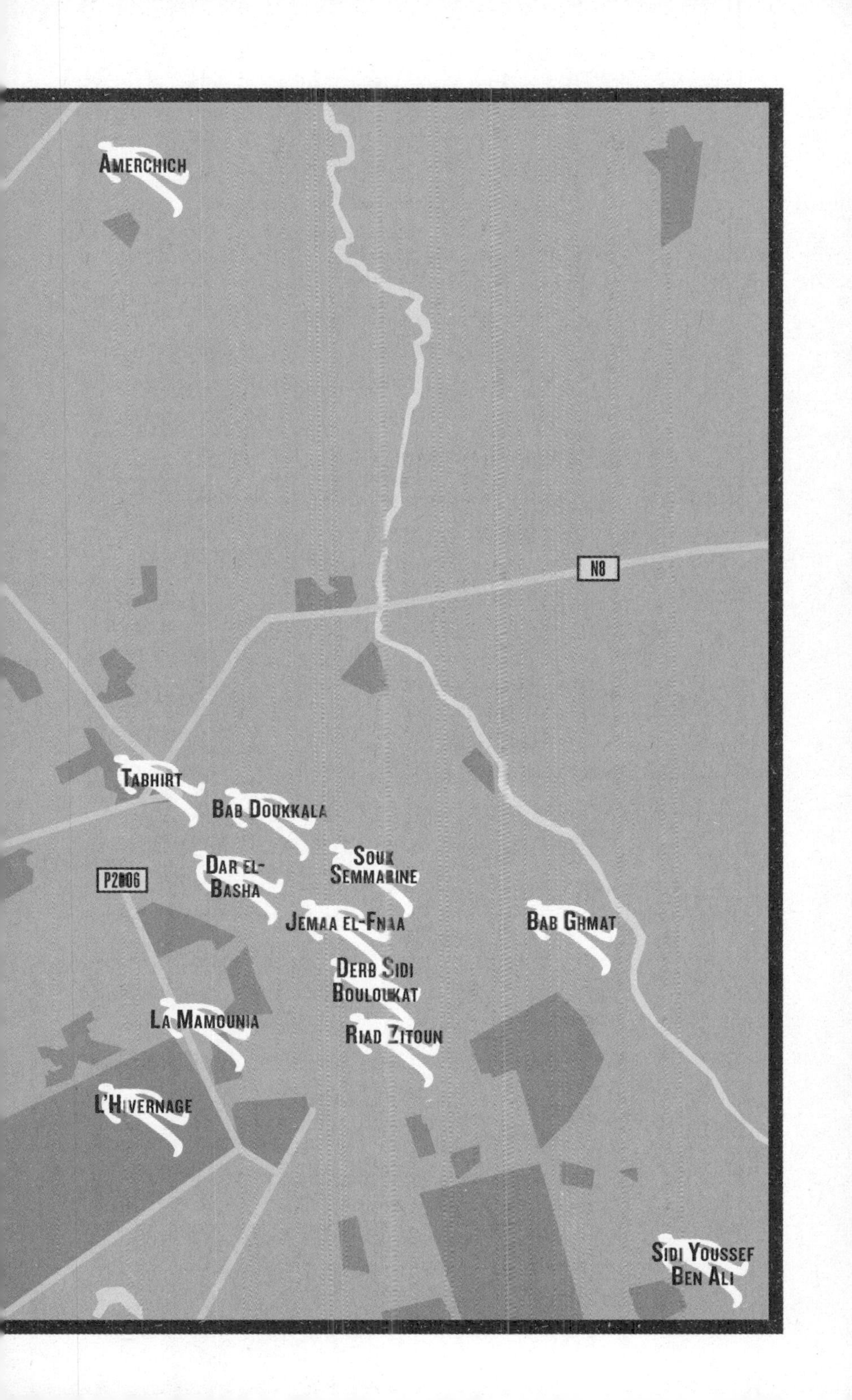

Amerchich
N8
Tabhirt
Bab Doukkala
Souk
Semmarine
Dar el-
Basha
P2006
Jemaa el-Fnaa
Bab Ghmat
Derb Sidi
Bouloukat
La Mamounia
Riad Zitoun
L'Hivernage
Sidi Youssef
Ben Ali

Table of Contents

PART III: OUTSIDE THE CITY'S WALLS

INTRODUCTION

City of Joy and Grit

When I agreed to edit *Marrakech Noir*, I didn't realize that I had just stepped into a well-laid trap. Marrakech—al-Hamra, the Red City, as Moroccans call it—has been linked to the color red since the Almoravid ruler Yusuf Ibn Tashfin founded the city in 1062. How could I change its color today? And to black, of all colors! For the city is red, and the people of Marrakech pray night and day to protect it from darkness, despair, and moodiness.

No one but palm trees remember that remote past, when bandits hid behind their slender trunks, waiting to ambush passing caravans. Whenever the convoys of al-Massamida tribes reached the place now known as Marrakech, they would whisper *morkosh* to each other in muffled fear, which meant *walk fast* in their language. According to some stories, this is where the city's name came from. But over the centuries the name has lost much of these dark connotations.

Moroccans today also call Marrakech "The Joyful City." The city is pledged to joy in all its forms, and the inhabitants actively seek it out. The city's days are bright and its nights are well-lit. Marrakechis are willing to read every type of story about the city—except those that are garbed in black. Even the storytellers of Jemaa el-Fnaa, the city's leading narrators, have always avoided dark tales in their enchanting *halqas*.

I used to frequent Jemaa el-Fnaa as a child, and I enjoyed listening to Gnaoua music as I rushed past snake charmers. Monkeys never appealed to me, and neither did the dancers and singers, but I would sometimes linger to watch an uneven boxing match, like a flyweight pitted against a cruiserweight. Sometimes girls faced off against boys, and many times the boys suffered a resounding defeat. But only the storytellers truly captivated me—stories such as *The Thousand and One Nights, al-Azaliya, al-Antariyah,* and *Hilaliya.* As soon as I spotted the so-called Doctor of Pests, one of my favorite storytellers, staggering toward one of the square's corners, I would drop everything and run to him. For me, he was the biggest star of the square. When he would disappear, I missed him. I knew that because of his addiction and his penchant for drinking in public he could be arrested at any time. When he would return, I would always ask him: "Where have you been, Doc?"

"I was in Hollanda," the doctor would reply quietly, using the Arabic name for the Netherlands. Thanks to the doctor, *Hollanda* became a euphemism for *prison*. The doctor once vanished from his *halqa* for many months—and when he reappeared again, I welcomed him with the same eagerness. That time, he claimed he had been in America. "I was working for the American army," he said.

No way, I thought. "That's too much, Doc," I said in disbelief.

"Don't get me wrong. I don't mean I was fighting beside them. God forbid! I was working with a special Moroccan delegation to prepare a salad for the American army," he explained.

The doctor's tall tale had attracted a great audience, all of whom hung onto his every word. The doctor told us that the American army was so big that they couldn't find a bowl large enough to prepare the salad. So they drained a huge lake and dumped in truckloads of tomatoes, onions, and green peppers à la marocaine while fire trucks pumped gallons of olive oil into the mix. As for the salt, pepper, and cumin, helicopters sprinkled them onto the vegetables from above.

"And you, Doc? What was your part in this fantasy?" I asked.

The doctor rebuked me with a look before he continued: "I had an essential role. They gave me an inflatable boat. I rowed across the lake and radioed the helicopters. *This area needs more salt*, I'd say, and the helicopter would respond to my order and add salt. *This area needs pepper,* I'd say, and so on."

The Doctor of Fests, the most famous entertainer in Jemaa el-Fnaa, told this outlandish story so he wouldn't have to confess that he had been behind bars. His storytelling helped him block out the dark memories of the prison and its guards.

Marrakechis can invent colorful stories to avoid the darkness of reality. The doctor thought it was important to protect his tale, and to preserve the joyfulness of the Marrakechi soul. My task with assembling this book, however, was to search for adventurers who could dive into the grit without any qualms.

One prominent Marrakech author refused, saying, "When you need a story about Marrakech, you'll find me at your service. I can write about the secrets of the city, its dreams, and its scandals—but not about its crimes."

Maybe he's right, I thought to myself. *This city is prone to scandals, not crimes.* The Marrakechis never tire of recounting scandals. They tell these stories with enthusiasm. They add a lot of spice to past events. But they quickly forget the dark stories, for the Marrakechi impulse is to always remain joyful.

Most of the writers I approached were eager to participate in principle, but they all asked: "Why darkness? Why crimes?" The questions are legitimate. Morocco has no tradition of noir literature. Under King Hassan II, defamation took the place of investigation, and fabrication took the place of interrogation. Moroccans had to wait for the death of the king, who ruled the country with an iron fist, to read the first detective story, "The Blind Whale" by Abdelilah Hamdouchi, one year after he passed. In this way, we are similar to our neighbors in Spain, where crime fiction didn't proliferate in earnest until after the death of Spain's dictator Francisco Franco in 1975.

In the last two decades, Moroccans have written no more than thirty detective stories. They are all novels—not one single collection of short stories among them. For that reason, I seemed to be seducing Marrakechi authors into some kind of virgin land, an untouched wilderness, which would be the ultimate challenge to tame. Some authors refused to participate because they didn't want to intrude upon a literary genre that they didn't know. Others tried but failed, while a third group succeeded.

The contributing authors took inspiration from old crimes that the city had kept hidden behind its ancient gates, as well as crimes that have happened more recently due to the changes Marrakech has experienced as it becomes a global tourist destination. Prostitution appears alongside arbitrary detention, violence, and terrorism. Poverty, corruption, and betrayal factor in too, as well as tales drawn from the dark reality of psychiatric hospitals.

Despite their variety, these stories remain rooted on Moroccan soil—allowing the contributing authors, writing in Arabic, French, and Dutch, to bring readers closer to the linguistic, cultural, religious, and ethnic reality of Marrakech, whether Arab, Amazigh, African, or Muslim, as well as its historic Mellah—the Jewish Quarter. Here is the capital of tourism, the city of joy and sadness, the city of simple living, the city linked to international capitals through daily flights, the city of the new European community, a winter resort for French retirees, and a refuge for immigrants from sub-Saharan Africa. Marrakech is also known for its sex tourism and a new generation of crimes. All of these aspects of the city are reflected in these stories, no matter how sordid. The authors haven't written only stories, they have tried to write Marrakech as well. Together their stories present a comprehensive portrait of the city, its sadness, violence, tension, and darkness, without neglecting its joyful spirit.

The stories take us into the ancient city to wander through Dar el-Basha and Riad Zitoun, from Bab Doukkala to Bab Ghmat, from Derb Dabachi to Derb Sidi Bouloukat. We pass through the ancient walls of Marrakech to the new neighborhoods which have grown since independence. Some have turned into pockets of poverty, like Sidi Youssef Ben Ali, and others have become middle-class enclaves, like Hay el-Massira or Hay Saada. One of the stories even takes us to Amerchich, both the psychiatric hospital and the nearby neighborhood that shares its name.

The place that no one can avoid in Marrakech, however, is Jemaa el-Fnaa—which is present in most of the stories. Either the story starts in Jemaa el-Fnaa or it ends there. Sooner or later, the reader finds him or herself at an intersection where dark storytelling crosses this square full of life, which UNESCO has designated as part of humanity's Intangible Cultural Heritage.

Jemaa el-Fnaa is a reliable source of joy—the square is a gathering place for singers and dancers, storytellers and charlatans, buffoons and dream snatchers, monkeys and snake charmers, fortune-tellers and women with henna-stained hands. Every evening the square transforms into the biggest open restaurant in the Arab world. Who would dare to follow these dark elements in the middle of such a joyous place? This, then, is what has made *Marrakech Noir* such a challenge for an editor, and for all the contributors as well. I will leave it for the reader to decide if we have succeeded.

Yassin Adnan
Marrakech, Morocco
June 2018

Translated from Arabic by Mbarek Sryfi

PART I

Hanging Chimes

THE MYSTERIOUS PAINTING

BY FOUAD LAROUI

Bab Doukkala

He walked through the door of the restaurant at twelve fifteen p.m., as he did every day.

Police Chief Hamdouch was a man of habit, *borderline obsessive* in the words of his dear departed wife, a Morocco-born Frenchwoman who'd died of a nasty case of tetanus after only a few years of marriage. Still a widower, and without any children, he ate lunch each day at Délices de l'Orient, opposite the Palais du Glaoui.

The proprietor, Driss Bencheikh, took great care to keep the chief's table open between noon and two o'clock. If a distracted tourist or an insouciant local had the gall to sit there, Bencheikh would direct them to another table. He was, in a sense, acting in the name of the establishment, and that lent a certain brusqueness to his behavior. The establishment never asked nicely.

And so, Hamdouch sat down in the same chair, every day, at twelve fifteen p.m. A large painting hung on the wall facing him. The object had appeared in a rather mysterious manner, upon the chief's third visit to the restaurant. He'd already grown slightly annoyed with it. Until his third visit, there'd been nothing in front of him but a dull ocher wall. He would eat his lunch staring into the middle distance, which suited him fine—he could think in peace. Then one day, without warning, this big, multicolored rectangle had materialized in front of him.

The chief was no art lover, even if he could appreciate old poems sung in dialect; in any case, he didn't know a thing about paintings. At first, he simply noted the painting's appearance in his field of vision, without attaching any more importance to it than was necessary. It was a small change in his routine, a tiny inconvenience. It vaguely bothered him, but it wasn't, as they say, the end of the world. He resumed his habit of watching the street through the bay window that projected out from the center of the wall, seemingly monitoring the comings and goings of passersby—a professional tic, no doubt. But then, we all suffer from this particular pathology.

One day, he grew tired of seeing the same people coming and going on the sidewalk, mixed in with the tourists who were of little interest to him—people who were here today, clumsy and yammering, but always gone tomorrow. So he shifted his gaze slightly to the left, and, glass of tea in hand, focused on the painting. He had to squint a bit against the light, but he finally managed to make out a scene painted in garish colors—a scene containing several figures. One figure drew his attention, and he examined it more carefully. *What the devil?* he thought.

Hamdouch furrowed his brow and called imperiously to the proprietor: "S'si Driss!"

The man hurried over, drying his hands on a white napkin, and bowed slightly, a timid smile on his lips, ready to be of service.

The chief gestured at the object of his irritation with his right hand, which still held the glass of tea, so that he seemed to be raising a toast to who knows what—to art, perhaps?

"That . . . This . . . *tableau*!"

The chief used the French word, probably because he didn't know the Arabic one, or had forgotten it.

"Yes, S'si chief?" replied the proprietor, in a tone that was equal parts cheerful and servile.

Hamdouch lowered his voice and spoke slowly, giving certain words an ominous inflection. He knew very well how to do this; he wasn't a police chief for nothing. "Is that His Majesty the

king, may G
painted . . . i

The pro
cupied the c
response wa
It's the pash

"And ye
handsome h
of tea and p
someone's
turned tow
Majesty du

"I prom
"Even if his
his beloved horse."

Reassured, the chief asked: "Well, which pasha is it? S'si Lamrani?"

"No, like I told you, it's his predecessor, Moulay Mimoun."

"I just wanted to be *sure*." The chief nodded, took a sip of tea, and went back to examining the lively scene that stretched out before him in evocative colors.

After a few seconds, the proprietor understood that he was no longer needed and went on his way, swatting at a few imaginary flies with his napkin.

The next day, when Hamdouch sat down at his usual table, it was the painting he immediately turned to, even before glancing out at the street. Gloomy-eyed and jaw clenched, he stared intensely at it. *That painting!* He had dreamed of it during the night.

The chief hated dreams. Whenever he remembered one upon waking, he was furious. He felt degraded, humiliated, and suddenly unable to cope. It was as if he'd lost all control of himself during these nocturnal adventures where everything seemed

ws what purpose. *Do cats*
hen why do I?

ld recite the traditional Muslim
n—but, not being totally uncultured,
time what a psychoanalyst might make
ns. There were, of course, a few psychoan-
ch—he had their information—but he wasn't
onsult any of them. To do so would be to admit
don't tell a police chief to lie down on the couch.
ob to grill suspects, not the other way around. And what
d be more suspicious than a follower of Lacan in Marrakech?

In his dream about the painting, the scene had come alive; it had engulfed him, in a sense. He'd found himself trailing after the chestnut horse on which the pasha rode, while everyone ignored him and jostled him around—what lack of respect for his rank! And in the surrounding chaos—the noise, the fury, the dust—one of the men in the painting had even tried to slip a gunnysack over his head. Yes, a gunnysack, like the secret police used in the old days, in the seventies, the *dark years*, when they would kidnap politicians, trade unionists, philosophy students. The shame! Him, Chief Hamdouch—*gunnysacked*! The world had been turned upside down! He woke up full of indignation and covered in sweat, trembling from head to toe.

And now he was eating his bell pepper–and-tomato salad, his gaze fixed on the maleficent painting as if he were trying to wrench some secret from it. In fact, a strange realization had come over him during his nocturnal intrusion into this frozen scene: everyone was looking at the pasha, which in itself was quite normal—even a dog looks at a pasha—but he'd had the impression that all these looks were . . . *fraught*. Not one of them expressed simple curiosity, admiration *(What a beautiful procession!)*, or even the famous "reverent fear" that was the foundation on which the entire structure of state authority rested. No, these looks said something else. *They were fraught*, the chief thought to himself again, frustrated at his inability to come up with a more precise description of what he'd realized; his stock of adjectives was rather limited, in both Arabic and French.

He sat solemnly scrutinizing the painting with his fork in the air, a long piece of bell pepper dangling from it. "I'm opening an investigation," he mumbled aloud.

Having caught a few indistinct sounds, the proprietor came hurrying over. "Monsieur Chief? More bread? Some water, perhaps?"

Taken aback, Hamdouch coughed, then pointed his fork at the wall, causing the piece of bell pepper to bob dangerously. "Who made this painting?" he asked.

The proprietor looked from the fork to the painting. He frowned. His forehead puckered up—he was pretending to be deep in thought—and he finally replied: "It's a young man by the name of Brahim Labatt. He lived on a street nearby, across from the blacksmith's souk." Driss leaned in closer to the chief and, adopting the funereal air that precedes this type of disclosure, whispered: "He committed *suicide* a few years ago. God preserve us!" He uttered the macabre word so softly that it could barely be heard. "It seems to have been the last thing he painted before he . . ." Driss didn't finish the sentence.

The chief registered the information and mentally opened a file under the name of Brahim Labatt, a young man who'd died under suspicious circumstances. He knew—the statistics didn't lie—that suicide was rare on Islamic soil. And so, the case would have to be investigated. With a flippant gesture that made the piece of bell pepper, still hanging precariously from the tines of his fork, appear vaguely threatening, he dismissed Driss, who hurried off to welcome a group of Japanese tourists at the door. The proprietor could be heard bragging in his eccentric English, punctuated with little sucking noises, about his restaurant and its cuisine *(The best in Marrakech, of course!)*.

The chief finished his meal, still unable to look away from

the work of art—was it, in fact, a work of art, or something else? And in any case, what *was* art? He began to lose himself in a labyrinth of reflections.

Back at the station, Hamdouch called in one of his employees, Ba Mouss, who'd been nicknamed "The Computer" because he possessed a phenomenal memory, at least when it came to the crimes, misdemeanors, and other incidents of note that took place in the neighborhood. Aside from that, he didn't know much about anything. Ba Mouss had never been transferred elsewhere, since transferring a computer would mean, in a sense, erasing all the files it contained—and what would be the point of such an operation?

Short and skinny, with big green eyes, the man-machine entered his boss's office. The chief didn't bother with preliminaries. "Ba Mouss, have you ever heard of a certain Brahim Labatt? A painter?"

As if Hamdouch had pressed the *enter* button, Ba Mouss stood to attention, cleared his throat, and recited: "Brahim Labatt, son of Abdelmoula, was a plumber. No high school diploma and the only son of the widow Halima. He lived with her on Derb Dekkak, then stayed there alone after his mother's death. He was also an amateur painter, you might say. He painted when he was out of work, which was quite often, and showed his artwork on the street, next to the barbershop. He managed to sell a few to some German tourists." A short sniffle announced a sad turn in the story. "Excuse me, chief . . . Brahim Labatt committed suicide seven or eight years ago. By hanging. May God have mercy on us!"

Hamdouch nodded his head, frowning. This was his way of thanking his subordinates. "Are we sure it was a suicide?" he asked.

"Only God knows, chief."

"And aside from God?" Hamdouch was growing impatient.

Mouss's last response had been close to blasphemous—but then again, what kind of computer invokes the name of God? Give us facts and figures, and leave God to the *faqihs*.

"Your predecessor, Chief Madani, closed the case," Mouss explained. "The poor painter had—"

"Hold on." The chief winced. "You say it was Madani who closed the case?"

"Yes. He closed it immediately . . . well, very quickly," the man-machine answered. "There was nothing suspicious about it."

"Very good, that'll be all. You may go."

Ba Mouss nodded and left the office without a word.

Hamdouch began to rub his forehead frantically with the fingertips of his right hand. A raging headache was coming on, a sign that one of his many intuitions had arrived, the kind that had helped him solve particularly tough cases throughout his career. His dear departed wife, Hélène, half-mocking and half-affectionate, had called these episodes *les migraines de mon Maigret*. Ha!

Still, he owed much of his success to his intuition. His most recent transfer from Safi to Marrakech had been a flattering promotion. He had solved several high-profile cases, including the Hay el-Majd killings, which had been all over the newspapers and had given everyone nightmares at the time.

What was presently setting his brain on fire was a coincidence he had just become aware of: the man in his dream who'd tried to put a bag over his head . . .

But back up, first things first: Madani, the ex-chief, had been forced to retire over a scandalous case of corruption (or embezzlement of public funds . . . it had all been very confusing) in which he wasn't directly involved, though he'd tried to cover up for the main beneficiary, who was none other than the ex-pasha Moulay Mimoun.

So, there were two *exes* in this story, a hanged man, plus a painting that connected all of them.

Suddenly, Hamdouch remembered the man in his dream who'd tried to put a bag over his head: it was Madani himself!

Without even knowing it, Hamdouch had recognized him in the painting—and now his predecessor had resurfaced, in the night, from the depths of his subconscious, with an air of murder about him. "The plot thickens," he murmured.

The chief rushed out of his office, down Boulevard Fatima Zahra, rounded the corner, and walked into the restaurant. The place was nearly empty at this hour of the afternoon. A cat was asleep in a corner, curled up in a ball. Only three French tourists, three men, were lingering over their cups of coffee.

Hamdouch ignored the owner's startled greeting and planted himself directly in front of the painting to confirm his suspicions.

Yes, it was indeed Madani there, beside the pasha's horse. You could distinguish his hideous mug, crudely painted though it was—on the verge of caricature. But then, nature seemed to have caricatured this man as the typical corrupt brute. The painter hadn't had to embellish much.

The chief noted another detail that aggravated his migraine. While all of the figures' gazes were *fraught*, there was an exception: Madani was not looking at the ex-pasha; he was staring out at the viewer of the painting. At that precise moment, Madani seemed to be staring into the face of the man who had succeeded him—Hamdouch. The ex-chief's expression seemed to depict a kind of confusion, a mixture of fear, arrogant disdain, and . . . something else. But what else could it be?

And what was more, his right hand, which at first glance looked to be stroking the horse's neck, was in fact placed on the left hand of Moulay Mimoun. The two men, hand in hand, seemed to be bracing themselves against the crowd's anger.

Yes, *anger*! That was the meaning behind the fraught gazes that Hamdouch had noticed before. That was it! The late Labatt was certainly no Rembrandt; he hadn't always pulled off the desired effect, but it was clearly anger that he'd tried to convey on the faces in the painting, with the exception of the ex-pasha and the ex-chief.

Turning to the three tourists, Hamdouch arranged his face into a cheerful expression despite the migraine that was stabbing at his temples, and called out heartily: "Welcome to Marrakech!" He said it in French, rolling his r's.

Surprised, the men hesitated a few seconds—long enough to reassure themselves that this elegant man, with his graying hair and dashing mustache, wasn't a beggar, a nuisance, or Clark Gable risen from the dead—before one of them returned his greeting: "*Merci, monsieur . . . ?*"

"Hamdouch, at your service." A pause. "I'm an art collector, and I'd like to ask your opinion." The chief gestured at the painting in a sort of invitation. "What do you think of that?"

Clearly amused, the three men got to their feet and moved toward the painting. They had polished off two bottles of Volubilia and, feeling mischievous, they spontaneously decided, without even conferring about it, to play the experts. It'd be fun—they were on vacation, they'd have a story to tell when they got back to Paris. What followed was a smorgasbord of clichés uttered in the most affected tones.

"That light, gentlemen! That light . . . it's like something out of Claude Gellée, *dit* le Lorrain!" one of the tourists exclaimed.

"See, the way that djellaba hangs! There, in the corner . . . lovely as the day is long," another added.

"That horse, the energy, the movement . . . pure Delacroix!" the last man in the group added. "And what a noble-looking chevalier—is that your king?"

The chief, whose migraine was wearing down his patience, said, "Gentlemen, calm yourselves! If you'll allow me, I'd like to ask you a specific question: what do you see in the eyes of all these men? Forget the horseman, it's the others who interest me."

The tourists went to work, no more messing around. They

examined the faces frozen in time by the painter, and the verdict was unanimous.

"*Oh* là là, they don't look too happy . . ."

"No, no, they don't look friendly at all . . ."

"I would even say they're angry."

Hamdouch, satisfied, pointed to the ex-chief. "And this one?"

The three men brought their faces up close, their noses nearly touching the surface of the canvas. This time, their opinions differed.

"A nasty fellow," the first Frenchman decided.

"Arrogant," said the second.

The third, a gangly redhead, took his time before answering. "Not quite, *messieurs*, not quite. I'll tell you: he looks *guilty*. Like a delinquent caught in the act. Like a good-for-nothing who gives himself away just by the expression on his face."

All four of them studied the nasty fellow's face. There was no doubt about it. That was it: Madani looked guilty.

"Bravo, Christian!" the first tourist cheered for the redhead.

Delighted, Hamdouch thanked the Frenchmen for their observations.

"And now, are you going to try to sell us this daub?" one of the tourists asked boldly, grinning. "Not a bad technique! Bravo! We fell for it like a couple of chumps. How much?"

Hamdouch fixed the man with an icy stare. "I'm not an art dealer. And for that matter, this . . . this thing doesn't belong to me. *Au revoir, messieurs*!"

The three men headed back to their seats, tickled with this little interlude. But just when the chief was about to leave, the redheaded Christian called out to him: "Ho there! There's something not quite right with your daub . . . sorry, your painting." The redhead stood up again, walked over, and pointed to the left-hand corner of the painting. "I'm not an expert, obviously, far from it! But I've never seen *zellige* tile on a wall. That's *zellige*, right there, isn't it?"

Hamdouch, already standing in the doorway, turned around and walked back. With his index finger, he touched the spot that Christian had pointed to. "You're right," he murmured, perplexed. "Yellow *zellige*, on the exterior side of a wall—it makes no sense."

How had he not noticed this detail? Were his powers of observation in decline? He felt sheepish for a moment, but didn't let it show.

Christian returned to the table where his friends gleefully teased him ("He's got an eye, this one," "Good work, Sherlock!") while Hamdouch slipped away, lost in his own thoughts.

Back at his office, the chief left his door open and called for his computer: "Ba Mouss!"

His voice echoed through the station and the little man appeared almost instantly, his eyes more greenish than ever. This melancholy shade seemed to spread out over his entire face, so that he looked like a tiny Martian who'd been woken from his nap.

"I want you to tell me everything you know about the ex-pasha, Moulay Mimoun!" the chief barked. "Everything! Facts, fiction, rumors, gossip . . . everything!"

Ba Mouss sighed and began to drone on about the rich life of the pasha.

The chief let this flood of information flow past him, interrupting the human computer every now and then to ask for clarification. When Ba Mouss had finished, the chief was silent for a moment. Then he said: "This story about the murder of a rival. Can you tell me more about it?"

"It's only a rumor, chief. And there's no proof that there *was* any murder. A coppersmith, a certain Dadouchi, had asked for the hand of a very beautiful woman in the Kennaria District, and it was granted to him. The marriage preparations were coming along nicely, but alas! The pasha, Moulay Mimoun, had designs on this same woman. Then one day, the coppersmith disappeared. He went to see a customer and didn't come back. In fact, he was never seen or heard from again. And so, after a few months, the pasha could add the lady to his stock of wives. But he rejected her a few months later, to the great anger and shame of her family." Ba Mouss lowered his voice. "Word spread that it was he, the pasha, who'd made the coppersmith disappear."

"*Cui bono?*" Hamdouch whispered to himself. He knew a few Latin expressions of great practical value that had circulated at the École de police, a legacy of the French.

"Pardon?"

"Nothing, nothing. Go on."

"I was saying that word spread that it was the pasha who'd made the coppersmith disappear. And there's more: rumor had it that the evidence of his crime still existed somewhere, and that one day it would appear in plain sight." Ba Mouss hesitated a moment, then blurted out: "It was said that the truth would be revealed by a magical bird."

Just as Ba Mouss had expected, the chief shrugged his shoulders in irritation. "A magical bird? Why not a flying elephant? You'd think we were in *The Thousand and One Nights*. Could you be any more gullible? It's up to the police, not the birds, to find evidence!"

Without entering into the debate between science and superstition—a debate the chief always won by force of his arguments and outright threats—Ba Mouss concluded: "Voilà. That's all we know of the story."

"Thanks. You may go."

The computer seemed to shut off, and disappeared. The chief went to close the door, then settled in comfortably at his desk; with his chin resting on his folded hands, he began to think. This business of the magical bird annoyed him to no end, but the more he tried to ignore it, the more it refused to leave him alone. He imagined a sort of giant, multicolored simurgh that soared to the heavens, then plunged back down to earth, carrying a violently writhing snake in its talons. *I'm getting all worked up about a silly legend,* he thought, peeved.

Then he remembered an expression that Hélène had sometimes used: *oiseau jacasseur*. She'd had to explain the verb—*jacasser*—to him: *to talk very quickly, in an annoying manner.*

A *talking bird?*

That reminded him of something. He closed his eyes and concentrated on the image. Memories of his childhood and adolescence, things he'd read or heard, appeared in a sort of halo . . .

After a few minutes, he opened his eyes and shook his head. Then he picked up his telephone and, after the usual greetings, asked one of the guys from the archives: "Do we have access to a list of the assets belonging, or having belonged, to the former pasha? . . . Yes, Moulay Mimoun . . . Can we get that? . . . It'll take time? I have all the time in the world!" He let out a slightly bitter laugh, thinking of his status as a childless widower. "You'll send it to me by a trustworthy messenger?"

He hung up, lit a cigarette, and randomly opened one of the files scattered on his desk.

A few days later, Hamdouch received the list he'd asked for. He ran his finger feverishly down the page and stopped at a name—the name of a riad that had belonged to the pasha.

"Bingo," he said out loud, smiling.

At the end of the alleyway, most passersby would turn left. Rarely did anyone turn right. On the ground, black marks left by thousands of mopeds over the years indicated only one direction: left. This was the way leading to Bab Doukkala, the main road that wove through the medina.

The chief, accompanied by his deputy Hariri, turned resolutely to the right. He knew where he was going.

In front of the riad, an old watchman was seated on a stool.

The watchman saw Hamdouch and Hariri approaching and stood up straight, discreetly dusted off his clothing, and seemed to come to attention.

"Assalamu alaikum!" the chief greeted.

"Alaikum as-salaam, S'si Chief," the watchman replied anxiously.

"Are the French people here?"

"No, sidi, they went out to buy some fruit and vegetables. But you may come in if you wish."

"It's fine, I'll wait until they return," Hamdouch told him. "And don't ever let anyone enter a house in the absence of its owners. Not even me! The law forbids it."

Fifteen minutes later, the owners, François and Cécile, came back from the souk. The chief greeted them with a smile and gave a sort of salute by bringing two fingers to his forehead, then introduced himself and his deputy.

"The police? Nothing serious, I hope," François said.

"No, no," the chief assured him. "I just wanted to take a quick look around, with your permission. This has to do with an old case that has no connection to you whatsoever. It all happened long before you bought . . ." Hamdouch paused, then gestured vaguely at the door to the old building.

François and Cécile exchanged a look and raised their shoulders in unison. "Well then, come in," François said. "We can't offer you any tea, just some fruit juice."

"No thank you."

The four of them entered the house while the watchman stayed outside. The chief started looking around, turning his head every which way.

"Are you searching for something?" François inquired.

"Yes, I'm looking for a part of the wall covered in *zellige*," Hamdouch responded. "Yellowish *zellige*."

"*A little patch of yellow wall*," joked Cécile.

"I beg your pardon?"

"It's nothing, just a literary reference," Cécile said. "But there is a similar wall here. The phrase is from Proust's novel *In Search of Lost Time*."

"Research? That's my department," the chief noted approvingly. "Your Proust, did he write about Marrakech?"

"No, no . . . the patch of yellow wall is in Delft, in the Netherlands, it's the birthplace of—"

Hamdouch raised his hand and interrupted Cécile: "Forget that, the Netherlands aren't in my jurisdiction. Where's the wall?"

They led him to one of the side rooms, with Hariri bringing up the rear. One of the walls was covered up halfway in ocher *zellige*. Curiously, there were no more tiles beyond this patch, and it looked as if someone had begun to cover the wall, then changed their mind without going to the trouble of removing the tile. Hamdouch studied the wall carefully, kneeling down to examine its base, then tapped it in several spots while pressing his ear to its surface. Hariri and the French couple watched him, baffled.

"You think there's something behind it?" Cécile asked. Without waiting for a response, she turned to her husband. "You remember the Héberts? They bought an old house in Paris, in the Marais. While they were doing some renovations they discovered a fake wall, and behind it, in a case, they found a very valuable violin. A Guarneri, I think."

"Well then, we just might hit the jackpot," François said.

The chief stood up with difficulty. "I don't know if you can get rich in the skeleton trade," he muttered. "If you can, then you're in luck: there's a coppersmith's skeleton behind this wall."

Cécile swayed and fell right onto a chair.

"What do you mean?" François asked, stunned.

Hamdouch shrugged and told his deputy to go find a bricklayer and two strapping policemen—and to bring mallets, hammers, and a large plastic bag.

While François tended to Cécile, who was hyperventilating,

the chief explained: "With your permission, we're going to make a hole in this wall to extract the corpse that's hidden behind it. But don't worry, we'll seal everything back up again."

Hamdouch went out to smoke a cigarette in the shade of an orange tree.

A few days later, Hamdouch was seated in his usual chair at his usual restaurant, in front of what was left of a chicken tagine with olives. His hunger satiated, he burped quietly and then ordered a mint tea. Finally, he agreed to rehash the case for the proprietor, who'd been hovering around him all evening.

"You know that Brahim Labatt was also a plumber? He'd probably been hired to do some odd jobs around the riad, and discreet as he was, they'd completely forgotten he was there. Without meaning to, he witnessed the coppersmith's assassination by the pasha, or rather by the pasha's henchmen. They must've lured the guy there to place an order for copper trays, or something of the sort. Poor man, I hope he was already dead when they walled him in. Otherwise, what a horrible end . . . Anyway, Labatt got out of there without anyone noticing him, and within a few weeks he'd finished the painting. It was, in a sense, his only way of speaking out about what he'd seen."

"But why didn't he just report the pasha to the police?" the proprietor asked.

"In those days, no one trusted the police, least of all a simple worker, a *son of the people* like Labatt. And then, to turn against the pasha . . . few would have dared."

"What a vile era," the proprietor lamented.

"But he couldn't bear to keep such a dark secret. He must've told someone. He claimed to have evidence, to have gotten it all down. His confidant spoke out in turn, and the rumor spread. Chief Madani got wind of it, and since he was in cahoots with the pasha, he warned him. The painter was discreetly arrested—and tortured, no doubt—before they finished the job by hanging him and making it look like a suicide," the chief concluded. "They searched his house from top to bottom, looking for papers that would incriminate the pasha. They were desperate to find a notebook, a letter, a few words scribbled on a scrap of paper, but no one thought twice about the paintings—the daubs that lined the walls! That's where he'd made his accusation in the most precise detail. Even then, you had to know how to look for it."

"But how'd you get the idea to go nosing around that riad? How did you know?"

Hamdouch smiled. "Riad Boulboul? *Boulboul* doesn't ring a bell to you? The talking bird in *The Thousand and One Nights*? As soon as I knew that the place had belonged to Moulay Mimoun, I understood the origin of the story about the magical bird that would reveal everything one day. Labatt had mentioned *boulboul*, and by word of mouth, the reference to the riad had been lost; people preferred to find magic in it rather than a simple physical address. But me, I'm a rational thinker. *Cartesian*, my wife used to say, God have mercy on her soul."

"So, what'll happen to the ex-pasha? And to the ex-chief?"

Hamdouch shrugged. "Nothing. Well, not much. Moulay Mimoun has always been protected in high places, and in any case, he's very old, he's become senile and forgotten everything. What judge would want to reopen the investigation? You can't send a doddering old man to prison. As for Madani, he's retired. If Moulay Mimoun got off, there's no reason to bother with his accomplice . . . an *âme damnée*, as the French say—a damned soul. You know that expression?"

"No," Driss sighed. "I'm a little sad to know that justice won't be served."

"Ah, but in a certain sense, it has. The reputations of these two scumbags are ruined. They'll end their lives in shame, detested by everyone, even their loved ones, waiting to go straight to hell."

"They're both . . . how did you say it? *Ânes damnés*."

"Bravo! S'si Driss, you're a quick learner. You've still got to work on your pronunciation, though," the chief teased. "It's *âmes,* not *ânes* . . . a matter of souls, not donkeys. Though Madani did always come off as an ass to me; one wonders how he managed to have a career. My guess is by doing favors for the powerful. Just like in this sad case."

The chief took a long sip of his tea and then pointed at the proprietor. "There's still one piece of this mystery I have to solve. The painting wasn't here when I first came in. Why did you hang it in front of my table a few days later?"

Driss Bencheikh shook his head, grabbed a chair, and sat down beside the chief. "Well, you should know that Brahim Labatt was my mother's cousin. I inherited this painting, in a sense. I knew it contained a secret because it was his last work, and nothing like what he normally painted. It couldn't be random . . . it had to *mean* something. I never believed that Brahim had killed himself, but I couldn't figure out what happened. When you started coming here for lunch every day, I seized my chance. A policeman's brain like yours would surely get to the bottom of it."

The chief remained silent for a moment, then raised his glass in the direction of the painting.

Driss did the same and, with tears in his eyes, murmured: "To the artist!"

Translated from French by Katie Shireen Assef

A NOISY DISAPPEARANCE IN AN ILL-REPUTED ALLEY

BY ALLAL BOURQIA

Derb Sidi Bouloukat

1. The Mayor in the Heart of the Labyrinth

News of Spanish film director Enrique Aldomar's disappearance spread all over Marrakech one October afternoon. To be precise, after four days without his family and those who knew him having heard from him. The mayor of Marrakech had already been informed of the director's disappearance before it circulated among the media and general public. The mayor was right in the middle of preparing the massive celebrations marking the nine hundredth anniversary of Marrakech's founding. The upcoming anniversary coincided with two other incidents that had also occurred over the last few weeks—prompting the mayor to view them in a new light due to the disappearance.

The first incident was the fire that had broken out in the Cinema Mabrouka, destroying half the theater. The second incident was the theft of Mohamed Ben Brahim's statue. Ben Brahim was a prominent Marrakech poet and his statue had recently been placed in Moulay Yazid Square in the casbah. While thinking about these two incidents, no meaningful conclusions came to the mayor's mind—except that a horrible coincidence had befallen him and the city he was entrusted to run. *It's nothing to cry about*, he told himself, as if the next few hours would be enough to solve the three mysteries, or as if he were certain that the director who had suddenly disappeared from a small hotel in Derb Sidi Bouloukat would show up unharmed. He remained locked in his office for the entire afternoon, doling out orders to his subordinates, a task he thoroughly enjoyed.

After receiving a phone call from one of the highest-ranking officials in the country, the mayor couldn't sleep that night. The call had put him in a state of high alert. He realized that he was facing a test he couldn't run away from. Marrakech seemed to be nothing but an enormous trap. He turned on his computer and began to read about Aldomar. The search engine delivered a stream of information replete with details about the director and his cinematic world. The mayor stared at the many pictures of Aldomar, wanting to imprint the man's face in his mind.

The following day, the newspaper headlines were obsessed with what came to be known as "The Case of Enrique Aldomar's Disappearance." The articles raised difficult questions: How does a famous director disappear in Marrakech, where cameras capture images of famous people from the moment they set foot on Moroccan soil? How did Aldomar disappear in a street known for its prostitutes, homosexuals, drug dealers, and counterfeiters?

Shortly before his disappearance, a national newspaper reported that Aldomar had refused to participate in an international film festival taking place in Marrakech. Aldomar claimed that the festival was tacky and without any artistic merit. In a tone that was somewhere between sarcasm and disapproval, the reporter had asked: *Did someone want to teach Aldomar a lesson for his disrespect toward a world-class festival and the liberal values that it represents?*

The people of Marrakech devoured the daily papers like they never had before. Everyone was baffled that Aldomar would stay in a shabby hotel in Derb Sidi Bouloukat in the first place, which was the last place he was seen. Most people linked the disappearance to what had occurred with the Cinema Mabrouka fire and the theft of the Ben Brahim statue, just as the mayor had.

The city was flooded with rumors that people outlandishly spun and disseminated. Once they found out that the missing director was gay, these rumors were followed by stinging jokes of a sexual nature.

After another long, sleepless night, the mayor awoke ready to search for the director, an operation he didn't really know how to undertake, save for the strict order he gave to his aides to turn the city upside down until Aldomar was found.

That afternoon, the mayor held a series of emergency meetings with members of the security forces and other influential people—afterward, he left furious at himself, at Marrakech, and at the people who lived there.

He drove slowly through the streets, despising his impotence, glaring at all the places and people he passed, as if condemning everything and everyone in his wake. It seemed to him that, on this morning, Marrakech appeared ambivalent to the matter of the missing director. A stupid idea occurred to him: his political enemies, both inside and outside of his party, could have been the ones who had come up with this scheme in order to knock him off of his mayoral throne. There were many who mocked him for his lackluster political skills, people who described him as *the failed administrator*, *the thief*, and *the empty-headed one*.

He swept the idea away angrily, recalling words he had heard in one of his meetings just a short while ago: *The formation of a cell to engineer the crisis*. The words had a touch of magic to them and were spoken by Omar Kusturica, the mayor's brother-in-law, who wasn't there in any official capacity other than his familial role.

The mayor's fatigued head boiled over with strange ideas caused by the dread that had been smothering him since yesterday. The fact that the city was teeming with more foreigners than before caught his attention. His paranoid mind assumed that these foreigners were undercover investigators, television reporters, and journalists on special assignments for international newspapers. It was clear that they had come here to get to the bottom of the disappearance of Aldomar, whose name, up until now, the mayor hadn't even known how to spell.

He wasn't sure where to go or what to do. He shifted his eyes between the road in front of him and his cell phone, which was on the seat to his right. If only the phone would light up and ring, pronouncing a miracle that would end the case of Aldomar's disappearance; a voice on the other end of the line telling him that they had found the man wandering around in Arset Moulay Abdeslam Cyberpark, for example, or sleeping in the back of a horse carriage in Gueliz or anywhere, really—as long as he was found.

The mayor undid the top button of his shirt and his tie, suddenly finding it hard to breathe. He parked the car on Agnou Street in front of the Cinema Mabrouka and got out. He carefully studied the theater, realizing that he had never been here, neither before nor after the fire. The sight of the charred building made him think of his own decrepit self, so he turned away and rushed back to his car.

As he continued to drive aimlessly, his phone rang and jolted him out of his daydream. It was the Spanish ambassador to Morocco on the line, jabbering away in mediocre French. The ambassador wanted to know where the investigation stood, reminding the mayor that Aldomar was a cinematic icon of Spain, and that the search for him should be considered a search for his country's lost treasure. All the mayor could do was assure the ambassador that the end of the ordeal was in sight.

The mayor hung up the phone with the ambassador's voice still ringing in his ears—an air of arrogance and superiority, mixed with a commanding tone that made him feel even more crushed under the pressure of the disappearance. He thought about taking off in his car, leaving Marrakech, traveling beyond the edge of the world. He wanted to keep driving toward the infinite, until he himself disappeared. The ambassador's voice wouldn't leave him be. But then the mayor decided to consult with his brother-in-law.

2. Omar Kusturica and the War Against Cinema

Omar Kusturica was one of the leading personalities of the Cine-Club during the mideighties. He was nicknamed *Kusturica* because of the way he obsessed over the film *Time of the Gypsy* by the director Emir Kusturica. Omar's connection to cinema was intense, almost pathological—he only saw the world and all of its complications through the camera's lens. He was related to the mayor through marriage—the mayor having married his oldest sister. Omar Kusturica was known as the mayor's confidant, and as the man who whispered strange ideas into his ear. People who knew about the mayor's affairs also knew that Omar Kusturica crafted his speeches. He was a technical advisor too, as needed. Some alleged that he was behind the idea to erect a statue memorializing the poet of Marrakech, to celebrate Marrakech's nine hundredth anniversary with festivities, as well as to establish a sister-city relationship with Bahia in Brazil, among others. Omar Kusturica stood by the mayor's side in all of his private meetings, to the point where rumormongers began to whisper that he knew all of the mayor's secrets. His face was dotted with pimples and his eyes shined haughtily behind glasses that resembled those used by welders, with their metal frames and thick lenses.

Omar was standing at the door of his house when the mayor arrived. He understood that the mayor was in a bind, just like the city was. He also knew how fragile the mayor could be, and how frazzled he could get over even the most trivial of issues.

"How does Enrique Aldomar disappear in a city that adores both foreigners *and* cinema?" Omar asked as the mayor walked toward the sitting room.

The mayor glanced at the newspapers strewn across the coffee table while he briefed Omar on the case and its implications for Moroccan-Spanish relations.

"This disappearance is *your* case," Omar stressed, like he was expounding words he had carefully prepared. "You have to emerge from this crisis victorious, no matter the price."

"But how?" the mayor asked in a feeble voice. "How do you even interpret this disappearance?"

"I think it's perfectly clear. There are enemies of the cinema who live among us. They're the ones who set the Cinema Mabrouka on fire, and they're also the ones who kidnapped Aldomar. Are you going to ask me the reason for this chaos? Let me tell you—these enemies want to destroy the idea that Marrakech is a city that loves the cinema. They want to sink the future of its renowned festival. You know well that there are those who don't like the huge amounts of money that are spent on the festival, one they describe as gaudy and unnecessary. The case is perfectly clear: they've declared war on cinema."

The mayor grabbed onto his brother-in-law's words like a life preserver tossed over the side of a boat to save a drowning man. His face relaxed now that he could see clearly. He stood up. He wanted to take Omar into his arms and release all of the anxiety that had built up inside of him since yesterday. But the pride and power that came with his lofty office kept him from doing so. Before leaving Omar's house, the mayor needed the answer to one more question: "What do we do now?"

"We must fight the enemies of cinema with cinema itself," Omar replied with an air of malice. "We need to flood the market with Aldomar's films. We must distribute them to everyone for free until the need for a war is rendered obsolete. All you have to do now is focus on the investigation—by releasing a statement aimed clearly at the accused."

The mayor left Omar's house with the feeling that his Machiavellian brother-in-law had arrived at a suitable solution. His head was filled with dark thoughts as he mulled over Omar's words.

Meanwhile, Omar began to prepare the speech the mayor would give to the press.

As Omar wrote the mayor's statement, trying to craft the right tone, he realized his mission was no less than delivering the city from disaster. The statement was brief and resolute in tone. The words declared war on the enemies of cinema who had taken aim at Marrakech.

Omar was certain that the city would inevitably emerge from this mess, but in an ironic way, he was also convinced that the conspirators' plan wouldn't be thwarted so long as Marrakech attempted to transform itself into a city for the international elite at any cost, as the hovels of Massira, Daoudiate, Socoma, and M'hamid continued to fester. Perhaps the enemies of cinema would one day prompt people to burn the city to the ground.

He lamented the mayor's condition, and that of Marrakech too. The disappearance had become stranger than strange. Omar was convinced that the disappearance of the director would not have had the same impact in a city such as Casablanca or Tangier or Fes.

3. A Moroccan Chaos

In the days that followed, every inch of Derb Sidi Bouloukat was searched, but the police didn't find a trace of Aldomar. People who were following the case began to doubt that he had even been in Marrakech recently—they believed that it was all a Spanish ploy to twist Morocco's arm after Morocco had been accused of cutting off the livelihoods of Spanish fishermen. But Aldomar did not emerge from wherever he was in order to refute these charges.

Then, one morning, the people of Marrakech discovered a communiqué—copies were plastered on walls and doors, and left on the streets. The communiqué—written by a group that called itself the Band of Merry Men—claimed that they had kidnapped the director and they were now demanding a ransom. The communiqué didn't say whether they were motivated by political or religious ideology, or whether they were a traveling circus troupe or a band of highway robbers; nor was the communiqué directed toward anyone in particular.

Investigators spent hours coming up with endless hypotheses about the nature of the kidnappers and their reasons for choosing Aldomar as a target. The police raided shops and houses throughout Sidi Youssef Ben Ali, Bab Ghmat, and Bab Aylan. People with prior convictions were yanked from their beds before daybreak and dragged out in full sight of their relatives and neighbors. Families were intimidated in order to extract any information that might lead to the kidnappers. As the hours wore on, the authorities even recruited the services of a popular private investigator who ran Revealing the Hidden, a renowned detective agency.

As the operation continued without any notable results, the pressure increased, the police became more frenzied, and the suspects were shipped out in trucks to unknown places, despairing at the thought of the torture that awaited them. Many fled Marrakech for the relative calm of the capital. As all of this was going on, merchants' stalls were packed with pirated Aldomar films. People were snatching them up as if they would provide hidden clues as to the director's whereabouts.

For the residents of back alleys and poor neighborhoods, where crime, unemployment, prostitution, and theft were rampant, the frenzy felt like an earthquake. Everything made the residents of these hovels look guilty—their hostile bronze-colored faces, their large hands, and their haggard appearances.

The police cordoned off these neighborhoods for days, until the people who lived there believed that the authorities were intending to send them en masse to another location, like they usually did with beggars before each royal visit to Marrakech. The people in these quarantined neighborhoods heard rumors about another city that was in the process of being built for them, about surveyors inspecting some barren land on the outskirts of Marrakech. Theories circulated that a Chinese company had been brought to Marrakech to replicate a part of the city in the empty wastes. People in the know confirmed that it was actually an old project which had been kept under wraps until the authorities saw that the time had come to execute it. This fate seemed sealed when a newspaper published a photograph of the Chinese company's previous city-replicating work—the Austrian village of Hallstatt.

These devilish Chinese imitated small and large architectural designs with equal skill, from colorful houses to windmills, lakes, streams, and churches. They would be able to create another Marrakech entirely—duplicating Jemaa el-Fnaa, the Koutoubia Mosque, the Bahia and Badia palaces, the mausoleums, the historic gates, Majorelle Garden, and even the Old Medina's alleys. They could replicate anything, except for the actual inhabitants. So people told each other what they wanted to believe in their customarily cheerful way, and they made fun of the proposed city.

It was in this atmosphere that Pedro Soldato—a Spanish writer who had been living in the Old Medina for over thirty years—emerged seemingly from out of nowhere. He appeared on the seventh day of Aldomar's disappearance. He wandered aimlessly through the city, as if he wanted to join the search for the missing director. The intelligentsia knew, as did some laymen, that Soldato had previously experienced his own disappearance. The story became well-known. It was said that when he'd returned from a trip abroad, he made his way to his favorite café overlooking Jemaa el-Fnaa Square—but he didn't find it there. The missing café alarmed him, so he had walked over to the cell phone store that had taken its place. The spirit of the old café, now effaced but still trapped within the new space, hit him hard. Horrified,

Soldato left. He turned around again toward the lost café in disbelief. Then he walked toward the square, stumbling along in his disappointment. He asked himself a terrifying question: *What if Jemaa el-Fnaa Square were to disappear too?*

That evening, Soldato drafted a long letter to the director-general of UNESCO about the café that had disappeared and the tremendous fear this startling discovery had borne inside him. He really believed that Jemaa el-Fnaa would disappear too. He implored the director-general to designate it as a World Heritage Site.

Soldato was reliving that time as he thought about the state of the city he loved. Going out for a walk was his usual way of coming up with ideas. After what seemed like many long days since the director's disappearance, and after gathering enough information to form an opinion on the matter, Soldato was ready to say his piece. He thought about writing an article in which he would talk about his relationship with Aldomar—they'd met several years before, shortly after the release of the film *Palace of Desire*. Soldato had learned about Aldomar's artistry, and the poisoning of the relationship between his native country and *the city he was born for* (his words). Soldato decided to draft an emotional essay about the director's disappearance rather than an investigative one, for it wasn't within his abilities to put forth answers about how, when, and why Aldomar had vanished.

4. The *Malhun* Singer and Her Collapsed Dreams

A second communiqué from the Band of Merry Men arrived one morning at the apartment of Souad Laamari, a thirty-two-year-old *malhun* singer and the mayor's paramour of three years. It terrified her that the communiqué had found its way to her inconspicuous apartment on Avenue Khalid Ibn el-Oualid, close to Marrakech Plaza, as she strove to keep her intimate relationship with the mayor discreet. She read the brief communiqué with astonishment. When she finished, the paper fell from her trembling hand. She called the mayor's private line, but there was no answer. She tried his other number without any success. The mayor was cut off, for the first time, from her world. She recalled that she had only been in contact with him once since the announcement of the director's disappearance. It was a quick call that had ended badly. The mayor had asked her not to call him until the crisis was over. But the Band of Merry Men's communiqué had forced her hand. She continued to call the mayor for hours without result, until she finally decided to go to city hall herself.

At the front gate she ran into Hocine el-Tadlaoui, one of the mayor's close associates. He was a real estate broker during the day and a pleasure broker at night. He was also the man who had first introduced her to the mayor. Seeming uneasy, he asked her why she had come. "These are difficult times," he told her.

She took the communiqué out of her handbag, glancing around nervously. The broker took a cursory glance at the piece of paper without reading all of it, then explained that he'd received the same message yesterday, as had Kika the actress, Omar Kusturica, and a few others. "They're taking aim at the mayor himself," Hocine growled. "The bastards know his life secrets and what goes on in his private garden."

"Who do you mean?" Souad asked.

"Why, the Band of Merry Men, of course," Hocine replied.

"Who are they?"

"How would I know? Perhaps they saw all of you and your less-than-wholesome relationships," the broker uttered sarcastically. "You the *malhun* singer, Kika the actress, the distinguished advisor Omar Kusturica . . and perhaps they know that the mayor was the one who arranged for you to appear on the *Nights of the Red City* TV show."

"So because of that meeting they kidnapped a foreigner—to insult the mayor?"

"I don't know the reason, nor do our police, who can *usually* be counted on to know the exact number of hairs on every Marrakechi's head," Hocine drawled.

"Where is he?"

"The mayor has been in a meeting since this morning with high-ranking officials who came from the capital. May God protect him. They've been grilling him for three hours, as if he were a student taking his baccalaureate exams."

Hocine gripped her left wrist and guided her to the stone bench in the middle of the building's courtyard. They sat down and watched the constant stream of people going in and out.

"My God, where did this disaster come from?" Souad said angrily, raising her eyes toward the sky as if she expected an answer to fall on her head.

"I don't know! Couldn't this Spanish bastard have found a city other than Marrakech to disappear in?" Hocine said.

"Do the investigators have any leads?"

"The mayor is saying that the people who pulled off the kidnapping must be *enemies of cinema*."

"What did the cinema ever do?" the singer wondered. "And what will happen with the festival?"

"Let the festival and all those people involved go to hell!" the broker snarled. He turned to look at her and noticed a look of apprehension. "Ah, I forgot. You're a permanent guest at the festival. I apologize. I completely understand your anxiety. I suggest you look for another festival, perhaps even another man—because even if the mayor emerges from this predicament with his heart intact, another organ may not be spared. In other words . . . no more erections. Know what I mean?"

Hocine's frankness silenced the singer. He knew the pleasure of her body firsthand, since he had slept with her before placing her in the mayor's bed. She suddenly felt ashamed, but that feeling soon gave way to another—the fear that her dreams of achieving glory and stardom would flit away like a bird. Her relationship with the mayor was never anything more than a way to further her fierce ambitions, which had motivated her every move since her onstage debut at the age of seventeen.

Souad never denied her debt to the mayor, for she was able to rise, step by step, by virtue of his kindness and grace. She perfected her art and had been able to enter the world of theater by playing a respectable role in a film that the mayor had arranged specifically for her. The case of the mayor and the missing director was her case too.

"We're all being held hostage, not just the director," said Hocine, in an attempt to shake the singer out of her reverie.

"All of Marrakech—all its people, and everything in it—is being held captive by this disappearance," she stated with an air of finality.

At that moment, a loud mob of men had materialized by the door. In the middle of the ruckus was the mayor, his face flushed, loose skin hanging from under his chin moving in rhythm with his body. He had clearly lost weight as a result of the incident. Hocine and Souad followed him with their eyes. The mayor's steps were slow, his body stooped over, surrounded by a throng of people. Marrakech was no longer under the mayor's control.

5. Kika, or the Beautiful Illusion

Kenza Laayadi—better known by her stage name Kika—came from a wealthy Marrakech family. She received her education at the Lycée Victor Hugo, but didn't complete her university education despite her father's pleas. She discovered the cinema through Omar Kusturica, who encountered her while her father was meeting with the mayor. She fell in love with the cinema after accompanying Omar to a studio where a film was being shot. The movie, *Seekers of Good Fortune*, was about an accident where a bus full of infertile women crashes en route to the Moulay Brahim shrine. This was her first foray into the world of cinema, which she would grow to love.

Kika didn't possess much innate talent, but she was armed

with a powerful femininity that practically exploded in the faces of those around her. She had a captivating, coquettish aura that distracted even the most focused of directors. Her willingness to work for little or nothing allowed her to take both small and large roles. She realized too late that the heights she dreamed of reaching existed only in other realms. Cinema in her own country was a plateau without a summit. Only those with an insatiable yearning for fame and self-realization could ascend to stardom. But she never stopped dreaming, and she played around with them, took pleasure in tickling them until they materialized.

She bought Aldomar's films from a vendor and watched *The Return* and *All About My Father* back to back. She envied Penelope Cruz for her roles—roles that Kika wasn't lucky enough to play.

Kika didn't receive the Band of Merry Men's communiqué, but she remained calm—unlike the *malhun* singer—held together by her wealthy family, which granted her a degree of security, even in the event that Marrakech were to fall apart entirely.

On the tenth day of the director's disappearance, the website *Marrakech Press* published an interview with Kika. The actress said that a film producer had called her days before Aldomar's disappearance, wanting to negotiate with her about doing a film in Marrakech under the direction of an unnamed Spanish director.

Her interview rocked the investigation, revealing missed essential details.

Kika continued to spew out the same story as she did the interview circuit. The various news outlets lured her to speak, hoping that she would say more than what she already had. Each time she was questioned by a reporter she would add a new detail that caused everyone to talk about her, until her dangerous game brought her to the office of the lead detective assigned to the case.

There, everything was squeezed out of her. The police felt

that she was causing unnecessary uncertainty and obstructing the investigation. They kept her under guard, and would do so until the investigation was completed, which doubled the curiosity of the press. They suspected the actress knew even more than she was letting on.

Standing on her balcony, being watched by policemen, journalists, and other onlookers delighted her to no end. It placed her in a world she had always wanted. She was like someone playing a role that, this time, she had chosen for herself—a role that could only have been written for her alone.

6. The Disappointed Investigator's Loss

He had to end his vacation in Tangier just as it had started in order to get back to his office in Marrakech. They told him over the phone that an investigation was awaiting him—something about an important Spanish man who had vanished. On the long road to Marrakech, he contemplated the huge number of cases he had dealt with during his tenure as an investigator. There had never been a case where a foreigner had gone missing. They hadn't even informed him of the missing person's name; they only told him that he was an important Spanish man. *How am I supposed to deal with a situation like this?* he thought bitterly.

The night's silence surrounded him. The highway was empty save for a handful of cars, allowing him space to leisurely mull things over. When he arrived in Marrakech, he briefly looked over the file before giving in to a power nap. During his short slumber, he dreamed that he was amid a group of people pressing up against him, their intertwined bodies demanding that he solve the case of the missing director that had so disrupted their lives. He woke up disturbed by what he had seen in his dream. He knew that this investigation would be tough.

He reread the file, then headed for the Kenz Hotel in Derb Sidi Bouloukat, mere steps from Jemaa el-Fnaa Square.

* * *

He learned from the desk clerk that Mr. Enrique Aldomar had checked into room 9 for one night (although he had spent only two hours there and then left without coming back), and that his name was recorded in the hotel guest register on October 5. The investigator examined the room for a few minutes, then asked the clerk whether the director had been carrying any luggage.

"It was strange—he had no luggage," the clerk said.

The investigator's visit to the hotel didn't provide any answers. It only uncovered a string of questions such as: Why would a foreigner check into a room for only two hours? Why come without luggage? Why would he choose such a sad hotel, in an alley such as this, if he was such a major director?

More questions came as time went on—but the investigation didn't move forward enough to deduce even the vaguest of answers. Hundreds of reports and testimonies were extracted from suspects taken randomly from the Old Medina. So-called experts attempted to glean answers from these statements, but they couldn't. That is, until the investigator crossed the street by the el-Baradei Fountain in Freedom Square. Thousands of pieces of paper flew around on the sidewalk or were pasted to the walls, or rolled up in the hands of passersby, or in the hands of coffee-shop regulars who studied them while sipping their drinks. The investigator grabbed one and read it incredulously—it was from the Band of Merry Men!

He sat on the café's terrace, taking a spot among the customers, perhaps fishing for a stray piece of information here or there about this gang. People in the café were talking about the ransom, surprised that no amount was specified in the communiqué. Soon, they began to joke and one of the wittier customers among them asked whether it was birds that had dropped this paper rain.

"No, it was the sky itself," someone else replied.

The investigator guessed that the omission was intentional, and that the next communiqué would no doubt be released soon with more information. The investigator thought that the kidnappers were testing the waters to see who was with them and who was against them. He finished his coffee and got up, folding the communiqué before stuffing it into his pocket.

He wandered around after that, driving through Massira and Sidi Youssef Ben Ali. Here he didn't see the communiqués anywhere. His eyes scanned people's hands, but to no avail. He got out of his car and asked everyone he bumped into about the Band of Merry Men and their communiqué. No one knew anything about either. He continued in this fashion until he came to the conclusion that the circle was closing around the kidnappers. He started to plan the next phase of his search.

But a second communiqué from the Merry Men gang didn't allow the investigator time to maneuver These new papers were distributed in huge numbers across the city. The new text included the ransom amount, set at two million euros.

The communiqué was glued to many doorways throughout Marrakech, including Bab el-Futouh, Bab el-Khemis, Bab el-Jadid, Bab Doukkala, and Bab el-Rouha. No one could solve the riddle of why these particular gates had been chosen. The Band of Merry Men's demand that the ransom's sum be paid in euros prompted people to think that the kidnappers might be a group of former immigrants, perhaps people who had come from Spain or Italy. This speculation reached the ears of the investigator, and he immediately recalled the story of some young Marrakechi men who had been kicked out of Spain at the beginning of 2011 because of their undocumented status. However, the story that circulated about them here in Marrakech was something entirely different, especially in Sidi Maimoun, where they had been born and raised. It was said that they had been detained in Spain for their involvement in a plot to steal the World Cup trophy that the Spanish national soccer team had won in South Africa. The Spanish police had arrested them while they were lurking around the Royal Spanish Football Federation headquarters in Madrid, where the World Cup trophy was stored in a safe on the seventh floor. The men confessed to having planned to steal the cup and bring it to their country; they had wanted to melt the trophy down. The investigator laughed every time he recalled this odd story.

He dug deep without reaping any results, and he was beginning to grow despondent. At the beginning of the investigation, he didn't think that a kidnapping case could be more frustrating and unsolvable than an everyday crime, or a rape, or even a terrorist bombing—that is, if the kidnapping were even real. The communiqué suggested it was, but what was this Band of Merry Men? No one had even heard of them before this.

After nine days, the investigation was wrested from the investigator, just as power had been taken away from the mayor. A new group of men described as resolute, powerful decision makers came from Rabat to take control of the case.

7. The Mysterious Enrique Aldomar Suddenly Appears

His name had been on the tips of a million tongues since his disappearance, and in less than a week, he had become the most famous missing person in the world. The burning question swirling in everyone's heads: *How will this affair end?* Everyone imagined the end differently, but Enrique Aldomar alone determined its conclusion.

His appearance was preceded by mysterious hints of his presence in different locations around Marrakech, sometimes even in two different places at once. Many recognized him from the ubiquitous photographs. They were enticed by the high monetary reward that the authorities offered to anyone who discovered his whereabouts. But the most astonishing thing was the testimonies that came in confirming that the director had appeared and then disappeared like a desert mirage. As soon as one person was sure they'd recognized him, he would evaporate into thin air without a trace.

It was difficult to believe all of these stories. The places where Aldomar was seen were as diverse as Marrakech itself. He appeared, according to eyewitness accounts, in Hay Hassani, Unité Quatre in Daoudiate, and even Avenue el-Mssalla in Sidi Youssef Ben Ali. The times of his appearance were just as varied—at midnight, at dawn, in the afternoon, at dusk. A myth was quickly established about the director, a man who appeared and then vanished. People had fun with his game of hide-and-seek, and they began to weave tales for one another of Aldomar's visits to their homes, how they had shared food and drink with him, only for him to vanish all over again.

A reporter for the Spanish newspaper *El Mundo*, which had been following the story from the beginning, used the expression *the wandering specter of Enrique Aldomar* in one of its articles, and published reports of his appearances and disappearances. Despite that, not one person on the Spanish shore could definitively confirm that the man was still alive. As for the Moroccan side, the ones calling the shots remained cautious, and this was the word that was repeated endlessly in news reports.

For reasons only he knew, Enrique Aldomar decided to reappear without warning in the infamous Derb Sidi Bouloukat neighborhood. He was in the lobby of the Hotel Kenz, sitting in a director's chair, with an innocent look on his face, his lips drawn into a sly smile. There was a large crowd of photographers surrounding him, as well as newspaper and television reporters from around the world. A few special investigators came along with aides. It was apparent that most of these people had been informed of the director's return ahead of time.

They all stood there without speaking, waiting to find out who was responsible for the director's disappearance—the cameras flashed and clicked. Then Enrique Aldomar's voice flowed low and soft. He praised cinema and children and their imaginative energy, and spoke about Spain, struggling with its immigrants and its Arab heritage; he spoke about misunderstandings being like an engine of history, and about literature as the twin brother of cinema. The director also spoke about fantasy being intertwined with reality, and about how all it takes to see fantasy in full relief is to lightly scrape reality's surface. He spoke about his upcoming film, which would examine the fallout from the disappearance of a famous foreigner in one of Marrakech's shabbiest alleys.

That afternoon, Aldomar talked about many other things—but he wouldn't say a word about the story of his kidnapping by the Band of Merry Men, where he'd been hidden, or the circumstances surrounding his disappearance in Marrakech.

Translated from Arabic by Alexander E. Elinson

LOOKING AT MARS IN MARRAKECH

BY ABDELKADER BENALI

La Mamounia

1.

Marcel had bad memories of Marrakech. But it hadn't always been that way. The first time he saw the city it took his breath away. The red light sliding over the walls, the snowcapped mountains of the Atlas in the background, the swallows that wove through the palm trees, and the three gleaming balls on top of the Koutoubia Mosque that storks flew around like satellites. The long, wide streets seemed to be endless. Everything looked as if it had been made for another time, perhaps another planet; a city that had been built for the inhabitants of the future.

One day, Marrakech's beautiful curtain was drawn back and revealed another face—indifferent, aloof, and criminal. Marcel had been ripped off, robbed of something dear to him, and he had left with his tail between his legs, never to return.

Once home, he never spoke to anyone about it. It lay stowed away in a place that never saw daylight.

"It'll be different this time," his agent said. "And you do have to start working again, don't you? A broke writer can't write. The imagination won't work."

The hopeless financial situation he had ended up in had come as a complete surprise. With the money he had earned from extracting oil on Mars, he had hoped to buy time to write.

Mars had been good to him. The vast quantities of oil that had been discovered there ten years before had created a boom.

When they devised an ingenious system that made traveling to Mars take only a couple of months, the amount of traffic back and forth increased exponentially. The shuttles went faster and faster, and he received a job offer that made use of his analytical abilities. The remuneration persuaded him, not Mars. He supported a drilling team on the red planet, which creamed off the oil fields by setting up a system to find buyers within a couple of hours of the source being discovered. The first to make an offer benefited from the small margins. It wasn't difficult work, but it was intense. The drilling team worked twenty-four hours a day, which meant that he hardly got any sleep. He had to be on alert in case of new discoveries. But the money compensated for everything. When he lay in bed, he made the most wonderful financial calculations, involving acquisitions and investments, and had money left over to go traveling. He even returned to Earth with an extra bonus. The red planet had made him happy.

When he did get back, however, he discovered that inflation had evaporated the capital he'd built up. The oil boom had flooded the markets with cheap money, which had pushed up prices. The cost of a good television—one he'd had his eye on—had gone up so much that it was beyond his budget. Only six months after his return, and he had to start over again. Now he cursed his time on the red planet. And to make matters worse, his wife had lost her job as well, a blow she took without concern, because she had become devoted to a charismatic guru who had convinced his disciples that the only real capital was the "courage to let go." She had started to *let go* of things, and she did that so well that her nonattachment led to her being able to levitate above a mat.

"I'm the only one in the group," his wife said proudly. And she parried his requests to think about the future with: "The future is now."

There is something in that, he thought. *The future is always now.* Amid the male company on Mars, he had forgotten how to talk to a woman. After a few days, he had a riposte for her, particularly because the bills had started to arrive. "If the future is now then it's still a shitty situation we're in."

"Everything is just a question of perception," she reasoned. "You're only seeing it with one eye."

"Only seeing it with one eye?" Marcel put his palm over his left eye and examined the bills. "Even if I do look at it with one eye, I can still see that we've got a problem. The bills haven't been halved." He turned to her; yoga had kept her fit and healthy. It had made her younger. Her calves were hard, but he knew that if he touched them, they would feel warm and soft. When they got bored, they had sex. It was never a disappointment and he forgot his financial problems for a little while. In bed, even he had the courage to *let go*.

"If you close your eyes, you can see a new universe," she said.

He'd had enough of new worlds for now. "The universe is empty and indifferent. You make more of it than it is."

On Mars, he'd hardly had any time to gaze into the universe; everything had revolved around drilling. Luckily, there had been a good satellite connection with a couple of his favorite talk shows, which offered a bit of relief. He lived for those moments of reprieve between shifts.

2.

In the evening, Marcel looked through a telescope at Mars, where he had left his colleagues behind. He never should have left. He cherished the long conversations they'd had with each other. What he'd told them about Marrakech, the Red City. "We're on the red planet, but the Red City is also special," he would say. Then he would tell them about the couple of times he had been there. But he only told them the good things. The men were not travelers—they hung onto his every word. Some had never been more than sixty miles from home before their journey to Mars. Most of them came from little American towns he'd never heard of before, and weren't planning to ever go anywhere else again once they got back.

"When we return, let's all go to Marrakech together," proposed one of the men one night.

"I'm never going back to Marrakech," Marcel vowed. "Apart from everything that was wonderful, I had a bad experience there."

"And that's why you're on Mars," they told him supportively. "You can't be farther away from your problems."

"Yes I can," Marcel had said. "Because I'm so far away, I feel less—but what I can feel, I feel all the more."

It went quiet around the table. He realized that he had expressed a feeling that they all understood. The men respected his privacy. They all had something to hide. If being on Earth was always painful, then there definitely must be something to hide. Could someone be so far away without suffering? They all felt better on Mars than at home.

3.

The agent kept ringing. He was a persistent type who owed his success to hard work rather than big breaks. *Getting rich is like threading beads* was the man's motto.

The job was to write the biography of the major media magnate Max Hirschfeld. *What a name!* Hirschfeld always appeared on the lists of movers and shakers around the world, and he had taken up residence at the Mamounia, the famous luxury hotel where the British prime minister Winston Churchill had spent his summers. The man had painted hideous pictures there that raised huge amounts at auction. Marcel was already anticipating having to spend two weeks with an egocentric, conceited, rich narcissist who wanted his every fart recorded for posterity. Marcel could use the money, but it would be at the cost of his psychological well-being.

"When I suggested that you be the one to write it, he agreed immediately," said his agent.

"Does he know my work?"

"No, but he liked your name," his agent told him. "His favorite grandfather was named Marcel."

"It's always something like this," Marcel said, exasperated.

"Don't knock it!" The agent had called on a Friday morning; the man smelled money. "If it makes it any easier, I won't charge you any commission . . . just the other party. What do you think of that?"

Marcel didn't try to explain that he really did not want to go to Marrakech. "I'll gladly go to New York or London or wherever else he lives."

"As long as he likes it there, he's staying in Marrakech."

"Can't it be done virtually?"

"Don't be daft! You've got to see the man," his agent scoffed. "Smell him, experience him. Otherwise, we'll find someone else to do it."

His wife was levitating above the yoga mat in a side room. It was a mystery to him how she managed it. It made her attractive: freeing her exceptional body from weightlessness with one jump, throwing her on the bed, and calmly unrolling the Lycra clothes so that she was as naked as light. He had never known that she had so much inner power. After his journey to and from Mars, he'd had enough of weightlessness. The sensation of floating didn't compensate for the inconvenience. His wife mumbled something in his ear about self-awareness and transition. The last thing Marcel wanted to hear about was self-awareness and transition. What he wanted to hear was that she'd had enough of living in the here and now and that she had applied for a job. But there was no point in bringing that up, since he had fallen a long way in her esteem. His reluctance to talk about his time on Mars didn't go over well with her, either.

"Your lack of communication is appalling," she chided, as she began slamming doors. After which they had sex; that's the way it went every time. He never got used to it, but it was always enjoyable.

It wasn't a bad thing that he ultimately hadn't earned any money on Mars, of course, but she would have appreciated the trip more if the journey had *changed* him . . . and it hadn't.

"I was too busy working to change," he'd told her.

She found that strange. "You're not living in the here and now."

4.

It was Saturday night. Marcel had difficulty sleeping, so he read about potential investments on the computer. Perhaps it might be better to invest what he had left to make good on some of his losses. Good times always follow the bad times. On Mars, his friends had told him about what they did with their money. Investing seemed a sensible option, according to some of them. Everyone did it in the United States. He should do it too. So, in the middle of the night, after three glasses of whiskey, he bought shares with what was left of his capital.

It was fast—faster than he'd expected. He prepared his portfolio after just two swigs of whiskey and went to bed cheerful. His wife was asleep, but he woke her and convinced her to make love. She enjoyed the smell of whiskey on his breath.

5.

The stock exchanges opened with huge losses on Monday. The Central Bank responded to the panic by printing a substantial amount of money. It had to be done to preserve what was left of public confidence in the monetary system, otherwise it would have meant disaster. "They're Printing Money!" was the news headline.

Again, Marcel thought.

Even more inflation! It would take months, perhaps years, for his investments to recover their value. He had little, he had nothing, and what he did have was worth even less. He had never been so miserable in his life. Marcel hid his wife's yoga mat to stop her from making his mood even worse with her levitating. The panic in her eyes when she couldn't find it was somewhat of a comfort. If he had to suffer, then she had to as well. He didn't tell her about his losses. He had become a heartless man because of what had happened to him. So, in desperation, he rang his agent.

He told his wife that he would be away for a month, which was not too bad in comparison with the four years on Mars. But she was more emotional than the last time. It almost certainly had something to do with the crisis.

"You will send money for the housekeeping, won't you?" she asked.

"Wouldn't it be a good idea if you went and looked for a job?" Marcel retorted.

"I'd rather be dead than hear you say things like that."

"I hate it when *you* say that sort of thing," he snapped.

"Come back with good news," she said.

"I'll be coming back with material for a book."

He wondered if he should tell her why he didn't want to go to Marrakech. He would rather go to any other place on Earth. Would she understand? But then he would have to tell her that Marrakech had been an experience that had changed him, that had made him who he was. Without that period in his life, he would never have begun a long-term relationship.

She waved her hand in the direction of the door. "I think the taxi's here. Quick. I can't stand it any longer. I have to go to my yoga class."

6.

Marcel could see Marrakech crystal clear from the air. It was a pleasure to look at it. It was only later that he understood that the transparency was deceptive. It was difficult not to be overwhelmed. The city had proved itself resistant to the tourism hype. It had not only survived it, but it had given it a twist. Tourists did their thing, the residents did their thing—it was a city that began each day trying to remember who it was yesterday, and had already forgotten again by the end of the evening.

When he smelled the air he knew that it had been a bad idea to come to the city. The best thing he could do was go straight to the check-in desk and catch the first airplane back home. He had hardly any time to think it through before the taxi driver who'd come to pick him up was standing in front of him, frantically waving a board with his name on it. Incorrectly spelled. The man embraced him as if he were a long-lost family member. And perhaps he was, a little. Anyway, he was already sweating. He wanted more than anything else to go to his hotel room and lie under a bedsheet with the curtains closed until this oppressive feeling had subsided.

It was not to be, however. The driver sped to the hotel as if he were being chased by people he owed money to, all while alternating Marcel's name: *Monsieur Marcel, Monsieur Marcel,* the driver said, *Monsieur Hirschfeld, Monsieur Hirschfeld,* like he was a small child who had just learned the words. It was only a short way to the Mamounia from the airport, but the driver seemed to know an even shorter route. The buildings Marcel remembered from his last visit flashed by left and right, pushed back in the course of time by more recent, more prestigious buildings, like old masters surrounded by voluptuous young women. As soon as evening came, the lights would be turned on, and Marcel would be able to see just how big everything was—the lights gave the decadence contours. He'd once been a part of it. Before they came to a halt in front of the Mamounia, the driver asked: "Have you been to Marrakech before?"

Marcel bit his lip. "This is the first time," he lied.

"You are a lucky man," the driver said as he opened the door.

If only he knew.

He would need something to drink first, to calm himself, so that he could cope with his pending conversation with Mr. Hirschfeld.

The Mamounia Hotel impressed him. Mr. Hirschfeld was paying for the cost of his stay. The way in which the attendant met and escorted him confirmed to Marcel that Mr. Hirschfeld was an important guest.

"Mr. Hirschfeld receives for dinner in his suite at nine o'clock," the attendant said.

"Can you tell me where I have to be?"

"You will be collected."

He installed himself in his room. He hung up his suit, shined his shoes, and quickly ironed a shirt. In the city evening fell, the time for people to drift to the old center, the hum mixed with the excited chatter of the exotic birds. From his room he could see the Koutoubia Mosque with the Atlas Mountains behind it. The city was seething. Sitting here inside, protected from the cacophony, made him feel small. He felt isolated, not really a person. He should have been out there, anonymous, just wandering, no real objective except the longing to be entertained and to meet new people. The city was good at that, giving the feeling that anyone could be friends with anyone else. "Who am I kidding?" Marcel asked aloud, trying to pull himself together. "I'm not welcome here. If I take one step outside the door, I'll suffocate. Everywhere I go . . ." It was pointless thinking about it. It was history. Marcel breathed air in through his nose. Air he was addicted to.

7.

Three rather insistent knocks on his door awoke him. The three miniature bottles of whiskey he had thoughtlessly knocked back had done their work a little too well. It was five minutes to nine and he had an erection. He wanted to have sex. He missed his wife. He was going to be late and wouldn't make a good impression on a billionaire that way. For a rich person, time is a fetish.

"I'm coming, I'm coming!" Marcel shouted in his best French as he pulled on his blue suit. It had been a long time since he had slept so deeply in the daytime. He couldn't tell from the face of the attendant who led him to Hirschfeld's suite if anyone was irritated with him. But did it matter? People fell asleep. It would have been much worse if he had stayed asleep.

With a knock on the door, they were allowed in. The attendant handed him over as if he were a parcel—only they didn't scan him. The spacious room proved to be an antechamber. There was a gigantic cage in which a Brazilian parrot was enjoying some nuts. It was being spoiled, and yet the bird did not seem to be at ease. It didn't move and looked suspiciously at the new guest. *Max Hirschfeld's parrot doesn't like strangers,* thought Marcel. *And I don't like his parrot.*

He was allowed into the next room. The attendant left him alone. They did that, of course, to heighten the effect—this man could only function by creating distance, by giving you the feeling that you were small. And the longer he was left alone, exposed to the décor around him, the deeper the realization that he had come a long way to meet this man. *What an extraordinary meeting this will be!* Marcel knew he couldn't give in to the depression that was hanging over him, throwing a blanket of melancholy over everything. It was the last thing he needed at the moment. He was contractually bound, by all sorts of clauses, to exude energy and enthusiasm. The billionaire must have zero doubts about him.

Suddenly, the billionaire stood in front of him and thrust an enormously big hand toward Marcel, fingers outstretched like a ship. Hirschfeld was bigger and more agreeable-looking than Marcel had expected. The corpulent, somewhat sickly looking figure was actually a friendly man, who moved easily and looked at him with welcoming eyes. His feet were in comfortable brown loafers and his face was well polished by the Moroccan sun. No sign of arrogance.

"Marcel Ophuis," he said, shaking the billionaire's hand.

"Hirschfeld, but call me Max. May I call you Marcel? Formality is for people who are on their way to the top, but we're there already. You as a writer, me as a newspaperman."

Rich people and people of standing found it difficult to relate to ordinary people. Not because they didn't understand them, but because they didn't know the context well enough, and they were afraid of making a mistake, of being confronted with their ignorance of ordinary things. This man was one of the few rich and successful people who had something of an ordinary life. That made him human. Marcel was immediately fascinated by him.

"Haven't they offered you anything to drink?" Hirschfeld asked. "The scoundrels. Please, sit down."

They sat close together. He found the intimacy, which Hirschfeld seemed to take as a matter of course, not unpleasant. It was important to leave a good impression and Hirschfeld understood that. Marcel was silently grateful that his agent had insisted that he accept the job. He sat opposite a true mensch.

"We're going to do it right. A biography has to have a face. Everyone makes mistakes, but few have the courage to admit them," Hirschfeld explained. "I'm able to say that I wouldn't have been who I am today without those mistakes. That's what the book has to be about."

"You already have an idea. That's good."

"I'm an open book. People have always underestimated me. And do you know why? Because they didn't know any better. And I made use of that. I regret some things . . ." the billionaire admitted. And to make it immediately clear that he meant what he said, Hirschfeld rattled off a number of names that Marcel had read about in preparation. The bottom line was that a lot of Hirschfeld's wealth had fallen into his lap because people had thought that he would mess it up. "They underestimated me, the idiots. Underestimated. And instead of giving me respect every time that I showed that I could do it, they gave me an even bigger commission, just to see how I would mess that up. But I didn't. I won and won and won." The last comment came out embittered.

So there *was* a pain that could be lived off for a lifetime. Pure kerosene was needed to keep on flying and to cross time zones. Hirschfeld's drive to make something of himself reminded Marcel of his colleagues on Mars, always trying to show the world that they were decent, that they were doing the right thing, that they were good people. It was a glimpse of a damaged man. That could be used to fill a very good book. He was a success in everything, but still he always had the feeling that it was thanks to the stupidity of others.

Hirschfeld clapped his hands. In no time, all sorts of dishes were placed in front of Marcel. Exquisitely flavored Moroccan food with a well-seasoned choice of spices. While Marcel ate, Hirschfeld watched him intently. Marcel's agent had warned him about this: Hirschfeld couldn't stand thin people. Marcel had to eat.

"Have you had enough?" the billionaire asked.

"Yes, it's delicious."

"Good. I'm impressed by your appetite," the billionaire said. "Your agent told me you could eat like a horse. That makes me happy. My father was like that, and my grandfather was as well. Cigar?"

"No thank you. I don't smoke."

"Smoking at my age is like unwrapping a present. I don't let anyone tell me what to do anymore," Hirschfeld joked. Then he burst out into an incoherent tirade about his four ex-wives who had tried to prevent him from smoking. He visibly enjoyed losing himself in such bouts of anger; his eyes shone with pleasure as he verbally got even. He tore his wives to pieces, but he did it with style. As if all the pent-up anger over the years had delivered the jackpot: passion, release, and relief. Before Marcel knew it, the two men were laughing together. The evening had somehow become enjoyable.

"But haven't they helped you live longer by stopping you from smoking?"

Hirschfeld moved a little bit closer to Marcel, and his voice smoothed into an almost whisper: "Better a short and happy life than a long and unhappy one. They were bitches. I tied myself up in knots trying to keep them happy, while they were just planning to fleece me."

Marcel couldn't do anything else but change his opinion: there was a book in this man. Maybe even two or three. If they became friends, it could turn into something big. If Marcel could place his talent in the service of a man who had not only made it, but who had seen enough to be able to tell a truly remarkable story, then it would also help his own career as a writer.

"Luckily, I now have a wife who really loves me," the billionaire said, his anger melting with a smile.

"Such luck is scarce. To fall for someone so late in life." Marcel quickly realized that he had said something stupid. He had to correct himself fast: "I mean . . . not that you're old."

Hirschfeld leaned into him. "You speak from the heart," he reassured Marcel, placing his hand on his own heart. "I like you. Because I'm old and my life is behind me, it allows me to see the time that I have left as a bonus. I don't talk to people that often anymore. And people don't talk that often to me. Do you know why? After a certain age, you don't trust people anymore. I've had bad luck. Each and every one of my children—and I have twelve—are unreliable, opportunistic, and dishonest. They're lucky in business and unlucky in life. If they call me it's only to ask for more money . . . What did you do before?"

"I was on Mars," Marcel answered.

"The planet?"

"Yes."

"That's good, there's a nightclub here called Mars. Wasn't it incredibly cold out there?"

"We were inside."

"You weren't there to write a book, were you?" Hirschfeld asked.

"Work."

"Were you a part of the oil boom that brought our planet so much wealth?"

"It was a good time," Marcel said.

"You must be happy to be home."

"It's okay. The money I earned turned out to be less than I thought."

"And the damned inflation as well," Hirschfeld said. "You couldn't see that coming on Mars, of course."

"You couldn't see it coming on Earth either. Money didn't interest me until I didn't have it anymore," Marcel admitted. "And then I became very interested. But I'd rather not talk about it. We're in Marrakech and we're having an interesting conversation. That is worth a lot to me."

"Come with me." Hirschfeld led Marcel to the window. There was a telescope on the balcony. "Part of the hotel service. Show me where Mars is."

Marcel began to point the telescope. He gestured to Hirschfeld. "There."

The man bent down to peer into the lens. Marcel saw that he enjoyed what he could see. "We're looking at Mars in Marrakech," the billionaire said, his tone full of awe.

When they went back inside, Marcel saw the woman who had brought both Hirschfeld and himself so much unhappiness. She was four years older. She had only put on a few pounds. She was beautiful, sensual, and sly—her name was Sarah, even if she didn't look like a Sarah.

"Ghizlaine, *ma chérie*," Hirschfeld said. "You were going to bed early. Did you miss me?"

This new name matched the off-white silk nightdress that fit perfectly over Sarah's copper-colored body, like a sumptuous art deco vase draped in silk. Yet the dress wasn't vulgar; she could never come across as vulgar. She had learned over the years that a man would surrender himself entirely to a woman whose appearance was based on a sort of shock effect. It was impossible not to want to hold her, to want to love her, destroy her, and then resurrect her—if that was even possible.

When she had financially and sexually drained him, had utterly humiliated him by disappearing without a trace, just before he was to leave Marrakech—he'd even been followed by boys who kept bothering him after he had asked around for her in the neighborhood where she lived—Marcel became so damaged that just the mere thought of her made him sick. But in her renewed vicinity, there was nothing of that. It was just possible that somewhere in his heart there was room for forgiveness. He would once again have the chance to enjoy her delicious presence—that promise which emanated from her broke his resistance.

They once had to leave a restaurant in a hurry while quietly waiting for their main course because his agent had discreetly whispered that a man at the bar could not stand that Marcel was with her. "Such a gentleman is sitting with such an interesting lady. It might be better for you and her *and* the furnishings if you continue your evening at another address. I can recommend somewhere for you," the waiter had told him.

Sarah was so beautiful. He was proud of her—his attention made her lively, and every time she'd disappeared with his credit card, she came back more richly clothed and more gorgeous.

"I can't sleep without a good night kiss, just like the French writer you told me about," Ghizlaine said to her husband. "I thought for a long time that I was the only one like that. It made me lonely."

Proust had felt that way as well. She had done some more reading since he last saw her: the change wasn't just on the surface. She couldn't return to the working-class area she had left like a missile. It had become a strange planet for her.

"Is this the *monsieur* you've been talking about? The writer?" she asked, tilting her head to get a better look at him. "Don't I know you? Haven't I read a book of yours? I'd like to. And then talk to you about it. Preferably in the shade in the afternoon."

She didn't walk toward him, she floated, as if a gigantic wind turbine blew her along. The refinement that hid her dark past as if it were a secret weapon had become even more intense.

"We have seen Mars. He's been on the red planet," Hirschfeld said.

"Extraordinary—an astronaut. Weren't you afraid up there?"

"You take your fear with you—and it's just as bad anywhere else," Marcel replied.

"Philosophical." She looked at him charmingly, as if to reward him.

"Ghizlaine," Hirschfeld whispered, almost as an admonition, in a tone they'd invented especially for their relationship. It was a tone that excited them—a needy girl for a forceful man. That tone was stronger than a legal contract. That tone said everything. "In just a short space of time, I've become very fond of this man, and now you come and spoil it for us," Hirschfeld teased. "Be nice to him. You could have been nice to the other one."

"That man was not as nice as this gentleman."

"We had a writer here staying with us," Hirschfeld explained. "There was some tension between him and my girl."

"And the girl won?" asked Marcel.

"He found it difficult to settle in," said Ghizlaine. "I'm not very good in competitions. Can't you see?" The small, soft hand that she held out melted in his; it told him that she knew very well who he was and that she wanted him, that she hadn't forgotten him and never would.

"But the other guy had to go to make way for you. You're a true talent. Everything has a reason. He didn't believe that Allah preordained all things. But I do. Do you?"

"What was it like on Mars?" Ghizlaine asked, her hand still lingering in his. "You have to tell me everything. You can only go once, and I've heard so many things."

Translated from Dutch by Terry Ezra

OTHER PLACES

BY MOHAMED ZOUHAIR

Tabhirt

The boy whose father was a tart chaser, who had abandoned both him and his mother when he was just a child; the boy whose only future involved skipping school, wasting his childhood with a potter; the boy who was totally uninterested in his youth or his poverty; the boy who, after his mother's death from an asthma attack when he was a teenager, lived the life of a vagrant orphan in the wild; that same boy grew up and, at the age of twenty-five, decided that he wanted to travel. And so, responding to some obscure call, he left Safi for Marrakech in search of some other time that he had only dreamed about.

It was early summer when Najib the potter took up residence in Tabhirt, the area in Marrakech where potters and their ovens were located. The potters in Tabhirt soon discovered how skillful this newly arrived young man was, and they watched him with a mixture of admiration and envy. Merchants competed for his wares and his reputation soon spread. The master potter recommended him to Master Hasun, a wealthy merchant whose workshops were always busy, and whose ovens were never extinguished. They were always fired up, even during feast days and Ashura.

Hasun was an old man, but someone who still liked to smoke kif and pot, as well as drink strong tea all day. The master took Najib the potter to his riad in Mawqif, which ran directly parallel to Tabhirt. Najib immediately noticed the lovely figure of Badia, who was sitting in the courtyard with her maid Masuda. Badia was a woman in the prime of her youth. She was lithe, fresh-skinned, and had a beautiful figure. When Najib glanced at her, his eyes flickered, and a hot flash ran through his entire body. He assumed that she was Hasun's daughter but felt a kind of dagger thrust at the thought that she might actually be his wife: an old ruin like him with such a luscious creature—what did they have in common? The riad was spacious enough, but it was really nothing but an old fortress, and this lovely woman would waste the best part of her life within its walls.

Indeed, Badia's life rarely extended beyond its bounds. Only on rare occasions would she go to the bathhouse or visit her family in Bab Hailana, which was also close to Mawqif. Even then, Masuda would always accompany her: the maid was like a shadow dogging her mistress's footsteps.

Badia gave the young man a cold reception. Once she was alone with the merchant, she upbraided him. "A potter boy in our house? Why?"

"He has no family," Hasun explained. "He'll come here for the night and leave in the morning. He'll be going straight from the front door to his bed. Masuda can look after him. We need him."

"You mean . . . *you* need him?" Badia said.

"He's a skilled craftsman. His fingers are golden. If we don't take him, someone else will," Hasun responded.

She was testing his intentions; his tone of voice was that of a merchant looking for a profitable deal. So this young man would be spending his nights here, inside this riad with its abundant rooms and furniture, a place totally lacking in warmth or life. In the upper rooms, Hasun the merchant kept some rare trinkets for use on appropriate occasions; in fact, all the rooms except one were filled with those trinkets. Now that one room would be where this newly arrived young potter would rest.

"Here's where you'll be sleeping, and there's the toilet."

Those were the terse words of Masuda, laced with anxiety, as though to keep some sentiment under control.

When she brought him his supper on that first night, she did not say a word. She simply put the tray down on the small wooden table, glanced in his direction, and then left. For just a moment she leaned over the banister and stared up at the sky studded with stars, their gentle gleam shimmering delicately in the heavens. It occurred to her to go back to the young man's room and ask him if he needed anything. The door to the tiny room was still ajar, and from close by she could hear his footsteps. But she decided not to venture any farther and went down the stairs to find Hasun and his wife. The couple were passing the evening in complete silence. The coughing of the very old husband soon interrupted the quiet. Hasun had no idea what to do about her—and Badia had no idea what to do about him, either.

Some nights later, Masuda stared at Najib, admiring his powerful build, his pinkish complexion, almost clay-colored. She enjoyed his perfect proportions and his youthful energy. A powerful longing came over her. She felt as if she had been brushed by fire.

"Do you know my name?" she asked him.

"Masuda," Najib answered. "I heard Master Hasun use it."

"You seem to be Masud, the lucky one," she told him.

With that, she left. All the lights on the top story were out except for the one in his room. All the other doors were closed, their secrets locked inside. Najib would later discover that they were all inhabited by pottery ware; he would develop a sense of companionship with them, even though the doors were locked.

Masuda did not go back downstairs. When she left his room, she went over to a corner directly opposite the door and stood there. Through a hole in the door, Najib watched as she took off her headscarf and threw it to the ground. Loosening her belt, she let her dress fall where it would. Removing her shoes, she started moving around like a silent dancer in the darkness. He saw her taking a few cautious steps toward his room. Pausing for a moment, she looked over the banister to the courtyard below, and then went back to the corner, put herself in order, and returned to her own room next to the kitchen.

After taking off all of her clothes, Masuda threw herself on her bed and surrendered to her powerful fantasies. Here she was, an unmarried woman, over thirty years old, olive-skinned and a bit plump, with a harsh voice, plain features, and ample breasts. Her devotion to her mistress Badia implicitly involved a silent love for the woman's body, something that she was pursuing breathlessly in her dreams as though chasing a mirage.

Another mirage was pestering Badia in the wide courtyard below, one that gave her heart a jolt. She could not get the image of the new arrival out of her mind: it pierced the veil of darkness and besieged her dreams. A fitful sleep turned into a raging insomnia. So near, yet so far, her husband rolled over in his bed with the nasty smell of kif on his breath. Once he finished his dinner and concluded the nonexistent conversation with the woman who was a prisoner in his mansion, he got up to spread out in bed next to her like an old dried-out twig lying beside a pure, coursing spring. Was Hasun completely unaware that by bringing this young man to the house he was providing what had been missing for some time? Did he not realize that he was introducing a spark to set off other sparks? The evidence was the chronic insomnia that was having such an effect on Badia. This spark was the breath of life infiltrating her existence, held in death's own talons. When the young man was in his room or if his image came into her mind, she would deliberately put on a show of cold indifference and even resentment toward him, all with the aim of keeping him and her conflict inside her—and what a dire conflict it was! If you place your hand on a piece of ice, it can burn you like fire, but when that ice is actually placed in fire, it melts into water.

Najib spent his days at the pottery workshop, singing of love as he kneaded clay. The clay would respond readily to his skillful fingers, which pulsated with the rhythm of his heart. Whenever he saw a lovely female body, he would be inspired by its beauty to create a statuette. Once the human eye fell on such a statuette, the heart was drawn to it and the hand was eager to purchase it.

"This is beauty's gift to beauty," he would proclaim each time he finished such a statuette.

"They are sources of income," had been Hasun's response, as he watched the statuettes fly off the shelves almost as soon as they were stocked. Rumors spread that they were possessed by good fortune; their new owners cherished them.

"Beauty's own gift to beauty. They should be donated to beauty, not sold!" Najib had objected.

"Get me the money, and I'll give them to whomever you please," Hasun had compromised. He would say this whenever he was feeling relaxed and at ease, stoned on kif, otherwise he simply ignored the whole thing, as worthless as a drop of water or handful of dirt.

The young potter thoroughly enjoyed making statuettes inspired by women who appealed to his heart, and it upset him to watch as the merchant bartered over them. Najib did not like the idea at all, but the only person he could share his feelings with was Masuda. He told her about the women who inspired him to make the statuettes, and that made her pale. He conveyed to her the sadness he felt at the way Hasun was selling them, as though they were merely decorations rather than art with his very soul attached.

Masuda went downstairs tense and hurt. The next morning, she told Badia what he'd said, and that only increased the pain of Badia's desire. Masuda felt the fire burning inside her as she listened to the stories of Najib's statuettes, while Badia listened to the very same stories as told by her maid. The same feeling of desire brought the two women together, but it also pulled them apart. No matter how hard they tried, they could not keep their feelings a secret from each other. Every night Masuda would hear the story, and the next morning she would relate it to her mistress. The nighttime account was repeated the next day, and the wait for the next story involved both tension and desire.

"So, tell me about your statuette women today," Masuda said to Najib one evening.

"Today, a woman came at midday when the quarter was taking a nap," he recalled. "I was on my own in the store next to the pottery. She came in, called me by name, and let her veil drop. Her face gleamed, a gorgeous blend of pink and white; her eyes positively oozed seduction. *Take a good look at my face*, she'd said, and that is precisely what I did. *If my face is not enough*, she went on, *then I'll take off my djellaba and even my underclothes, so you can see my entire body.*"

Najib paused in his tale for a second, his eyes glazing over dreamily before he continued: "*Your face is quite enough*, I told the woman. *Don't deceive me, my heart is soaring in the blue heavens*, she said. *No statuette-maker can possibly deceive a figure of such beauty*, I responded. She laughed heartily. *I'm going to wait for the craftsman's product*, she said. *You shouldn't wait too long, the statuette will emerge in good time,* I told her. And with that, she put her veil over her face again, while I filled my soul with the vision of those black eyes. I got the impression that she was pleased at the way I looked at her, as though to acknowledge that an ineffective model—one with no inner sense of the various concepts of wine not found inside the grape—will never lead to the creation of a fine statuette. When she left, a gentle, dewy breeze imbued with the scent of lavender had cooled the heat. I will confide to you, Masuda, that at that moment I could hear the clay calling out to my very soul. I flew to it on wings of sheer desire. It responded to me with relish. That statuette is hidden now. It is intended for that lady, and I shall give it to her as a gift, expressing my heartfelt thanks for her beauty, the kind from which you can unwrap a loveliness of a different type."

Masuda's eyes were downcast as she listened in silence, keeping her own desires suppressed. Sometimes she shuddered a little, other times she looked up at him to hide a tear that she could not control. When he finished, she stood up without saying a word, closed the door behind her, and went back downstairs. During the nighttime darkness she burst into tears.

The next day, when Najib and his master Hasun had left, she was obliged to tell Badia the story from the previous night. Her mistress listened with her entire body on fire. By the time Masuda had finished, Badia was bathed in sweat, her breathing was short, and she was practically having convulsions.

"What's the matter, my lady?" Masuda asked.

"Nothing," Badia said. "I need to have a bath."

Badia dashed to the bathroom, poured water all over her sweat-slicked body, and started screaming. Her voice was hoarse, full of longing. As Masuda listened to her cries, she too was deeply troubled, although the feeling couldn't be expressed in words.

In the old days, an Arab poet would flirt with a woman. His *ghazal* poems would be objects of pride for her, a celebration of her femininity, something she craved even while her family disapproved. They would pursue the poet and prevent the two of them from communicating with each other. They would even declare war on him; they would kill him or encourage others to do so. There was no precedent for a woman rejecting her poet-lover; indeed, she might've been the one taking initiative. The woman's family was supposed to take charge if someone composed a poem about a woman of their tribe. *Ghazal* poems transformed a piece of clay into a statuette in celebration of beauty, the very thing that Najib the potter did when he revealed his inner emotion to the clay and exchanged secrets with it.

Did the girl named Sara not discover that very fact when she spotted a statuette that looked exactly like her at the pottery store? When she visited the store, Najib was arranging some of his creations on the shelves. Those statuettes would always attract the eye and give rise to hidden emotions. However, this girl Sara pretended not to know about such things—indeed, not to like them at all. Once Najib realized that, he stole a glance at her features and figure. For her part, she stood in the sunlight and allowed him to take a long look at her as she examined others' pieces. Soon a nonverbal conversation between them transpired, before Najib addressed her politely: "Next time you'll see something you like."

"I'll wait then," she said. "Goodbye!"

Sara did not have to wait long. Just a few days later, a statuette that looked just like her, one that she felt expressed a distinct feminine feeling, vanished from the shelves. She acquired it at the price demanded by the merchant, then put it beside her bed and admired it often.

The stories kept coming, and Badia expected to listen to them every morning. If she didn't have to sleep with her husband, she would certainly have listened to them before the rooster crowed, like Shahriyar in a womanly form. But in this case, the young potter was Shahrazad in a masculine guise, and Masuda was the go-between. The nighttime stories came in various shapes and sizes. Were they supposed to postpone the death of Najib the potter—or hasten it? Was Masuda telling them so as to relieve her own stress or to increase Badia's? Did Masuda tell them to prove to Badia that she was closer to the storyteller, or as a way of concealing her own despair about him? Did she sense that her role merely involved conveying the story to the person for whom it was intended? Was this intended person just the story's subject and the story itself a rose on the statuette's body? Yet the primary topic was operating in a different universe, distracted or seemingly so. Afraid? Hesitant? Nonchalant? Whatever the case, it was Badia who was on fire; she was further enflamed every time she heard a story about the other women.

As long as he doesn't take the initiative with me, she told herself,

I shall do it with him. And let whatever happens happen! She believed that her own story should be recorded, or else she should move to act. She had never been aware of her own femininity for a single day, or of the woman hidden inside her. Her very existence was like nothingness. As her own body opened up to its potential, she had been buried in a marriage to a frigid and inadequate husband.

Her father had been a potter working for Hasun. One of the employer's ovens had collapsed on top of him, and her father had burned to death in its ashes. Hasun had arrived to convey his condolences and had spotted her as a teenager, having known her previously as just a child. Only a few months went by before he came back and asked her mother for her hand in marriage, in exchange for support for the widowed woman and her four children, of which Badia was the oldest. Her mother gave her to him, and so he hurriedly divorced his fifth wife, claiming that she was barren, whereas he knew full well that it was not his wife's fault but his own—he was the sterile one. Changing wives for him was just like changing clothes. So Badia arrived at the riad of an infertile man who was older than her own father. He constantly craved money, his only obsession. She had been handed over to him at the age of seventeen, and now she was twenty-three, a prisoner in the guise of a wife, married to a man thirty-six years older. Her husband was addicted to kif, hashish, and other vices that made his sweat and breath stink. He had nightmares. What time had wrought could not be put right. He was cold in his daily contacts, and foul to be near. *So, here I am,* she told herself, unable to sleep, lying awake in these days of torment. She was served in her own relentless fashion by an old maid who had no purpose in her life either, but simply handed Badia over at night to a senile old merchant as though consigning her to a grave of ashes. *But here you are, with heart tremors and calls to desire. Your stories hit me like so many arrows and tongues of fire. Where should I turn, and what should I do?* Badia wondered.

Meanwhile, Masuda had started smoking some of the kif she prepared for her master, stealing a little for her own enjoyment. She also took some hashish. Hasun was aware of this, but chose to ignore it. He was relieved that someone else was sharing in his habit. One time when she got stoned, she raised her voice in song.

For Badia's part, she was having her own daydream—where she was naked in front of Najib. *Isn't this spectacular display enough, using all the eloquence of my body to make even the dullest stone excited?* Badia had asked the dream potter. She watched him while he stared at his delicate fingers stained with clay. He did not look at her. Masuda's singing blended with her own day-dream, and deliberately interrupted them like a planted spy. She looked on as Masuda stripped naked in front of him and kept on singing. He peered over at Masuda, but not at her. *Bring me a knife!* Badia yelled. *So I can cut off his fingers. No, instead I'm going to kill him, and her as well.* At that point, Badia woke up to hear Masuda's shrills reverberating through the riad.

Masuda started spending more time with him and devoting more attention to his stories. The whole thing became more complicated. Did Masuda tell her his stories to uncover Badia's secrets or her own? Every morning her ringing laughter greeted Badia as she perfumed the sleeping quarters to get rid of the stench of her decrepit husband's body.

"Why are you laughing, Masuda?"

"Because I've failed," she replied.

"Failed?"

"Yes, failed in love," Masuda said.

"Who do you love, Masuda?"

"The summer clouds, my lady."

"Is that a riddle?" Badia questioned.

"The whole of life is a riddle," Masuda said.

"What do you mean?"

"I want to roll around naked in the dirt," Masuda said. "In

the end, that's what we revert to, so our bodies need to embrace it. Fresh and warm before they're buried beneath it . . . cold and stiff."

Badia said nothing. She noticed how tall the trees inside the riad were as they opened up to the warmth of the sun and the blue sky above; dead, yellowing leaves dropping from their branches into oblivion, leaving behind fresh ones, alive. She also watched sweet basil leaves being tossed into the oven of her husband, the pottery seller with his brittle bones and feelings. Inside her, the fire burned to ashes.

That year, the summer hung around with its different moods. Sometimes the sky was clear, other times cloudy. The atmosphere was hot and steamy. Even so, the window in Najib's room was only open a tiny crack; it looked out at the riad's courtyard, where Hasun and Badia used to spend their summer evenings. Not a word was ever spoken, and eventually the merchant's eyelids would sag, and his whole body would slouch with them. He would go upstairs to the bedroom followed by his solitary wife. Then, the only thing to interrupt his sleep would be a coughing fit. Badia's heart would remain on fire, and she had trouble falling asleep. Time will always synchronize with whatever is weighing on the soul and force it to continue, like carrying a heavy rock up to the mountaintop.

Recently, Masuda's behavior had changed. She had told her mistress, frankly, that she was unhappy about being single. She was certainly aroused by Najib's stories, but at the same time they distressed her, like a false pregnancy. A few months before, there had been a blond cat inside the riad; the cat had an overwhelming desire to mate during the spring, and had started a feverish meow, raising her voice and turning it into a kind of chant. The cat had wandered all around the riad with her tail up, rubbing against everything. Her meowing attracted the attention of a huge gray male cat; the gray cat stared with lustful eyes at the female from all the way up on the roof. The felines started consorting with each other, but one night the female cat slunk out of the riad and disappeared, never to return. Surprisingly, the male cat kept looking down from the roof, searching all over for his mate. He called, cajoled, and waited. He went away, came back, and called again, but there was still no sign of the female cat. One night, he leaped down from the roof to the uppermost story in the riad and looked through the balcony window. Masuda smiled at him, and he stayed where he was. When she went over to him, he stood still and gave her a cautious look, seeking affection. She stroked his warm fur and he relaxed a little; he snuggled down comfortably. She took him downstairs, and looked over the balcony. Hasun and Badia were in bed.

The cat went into her room, so she gave him something to eat and drink, stroked him, and hugged him to her chest once again. He purred contentedly and pushed his head into her underarm, sniffing the scent of hair, sweat, and insomnia that nestled there. When Masuda woke up at dawn the next day, she started looking for her nighttime visitor, but found no trace. She expected the cat to come back, but he didn't. That one night became ingrained in her mind like a flash of lightning, leaving behind a painful memory.

With the cat came a desire on Masuda's part: she wanted a man whose very fire would impregnate her. Najib, meanwhile, kept insisting that she simply listen to his stories at night and let her tell them the next day: "Listen to me, Masuda! This morning a lump of clay refused to respond to me; I wanted to knead it, but it stayed solid between my fingers. When I poured some water on it, it went soft and then expanded. I added some more clay, and it all went solid again. I told myself that anyone who cannot sense the clay's sensitivities is no potter. So I listened to what this recalcitrant lump of clay actually wanted. So, Masuda, do you know what this lump of clay wanted?" Najib asked.

Masuda did not reply, she simply stared at him in amazement.

"It wanted some milk from a woman's breast!" Najib said.

"What do you mean?"

"In order to submit and be shaped, it wanted some milk from a woman's breast," he explained.

"Have you found any?"

"Yes, there are lots of nursing mothers in the quarter."

"Except in this household," Masuda pointed out. "What did you do?"

"I approached an elderly woman and asked her to get me a few drops of a nursing mother's milk. I told her it was a cure for a worker's eye that had been pierced by a splinter."

"So what happened?"

"The milk arrived, and I poured it over the clay. It immediately became fully malleable," Najib told her. "It was like a truly beautiful woman suckling a truly beautiful baby."

"So where is that statuette?"

"I'm keeping it for myself," Najib said. "Moments of inspiration like that don't happen all the time."

Masuda stared at the potter, her eyes aflame, while he was distracted and still thinking about the statuette. Then, silently, she stood up and left. In the small hallway opposite his room, she paused and exposed her breasts to the distant stars, to the sultry breeze, to the mirage . . . "There's no milk in these dangling breasts of mine!" she said aloud.

Slapping her thighs, she mumbled some unintelligible words and went downstairs again. By the bottom step she leaned her head against the wall, her body quivering, as she let out a hauntingly gruesome laugh mixed with tears.

The next morning, Badia got to hear about the clay that wanted a nursing mother's milk. Screaming like a woman in mourning, she signaled to Masuda to stop. "I'm going to kill that wretch," Badia growled, her eyes fixed on the potter's window, "before he kills me!"

Going up to her bedroom, she closed the door and burst into tears.

Masuda followed her to her room and opened the door, prepared to get some answers. "What's the point of crying?" she asked. "You can drown the entire house in tears, but not a single stone in the walls will pay *me* any attention!"

"So what?"

"I'll plan something to put an end to this torture," Mausda promised.

"Won't that be risky?"

"What am I risking?" Masuda remarked. "A life that is already lost?"

So here was Badia, battling with her own noble self. That very same night, the first phase of the plan took place. Wearing a thin dress, she sat next to her husband. As was the case every night, he was stoned. She poured him some tea and caressed him.

"You seem to be in a good mood tonight," Hasun said.

"When it's this fresh, it opens up the soul."

Her soft hand clutched his veined wrist and he surrendered himself to her. The scent of her ripe body overwhelmed him, and he inhaled the entire atmosphere; he felt sated.

"It's as though you've never seen me before," Badia said.

"I'm seeing you now as I want to see you."

"Do you know what I want?" she asked him, stroking him and whispering in his ear.

"A gold bracelet?" he asked.

"No."

"A ring or kaftan?"

"No."

"So, what is it you want?"

"I want to dance for you."

Another wave of intoxication enveloped the merchant's head. She had arranged it all so that he would beg her for this prize.

"Please dance for me, Badia, please do," he pleaded.

"Here, in the courtyard?"

"Yes, here in this wonderful atmosphere. Before I fall asleep in your arms."

His speech was slurred, and his legs could hardly support him. Like a white cloud, the image of Badia's body in her thin dress floated before Hasun's eyes—coming close, then moving away. Her clothes revealed the spectacular details of her athletic body, and her dance was white-hot, only adding to his inner fire. The dance pulsated from every part of her body; there was no need for other rhythm. Her only goal was to be seen by the eyes of the one who inspired such feelings, not the sleepy eyes of a cracked seashell. The dancer was instinctively aware that other eyes were watching her from behind the window on the top floor, and through the crack in the door of the room next to the kitchen. Only someone with no emotions could fail to be drawn to such an exuberant display . . .

"Oh, I'm so tired," Hasun mumbled.

That was the inert response of the feeble old man . . . but the same dance penetrated the heart of the young potter and fired up his very soul. The sensation moved to Najib's fingers, which responded positively. He wasn't afraid, hesitant, or nonchalant. What he needed now was a truly exceptional opportunity, one he had never encountered before, but which was certainly afire at that moment. He had a pressing urge to deal with clay right then.

Once the sleeping merchant started snoring loudly, satisfied with the nighttime performance, Badia slunk out and went to the room alongside their bedroom. Wrapping herself in a brown coat, she stood there for a moment, listening. She could hear cautious footsteps. *Does anyone else hear them?* she wondered. She looked out into the pitch darkness outside the room but couldn't see anything. Even so, through the total silence she managed to hear the riad's door being opened from the inside. The hand involved knew the bolts very well and closed it carefully. Could anyone else be opening the door at this time of night? Why was he leaving his room, going downstairs, departing? Was he running away from her? Running away after such penetration of the very depths of their souls?

The potter left the riad's alley in Mawqif and headed for the workshop in Tabhirt, followed by a shadowy figure wrapped in a coat. The streets were deserted besides a few stray night creatures. The young potter was in a hurry, like an arrow shot from a bow. He felt a pain inside him, this burning need to work with the clay, and all the while the shadow was trailing him from a distance. When he entered the shop and turned on the lights, he spotted a lump of clay that seemed ready for kneading and shaping. He bent over it with all the enthusiasm of a lover. His soul was overflowing, his fingers were poised and ready, and the picture was still shining in his heart and imagination. Just as Badia's body had been dancing a short while earlier, so now were his fingers dancing as they gently molded the body of clay. The statuette was gently stroked into shape, as though it were being formed spontaneously from his passion. One stroke and the basic features were in place; another stroke and the gesture was there; another and the pulse of movement was added; a series of concentrated, interlinked strokes and the statuette was finally ready, enveloped in its own halo of light. The potter was so happy that he burst into song in celebration of this heavenly presence, while the watching shadow sneaked a look through a crack in the door. The statuette did not look anything like its model, since the artist had been wary about his hidden passion being revealed. This was a statuette based on an imagined conception of love, keeping the real shape ambiguous while preserving the essence. Here was the symbol that embraced every conceivable aspect of symbols without revealing the inner secret.

With the approach of dawn the potter carried his new statuette—this symbol—to the oven for heating. He finally saw the person who'd been watching him.

"This statuette doesn't look like me at all," the shadow muttered. "So, it's not for me. The wretch is still ignoring me in spite of the flame that I aroused."

Underneath her coat, this relentless shadow was clutching the hilt of a dagger. The young potter had hardly emerged from the pottery's threshold before the blade was thrust into his chest, aimed at his heart. His blood gushed out to moisten the new statuette, which he continued to clutch to himself in the fervor of his passion, as his life exerted itself fully in its confrontation with the finality of death. Then, everything collapsed and he crashed to the floor, the clay mixing with his freshly spilled blood. The shadow now slipped away, the bloody dagger concealed under the wrap. She disappeared into the gloom of the predawn morning.

Before the sun was even up the next morning, there were loud bangs on the merchant's riad door. When he heard the news, he quickly left the house. There were two women in the household who bewailed Najib's death in the most intense fashion. Rumors and speculation spread like wildfire: How could Najib the potter have been murdered? Was it a jealous lover for whom he had never made a statuette? Or was it a woman who had wanted him to make a statuette, and he had not done so? Or was it another craftsman who was envious of him? Or had Hasun hatched some plot against him, spiteful because of the attentions that his beautiful wife was paying to the young man? Was it this, or that, or something else?

On the very same day, both Badia and her servant Masuda vanished separately from the riad without any prearranged plan. Neither of them spoke to the other—or even knew where the other was going.

As the murdered man was laid to rest in the Bab el-Khemis Cemetery, inquiries had not yet identified the murderer or the location of the two women. The murderer's shadow still managed to appear at the gravesite a few days after his burial, walking between the headstones until it reached his tombstone. Leaning over the grave, close to the heart of its owner, as it listened to the groans, the murderous shadow cried out: "Najib!"

"Yes?" he replied.

"Why are you groaning? Do you need anything?"

"Why did you kill me, Masuda?"

"Because I love you."

"Does the lover kill their beloved?" he asked.

"If the lover is desperate, and the beloved has refused to make a statuette of her."

"You treated me badly," Najib snapped.

"It was no worse than watching you go to someone else," Masuda snapped back.

"You were unkind, Masuda."

"Forgive me, Najib. Death was the only way I could see of being joined with you."

Walking toward the edge of the cemetery by Wadi Isil, she threw herself into the deep lake and disappeared into its depths, where she was to remain.

Summer was not yet over, and its steaming heat had not relented. Najib's fingers no longer danced over the clay. And yet a woman of faded beauty kept searching for him. For days, no one knew where she had vanished, or from where she had emerged on that searing-hot noon, shoeless, her clothes in tatters, her body weak. She was clutching a statuette with bits broken off and her tangled hair cascaded like a waterfall. She stopped by the door of the pottery shop where the dead man's fingers had danced over the clay, looked into its empty space, and called him by name. She laughed at first, and then she cried. She made the other workers cry as well, and passersby who gathered around her.

"It's Badia," some of them whispered to others. "Hasun's wife. She's gone crazy."

That same evening, she was placed in a hospital for especially dangerous patients, even though the only people who believed that were the very ones who'd poisoned their own perceptions.

As though nothing had ever happened, Hasun had searched all over his house when the people in his riad had disappeared, and then changed his old bed for an even bigger one. Refilling his supply of kif and his hashish pipe, he got ready to remarry.

Translated from Arabic by Roger Allen

THE MUMMY IN THE PASHA'S HOUSE

BY MOHAMED ACHAARI

Dar el-Basha

Patti sat in the garden of the house in Marrakech that she had bought ten years ago—her first home. She was listening with a genuine Sufi absorption to al-Sharqawi recount the story of the mummy in the pasha's house.

Al-Sharqawi had begun with the moment the governor's entourage, the police, the historic buildings inspectorate, and the procurator-general had all arrived at the *dwairiya*—a small house that contained a kitchen, storerooms, and servants quarters on one side, with the finer and more lavishly decorated Turkish baths, lounge, and other living spaces on the other. The house also contained a lounge for female companions, which was accessible by climbing an ebony staircase from the lounge. In this velveteen area of the *dwairiya*, the pasha had installed a plaster mosaic of blue, yellow, and green tiles that he had specially imported from Istanbul—his own Sulaymaniyya from the Ottoman capital. He would often brag about the mosaic, even though he knew nothing at all about that particular Ottoman palace—people living in the *dwairiya* even called the house the *Sulaymaniyya*, their belief being that the use of the title implied that some demon followers of King Solomon were to be found there, all subject to the pasha's instructions. In the dead of night, when the inhabitants could hear the sound of the pasha's retainers and soldiers being lashed by a leather whip, they would put their fingers in their ears and their knees would knock together in horror as they listened to what the fiends were doing to the victims locked inside the vaults housed below the stables.

Al-Sharqawi confirmed that the group of delegators headed straight for the crumbling wall in the lounge, the one being rebuilt by craftsmen, since more mosaic pieces from Turkey were being imported. Inside the hole—which made itself evident as soon as they started removing the debris from the wall—was a coffin made of fine wood. The senior craftsman announced that a perfectly mummified body, still wrapped in its shroud, was inside the coffin. When the foreman asked that the coffin be brought out of the wall and opened in front of everyone so that a report could be filed on the mummy's discovery, the workers refused to do so.

The foreman had then been forced to open his shirt, displaying to the members of the delegation the painful wounds he had suffered after opening the coffin himself. Through his sobs, he insisted that the gaping wounds on his body were the result of a savage beating, although there had been no one there to hurt him and no whip to administer such damage.

The foreman had been compelled to bring in helpers from the department of national restoration to undertake the task of transferring the coffin. They moved the casket from the wall to the police vehicle, preparing to show it to the archaeological experts whom the government had brought in from France and Egypt—these experts would examine the mummy and probe its shriveled entrails.

The next day, a helicopter transferred the foreman to a university hospital in Rabat, where they would examine the severe wounds caused by the inexplicable beating, which apparently had no human source.

Patti loved al-Sharqawi's stories. Even though he didn't have a regular group of listeners in Jemaa el-Fnaa Square, to whom he could hold out his skullcap to receive donations after every tall tale, Patti still considered him to be the quintessential modern storyteller. She believed he was someone who deserved all sorts of gifts and recognition. Patti usually gave him something when he came to narrate one of his wonderful stories—stories that remained fresh from his time at the Mamounia Hotel, where al-Sharqawi had been a doorman ever since the seventies.

At first, al-Sharqawi had latched onto the legendary tales of the hotel itself, with its world-famous visitors: Churchill, Hitchcock, Orson Welles, Marlene Dietrich, and de Gaulle (in his case, for just a single night, and they had to make a special bed that was long enough for him). Soon enough, al-Sharqawi had complete command of all the secret worlds inside the hotel—scandals, spectacular soirées, and many love affairs. From all these intimate threads he would weave his stories; he always had a role to play in their construction, even if that required him to skip or blend time frames or to mix facts with nebulous claims. Then he organized a network of hotel workers, suppliers, and taxi drivers to provide him with news about the city as a whole—sporting events, lavish weddings, Don Quixote–like confrontations, newly opened restaurants, and swank apartments. News of prostitutes, demons, gay people, sex clubs, hideaways for disobedient minors, and pornographic shoots were also welcome. He would fuse all these true details together and end up with tales about the city as it really was, and as it might be—cloaked in legend.

He had no qualms about raising the dead and dispatching them to the city's markets and quarters; his sole purpose in doing so being that he got to meet them himself and put them willingly or unwillingly into his stories, which he wove together using dreams and illusions. Patti loved it all, and her weary eyes would tear up—her whole body would laugh with gusto. She told herself that the best thing she could do in her own life was to place her destiny into the hands of this magician. He could then incorporate it into the city's very soil, till it became part of its reddish clay or the dark green of its palm trees. After all, the best way to be integrated into a recalcitrant city is through wonderful tales.

There was no one else in the world that al-Sharqawi loved as much as Patti. He loved her more than his own mother, who it was said gave birth to him twenty months after his father's death. With the innate intelligence of an embryo born into sorrow, he'd sensed that life in the dusky old city without a father would be unbearable. So he'd decided to remain inside his mother's womb till he almost turned into a piece of stone.

He didn't love the old American woman just because she was so generous with him (she had even been thinking about buying him a house in one of the Imran Company quarters), but also because she listened to his tales so meekly. When he finished a story, she'd shed a few tears before her entire face lit up with a burst of laughter. Once in a while, he would think about the charitable acts that this good American woman did for the street kids—and she wasn't even a Muslim. Patti also took time to teach the suburban girls. *This woman has to be a Muslim*, he would tell himself. *If it were up to me, I would make her head of the Scientific Council of Marrakech and its precincts*. Patti was unmarried, but with her good heart, she was the one who paid attention to the ancient pulpit at the Koutoubia Mosque. It was originally made in Cordoba in the eleventh century, then was transported in pieces over the sea and by camel from the north of Morocco to the south. For centuries the Friday sermon would ring out from its iconic tower, but then, inevitably, its engraved woodwork began to fall apart. It was pushed to a remote corner of the Koutoubia Mosque, with a disconsolate jurist seated alongside it. He chipped off small bits of tracery and claimed that they were effective treatments for people who had migraines and toothaches. Patti was the one who saved it from turning into a false sort of aspirin.

She, along with the Metropolitan Museum, made a very

generous donation which saved the woodwork and gave it new life—as a one-of-a-kind example of Islamic art. So, here was this sensitive lady, who continued to lay a place at her table for her life companion, who had died a quarter of a century ago. She always included his favorite meat and a glass of his most-cherished wine. She would ask, with a smile, if he was going to eat his lunch, because these days he ate hardly anything at all! Al-Sharqawi loved all this—and Patti too. And he loved Marrakech, the city that gave its inhabitants such wonderful stories and provided for its citizens, who were so sincere.

Al-Sharqawi could not believe the stories about the mummy. If it were one of the pasha's enemies, as the gossips claimed, or one of his soldiers, or even a runaway slave, then the pasha would certainly not have gone to all the trouble of wrapping up the corpse, embalming it, and putting it in a coffin of stained wood—just to make sure that worms didn't eat away at it inside the wall. The pasha would simply have done what Moulay Ismail did when constructing his capital city of Meknes: bury the exhausted construction workers alive inside the building itself to make them an intrinsic part of the structure's defenses.

It was basically impossible to fabricate a mummy out of anything but the distant past, and the whole idea of murder was ridiculous. That at least was the conviction that led al-Sharqawi to make use of every means possible to get information from the research team that was examining the mummy. He even abandoned his post at the Mamounia for the first time since he had started working there to hurry over to Patti's place in order to tell her the story of the mummy.

Patti was still in the Jacuzzi, bubbling water soothing her limbs. She immediately realized that al-Sharqawi's early arrival implied that some urgent matter had come up, something that could not be delayed for a single instant. Much to the astonishment of her servants, she gave instructions that al-Sharqawi was to be admitted without delay. She was completely naked as she welcomed him, her aging body sagging somewhat. She paid no attention whatsoever to his total shock.

Al-Sharqawi saw that she was a woman. Yes, a woman indeed—a woman who'd been murdered by a severe blow to the base of her skull which had occurred last century—or, in other words, almost sixty-five years ago. That was all there was to it. "This is the way it has to be," said Patti, with a devilish glint in her eye.

Al-Sharqawi went back to his post—doorman to the world, as he called it. He kept thinking about her naked body, and her flashing eyes. He told himself that when the eyes of an eighty-six-year-old woman gleamed in that way, she could still be a veritable cauldron of desire. For the first time in his life, he didn't feel any kind of revulsion toward the aged, foreign female guests at the Mamounia Hotel. He could remember well the way that they would regularly grab handsome young men by the arm, play coy, and then dance as though they had just emerged from the grave.

When Patti sat down to breakfast, she was still thinking of the news that she had heard. It disconcerted her. Her mind kept moving between her table in the present and another one far away—the one where she'd sat with her friend Anais in Paris back in March of 1938. The two girls had decided to go to Marrakech after a crazy week that had started when Patti opened an old newspaper and found a picture of the pasha riding horseback on the first page. He was wearing a white suit and staring up at the sky. He looked like a prince who had just sprung out of a fairy tale.

Patti told Anais that she was going to marry that pasha. She knew that he gazed at her in his magical way in order to seduce her. Anais had done her best to convince her friend that his violent passion was only romantic extravagance; after a noisy night in Paris it would dissolve. Still, Patti couldn't stop herself from running all over Paris searching for details about the pasha and his life. Eventually, she learned all there was to know about his palace, his harem, his campaigns, his wealth, the nights he spent in Paris, and his piercing magical gaze, something that made him as much in vogue in Paris as jazz and cubism. No one could claim to be a man of the world if he had not sat down with the pasha at least once. Patti had gathered all these precious details, then persuaded Anais to accompany her on the scary journey into the African jungle, where the magic commander still hung severed heads on city gates, shot tigers and lions in the bush, and returned from combat to his harem of beauties, all of whom competed for his virile powers.

That evening, al-Sharqawi returned to Patti's home, eager to see what effect his news had on her and whether his eyes had affected her when he'd encountered her in the Jacuzzi. He found her relaxed, her complexion blooming with total self-satisfaction, but the cause remained a mystery. All of which encouraged him to open his story box: The mummy was a woman whose identity remained unknown. Whoever entombed her had put a message into the coffin, which consisted of a gold necklace with a cross at its center.

At this point, Patti jumped up. She would have said that she knew the woman in question and the necklace too, had al-Sharqawi not been too distracted with telling his story: "I know the lady in question . . . the youngest of three sisters brought from Syria by the pasha. She played the lute, and her two sisters danced. The pasha adored the lute-playing sister and took her with him to Paris, escorted her to a soirée at the Lido, and dressed her in clothes purchased at the finest department stores. In a single week he decked her toes in ten spectacular rings from the very finest jeweler in Paris. But then she vanished, as though the earth had simply swallowed her up. No one dared ask about her, regardless of whether the pasha was present or not. The middle sister was still alive and, with the pasha's permission, married a merchant from the old quarter. She gave birth to the most famous singer in the city. These days, she stands by Bab 'Amala, yelling at the top of her lungs that the authorities need to hand over her sister's body, so she can be buried and her soul laid to rest, instead of hovering between heaven and earth."

"What about you?" Patti asked, a sudden frown across her face. "What do you think?"

"Me?" al-Sharqawi replied. "I don't believe a single word of it!"

When Patti and Anais reached Marrakech in March of 1938, the city was bathed in an enchanting light; palm trees and orange all blended together. The city's aromas were steeped in spices, coupled with roses and lemon blossoms, which made everyone glide as if their feet weren't even touching the ground. It all imbued the city with an indefinable allure, one that made people fall in love in a heartbeat. So Patti didn't even wait until she reached the pasha's house before revealing her heart to him, offering it up in sacrifice to the sheer magic of the place. But things went awry, as they sometimes do.

They had arrived at the pasha's reception hall just before sunset, attended by his personal portrait artist. The entire courtyard was teeming with European guests, a few army generals, administrative officials, and grandees; the whole meeting resembled a welcoming reception like the art openings in Paris. The salons surrounding the courtyard hosted small groups of the pasha's most important guests. In one of the salons was the pasha himself, looking well dressed as always, with a determined glint in his eyes. Patti and Anais had moved forward to greet him on a signal from the painter; the pasha had beamed a smile and held Patti's hand in his own, while Anais finished introducing her friend. Anais then translated Patti's description of her work to the pasha, telling him that Patti collected European paintings for museums in New York. With that, he had grabbed ahold of Anais's hand.

"So young?" the pasha had asked Patti.

Patti could not reply. She had stared in amazement at the pasha's figure, as he bent over slightly to put his arm around Anais and took her on a tour of the palace—beginning with the huge cedarwood door at the entrance, then turning right toward the doors made of inlaid wood, with carved arches painted in natural extracts of saffron and anemone. Once in a while, the pasha pointed out the gilded ceilings and the way that their leafy patterns matched the geometrical shapes on the walls. He paused in front of the lions' claws decorating the columns and the patterned mosaics that covered them. He then brought her back to the reception hall with its own splendid columns, pointing out details concealed by the wonderful structure—wickerwork, clusters, and miniature crowns, all exquisitely proportioned. From the hall, he took her out to the Andalusian courtyard, the harem rooms, and his study. Eventually, the couple reached the private quarters, where they passed through a huge engraved doorway. The pasha escorted Anais inside and two guards closed the doors behind them.

Patti and the pasha's painter were left to wander around the palace until someone arrived to take them back to the hotel. Patti then spent an entire month in her room doing nothing but crying, eating, and sleeping. She didn't see either the pasha or Anais again. The painter came to visit her every day. He spent long hours with her, painting her and talking to her about the pasha. As he began to seduce her, she started paying closer attention to him. Every time he tried to get her in bed, she told him to bring Anais first, and then he could have what he wanted. In response, he told her that it would be much easier to bring her a lion in a hemp sack.

And then, one steaming hot day, Patti suddenly decided to go back to Paris—and then to New York. Later, she married a young man whom she had gone out on innocent strolls with. They spent many years together, traveling to remote spots to acquire rare works of art. Patti's only search was for those obscure feelings that had overwhelmed her on the day after the mirage. Through this marriage founded on profound mutual understanding and an equally profound misunderstanding, the couple shared the experience of enormous wealth, and collusion unaffected by the ebb and flow of life. She hadn't told her husband about her emotional collapse in the past, until the very last day of his life, when he asked her why she always cried when looking at the ugly painting she had kept—the one that had been made by the pasha's painter. She told him that she was actually crying for Anais, whom the pasha had snatched away from her. When her husband did not seem completely convinced, she told him the whole story.

When al-Sharqawi told Patti about the lute player from Syria, he sensed that something bad had happened. She looked flustered and angry, and terminated their session with an insulting curtness. To get rid of this bad feeling, he headed straight for the café where his closest friends would spend many hours sipping mint tea and indulging in the kind of laughter known in Marrakech as *tamshkhir*. They would laugh at each other, at the city that sold itself to foreigners, at those same foreigners who sold themselves to the city, at the disputes over palm trees being destroyed by apartments, at other apartments where intimate soirées took place, at Tangier—and at laughter itself; laughter being the most stubbornly historical feature of Marrakech.

Al-Sharqawi reached the café, where everyone was talking about the mummy. One of his friends asked him in a disgusted tone what all the fuss was about over some neglected bones in a wall. Al-Sharqawi told him that they were not just bones, but rather a long-forgotten crime.

"All of Marrakech is full of dead men's bones," his other friend said. "Just dig under your own pillow and you're sure to find a forgotten skull, or one of the bodies that the pasha used to hang in the Old Medina's alleyways—"

"Why dig under his pillow?" another man interrupted. "The only skull under the pillow is his own."

"Whose?" al-Sharqawi asked.

"The person in front of you," the man answered.

Al-Sharqawi turned to his friend. "Why do you put your head under the pillow?"

"I'm scared! All the people who were beheaded come out in the dead of night," his friend roared, his disgust turning into hysteria. "They wander around the neighborhoods and houses while people are asleep. Bodies are looking for heads, and heads for bodies!"

"That's all from smoking bad grass," al-Sharqawi assured him. "You're mixing hash with Marlboros, and it's affecting your minuscule brain so that you're scared to death. That's what happens to people who abandon the old ways of clipping kif they inherited from fathers and grandfathers, and start using the kinds Christians use."

Al-Sharqawi told them all about the woman whose body had been found in the wall, and that caused a general commotion.

"Which woman? God forgive us, and you! Were they a woman's bones, a man's, or a gremlin's?" his hysterical friend inquired.

"Religious scholars will grab everything. Root and branch," al-Sharqawi replied dismissively, "while some stray remains are involved."

"But we're only prepared to acknowledge flesh. So go ahead, esteemed sir, and put some flesh on those bones!"

But al-Sharqawi insisted that there was a murder victim involved. He wanted the whole of Marrakech to know of this event, and to be aware that a crime had been committed one year, or maybe even sixty years, earlier.

"It doesn't matter," his other friend said.

"Yes, it does matter!" al-Sharqawi protested. "Sixty years

ago the pasha and others were killing people just as easily as we're drinking tea here. Those who kill suffer an incredible, never-ending punishment for it."

Al-Sharqawi experienced for himself the extent of people's involvement in his stories, as he left his house the next day and walked for over an hour deliberately through the alleys and markets of the Old Medina. Two people asked him with a snide tone what God had done with the bones in the wall. He corrected them first, by saying that it was not just a few decaying bones in the wall, but rather a complete mummy, and that on its neck was a gold necklace with a cross. Secondly, he called them heretics, and told them that Marrakech had its own mighty pharaoh whose dead were embalmed. "If he had indeed survived," he explained, "maybe you wouldn't be so stupid and arrogant, like the mustaches on vain and ignorant people!" And with that he'd continued on his way, the notion sticking in his throat that a significant transformation had taken place in the city.

The story no longer fired people up; it had come and gone in the flash of an eye. It was almost as though some kind of curse had afflicted people, turning Jemaa el-Fnaa Square from Shahrazad into a huge kitchen reeking of garlic and chopped onions. The only thing that managed to clear the block in his throat were the greetings he received by the door of the Mamounia Hotel—from taxi drivers to buses of tourists to travel-agent employees. When they asked him about the latest developments in the case, he emerged from his gloomy mood and started rebuilding the story with all the enthusiasm of someone who would not be deterred from finding a suitable conclusion—regardless of whatever may have actually happened.

His real task was to bring all possibilities into the story, however likely or remote they may have been. Even the authorities had declared the matter closed. Not only that, but the reports written by the archaeological experts the official medical doctor, and the head of the Sixth District described in detail what happened and how. But he just couldn't find any link to connect the skeleton they'd discovered to the Syrian lute player who, according to her older sister, had disappeared sixty years ago. That detail was particularly significant, since a new report had reached the procurator-general. The report claimed that a French woman named Anais had also disappeared about sixty years ago, along with a necklace with a cross that she used to fiddle with while sleeping naked in the pasha's arms.

When Patti arrived in Marrakech some forty-five years after her first tragic visit, her intention was to use the city to salve the wound that was infecting her life. For some years, she had developed the habit of constructing a blooming garden in her memory, one where leafy trees would brush against each other and no disruptive plants would grow between them. She always reckoned that the nasty things that happened to people stayed in the places where they first occurred, but also remained in their memories the very same way. The only way to get them out was to come to terms with the places that served as their original stage, thus erasing the painful traces that are associated with them.

Patti used to recall all the moments in her life that were linked to specific places. Whenever she remembered Marrakech, the sting of that evening when the pasha took Anais into his private quarters would hurt her—and of course she had never seen either of them again. So she came back to Marrakech right after a serious heart operation, believing that a profound reconciliation with Marrakech would make all the places in her life seem like the blossoming cloud that hovered over her as she emerged from the anesthesia.

She came back to Marrakech in the midnineties, and all she could remember of the city was the huge gateway to the pasha's palace and the painted door that was shut in her face. She could still see herself leaving on the desolate train to Casablanca Airport, feeling tense and very upset. It wasn't because of what had happened, but rather because the pasha's painter had insisted on giving her a painting with no artistic value. In spite of that, she had no choice but to add it to the weight of her baggage, as though she were running in the opposite direction of her dreams.

So here she was on her second visit, as her every sense soaked up the light and pungent aroma of the city. She came to realize that mankind was the tree that concealed the city's own forest. When that handsome warrior led her to Marrakech, he was also the reason she didn't get to see much of the city. From that moment, he didn't constitute a wound, but instead became a distant tale, one that was almost laughable. She would devote herself to her own narrative, whether the occasion demanded it or not, if only to dazzle her companions with this romantic madness that once swept through her life like a heavy rainstorm, only to swiftly open up a space for serenity that no sense of loss could spoil.

Patti bought a number of mansions in the golf course section of Marrakech, far from the alleys of the Old Medina and all their sad mystery. Her practical instincts made her feel like she could make large profits from this Marrakech dream—a dream that offered an entire mountain covered with snow, and a desert where mirages and expansive gardens bloomed as though recently arrived from Andalusia.

From the very first day, she turned down offers from agents who were used to selling riads in the city to foreigners who imagined that *The Thousand and One Nights* would emerge from cracks in the mosaic. Patti termed this hankering after Old Medina riads the *returning colonialist syndrome:* a desire to rewrite the history of colonial occupation on the basis of touristic goodwill. But having no historical hang-ups, Patti bought five mansions linking the golf course area to the pools, palm orchards, and orange groves. She started selling her rich New York friends magical stays, without sex, soirées, or tacky folkloric performances.

During Patti's prolonged stay in Marrakech, she herself was

subjected to trickery, rip-offs, and fraud of a wide variety, but she didn't nurse any lingering resentment about it. Sometimes she would even let herself succumb to the tricksters' maneuvers as a kind of entertainment, regarding it all as part of the spice involved in risky ventures. When she finished repairing the pulpit in the Koutoubia and saw it on display in the Badia Palace, she had a sudden inspiration, one that occurred to her fully formed: she would donate a museum to Marrakech—where all the works of art that she had collected from China, India, South Asia, Mongolia, Turkmenistan, Bukhara, Tashkent, and elsewhere around the Orient would be put on display. This international museum seemed to be the sweetest possible gift that she could give to this city, which had been known to inspire thrilling journeys of its own.

A Moroccan government bureaucrat had suggested to Patti that she might help finance the restoration of the pasha's palace, which could then be the site of her amazing new museum. It gave her a jolt, and she felt as though she were hovering between the earth and the sky. For the first time since her return to Marrakech, she went to take a look at the pasha's palace. Once again, she was transported right back to that hotel room from forty-five years ago, and the tears fell. She cried because, after everything that happened, she could envision a beautiful fate being woven for her by the pasha's own hand, like a legendary warrior who bitterly regretted the way he had treated her.

With the discovery of the remains, the restoration work on the pasha's palace had stopped. The remains weren't particularly significant in and of themselves, but the story made them appear that way. Since the authorities were more worried about the story than they were about the raw materials involved, the entire restoration workshop was closed down. The young engineer who was supervising the project began to imagine all sorts of provocative ideas that poisoned Patti's life. "An interest in anything linked to the pasha," the engineer suggested, "would get on the authorities' nerves." They were worried about the pasha's reputation, which was that of a vicious southern commander who had been an agent of French imperialism, a coconspirator against the crown, and a terrible governor—whose name alone was terrifying enough to make people wet themselves.

Using a subtle strategy the authorities had set about eradicating the pasha piece by piece. They started by sequestering all the properties he had appropriated when he had a free hand over the country and its population, and ended by erasing every vestige of his era. When the pasha welcomed European grandees to his eighteen-hole golf course—Winston Churchill being chief among them—he would drink champagne, organize soirées at the lido, and hold parties in the palace hall, at which Farid al-Atrash would sing, Samia Gamal would belly dance, and Egyptian and Syrian poets would praise him. All this happened in the thirties and forties of the last century—it was also a period when most Moroccans could barely afford to buy the most meager clothes.

When viewed through the prism of the new museum permitting the pasha to return gracefully to the city, in the form of a new artistic foundation that would once again place him on the throne in Marrakech, then the entire project became an aggressive attack on the country's symbolic security.

When Patti heard these astute observations from the engineer, she had a sudden panic attack. She envisioned the very thing that had happened to Anaïs happening to her as well. But al-Sharqawi soon arrived to calm her with his daily stock of stories about the city, about the film stars staying at the Mamounia, about the pasha's restaurant and dance hall, an international chain which obviously had no connection with their particular pasha, and about riads in the Old Medina.

"Do you love the pasha?" Patti asked al-Sharqawi as he was about to leave.

"It's you that I love," he replied sincerely, with a sparkle in his eye.

She guffawed loudly, and that encouraged him to go on: "You're more remarkable than all the pashas in the world!"

Patti said she knew nothing about the pasha. She had received a number of books about him from the engineer, but had not opened even one of them. Ever since the very first time she had glimpsed him in the newspaper, she had always regarded him as a dream beyond reach.

Al-Sharqawi liked toying with this idea in particular, claiming that the pasha would emerge and visit people in their dreams. Getting out of bed, people would wander around the city's alleyways until they passed by his silent palace. They would come to realize that he was no longer to be found, since he had died in the midfifties; all that remained was the terror that could bend people's backs, and laughter that could make people cry.

"The pasha used to live for the love of women," al-Sharqawi remarked. "Everything else was a swamp of illusions. He had two wives from Turkey: one was from the Atlas Mountains in Morocco, and the other was the daughter of al-Maqqari, the Ottoman grand vizier. When his brother died, he already had ninety-six women in his harem, and he simply added another twenty-four that he expropriated from his brother's harem.

"He had his own hunters in Paris, Tangier, and Marrakech," al-Sharqawi continued, "who would supply his bed with beautiful female tourists and other companions. He used to give them valuable jewels and rolls of silk. In addition to all this, he had European lovers, among them the wives of prominent diplomats who would spend days and nights in his palace. The diplomats all knew, but they received the most incredible gifts in recompense. There were so many births, both known and unknown, that hardly a day went by without a baby being seen who looked just like him. Both the elite and general populace thought the pasha was a father to enough children to fill an entire city. In every case, people looked at the child's features and saw the pasha's likeness. So, my dear lady, this is the man you dreamed of marrying. Had you done so, today you would be the most miserable woman in the entire world."

"But I still have the dream, even though I didn't win the pasha's heart!" Patti said with a laugh.

Not even a week went by after the discovery of the remains before amazing things started to happen across town. They all emerged from stories told by al-Sharqawi. He insisted that they were fresh and came from sources whose veracity could not be doubted.

The story of the savage beating with no known assailant had now extended, and had claimed some new victims among the archaeologists and local authorities. Then the mummy escaped, and people started to see the dead corpse roaming the pasha's palace, still wrapped in its shroud, by Bab Doukkala. The mummy vanished for a while then reappeared by the Telouet Kasbah. One of the restoration workers saw it playing golf without a club or ball at the course where dirt and dead trees were piled up. Patti and al-Sharqawi saw it in the Jacuzzi, warming its decrepit bones. Each time the rumors initially amazed people, but before long, popular enthusiasm elevated them to a level of unadulterated truth.

As part of this general fever, al-Sharqawi grew moody and unpredictable, slamming doors at the Mamounia Hotel right in the face of visiting tourists, especially after people demanded to hear some of his amazing stories. These feelings grew more pronounced when Marrakech started preparing for the crowning of Jemaa el-Fnaa as a World Heritage Site. For many years, that square had been *his* square. As night fell, he would establish his circle of listeners, and they would grow and grow till they became a swarm of bees buzzing around his tales. At night's end, he would send them all away. But what happened had happened, and he was no longer who he had been, and neither was the square itself.

He used to recite from *The Thousand and One Nights*, from the sagas of Abu Zayd al-Hilali, Antarah Ibn Shaddad, and Sayf Ibn Dhi-Yazan; about the tales of the jinn, sorcerers, and also pious men of God. Then, a nasty worm made its way into his little mind and urged him to start including contemporary tales into his evening sessions. He discovered that the pasha was a very dynamic subject, one that the people of Marrakech listened to carefully. They were secret stories that had never seen the light of day:

The pasha, alone at night in his palace, walking around his bed, using sweeping arm gestures to dispel the sounds of legions of people fleeing his fighters as they advanced in the High Atlas, while being fired at by a 77mm Krupp gun, the only one of its kind in the entire kingdom—the one that Hasan the First had given to al-Madani al-Klawi, so that he could exert complete control over the south, as far as the edges of the Sahara.

Then there's the pasha, left on his own and scared out of his wits in his dark room, as he goes through his daily ritual of experiencing visions of precisely the same kind of terror that people felt when thinking about his own tyrannical behavior. There would be a grisly hour of panic, weeping, and groveling as he imagined his brother al-Madani coming through a crack in the door, even though he was dead, and yelling at him: "You're no use to anyone! France is stronger than you are and so is the tribe! The only thing bigger than you is what's between your legs!"

The pasha would listen, as his brother spoke to the French general: "It's just a dagger. I'll stab him and then put it back in its scabbard."

The pasha would prostrate himself at al-Madani's feet

and beg him to let him have just a little bit of his cunning, so he could feel something other than raw fear.

The pasha used to dress the Syrian lute player in ten jewels, one for each toe. He would ask her to dance on his chest like Samia Gamal, as though she were dancing in a demon's palm.

The pasha frothed at the mouth in rage because the caid, Hmmu, would put on a big show of opposing the French while he was actually biding his time, never missing an opportunity to show his contempt for the pasha as an agent of colonialism.

The pasha had dreams of liberating the Telouet Kasbah from the clutches of his brother and nasty brother-in-law who stuck in his craw.

The pasha's enormous harem consisted of Egyptian and Syrian dancers, Turkish lute players, and Chinese masseuses.

Then the pasha was involved in a parade that he'd organized to welcome Theodore Staigh, Lyautey's deputy, with the aim of providing proof that the deputy's predecessors had been right about the pasha, and also to convince the people that the presence of France in this difficult country was something to which he was personally committed, no matter the cost. Up to that point, it had already cost France fifteen thousand deaths, while the number of Moroccan souls lost was 400,000.

Al-Sharqawi was convinced that the pasha was one of Marrakech's greatest miracles. He spared nothing in providing details of the huge parade, one in which Hmmu played a leading role in order to scare the newly arrived official, while the pasha's goal was to impress him. He described the way the procession set out from Marrakech toward Mount Tichka, amid crowds of tribesmen who lined both sides of the road of melted ice. They were ready at any moment to pick up and carry the cars in the official procession across the valleys and muddy roadways. Once the French delegation reached the Tichka crossing, they found white goat-hair tents set up to receive them. Thousands of horsemen surrounded them, firing dozens of continuous shots under instructions from the pasha, as a way of greeting the newly arrived French official. The 200,000 shots fired left a cloud of smoke that lingered in the Tichka sky for a considerable time.

Al-Sharqawi used to bind the people listening to him to what he referred to as *the new eternity,* and yet the level of fear associated with the pasha's name led people to ask themselves whether the authorities supported his remarkable tale.

Then one evening the authorities arrived and grabbed al-Sharqawi from the middle of his circle. For several months, he was gone. When he finally came back to Marrakech, he was a broken man—and once again the doorman at the Mamounia Hotel.

On the very first day back at his job, a shy passerby approached and asked, "Wasn't it the pasha who killed Hmmu so the entire scenario with the French could be cleaned up?"

"Yes," al-Sharqawi replied. "He's the one who killed him. There's no doubt about that. But it had nothing to do with the French. He wanted to marry Halima, the caid's wife, and get ahold of Hmmu's harem, which included the gorgeous Mina, al-Haddad's daughter!"

Before the passerby moved on, al-Sharqawi stopped him. "Make very sure," he cautioned the man, "that you don't tell that to any other human being!"

Other stories later took over and replaced the tale of the mummy. But Marrakech never forgot stories, even though it may have pretended to do so. It left them burning in the ashes, but only in order to bring them out again at the right moment, to use them to provide warmth on chilly nights.

Work began again on the restoration of the pasha's palace

and people went back to the old stories; and, indeed, the old stories returned to the old square.

Nobody paused when Patti died. She had gone back to New York to supervise the transfer of her museum collection to Marrakech, when her heart had stopped. Al-Sharqawi shed only two tears—one for her, and the other for the apartment that she had not lived in till it was too late!

No one in Marrakech thought that Jemaa el-Fnaa would ever revert back to the days of old—the square where people used to gather around performers and storytellers, in clusters or alone, spinning in a circle around flute and cymbal players, magicians, and fortune-tellers. UNESCO did designate the square a nonmaterial World Heritage Site, but it was brought back to life because people liked to blend the serious and frivolous. Marrakech people liked to play jokes: they put harmless snakes around tourists' necks, hid fortune-tellers under Coca-Cola umbrellas, and performed wild dances every time Scorsese, Spielberg, Coppola, or Rampling walked by. They were now doing things they had never done before—leaving behind the old atmosphere of turmoil and perdition and instead surrendering its spirit to globalization. So here they were, stuttering their way through disjointed tales, trying to mix accounts of Antar, the pre-Islamic poet-hero, with the movie *Cotton Club*—all to please UNESCO. No one had the slightest desire to sit in a dreary circle and listen to these phony narratives, of course, because any storyteller had a thousand more interesting tales crowding inside their head, which could turn into a river of laughter at any moment.

Marrakech was a truly magical city, painted by great foreigners, with rich people both old and new. However, with nightfall, the city opened its ten gates to the simple folk of the Amazigh and Hauz, to the Rehemna Bedouin and desert nomads, so that it could be reborn every day.

Jemaa el-Fnaa was a square that slept alongside its food carts.

Then came the winter, when it woke up to notice the circles that had come back and clustered around experts. In a distant corner of the square, people were amazed to discover a circle they recognized, just as they did its convener, with his Meccan-style turban and camel-hair burnoose. Nothing had changed except that al-Sharqawi was no longer telling stories to an eager audience. They were there merely because of the nice lamp that the government had given him.

He was telling the story of the British girl who was a friend of the pasha, the one who used to play golf and ride horses with him. She sat down with him for hours, chatting about music, horses, women, violence, and fear. Every time the conversation became more serious, she would disappear. He desired her without touching her. This all-powerful pasha who could seize the entire world by force found himself overcome by a powerful feeling of timidity every time he wanted to touch her. This girl would be intoxicated in his presence and turn into a ruthless prison guard, one who was enraptured by his stories. She listened modestly while he unloaded all his fears and sorrows and confessed to her what he used to do to himself during his daily encounters with terror in his dark quarters. The pasha—who'd been thrilled when the Krupp gun destroyed the tribesmen's bodies—almost prostrated himself when faced by her smile. He admitted to her how much hatred possessed him when he remembered his brother and the subtle way he could entrance people. Whenever he remembered Hmmu he would stare at her features and come to the inevitable conclusion that the English would make excellent colonialists, much nicer than the French. The British girl would blush modestly at his flirtatious efforts. The pasha drank in the sudden blush on her cheeks. But he was still unable to reach out and touch her. At this point, the pasha had bedded over two hundred women. He couldn't even remember the features of some of them, but here was this British woman whose face had captivated him—yet he couldn't make love to her in his bed.

She spent all her time with him, and then left him wandering around his huge harem in search of someone who resembled her. Eventually he would collapse in bed with no heart. She traveled and returned. While she traveled, the pasha would become sick and go to Telouet to immerse himself in the rigors of the ascetic life in the mountains. With cloudy eyes, he observed what his successor and rival was doing with hundreds of prisoners who were crammed into cells and tethered in chains. They had all lost their minds, hearing, and sight. Some had died in his custody and fallen to pieces, with no one even aware.

In Telouet, the pasha watched the horses and fighters, and tried to read into Hmmu's movements for signs of a secret conspiracy. Returning to Marrakech, he tried to come up with a way of removing this thorn from his foot and that of France as well. He was consumed by a sense of frustration at what was happening to him in general, and more specifically with the British girl—not to mention this foul caid who had managed to build his tiny kingdom using iron and fire. He may have been pretending to stand up to the foreigners, but all he got was a reputation as a double agent!

When the girl returned to the pasha's palace, a set of enigmatic candles were lit inside him. He spent long hours chatting with her again, discussing the paintings he had to acquire and the interior construction, decoration, and furnishing needed at the Telouet palace. He told her what he needed to do about the *Mas* newspaper, which he had just taken over. The pasha's remarks were bursting with hints, allusions, doubts, and expressions of authority. He was not by any means lacking in concubines, but he never spoke to any of them either before, during, or after intercourse. Shockingly, a thin but forceful blond girl had deeply affected this tyrant. She knew how to deal with his tongue, but only his tongue. He took her on a tour of various parts of the palace, but when she decided to leave, he said farewell with only a handshake. In a fit of uncontrollable fury, he then sent an army of spies to follow her. He was anxious to find out whether their conversations were going in a particular direction and, if so, which one. Day after day he dispatched these spies, and became sheepish when they came back with nothing worth mentioning. Until one day, when finally there was definite information: the girl had gone out in all her finery with an Italian pianist and attended a reception at the Italian Embassy. The pasha didn't like Italy, let alone the pianist—and he didn't like how the Italian government had occupied Ethiopia several years ago. Ethiopia was the homeland of his mother al-Zahra Umm al-Khair. The Italians had killed her family. He could never forgive Italy for the evil things it did to his mother. He couldn't forgive Italy for coming between himself and his English girl, nor could he forgive her for going out with this entrancing pianist, who would come to lose his fingers a couple of days later.

The pasha was heated with rage like never before, not even on that day when Anais had told him: *You're just a beast. My friend knows better than you!*

And what happened had happened.

Passion toppled the warrior from atop his steed and dumped him into a hellish castration from which there was no escape. The pasha was drinking alone, naked in the palace bathhouse, when he spread his huge hand over the wall where the beautiful woman had slept.

People in Jemaa el-Fnaa Square despised spicy food. They listened in confusion to a new storyteller, who used exaggerated gestures to tell the remarkable tale of Ibn Rushd. All the while, they were thinking about the mummy that restorers had removed from the palace bathhouse. Amid its shrouds, the archaeologists had found no trace of the love story that the pasha forgot to bury there.

Translated from Arabic by Roger Allen

PART II

THE RED AND THE BLACK

A WAY TO MECCA

BY HANANE DERKAOUI
Riad Zitoun

It was five a.m. in the old neighborhood of Riad Zitoun, in the ancient city. The first Friday in the month of June. The voice of the muezzin chanted the call to prayer; two young men from the neighborhood were on their way to the mosque, when they encountered Hmad returning late from work. Their neighborhood was small, but Hmad didn't speak to anyone. All that anyone in the neighborhood knew about him was that he had moved from an Amazigh village close to Ouarzazate, and that he worked as a waiter for a Christian in one of the ritzy neighborhoods in Gueliz.

"Listen, Ali, this serving job of Hmad the Chelh's is really weird, 'cause every day he comes back at five in the morning."

"It's true, Brother Ibrahim, every morning we run into him when we're on our way to dawn prayer."

"But we don't go to the dawn prayer every morning," Ibrahim said.

"I know, I just mean that we see him whenever we do go to morning prayer."

The two young men were late for the prayer, so they hurried their steps toward the mosque. Since their vigilance in matters of faith was only recently acquired, they were earnestly trying to project the appearance of being genuine believers who go to the dawn prayer every day, and who sit afterward with the *faqih*, debating aspects of the *hadith* with him, and asking innumerable religious questions. After the prayer, they were sitting far from the mosque smoking the only cigarette they had left after going completely broke.

"Why don't we follow Hmad?" Ali suggested. "We could con him and get some money out of him."

"Didn't we say that we've repented getting money like that?" Ibrahim replied.

"We've been diligent about going to prayer for a month now and nothing has changed; besides, we've squandered the last of our money."

"But we've repented, my friend," Ibrahim repeated. "Stealing is forbidden. The *faqih* said that God will open the way for us and guide our steps."

"God guides the steps of those who are educated and who have a university degree, or at the very least those who have a trade. As for us, what will He guide our steps toward?" Ali lamented. "There's no diploma in picking safes or five-finger discounts . . . we have no experience except for stealing."

Back before the tourist police proliferated, Ali and Ibrahim had worked as unlicensed tour guides. The license that allowed you to practice the trade with your head held high was only issued to people who paid a bribe at the new Institute of Tourist Guiding. This option was financially out of reach for them. Undeterred, they had wandered around Jemaa el-Fnaa and other historical monuments ambushing tourists. However, the tourist police kept a close eye out for them, harassing them and their peers. They were each arrested as many as forty times over the course of five years. They ended up abandoning the tourist trade and entering into the world of delinquency through its wide and welcoming door, by working on their burglary skills and organizing a few petty fraud operations.

Two months ago, they had both been overcome by a sudden religious impulse that shook their world. Their life was racked with turmoil, and they wavered in an ambiguous place between following the right path and straying from it. For they truly did want to be sincere, submissive Muslims like the ones the imam described. However, in the moment of temptation itself, they knew only too intimately about the bottomless depths of the city: its licentious underworlds, prostitutes, nightlife, and hashish establishments. But the explosive change came after they had robbed the house of an old lady in Sidi Youssef Ben Ali, and the old woman had said to them: "Take everything in the house and just leave me alive."

Ali was the first one to be affected by the incident. He tried to talk to his friend about it while they were returning with the day's loot on the back of a motorcycle: five hundred dirhams and a gold signet ring. When they got back to their room, Ali wanted to talk to his friend about this lady who reminded him of his grandmother. She had raised him in a village called Smimou near Essaouira before he left for Marrakech fifteen years ago. After splitting the loot, Ali had told Ibrahim with pain in his voice: "That lady really broke my heart. I don't want to do this to old people anymore."

"But who will we rob if not the old and weak? That's the nature of the beast. We don't have a choice," Ibrahim had reminded him.

"What if we switched professions, turned to God in repentance, and became like other people? What do you think about us going to pray with the congregation?"

"Why not? This might be another way to stay clean and to find some peace of mind," Ibrahim had replied, having felt the same shame as Ali.

Going to prayer in the mosque was an idea that had never enticed them before this. It was an entirely unexpected proposition. The young men thought that only those who had a lawful profession could enter the mosque, and because of this, they'd always kept away from the kingdom of God and the world of the faithful.

They had learned how to perform the prayer and the ritual

ablution during their primary school lessons, and they had not forgotten. Ali and Ibrahim had not learned this at home because their families were poor Amazigh speakers in the Essaouira province who were not proficient in Arabic.

Ibrahim and Ali started to frequent the mosque, warily and curiously at first, but eventually they began to enjoy the Friday sermon and to delight especially in the ambiance of the dawn prayer. However, throughout the rest of the day, they weren't seriously tempted by the mosque. Dawn prayer with the congregation was sufficient to purify their hearts; they had not committed any burglary or break-in for more than a month now. But what could they do for work? The money had run out and they hadn't found any respectable employment yet. In truth, they had not looked for any real work. With the onset of faith, an unaccustomed indolence descended upon them. During the nearly two months of visiting the mosque twice a day, they hadn't much felt the desire for adrenaline that had driven them to their risky way of earning a living. Faith had succeeded in quieting that impulse, but had not eradicated it completely. Now they felt the craving for adrenaline return while they watched Hmad close the window of his room.

"What exactly does he do for work?" Ali wondered.

"Why do you want to know?"

"Maybe we can get some money from him, or from the Christian he works for," Ali said. "Maybe we can find something to blackmail him with? You know, Christians are easy pickings."

"That seems complicated," Ibrahim said. "We can't even go into stores anymore. We're complete outcasts in this city. All that's left to us is old people in remote neighborhoods. We jump them, scare them a little with the knife, and take our share."

"I'm begging you, not the old people. Let's follow Hmad to the Christian's place."

The thieving duo finished their talk, and went back to the wretched room that their poverty confined them to.

* * *

Hmad was shedding his clothing so he could don his coral-colored silk robe, wrap his hair in a matching kerchief, and dab on a little perfume. He got into bed and tried to sleep while he thought over his night, which had been full of surprises. Important people had come to the party and he had earned a tidy sum of money. There had also been this man among the guests who had besieged him with stares all night long. He didn't ask Hmad to join him in one of the rooms like the others did. He only gazed at him and looked into his eyes. The others didn't usually look into his eyes. At these soirées, all of them only looked at his ass which he knew how to shimmy and shake so well.

He thought about the first time that he'd noticed how different he was from the other boys. He was twelve years old, and the other boys had started to talk about the length of their penises and such. Hmad had wanted to talk to them about what happened in his backside, about the tingling sensation that spread through it sometimes. He didn't know what was happening to him. When he stood close to his male friends, he wanted to move even closer. In time, the boys began to go to where the river grew large, and there they examined each other's privates, which had started to grow bigger. Hmad wasn't interested in scrutinizing his *thing*. But he did want to get closer to the other boys, to touch and lick *their* amazing things.

He even used to play house with the girls, and considered himself an excellent housewife. He knew how to roast the birds that he'd caught, and how to make *zamita* from ground pearl barley. Sometimes he made the *zamita* from *wari*, which was a thorny plant that sprouted seeds; it was then made into flour. The *zamita* with *wari* was just like the *zamita* his mother made from time to time. Hmad had to live with his mother and his sister since his father had disappeared one year after he was born. Many people said that they'd seen his father in the village of Tighassaline, living with a prostitute there. In any event, his mother raised him on her own. She used to work in other people's fields until the drought years hit the crops and the livestock, and then she was without work for some time. Later, one of her former employers from the north hired her on as a servant in his house. Hmad remembered those days with the greatest tenderness. His mother was an affectionate woman. She often hugged and kissed him, and constantly spoke loving words to him, praising his beauty and charm.

When he reached the age of fourteen, he didn't go with the other boys to the one prostitute who remained in the village. The people of Tinejdad had driven all the other prostitutes from their village. Yamina had stayed despite their protests. She welcomed all the young men just becoming acquainted with their bodies for the first time. She taught them the fundamentals of desire and showed them sensual delights that were forbidden in the very conservative village.

Hmad didn't go with his buddies to visit Yamina, so his friends became suspicious, and news spread about him: *He's one of* those. *No doubt about it. He really is a bit off . . .*

It didn't bother him that people alluded to this early and muddled manifestation of his femininity. He found freedom in it. He became more fastidious with his clothing, wore rings on his fingers, and sometimes painted his nails, delighting in his expressions of femininity. Ali Oukoubach paved the way for him in this department. Oukoubach was openly feminine even though he was forty years old. Oukoubach was Hmad's beloved role model. The forty-year-old wore women's clothing, painted his nails, and darkened his eyes with kohl. He performed at weddings and he had a pleasant singing voice that everyone admired. Everyone knew what Oukoubach did with the men that visited him every night, but no one expressed outrage.

Hmad was happy in his village. He thought that he too would grow up and everyone would accept him, and that he would entertain at weddings. Hmad also loved to sing; he had a beautiful voice. In fact, he didn't learn a trade because he knew that his profession would be singing at weddings and pleasing men—just like Ali Oukoubach. Then something unexpected happened: Ali Oukoubach was found murdered. They discovered his body rotting in the grass by his house in Ksar Aït Assam. He'd been decapitated. The crime shocked the village and shook Hmad to his core. Hmad feared staying in the village and he no longer felt safe there.

When he reached the age of seventeen, he told his mother about his desire to leave. She gave him some money and saw him off with tears in her eyes.

"I'm going to work in Marrakech," Hmad told her. "As soon as I have a house I'll come get you."

"My darling, may our Lord open a path of plenty for you," she'd said in blessing.

Hmad stopped in Ouarzazate, also known as the City of Games, while on his journey. He even worked there awhile. He wore women's clothing and danced. He loved his time there. But the time of games was soon over, and so Hmad left to continue on his journey toward Marrakech. In a big city like that, he thought that no one would bother him.

The thing that most captured Hmad's interest in Marrakech was Jemaa el-Fnaa. In the first days after he arrived, a veritable giddiness took hold of him, and he roamed among the barbers, snake charmers, and singers; he would spend the night wandering from one group to the next. The smell of food assaulted him, but he didn't have enough money to eat what he wanted, so he had to make do with one meal a day.

Hmad didn't find a job in the beginning because he wanted artistic work like singing or dancing. He mingled with the leaders of various performance groups in Jemaa el-Fnaa until a folk music troupe took him on. The leader asked him to dress up in women's clothing and to dance to the rhythm of their music, embellishing the entrance of their troupe with his coquettish sashays. This was delightful for Hmad. It had been his dream since he was a small child to become a woman, to sprout breasts, to have a woman's sexy ass. He knew that sex-change operations were very expensive, so he made do with dressing up and applying the beautifying powders that were capable of transforming him into a woman.

He found a room in the Riad Zitoun neighborhood. He only had to cross from Riad Zitoun to Arset el-Maach to get to Jemaa el-Fnaa. Sometimes he took the route through Kennaria so that he passed in front of the Café de France, and there, he was really in the heart of the square. He was keen not to get to know anyone from the neighborhood so that he would be safe from offending them. He had briefly met some of the young men of the neighborhood and he'd told them that he worked as a waiter for one of the Christians. He was trying to steer clear of them all. He barely responded to their greetings. Hmad was able to make a living off of his dance performances at Jemaa el-Fnaa. He danced with kohl-darkened eyes and a white veil that revealed his two plump red lips, but which still concealed the features of his face. Jemaa el-Fnaa embraced him for many months before he met Gerard, who changed his life completely.

Gerard saw Hmad dancing at Jemaa el-Fnaa and liked him right away. He was a Frenchman in his fifties. His heart had scarcely started to recover from the shock of the death of his partner Albert, who was killed in a car accident in one of Marrakech's suburbs. Gerard had waited in the *halqa* until the end of Hmad's act and approached him as he was gathering his things. Gerard's breath blew hot in Hmad's ear as he whispered an impromptu invitation to a cup of tea.

Hmad and Gerard drank tea at the Café de France, then went up to the roof of the café that overlooked Jemaa el-Fnaa, its market stalls, open-air restaurants, the towering trees in the historical garden of Arset el-Bilk, and the four mosques strung around it. For the first time, Hmad saw the minaret of the Koutoubia Mosque from above. How terrifying that high tower was from this place! The square seemed even noisier from up high than when he was in the middle of it. Hmad wanted to work in a more tranquil place, and to live in a better area than the old neighborhood of Riad Zitoun. It looked to him like there were mythical gardens contained within the ancient city. There were also some majestic villas in Marrakech, which he had glimpsed in magazines at the barber. Exquisite homes with swimming pools, broad balconies, and real gardens with flowers and plants swinging loosely from the windows. It was his dream to see one of them from the inside, to find out how it was decorated, and how its owners lived.

In the oasis town of Tinejdad, Hmad had lived in a rickety, abandoned clay castle. Most of its inhabitants, and those in the surrounding area, were poor. In Ouarzazate, in the days of the City of Games, he had lived in a small room in a filthy building on the edge of the city. He had never been blessed with a single day of living in a house with a garden. He looked at Gerard and thought, *Maybe he lives in a house with a garden, and maybe he'll invite me there.*

Gerard did indeed invite him to his house. He invited him over and over again. He made coffee for Hmad on his first visit, then he started to invite him to lunch. Their relationship intensified. One night, they found themselves naked in bed. Despite his inclinations, Hmad had never before fulfilled his dream of sleeping with a man. There had been a few tourists who had offered him money in exchange for spending the night with them, but he wasn't looking for money. He was earning enough from dancing to meet his needs, and he didn't need more.

Hmad drank whiskey with Gerard, and his body became a little loose, which made the sex easy. Hmad let Gerard do whatever he wanted to his body. His fingers were magical, arousing all the titillating tingling in Hmad's backside. The old sensations that he had hidden for years bloomed once more. His mother had provided him with a deep unconditional love, and because of this, he wanted to save his body. So he hadn't shared it with anyone before Gerard. When he was in the oasis, he used to think that one day he would love a man with blue eyes. Gerard's eyes weren't blue, but he was blond with green eyes, and he liked that too.

Gerard wanted Hmad to change careers and work as a drag queen at his house. Gerard hosted three parties a week—for both gay tourists and Moroccans. Hmad didn't fully understand what it meant to be a *drag queen.* But Gerard explained to Hmad that he would prepare him for this thrilling assignment himself, supervising his makeup and arranging things. Hmad was delighted. Finally, he had found love and work that he actually wanted, and on top of it all, a job which required him to dress as a woman. From his understanding of what Gerard said about his new job, it would allow him the opportunity to be the most beautiful of women three times a week.

Thus began his new life: spending the day sleeping in his room and in the evening cutting a path across Riad Zitoun through Arset el-Maach to Jemaa el-Fnaa. In front of the Koutoubia Mosque he caught a taxi to Gueliz. He arrived at Gerard's house at eight, and prepared himself for the evening's soirée. The drag queen makeup took a very long time. Three hours of preparation—of doing his eyelashes, whitening his skin, and then applying makeup to the rest of his face. After this, he would dress in an evening gown and circulate among the guests. Most of them were tourists, both male and female, some of whom would secretly slip cash into his bra. He understood that these parties were successful because of him, and that Gerard was paying him well: a thousand dirhams a night. He sent three hundred dirhams to his mother and saved the rest. He no longer thought about bringing his mother to live with him, but he had started to fantasize about living with Gerard. Oh, if only it were possible for him to become his housewife. To look after everything in that house, from the cleanliness of the rooms to the dishes in the kitchen; from taking care of the plants in the garden to pampering Gerard's body. That house was heaven, and he dreamed every day of living in it. Gerard loved him and Hmad knew it was just a matter of time before he would ask him to move in. Hmad wanted to leave his room in Riad Zitoun and dreamed nightly of crossing the chasm between Riad Zitoun and Gueliz.

He thought about all of this as sleep began to overtake him at dawn, on the very day after he had met Ibrahim and Ali. He had responded to their greeting without even knowing them. He recognized their faces, having encountered them by chance here in the neighborhood more than once. *It seemed like they were on their way to prayer at the mosque,* thought Hmad. *I want to go to the mosque too, but God will not accept me. I don't think it's possible for someone like me to go through the door of the mosque.* He sniffed his perfumed body and thought: *I'm not unclean, so why would God punish me for this inclination which He Himself created in me?* There were many things Hmad didn't understand about faith, and because of this, he left the matter for a later time—when he would go on the Hajj. God would forgive him as long as he submitted his sins before Him and did not advance further into sin than where he already was. He was not overtly concerned with questions of faith—with the exception of the Hajj.

Hmad wanted to walk around the Kaaba with the other pilgrims one day. To throw stones at the devil and shout joyfully: "Here I am at your service, O Lord!" The phrase rose up in his mind as the room filled with the fragrance of Meccan incense; Riad Zitoun had become the way to Mecca, and he saw himself in white clothing entering into the Kingdom of God, just like the others. He used to dream of the day when everyone would call him al-Hajj Hmad. This dream had been forcefully unleashed once again, ever since he had surrendered to the temptation that had overwhelmed him after he'd set foot in Marrakech. Lately, these bouts of temptation had grown in frequency. So he had started to visit the graves of the marabouts and the pious saints, until he finally found protection in the mausoleum of Sidi Bel Abbès, the holy helper of the poor and sick. Nothing would heal his heart, though, except a visit to the prophet's grave and circumambulation around the Black Stone. He knew that the way to Mecca would open for him one day, for God does not shut His gates in the faces of good-hearted people. Hmad told himself that this dream would come true one day. He knew that things happened with time, and that the time for the Hajj would eventually come. His imagination was wandering toward Mecca when sleep finally conquered him.

Ibrahim and Ali woke up, then went back to watching Hmad's window, and to the questions regarding his secret late-night job.

"He said he's a waiter. Leave him alone," Ibrahim said.

"A waiter that comes home at five in the morning?" Ali countered.

"It's Marrakech, brother! There are places that never close." Ibrahim rolled his eyes.

"But he isn't working in a cabaret or a nightclub. He said that he's a waiter in one of the foreigners' houses, and there's no respectable house that keeps its doors open until five in the morning."

"We won't get anything out of this scam. Hmad is from Chleuh country, far away from here, and no doubt he's as inexperienced and naive as the rest of his people in Ouarzazate," Ibrahim argued. "He really could be just a waiter."

"I am almost positive that he isn't just a waiter. This guy has a secret behind him that we need to figure out. Let's follow him tonight and find out."

Ali and Ibrahim ultimately agreed to follow Hmad when he headed to work and to return only when they had solid information. They went out into the alley to try to borrow a few dirhams for food while they waited for him. They ran into Mubarak, who was an unlicensed tour guide, but who was smart and eager and not burned-out like them. He supplied them with twenty dirhams. They bought two sausage sandwiches from Doukkali, the owner of a grilled-meat cart, and sat with Aouicha, who made tea right on the ground. Aouicha had worked as a prostitute before her beauty withered and her value in the city's flesh market collapsed. She had not produced any children. When she retired, she set up shop on the ground preparing porridge in the early morning and making tea throughout the day. Ali and Ibrahim asked her about Hmad the Chelh, and she replied: "He is a well-mannered man who doesn't talk to anyone. He drank tea at my spot two or three times and did not utter a word. He is just a wet-behind-the-ears Chelh who lucked out finding work as a waiter at one of the villas."

"I don't believe that he works as a waiter," Ali told her.

"And why not? He seems to be clean like a waiter."

"Exactly—the problem is his cleanliness. He seems to be cleaner than necessary. He has a strange kind of style. It seems more like he is an employee or an assistant at a pharmacy . . . something like that. What if he's a cop?"

"And what would an undercover cop be doing in our stinking alley?" Aouicha challenged.

"Maybe he's spying on some big gang."

"You watch too many movies," Aouicha said, waving him off. "Our alley is nothing but petty crooks the police couldn't care less about."

They left Aouicha's spot and stopped by the cigarette seller, Zeroual, another person who was extremely suspicious of Hmad. Zeroual found him to be more stylish and tidy than was strictly necessary. In his mind, Hmad did not seem like the other Chleuhs of Ouarzazate, who were known for their uncouth appearance. As the three of them deliberated, their suspicions grew. The cigarette seller spoke with intense resentment. How could this Chelh peasant come from a village in the south and find work that easily in a villa of one of the Christians, whereas he was a son of Marrakech whose family had been here for generations and there were no prospects in front of him other than selling loosies?

"Marrakech only gives to outsiders," Ali agreed.

"Yeah, they come from far away, they take the ministry's permits, they become licensed guides, and we are left with nothing," Zeroual said.

Ibrahim and Ali remembered with regret their days as tour guides. Those were the days of contentment and easy living. They used to be so happy when the day ended and they could roll a joint at one of their places. The most important thing with the tourists was to provide hashish at their evening parties, and sometimes to supply sex too. The foreign women were sexually liberated; they gave pleasure and took it themselves anytime they wanted it. It wasn't necessary to have a relationship or to face all those obstacles that Moroccan girls put in front of you. Nothing remained of those glorious days except for the memories, nostalgia, and indignation toward the tourist police who had ruined their lives. They considered scamming the tourists an acceptable thing, because all of them were rich, and what they took from them through trickery and deceit was nothing but crumbs.

At the end of the day, the thieves left the cigarette seller and went to their room to change. They dressed in their most stylish clothing: nice shirts, jeans, and sneakers. Ibrahim put a chain around his neck and a watch that didn't work on his left wrist. They surveyed Hmad the Chelh's window. He stepped outside and the duo followed him across the back streets of Riad Zitoun to Arset el-Maach, and from there to Jemaa el-Fnaa. They lost him for a moment in the bustle of the square before Ali spotted him again.

"Look, look, there he is!"

Hmad was cutting a path toward the Koutoubia. They followed him, all the while hiding their faces behind newspapers like in the movies.

Hmad stopped at the horse-drawn carriage station and his pursuers hesitated. Ibrahim asked: "What do we do now?"

"We're going to ride the same carriage as him—we'll ask him where he's going, and we'll say that we are heading, coincidentally, to the same place."

They rode in the carriage with Hmad, who stayed silent the whole way to Gueliz. He avoided looking at them, and didn't ask them where they were going. He was thinking about the party that night and about Gerard. He was determined to ask him about moving into the elegant villa. Hmad was tired of Riad Zitoun and its clamor. Besides, the residents would find out sooner or later about his business, and then they'd harass him, or maybe even kill him like the people of Tinejdad had done to Ali Oukoubach. He trembled when he remembered the death of Oukoubach and his defiled body in the middle of the grass. He wondered: *Is someone in Marrakech going to do the same thing to me?* He comforted himself by thinking: *Marrakech is a big, open city. Its people are accepting of who I am.* He recalled all the jokes that were told about Marrakech men—about how they love other men, sometimes even preferring them to women, and about how this did not seem to be a problem for them. Despite all of this, deep inside he was afraid of being discovered, and of meeting his death like Oukoubach. He reassured himself that nobody, until now, knew the real nature of his work, or his hidden indulgences. His thoughts jumped back to Gerard: *What makeup will he have ready for tonight?* The previous night he had made his face up to look like an American actress named Marilyn Monroe. He felt very beautiful in Marilyn's clothing. No doubt she was bewitching. He loved the long fake eyelashes most of all, the slightly curly blond hair, and the dress with bared cleavage. He could feel everyone's stares and surging desire. He suspected that among the gazes were some looks of envy, for the partygoers knew about his relationship with Gerard, who had continued to praise Hmad's devotion, candor, and sincere lack of desire for material things.

Hmad really didn't covet those items; he only wanted to be partners in everything, and to live together as lovers.

Gerard had asked Hmad if he wanted to move to France like many other young men in Marrakech, but Hmad made it clear where he preferred to live: "I want to stay with you. So if you stay here, I'm staying. If you go, take me with you."

Their love was glowing and growing, especially since Hmad had become a drag queen and all those stares of admiration had been focused on him. Pride had succeeded in igniting and inflaming Gerard's love even more. Hmad was overjoyed when Gerard looked at him adoringly. This was why he was so elegantly glammed up, perfumed, and adorned with rings. He hadn't imagined that he would find his beloved this quickly. And on top of this, he was a sensitive and generous lover, despite being a foreigner. He assured himself that with Gerard he would live the rest of his life in love, bliss, and joy, not to mention the parties.

When he had left his village, he was determined not to live like Oukoubach, who had been killed by one of the many lovers he'd taken. Hmad wanted a stable life with only one partner to fulfill his desires, to look after him and his mother in the village. He had not spoken frankly with Gerard about the issue of helping his mother, but he felt sure that his lover would not fail him in this. Of course, he would help him send enough money so that his mother could live independently and with dignity. He decided, as he got off the carriage, to speak with Gerard about this issue as soon as the party was over.

Hmad was lost in his reveries and didn't see Ali and Ibrahim getting off at the same stop. The duo paused to talk with the driver because they didn't have enough money to pay the price of the carriage. Hmad continued on his way and almost escaped his pursuers before the pair bolted away from the carriage driver and trailed after him. Hmad entered a swanky villa surrounded by an enormous wall. It wasn't far from the

Ibn Tofail Hospital, where there were many other spacious colonial villas.

Ibrahim turned to his friend. "You have to believe him now, he really does work in that villa."

"Let's go inside and see what his work is like."

"They'll arrest us," Ibrahim protested, pulling on Ali's arm.

"They'll be preoccupied—it looks like the party has started. They won't notice us."

The pair circled around the tall walls of the villa and stopped at the back. Ali climbed onto Ibrahim's shoulders and pulled himself up on the wall. He stretched his hands down to his friend to help him climb up as well. Then they jumped inside.

Ali followed his friend, the sound of Western music filling the place. The guests flocked toward the house in groups. There were lots of fashionable male tourists with half-naked Moroccan girls on their arms. There were also chic young Moroccan men, more done up than was appropriate. It seemed like they were high-class elites—very clean and smelling of expensive perfumes.

"These are not our kind of people, brother," Ali whispered.

"Just look at the children of Gueliz."

"Yeah, high class, brother."

No one paid attention to their presence as they sauntered inside. Two servers walked by with wine and champagne on trays, and Ali and Ibrahim grabbed glasses as if they were invited guests. They downed the drinks in one gulp and went back to the server to ask for more.

"Are you sure we can drink?" Ali asked. "We go to the mosque now and alcohol is *haram*."

Ibrahim was already beginning to feel tipsy. "It's not forbidden! Honestly, there isn't a single verse that forbids alcohol in the Koran," he muttered. "It's only suggested to abstain. Anyway, we aren't going to pray while we're drunk."

"I am afraid of this act. Turn to God in penitence."

"God doesn't know we're in a villa in Gueliz, enjoying ourselves with all these exquisite drinks. Drink, brother, and don't annoy me. We will pray later on."

"You're right, Ibrahim . . . these drinks are great!"

It was clear that most of the guests didn't know each other. There were middle-aged foreign men trying to hit on stylish young guys while they drank champagne and beer. No one cared about anyone else here. Ali and Ibrahim wandered around the huge house. The gigantic living room was divided into two sections. One was decorated in Moroccan fashion, with cushions and sofas covered with green and purple brocade fabric, while the other section was furnished with sophisticated antique European canapé couches in orange and brown tones. The curtains were of the Moroccan patchwork style, sewn from recycled green and purple Indian saris. In the middle of the living room, a wooden stairway led up to the first floor, and in one corner a corridor crossed to another room that looked different than the others. In the middle of this room was a desk, and the walls behind it were covered with bookcases filled with volumes of all sizes, most of them bound in leather, and all neatly arranged.

Having never seen such an enormous number of books before, Ibrahim turned to Ali and said: "The Christian is educated."

"I don't think we'll be able to dupe him then."

"Educated people are stupid too, dummy," Ibrahim quipped. "He'll be an easy mark, just let me think of how."

But Ali didn't let him think. Instead he led Ibrahim across the painted hallway covered with authentic Moroccan *tadelakt* plaster until they found themselves on the way to the garden. The other living room in the European style was painted white, and led out to the open veranda beside the garden and pool, which was almost overflowing with water. They thought for a moment that they were in a dream. Or was this really the valley of heaven that the *faqih* had spoken about? *Without a doubt, heaven looks like this place*, Ali thought. What was heaven if not water, pure white surfaces, fruit trees, and a pool in the middle of a garden?

The thieves discussed the covenant of faith and how this place seemed proof of the profligacy that they had heard the *faqih* speak about.

"They are the people transgressing beyond bounds," Ali said drunkenly.

"They're infidels," Ibrahim responded, raising his glass high. "Death to the infidels!"

It seemed to them that this was a completely different life. For a moment, they felt filled with a compassion that left no place for hunger, which had hardened their hearts. For they had chased after this hunger since their childhood in the luckless village of Smimou. Their entire lives had been spent hunting for scraps of food, and this endless foraging transforms any human heart into a callous brick.

"Why don't we leave him and his business alone, brother," Ali said, more relaxed after another glass of champagne. "He didn't do anything to us."

"Wake up, Ali! If we go back to Riad Zitoun, we go hungry. The twenty dirhams we borrowed from Mubarak are gone, and tomorrow he's going to ask us to pay him back. What are we going to say to him, you thin-skinned sissy?"

"We are going to look for work, pay off our debts, and start a new life," Ali insisted.

"A new life—without a trade or education, and with the tourist police waiting to ambush us on all sides of the square?" Ibrahim drawled. "Rest is for the rich, for those people I saw coming into this villa as invited guests. As for us, we jumped the fence. No one wants us here."

"It feels like no one has wanted me here since I was born," Ali said. "My dad just shot his load into my mom's belly, and then she tossed me into the cold room of our shack. Nothing was prepared for my arrival into the world: I had no food or clothes, and I studied nothing, so why did my parents even bring me into this life?"

"They brought you to me so we could con gullible people and eat sausage sandwiches at the end of the day," Ibrahim joked. "That's the most he could do for you."

"Ibrahim, I want to get married. I want to have children," Ali blurted out, the alcohol loosening his tongue.

"It's like the proverb says: *Here you are naked and asking for a diamond ring.* Marriage? Are you nuts? We haven't paid rent in two months. Where is your stupid bride going to live?"

"Maybe I'll find a girl with a job to love me, and we can manage together."

"Why would a girl with a job want you?" Ibrahim asked with a laugh. "Girls with jobs are looking for guys with real jobs, not thieves like us."

The duo finally stopped probing their painful thoughts and surrendered themselves to the music.

"I'm going to get another drink, stay where you are," Ibrahim said as he headed back to the servers.

He brought back two flutes of champagne. They sat on the edge of the pool drinking and gazing at the fruit trees that surrounded them.

"No one is even picking the fruit here, look how it's scattered on the ground."

"I told you, they are the people transgressing all bounds," Ali said.

"Infidels."

Ali and Ibrahim were soon joined by a group of screaming young people—young men and women who threw their clothes in the water and filled the pool with their bodies. Some of them started kissing each other. Among them was a teenaged Moroccan boy who was passionately kissing a middle-aged foreign man.

"We are among the Sodomites, my friend," Ibrahim murmured.

"I told you, they are transgressing," Ali repeated.

"Infidels."

The thieves retreated from the pool, tipsy. They stumbled

toward the living room where everyone was dancing to *raï* music.

Cheb Khaled was singing: "*Didi . . . didi oh . . . didi . . .*"

Moroccan girls writhed to the music, and the foreigners accompanied them by clapping to the beat. People were clinging to each other with glasses in their hands; the drinks were flowing everywhere, and the neatly arranged tables were covered with dishes of succulent food.

Ali and Ibrahim were given plates. They piled them with pieces of fried meat, chicken, and unfamiliar salads. The pair ate greedily, and at that moment they were absolutely certain they were in heaven. They had never been to a party this lavish in their whole lives. True, Ibrahim and Ali had known tourists before, but the ones they knew were tourists of a different stripe—ones who could be found wandering across Jemaa el-Fnaa morning and night with their backpacks. Those were the ones they had taken advantage of and swindled, whereas the rich ones sought refuge in villas and luxurious gardens, and in parties like the one they were crashing.

"How do they go shopping, then?" Ali asked.

"Clearly they send their servants to do the shopping for them."

The thieves had just finished their plates and were preparing for another round when a voice suddenly shouted from the top of the stairs: "*Maintenant, la surprise de la soirée* . . . Mademoiselle Marilyn Monroe!"

Ali looked quizzically at Ibrahim. "Did you hear that?"

"Some kind of surprise . . . some kind of food, maybe?"

"He said Marilyn Monroe is here. She's an actress, stupid," Ali said, shaking his head.

"But she died years ago."

"I swear to you, he said that Marilyn Monroe is here."

They turned toward the stairs and saw a young woman of outstanding beauty descending, very deliberately, the wooden stairway in the middle of the room. She was blond, with large breasts almost bouncing out of her white dress that was slit open at the bust to reveal her charms. She was puckering her delicious lips as if to kiss an imaginary person, and she stretched out her soft arms invitingly. She came down the stairs slowly, stepping to the beat of the soft music. She appeared to be Moroccan.

Some of the men shouted: "*Oooh!*"

"Ay luv yoo, Marilyn!" one guy screamed.

She seductively lifted up the hem of her dress so that her translucent white stockings appeared, hooked to something even more alluring. The flesh wrapped in the tight muslin pantyhose looked even more tempting than the naked flesh itself.

Ibrahim imagined himself removing her stockings, taking his time kissing those tasty lips of hers. He hadn't touched a woman's body for months because he couldn't afford a prostitute, and he didn't dare flirt with the poor girls in Riad Zitoun.

In the days when they'd been tour guides, Ibrahim hadn't been deprived of sex. It had been available from the female tourists who generously offered their bodies and their bountiful love. There was no need for marriage, the women didn't get upset, and there were no protective brothers, chaperones, or uncles. Just total surrender to the heat of a throbbing body, giving pleasure and taking it. Most of the time they were both drunk, so Ibrahim couldn't remember exactly how many women he had slept with back then. When they were tour guides, he'd also had a relationship with Zahra, a married woman. He regretted not getting married back then. If he had done so, there would be children jumping around him right now. He pushed the thought of marriage from his mind and simply enjoyed the sight of Marilyn Monroe. He was truly astonished, because he knew that she had died a long time ago.

"I can't believe Marilyn Monroe is here," Ali said, his mouth still open in shock.

"I swear, you're so stupid. It's a man," Ibrahim responded.

"A man?"

"Yeah, I swear, it's a man," Ibrahim said. "Just look at his legs."

Ali looked at Marilyn's legs. They did seem manly. He turned to face Ibrahim. "It's true! She really is a man . . . wow! Where are we, my friend?"

"We are with the people transgressing beyond all bounds," Ibrahim said grimly.

"Infidels."

They could accept many things, but not a man dressed as a woman. In their opinion, this was something revolting—an unforgivable crime that violated all that was holy. Ali was reeling as he yelled: "I want to throw myself on that effeminate Christian and choke him."

"He isn't a Christian—he's Moroccan. See, his face isn't foreign," Ibrahim said.

"He isn't foreign?"

"I don't know why I feel like I know him. Something about him reminds me of someone I've seen before, but I don't know from where . . ." Ibrahim trailed off as he took a good long look at Marilyn.

"Yeah, he does seem familiar."

"Anyway, we came here because of Hmad the Chelh," Ibrahim reminded. "We should go look for him."

"I totally forgot about him . . . I didn't see him with the servers—where could he be?"

They circled the house once more, but they couldn't find him.

"I'm sure I saw him enter this place," Ibrahim said.

"Me too. I definitely saw him, but where could he have gone?"

"Let's try the first floor."

They went upstairs and encountered paintings and photographs of naked male bodies in seductive poses throughout the red hallway. Ali, fighting off his drunkenness and arousal, yelled: "They are the people transgressing beyond bounds!"

"Infidels!"

They opened the door of the first room on the left side and found a foreign man and a Moroccan girl clinging to each other. The foreigner was annoyed and bellowed in their faces: "*Allez vous faire foutre!*"

Ali closed the door and turned to Ibrahim. "What did he say?"

"He said, *Go fuck yourself.*"

"Goddamn you. Goddamn all of you. They are the people transgressing beyond bounds!" Ali said once again.

"Infidels."

Ibrahim and Ali said these things, but experienced at the same instant a powerful arousal.

"Oh, if only I was in his place," Ibrahim mumbled. "If only I could hold a woman right now, touch her waist, plow her until she moans."

"Unbelievable . . . not a single woman hit on me at this party," Ali griped.

"Have you seen the people here, have you seen their clothes? Their faces? We look like a couple of homeless bums and you wonder why they aren't chasing us?"

"No one has even noticed we're here," Ali grumbled. "Everyone is drunk, or in bed with a slutty girl, or a girlie boy."

Ibrahim opened the door to the second room and saw two young guys naked on the bed, hiding under the blanket in fear.

"I am about to explode. I want a woman now, any woman," Ali moaned. "I just want to go to bed with a woman beside me."

Like most young men of his age, Ali thought about sex obsessively. Nothing would cure this except for marriage, or being able to have a woman every day. But marriage was impossible for him. Sex had tortured him even more since he had been overtaken over by religious sentiments. He had started to feel sinful because of his urges, and the fact that he couldn't satisfy his needs in the legal way that the *faqih* talked about.

Ibrahim grabbed Ali's arm, pulling him out of his thoughts. "Quit daydreaming and help me look in the other rooms. Maybe we'll find that damned Chelh in one of them. I bet he's not even a server here. But someone must know what he really does in this place."

The thieving pair were Chleuhs themselves. But they considered themselves to be different from the poor and backward Chleuhs from Errachidia and Ouarzazate, since Ali and Ibrahim had been born and raised close to two cities: Essaouira on one side and Marrakech on the other. They were fortunate that they'd been raised in a village close to Marrakech, the center of Moroccan civilization. A city of achievements and the pride of the Berbers. A city open to all cultures. You only had to wander across Jemaa el-Fnaa to see the whole world, and you could hear half the world's languages while sitting in the humblest café. Being from Marrakech filled them with a particular pride. How could that damned Chelh be working in this heavenly villa amid all this bliss when he was from the godforsaken wasteland between Errachidia and Ouarzazate? The train didn't even go there.

Ali was still caught up in his dreams of having a woman to warm his body. He was nearing thirty and he still hadn't enjoyed the pleasure of daily sex that the *faqih* said marriage provided.

Ibrahim turned to him again, once more snapping him out of his reverie. "Focus, Ali. We're here to look for Hmad the Chelh and we haven't found him yet."

"And where will we find him in the middle of all this racket—with guests, servers, and suspiciously locked rooms?"

"We'll ask the owner of the house," Ibrahim suggested.

"There's an idea, we'll ask the owner of the house."

They went over to a group of people surrounding Marilyn Monroe but were roundly ignored. The music was loud and most people were occupied with their companions. They finally asked a drunk Moroccan girl and she pointed at someone else in the circle around Marilyn, saying: "He's over there, his name is Gerard."

Ali and Ibrahim turned toward Gerard, who was leaning against Marilyn's shoulder with his ass glued to her thighs.

"*Bonsoir, monsieur,*" Ibrahim greeted.

"*Bonsoir,*" Gerard replied.

"*Nous cherchons Hmad Chelh?*"

"*Il est* là; *c'est Marilyn, ma* drag queen *préférée*," Gerard said before turning away.

Ali whispered to Ibrahim: "Did you understand anything?"

"He says that Hmad is Marilyn."

"This damned Chelh is mocking us. He's a fairy and a faggot!" Ali seethed. "We're going to blackmail him and expose him to the neighborhood, or maybe to all of Marrakech, if he doesn't pay up. We're going to take so much money from him in exchange for our silence. Just like we did with Nadia the dancer. She paid us for months before she disappeared from Riad Zitoun. Where did that fornicator go? These people are transgressing beyond bounds."

"Infidels," Ibrahim said.

Thoughts raced through Ali's brain. He remembered his mother warning him about the consequences of leading a life of debauchery. He pictured his older brother warning him about what some boys do with each other, recalled the *faqih* declaring the secret practice of homosexuality to be *haram* and the gravest of sins. He suddenly smelled a strange fragrance that was neither perfume nor alcohol. A queer aroma that he remembered trailing behind Hajj pilgrims when they returned from Mecca. Or like the smell of the mosque—that pleasant smell of old books, cheap incense, and shoes.

Ali drew the knife that he always kept in his pocket. The knife that he used to threaten old people with before he had repented before God. He flung himself at Hmad the Chelh, chanting: "*For ye practice your lusts on men in preference to women: ye are indeed a people transgressing beyond bounds!*"

The *faqih* had explained this verse to them only a few days before, describing all the punishments for homosexuality, and explaining that God rejoiced on His throne when sexual deviants were stoned.

Ali threw himself on Hmad the Chelh, aiming several sharp stabs at his stomach. Hmad staggered before he fell to the white floor covered in his own blood. Gerard threw himself on top of Hmad, screaming hysterically and kissing Hmad. A great tumult arose. It seemed as if everyone in that heavenly villa awoke from their drunkenness.

Ibrahim roared at his friend in shock: "What have you done, you brute?"

Ali didn't hear anyone. He didn't see anything. He was only dreaming of heaven . . . of the huge quantities of red wine . . . the wonderful food . . . and the women . . . And he called out, hysterically: "They are the people transgressing beyond bounds . . . infidels! . . . They are the people transgressing beyond bounds . . . infidels!"

Translated from Arabic by Jennifer Pineo-Dunn

THE SECRET IN FINGERTIPS

BY FATIHA MORCHID

Douar el-Askar

They call me Scheherazade, a nickname Philip gave me to stress the fact that with my fingertips I tell tales as magical as *The Thousand and One Nights*. I adopted the name because it seemed to suit me even more than my own name, which I preferred to completely forget, convinced that deep inside every woman lies a Scheherazade. If the tales of Scheherazade were a shield for her against death, the language of my fingertips was, for me, a shield against poverty.

The language of fingertips, like any other language, can be be learned and mastered with some perseverance, and a gifted person can even practice it creatively. I discovered my talent by chance, as often happens with discoveries. Some would consider me a whore, for it is easy to cast judgment, but I do not consider myself so. You can define me as follows: an ambitious, somewhat smart girl, who life blessed with a gorgeous physical body, but who had been denied the material means needed for well-being. There are those who would see this as a definition of whoredom, or at least a hint at it. But in Marrakech, beautiful rich women are called princesses, while beautiful poor ones are called whores.

I said I was smart, but my intelligence was not the kind that would benefit one in their education, though I reached the baccalaureate level without great effort. What I mean is daily-life smartness, which some would call *heart smartness.* I don't like the latter label because I've got a silly heart, or otherwise it wouldn't have fallen for our neighbor Saeed—the drug dealer. I forgot to tell you that I am from Douar el-Askar, a neighborhood that hosts soldiers' families and hordes of laborers who work in the local food industry factories—particularly with apricots and olives. It's one of those suburban neighborhoods that sprang up like mushrooms outside the Old Medina of Marrakech. The city that was once red before turning as black as my own days.

I am sorry if I sound scatterbrained—*jumping from the rooster to the donkey*, as Philip would say. Let's go back to daily-life smartness. I realized at some point that success in school was no longer equivalent to success in life. That had once been the case, but our generation began to learn only as much as was helpful to engage early in the battleground of life. No one wanted to end up like Mahjoub el-Wafi, who studied medicine for twelve years only to open a clinic in Tameslouht. Poor thing! He would get his payment in chickens and eggs from the people of the neighboring *douars* . . . that's why I decided to be more practical than Dr. el-Wafi. So I asked myself the following question: what career guarantees a bright future?

After a prolonged consideration of things, I opted for a career in massage: relaxing massage . . . weight-reduction massage . . . Thai massage, Chinese . . . or even satanic massage. What's important is that it was an independent occupation that could be exercised in luxury hotels, beauty salons, and even private homes. It didn't require specific tools—just trained fingertips and some basic oils. Most importantly, it was in demand among the well-to-do. *Being with the poor makes one poor*, as Saeed says.

Aunt Mannana, the fortune-teller in Jemaa el-Fnaa, helped me make the choice while staring into my palm lines: *Your good fortune will come from beyond the seas. He will be older, wealthy, and renowned . . . but the secret is the fingertips.*

I didn't understand then what the fingertips of unskilled people can do except steal—until I learned how to massage.

After that memorable meeting with the fortune-teller, I began to secretly examine each foreign face I met. I wondered if that face was good fortune coming from afar.

You might see my consulting fortune-tellers as a contradiction with my practical approach to life, but you will understand the matter once you realize that every great thing starts with a dream. For me, fortune-tellers were sellers of dreams to those who dare not have any. Besides, they can fill a person with tremendous self-confidence, thanks to an amulet that provides one with a charm known only to Moroccans, which is called *qaboul* (acceptance). It's an alchemy that makes one lovable, attractive, and irresistibly charming.

I entered the world of massage with spectacular confidence, psychologically prepared for this new venture. It would suffice for me to add the ashes of some amulet to the basic oils with which I massaged the bodies of my clients, to feel my own miraculous abilities, to access their feelings, entrails, hearts, and pockets.

This is how I got to know Mr. Philip, or, rather, his body—only a massage allows you to know the body of a person before knowing their name. He had the traits of the foreigner the fortune-teller had prophesied. He was a Frenchman in his seventies who settled in Marrakech because of a dream he had shared with his deceased wife. They had both discovered the red radiating face of Marrakech: the hospitality of its people and their sense of humor, the delicious food, the magic sunsets over its palm-tree alleys, its markets alive with colors and smells, and the Jemaa el-Fnaa Square with its exoticism, its clowns, storytellers, dancers, snakes, apes, and clamor, bestowing a new life on its visitors. The Frenchman bought a house in Derb Dabachi in the Old Medina, a neighborhood that was a busy passageway to Jemaa el-Fnaa. Derb Dabachi was also famous for hosting in the famous Ghazalah Cinema, before they destroyed it, as well as the notorious gay shop called al-Gaman.

With renovations, the old house was transformed into a

wonderful riad where Philip wanted to live the stories of *The Thousand and One Nights* for the rest of his life. He called it the Riad of Dreams. He forgot that dreams could turn into nightmares.

At the time, I was a young trainee at a massage center in a five-star hotel. I got that job thanks to Saeed—the drug dealer. In Marrakech, you can manage your life if you're smart enough to adapt to all situations and take advantage of each one of them. But no one was smarter than Saeed when it came to taking advantage of people and things. He was the kind of person to whom the popular saying applies: *He lays hands on whatever he sees, and has a share in whatever he hasn't seen yet.* He worked sometimes as a tour guide and sometimes as a driver. He traded in everything from clothes to illicit goods, and had numerous clients—the kind of clients attracted to Marrakech's hashish rather than its palm trees. He would give me presents that seemed more expensive than what he could afford.

I don't know what exactly attracted me to Saeed. He wasn't handsome, but he had the charisma of someone who lived on the edge. Yet I felt safe with him, and this seemed another contradiction of mine. The cops could've arrested him any time they liked and thrown him in jail, even if he had friends among the police who benefitted from his deals in return for their silence.

Some policemen provided protection by ignoring your activities until someone stronger than you emerged on stage, and then you became a scapegoat. I had a passion for Saeed, but at the same time I didn't want to spend my whole life with him. My ambitions were larger than him, and men like him only loved my body and its charms.

I had a strong feeling that I was a princess who was born in the wrong place and in love with the wrong man. I resembled none of my family. All of them were ugly, including my mom who was a housemaid of pure breeding, one of those who labored in homes for meager wages, or worked every day at olive and apricot factories in Douar el-Askar for their daily bread. My father spent his life working in a tannery far away from our neighborhood. He died of lung cancer caused by inhalation of dyeing chemicals when I was ten years old.

I have two sisters, dark-skinned like my mom, short with snub noses and curly hair. I alone was fair-skinned with hair like silk and a slender shape. I honestly doubted whether we all came from the same father. My mom said, justifying the differences, that during her pregnancy she used to work for a beautiful French lady. She said pregnancy cravings had their own secrets and mysteries. Who knows what happened? Perhaps I am the daughter of some foreigner for whom my mom worked. If that's true, I can't help but thank her. At least she saved me from the ugliness that would have disqualified me from the world of massage.

I also have an older brother who took refuge from the family's poverty in faith. After he had failed his studies and given up all ambition, he grew a casual beard and spent most of his time in the mosque. As alcohol is forbidden in our religion, he replaced it with *maajoon*. In the beginning, he tried to exert his authority over me and my sisters as the man of the house, but the power of the pocket money I provided him with and the effect of *maajoon* made him docile, so he contented himself by asking God to lead us back to the righteous path.

If Mr. Philip were the foreign man destined to bring my happiness as Aunt Mannana had foretold, then the tree had to first be shaken for the fruit to fall.

"Do you prefer a regular massage or a special one?" I had asked him, feigning innocence.

"I want a relaxing massage," he replied. "But if the special massage is better than the regular one, why not try it?"

He seemed like the kind of person not used to the intimate caresses often demanded by foreigners his age. I thought that sometimes one learned nothing from the passage of years. I filled my palms with the oils prepared according to Aunt Mannana's recipes and passed my soft fingertips on his stiff skin after I galvanized them with smooth, sensual energy. I tried to make the exciting part of the massage inevitable. The soft music, the smell of Oriental incense, and the room's coziness all together completed the play of my fingertips.

Clients who developed an erection went from bashfulness to confusion, and then to laughter. There was nothing like laughter to establish communication. Here, I would intervene gently to puff up their virile ego, showing admiration for their male organ no matter how tiny it was, explaining that it was just a natural reaction in real men. Of course, I didn't give a damn about boosting their sexual prowess. I, as a matter of fact, cared only for the extra tip that I got from them. I developed the ability to manipulate any kind of human being, aside from Saeed, who kept manipulating me.

I don't know why I became so weak in front of him. Was it my love for him or my fear of him? Moments of tenderness in his company were accompanied by his fits of violence. He would sometimes beat me and then perch at my feet, crying and pleading: *Forgive me, my sweetie. I'm not cruel, but this hellish life is full of cruelty.* We would then embrace, cry together, and make love passionately, dreaming of a better tomorrow.

He taught me exciting massage techniques, which I practiced on his body. He taught me the art of using my fingertips, how to tempt and then deny, how to make the client pass gradually and slowly from relaxation to sudden pleasure. In fact, I was very perplexed when he told me all this, and I didn't understand how he could be so jealous yet at the same time tell me to indulge my clients. He said that it was not lovemaking and that my fingertips had nothing to do with my body. How could he say that when he knew that things sometimes did not stop at my fingertips? What if the client were to ask for oral sex?

Finally, I convinced myself that my body had nothing to do with my mouth either, and I immersed myself completely in massage. This was basically prostitution disguised as massage. However, after I started working at the Riad of Dreams, I discovered that prostitution was an essence with a variety of expressions. *Let any one of you who is without sin be the first to throw a stone at me,* as Christ said.

After the first massage session, Mr. Philip offered to employ me at the Riad of Dreams. I discovered later that our meeting was not a coincidence, and that Saeed had planned it all. Saeed told Mr. Philip that the Riad of Dreams lacked a beautiful lady with the skill of massage. Then Saeed sent him to me at the hotel for a trial session; afterward, he told him that I was his neighbor and close friend.

It saddened me that he did not present me to Mr. Philip as his girlfriend, but he justified his deed by saying that Marrakech had ears that were wide open and mouths that were gaping—everyone knew what was in everyone else's bowels—and that Mr. Philip's knowledge of our true relationship was none of his business. He added that he was to blame for considering my own good and my future. I thanked him with an embrace and closed the subject, as was the case after every quarrel. And so I began my adventure at the Riad of Dreams, and at first I was happy with my new job.

Unfortunately, exactly two months after I got this new job, my mother fell sick and stopped working. So I had to provide for everyone and bear the cost of medication and other household expenses, which compelled me to sometimes ask for help from Saeed, who began to get nervous about my endless demands.

One romantic night, while Mr. Philip was away in Paris to attend the funeral of one of his friends, we were making love in one of the luxury rooms at the Riad of Dreams. Saeed, to my surprise, said: "I have an idea for us to break out of this misery. You just need to make Mr. Philip fall in love with you and marry you . . . Then, Scheherazade can become the lady of the riad. Imagine changing its name to *Riad Scheherazade*. This can happen if you truly help me realize our dreams."

I was shocked by the suggestion. "How dare you ask me to marry him! What's in it for you? Wouldn't you be jealous? And what about *our* marriage?"

"I doubt his sexual potency," he laughed. "Of course we'll marry after we get rid of him and you inherit everything."

"What do mean by *get rid of him?*" I asked, terrified.

Saeed stroked my hair lovingly. "Honey! Don't you see that he's already one inch away from death? But that's my job. All you have to do is to make him fall in love with you and propose to you. After that, you'll see good things happening, my dear Scheherazade, my Lady of the Riad."

At that very moment, the face of Aunt Mannana the fortune-teller took hold in my mind. She had stared at the lines of my palm and said: *Your good fortune will come from beyond the seas. He will be older, wealthy, and renowned . . . but the secret is in the fingertips.* I wondered, *What if this really is the destiny written in the lines of my palm? Who can escape destiny?*

I admit that I actually dreamed of becoming the Lady of the Riad, especially since my life obligations were tearing me apart: moving daily from the choking misery of my family's home to the luxury of the riad and its clients who were obsessed with their bodies; tumbling between traditions, beliefs, and my veiled sisters who were submissive to the authority of my brother and his scary asceticism, and the world of massage and its licentiousness.

Back at home, together with my sisters and my mom, we would pray behind my brother, who enjoyed his role as imam. None of them, however, knew about my inner suffering.

I believe in God, but my brother's ambivalence was not a good thing, as he saw no problem in his reluctance to work or continuing to take pocket money from me. He also began to incessantly ask me to help the brothers who had also stopped working and devoted their daily lives to worshipping, even though working was an act of worship in our religion.

Plus, my mother pestered me with her usual question: *When will Saeed propose to you? Your brother is upset with people's gossip . . .*

I'm not the type of person who cares about gossip. I'd realized at an early age that I would either care about myself or about people's gossip, and it didn't take me long to make my choice. I started to enjoy the idea of being the Lady of the Riad. I would take quiet time to gaze at myself in the mirror. I would see myself as a princess strutting around in my own palace. Why not? Do luxury and beauty not go together? However, I wanted no harm done to Mr. Philip. He'd always been nice to me and preferred me to his other masseuses, saying that I was more beautiful and intelligent than any of them, and that I had the admiration of all the clients. But who knows? Maybe he hadn't even thought about the idea of marriage at all.

Saeed and I schemed together so that things would later take the course we had planned. It wasn't difficult to seduce Mr. Philip, who Saeed prepared slowly, the way Marrakech people prepare *tanjia*. After a few weeks, Mr. Philip came to our house to propose to me, carrying a bouquet of red flowers and red with embarrassment. He was led by Saeed, who was walking proudly and looking relieved.

My brother, who we didn't take into account, opposed the marriage, and threatened to burn down the whole riad. He was shaking with anger as he cursed Saeed: "How dare you do this, you villain? You are not a man . . . Having had enough of her, you now pass her on to an old Nazarene the age of her grandpa."

Saeed snapped back in the same violent tone: "It's you who is the villain . . . You just want your sister to keep supporting you and the family. If you were a real man your sister wouldn't have had to go to work in the first place!"

The marriage proposal turned into a brawl. At one point my

brother tried to grab me and threatened to kill me, while my mom cried and begged him to calm down. I don't know how I suddenly got the courage to stand up to him for the first time in my life.

"How dare you deny what Allah has permitted?" I bellowed. "Philip agreed to convert to Islam. Since I'm not a minor, the new family law says I don't need the permission of anyone. You'll keep receiving your pocket money as usual. As for me, I embrace my freedom whether you like it or not!"

We left the house—Philip, Saeed, and I—escorted by my mother's tears and my sisters' laments.

I married Philip after he converted to Islam by saying the *shahada;* we married before a cleric and two *adls: There is no god but Allah, and Muhammad is the messenger of Allah.* I never imagined things would be so easy, especially since I knew Philip to be an atheist. After the wedding, which was quite intimate, I became the Lady of the Riad but severed ties with my family—my brother disowned me and forbade my mom and sisters from having anything to do with me.

Philip was happy with our relationship and did everything to make me happy too, as I gave his life a sense of plenitude. One day, he confided in me about his past life in a tone verging on bitterness: "I was a bank manager and I had so many friends, but retirement revealed my shallow relationships with my colleagues. Once one retires, work-based relationships also retire. Those human ties rarely survive outside the walls of administrations and offices. Like chairs and files, they depend on space, not people. Only my relationship to my late wife grew stronger after my retirement, which is the reason why we decided to leave Paris."

While Philip was enjoying his new life, I was striving to convince myself that I'd made the right decision. A decision now spoiled with the taste of fear and anxiety, especially as Saeed's material demands and greed grew with time. Saeed asked to work at the reception desk next to Leila, so he would know every penny that entered the money box. I never liked Leila, there was something mysterious in her behavior that hinted at a big secret in her life, and, frankly, I didn't like her way of flirting with Saeed. She wasn't beautiful. She was one of those Marrakech girls with brown skin and curly hair, but she was attractive and witty in a way I could not be. Everyone called her Flifla, which meant *hot little pepper*—because she was so hot and sexy.

Longing for my mother and sisters began to tear me down, and I felt increasingly trapped by Saeed. He no longer showed any interest in my body. He justified that by saying he didn't want to draw attention to our relationship, since to Philip I was Saeed's best friend, and his flirting with Leila was only a cover.

I would cringe whenever Philip hinted at something going on between Leila and Saeed, while Leila would only lower her eyes and smile in the kind of hypocritical way my townspeople were so good at. My nerves were frayed. The virus of jealousy took hold of me and I began to experience an unbearable sense of tension as I became the Lady of the Riad, and thus bound to behave decently, especially with clients used to the special messages. Naturally, I stopped giving massages after I trained two new girls to do the job. This act impressed Philip, who took it as an expression of faithfulness.

Faithfulness is a term that has no place in the riad, where the client is king and everyone else a slave. The client gets to live out *The Thousand and One Nights* in the Scheherazade Riad (I forgot to mention that Philip changed the name of the riad on our wedding night). Saeed's drug trade started bringing a special kind of client to the riad, and the reception desk became a secret place for all sorts of illegal business behind Philip's and Leila's artificial smiles.

Saeed would be evasive whenever I tried to dot the i's. He would say, "Do not be stupid and spoil everything with your pathological jealousy. Am I jealous when you sleep with Mr. Philip?

Of course not, because it's just a plan to unite later in times of prosperity. This was our choice, together! Don't be crazy."

The problem was that I wasn't sure whether anything happening around me was actually my own choice. I was involved in a mean game, believing that I held all the cards, but the actual winning card remained in Saeed's hands. He ended up taking a room at the riad after making his presence necessary there, and winning the trust of Mr. Philip, who considered him almost a brother-in-law. And why not? Isn't he like a brother to me?

I could no longer understand Saeed. Sometimes he would express his impatience to get rid of Philip and I would urge him to wait. I became afraid of my own shadow. Other times I felt he enjoyed his new status and was in no hurry to change anything.

During one dismal week, news of my mother's death reached us. My sorrow was immense, especially since my brother, who blamed me for her passing, prevented me from attending her funeral. Philip tried his best to mitigate the impact of the shock, but my grief was as deep as my feelings of loneliness. A month after her death, he decided to take me abroad for a change of scenery.

While preparing for the trip to Paris, Saeed handed me an official-looking paper and asked me to make Philip sign it before leaving. "It's just a proxy for me to be able to purchase supplies for the riad in Philip's absence," he explained. "This will also help us plan for our future together."

"How so? And if he asks me about it, what will I say?" I asked him.

"Serve him a few glasses of champagne and massage him with your magic fingertips. I am sure he will sign anything you put in front of him," Saeed replied sarcastically. He then stepped forward and hugged me, and I suddenly realized how much I had missed his embrace. Then, he added: "It's in Arabic, you can translate it any way you want. Do this, my dearest Scheherazade, and soon we will get rid of the ghost of this old man."

I did as he said. Philip promptly signed the paper, which I presented to him as a certificate of residence, confirming that I officially lived in the riad. I added that my brother needed it.

We departed Marrakech, leaving the riad to the care of Saeed and Leila. Although I had always dreamed of traveling abroad, I could not enjoy my time in Paris. I felt bitter in Philip's arms. A feeling of dissatisfaction haunted me and a sense of guilt tore me down when I remembered the death of my mother, who had taken her grief for me with her. How strange that now that I had a car, wore expensive clothes, ate food prepared by chefs, and enjoyed sessions of personal massages, misery was creeping into my life. Laughter no longer tasted of joy nor smiles of satisfaction. I felt as if a void was growing larger inside me every day. My dreams had become real, but their color was gray.

Meanwhile, a voice inside me kept whispering that Saeed was lying to me. I could no longer stand Leila's presence at the riad. I wanted to kick her out, but Saeed was against the idea and kept saying that she was an important piece of the plan, that we had to keep her there until everything was over. I tried to put an end to my suspicions, and I convinced myself that jealousy was the cause of my tragedy, hoping that I would soon get rid of her. For now, I just had to trust Saeed and his secret plan. But things were not so simple.

After my return from Paris, I went to see Aunt Mannana, as I often did when I felt down.

She welcomed me early in the morning in her semidark room on the roof of a decadent building, amid the smoke of incense. She had fear in her eyes, as her henna-dyed fingers arranged the cards on a small table in front of me. "There's an adder in your home . . . wriggling under your bed. Beware of the adder, daughter," she said.

I was terrified as I imagined the snake coiling over my body. Who could it be? It was Leila, no doubt. I could no longer bear her yellow smile as she cast her shadow over me every morning and said in her Marrakech accent: *How are you this morning, Lalla Scheherazade? And how is Mr. Philip?*

The words of the fortune-teller stoked the flames of doubt in my heart as jealousy ravaged me. And so, during a dawn that was grim with insomnia and longing, I slipped from Philip's thorny arms and crept on the tips of my fingers and toes down to Saeed's room, seeking a little love. Overwhelmed with burning desire for the warmth of his body, I opened his door quietly so as not to wake up the servants. To my surprise, he was fast asleep with Leila, who should have been at home in her own bed. I almost fainted as I fled the specter of betrayal and rushed toward the bathroom where I vomited up my bitterness. Philip got up and rushed after me. He carried me back to the bedroom and called a doctor. The doctor said that it was food poisoning. He was correct in his diagnosis, for I had indeed swallowed the venom of the adder and her lover—the traitor.

I spent a week in bed utterly dejected with Philip playing the tender nurse. But tenderness was hard for me to accept as I began to hate men, the world, and myself. I thought a lot during that week about a plan to take revenge on Saeed—the ignoble creature whose trust with Leila polluted the riad and suffocated me. Yet what if I complied with his plan? Made him get rid of Philip alone, so that he could spend the rest of his life in jail while I eliminated Leila and poverty.

Philip was a nice man who really loved me, but he was old and had lived his life and realized all his dreams. As for me, I was still at the beginning of my journey, which would remain forever postponed if I didn't act quickly. I had only myself to rely on.

I met Saeed in private and questioned him: "What's your plan? I see you're no longer in a hurry to get rid of Philip."

"I prefer to keep the plan to myself so that I don't implicate you with me, dearest Scheherazade," he told me. "You're so sensitive. I'm afraid you might become weak and give away the secret. Let me act on my own. Stay calm and affectionate toward him, and let no one suspect us. Forget about Leila, she is good and loves you."

How dare he defend her in front of me? How impudent. I was about to tell him what I knew about his affair with Leila, but then I thought better of it. He kissed me passionately and whispered in my ear: "Do not let the devil toy with you, sweetie. You know I wouldn't do anything without you. You are Philip's wife and his only heir, and even if I did care only for his money, I'd have to marry you to get it. Besides . . . what good is money without your love?"

The power of his persuasion equaled my vulnerability before his affection. I tried to calm myself with the idea that Saeed's relationship with Leila was only sexual, and invented all sorts of arguments for that: she must have been coming onto him, and a virile male in our culture cannot repel a woman who makes such advances. Then I decided to confront her instead—yes, I should threaten her. Tell her that if she didn't keep away from him, I'd kick her out and take my bread out of her mouth. Maybe that would scare her and prevent her from further shenanigans with Saeed.

With this in mind, I seized an opportunity and invited her to Philip's office one afternoon. I told her: "We are women and we know about each other. This is why I want to tell you that Saeed is like my brother, and I know what's going on between you . . . I want you to put an end to your relationship with him or I'll kick you out of the riad."

I was surprised at her reaction. She burst into laughter and looked at me with insolence. She brought her face closer to mine and whispered mockingly: "Keep your lies for your Nazarene husband. I know everything about you. I know how jealousy is ravaging your heart."

I fumed with rage and couldn't control myself; I raised my

hand to slap her in the face. "Respect your mistress, slut," I hissed.

Leila returned the slap with similar violence. "You're nobody's mistress, you idiot," she tossed back defiantly.

I lunged at her and we started punching and pulling each other's hair while exchanging vile curses and insults like bullets. Suddenly, Saeed rushed into the office and tried to separate us.

"What's your problem? Everyone can hear your screams across the riad!" Saeed shouted. "Enough!"

I could feel my lower lip bleeding as he pulled us apart. "Do you see what you've done?" I yelled back.

Saeed turned to Leila, held her hands, and said almost soothingly: "Don't be silly."

"It's you who are silly!" I growled. "Don't defend her."

My limbs froze when I saw him hug her. "Calm down," he whispered to her. "It's not the right time yet."

"What do you mean by that, you traitors?" I demanded.

At that very moment, Philip entered as the room, anger illuminating his pale face. He took hold of Saeed and cried out: "How dare you do this to me? You robbed me, you son of a bitch!"

Saeed pushed him and Philip fell down. From the floor, he lifted his eyes to me. "And you, were you his accomplice?"

I didn't understand what was happening, so I asked: "What's the matter? What did you do, Saeed?"

"You see, it is the right time," Leila jumped in, as she ran a hand through her disheveled hair. She walked toward me. "The game ends here. Didn't I tell you that you were nobody's mistress? The riad is no longer his. It now belongs to someone else."

I asked for an explanation as I helped Philip to his feet.

"You've been outsmarted," Leila gloated. Then she turned to Philip. "What good is money to you when you're about to kick the bucket? Come along, Saeed, let's get out of here—we have what we need."

Saeed followed her to the door and Philip rushed after them.

"You can't get away from me so easily!" he barked. He grabbed Saeed's shoulder, but Saeed turned around and shoved him hard. Philip fell to the ground again and Saeed unleashed on him, punching and kicking him while he was down.

I screamed and tried to pull him away. "Stay away from him! You'll kill him!"

Saeed pushed me as well, and I fell to the floor as he turned his attention back to Philip.

Leila stood by the door, smiling maliciously. "Enough, darling. Let's go," she said.

Saeed got up, leaving Philip listless on the floor, and headed toward the door, his back turned on me. Shaking with rage and hatred, I jumped up, grabbed an iron statue from the desk, and hurled it at Saeed with all my strength. It hit the back of his head. Blood immediately gushed out of his skull and he fell to the ground.

Leila shrieked: "You killed him, bitch!"

At the sight of so much blood covering the floor, I lost consciousness.

I opened my eyes to the sight of a paramedic.

"Wake up. Are you okay?" he asked.

The room was crowded with policemen. The ambulance took Saeed to the hospital while Leila and I were arrested.

Leila turned out to be a fugitive from Belgium, where she was involved in a drug-trafficking ring. She confessed to the police that she was the one who had planned everything. Leila had known Saeed before he'd employed her. Together, they had sold the riad and its contents using the proxy that I made Philip sign, and were about to flee abroad with the money. They were each sentenced to ten years in prison.

Saeed was transferred to jail after spending several weeks in the hospital. Some police informants who used to protect him now revealed his involvement in prior criminal cases, which increased his sentence to fifteen years.

I myself spent a few months in custody before I was released on bail that Philip paid. He also forgave me. "Behaving badly once does not make someone a bad person," he told me. He did his best to save me from any further trouble.

I must say that during the time Saeed was in the recovery room, I oscillated between two contradictory attitudes: on the one hand, I wished for his death so that Leila would be deprived of her lover forever; and on the other hand, I prayed for his safety so that I wouldn't be deprived of my freedom. Luckily he didn't die, because freedom was far more meaningful than love.

I am now living at Riad Scheherazade as the undisputed lady there, taking care of Philip (my fortune come from afar). He recently suffered a stroke. I massage him with tenderness, using my painstakingly acquired methods. Who knows? He may recover from his hemiplegia. Isn't the secret in the fingertips?

Translated from Arabic by Norddine Zouitni

DELIRIUM

BY MAHI BINEBINE

Souk Semmarine

To share the same body with a wayward being is no easy feat. Kamal and I were in constant conflict, most often over nothing. We argued day in and day out, and our fights sometimes grew so heated that passersby, ignorant of our history, would take us for fools. We spoke as one on a single matter: our love for Mama Rosalie—an intense, unconditional love.

It would be hard for me to give you an accurate account of my companion, as we can only know ourselves subjectively. Mama Rosalie had drummed into us an old story her mother used to tell: *A rock suspended in the heavens is fated to fall on the head of the man who disparages himself on earth. Since the dawn of time, this meteorite has been floating in the firmament.* And so I can only speak well to you of Kamal because, whatever people might say, we have a certain affection for each other. He's a little bit of me, and I'm a little bit of him. We are, then, rather handsome young men: well-built, baby-faced, with those dull eyes—bloodshot, but kind—particular to men who've ceased to dream, who've thrown in the towel and no longer expect anything of anyone.

Our greatest asset was the language of Goethe. In all of Marrakech, we were the only tour guides fluent in German. We might as well have been oil barons. Not a Kraut in the land of the Moors escaped our nets. We were the rightful rulers of the coach buses crammed with white bodies, hormone-fed, laughing and avid, ready to spend a fortune at the Semmarine, the grandest souk in town. We would lead them into our friends' bazaars, singing the praises of our ancestral handicrafts, so elegant and refined, the work of a gifted people living in the most beautiful country in the world: *This carpet here belonged to the mistress of King Moulay Ismail, who took tea at her home on a hilltop overlooking Meknes all throughout his reign; that sculpture there was custom-made for the regent Ba Ahmed, who commissioned the Bahia palace with its 156 rooms in the Old Medina of Marrakech; this dagger, once belonging to Tashfin Ibn Ali, son of the founder of the Red City, served to cut the throat of an Andalusian rebel who'd come with his compatriots to build the wall encircling the old town; and this box before your eyes is an extremely rare piece: the bones of a mythical camel that crossed the Sahara a hundred times, encrusted in* thuya *wood by the chief of the Jewish artisans of Mogador*. We rattled off our string of lies without blinking an eye, with remarkable eloquence, a penchant for anecdote, and absolute conviction. Thomas Mann, Stephan Zweig, and Herman Hesse lent their music to our hoaxes; they were, so to speak, our accomplices. Their words peppered our speeches, helping us to justify the exorbitant prices that we charged with reassuring nods of the head. A good share of the booty was paid to us afterward.

Kamal and I made a small fortune each week, half of which ended up in Mama Rosalie's purse, and the other in the till of the potbellied owner of Café Atlas.

Once our morning work at the souk was done, we'd spend most of the day drinking beer by the case, in this godforsaken hole in the wall where we found a kind of peace. Our secret squabbles would die down; we'd admit to the snag in our argument on this or that subject, each of us conceding a point in the debate, even flattering each other, becoming affable and easy. If only we'd had two distinct bodies, we'd have embraced one another like a couple of drunks.

Come nine o'clock sharp—just this side of an alcoholic coma—we'd climb onto our mopeds and fly straight to Mama

Rosalie's. That we made it home safe and sound every night was no less than a miracle. If we sometimes took a spill in a narrow alley between buildings, it was rarely serious. We'd get to our feet and bravely continue on our way. As soon as we arrived, a good warm meal (the only one of the day) was served to us by a young housekeeper with sumptuous curves who we always swore we'd take advantage of, though we never had the energy to go through with it. Mama Rosalie stayed shut away in her room, refusing to cross paths with the pitiful wrecks that came stumbling through the door every night of her life. She'd wait until the next morning, at coffee, when we'd become human again and speak intelligibly. We loved these moments of reprieve, loved resting our heads on her knees and letting her fuss over us like in the old days, when she'd spend hours picking our hair for lice. We couldn't get enough of her caresses or her half-soothing, half-reprimanding words. Just knowing she was there beside us gave us the strength to face another day, to face the chaos of the souk and its hordes of tourists. We'd recharge our batteries, laughing at the same old jokes we'd told a thousand times. That just about sums up our existence, Kamal's and mine.

Café Atlas was a world teeming with the dregs and mold of the city, a lure for all kinds of human distress, an island of survival on a sea of torment, engulfing you in its smoke: stories sung by vagabond dreamers, the humid air filled with joyful chatter, and tears that fell from a thousand bursts of laughter. It was a place where you could be without really *being* there, a place closed in by dirty, smoke-stained windows that hurried passersby would brush against on their way to somewhere else, where the din of life was a faint, distant sound, drowned out by the omnipresent voice of the divine Umm Kulthum, and where the beer and wine flowed freely. Ah! Café Atlas was our paradise . . . or our hell, depending.

On that particular night, riding home on our mopeds, we'd

suffered a brutal fall. Our face was covered in blood. We couldn't move so much as our little finger. Kamal opened his eyes to see a dead child laid out beside us. A crowd had gathered, the people's accusing looks like so many blazing pitchforks ready to stab us. He saw horned serpents and yellow scorpions flowing from gaping mouths, the sleeves of the crowd's djellabas billowing around us in a ghostly danse macabre as people screamed and screamed. The child, dressed all in white, stood and began to join in the dance.

"He's dead!" Kamal told me.

"Who?"

"The dancing child. Black blood is flowing from his ears."

"I don't see any child," I said.

"He's lost in the crowd, that's why you don't see him."

"There's no crowd! We're alone in the street," I insisted.

"You don't hear them screaming?"

"I can only hear you."

"And the blood on the ground?"

"It's ours. Look closely, we've just fallen. It's not the first time!"

"You're lying. You refuse to see what's in front of your face!" Kamal shouted. "You never want to see anything!"

"Come on, get up. Let's go home. A warm meal is waiting for us."

"I hate you!"

"You'll get over it."

"I've *always* hated you," Kamal said.

"Because I see you. I don't judge you, but I see you. You don't like to be watched."

Kamal went silent. I'd never seen him in such a state. His fixed expression raised a kind of invisible wall between us. I tried to change my tone, to soften my words, to reason with him in every possible manner, but he wouldn't listen. It was as if, by some obscure trickery, he'd caused me to vanish from our existence.

He'd turned his back on me—on *me*, his companion for better or worse since childhood. My protests were in vain. I could see my words driving straight into that wall of silence, then rolling down it like drops of condensation.

He stood up, got back on his moped, and rode straight to the souk. Most of the stalls were already closed. The muezzin was calling for the evening prayer. He stopped at Morad's—a friend who owned our go-to bazaar.

"Hide me," he sobbed. "Hide me!"

"What's going on?" Morad asked.

"I hit a child," Kamal whispered. "I killed him."

"What are you talking about?"

"I'm a murderer!" he bellowed.

"Calm down and come inside."

"The kid was no more than ten!" Kamal trembled, and his bloodied face seemed to confirm his story.

Morad asked no more questions. Where we're from, we stick together and we take care of each other first and worry about the consequences later. He brought Kamal into his bathroom and made him take a shower. Kamal let himself be taken care of, his expression blank, his movements slow. Morad came back with a first-aid kit and attended to his wounds. The sting of the alcohol didn't even make him wince. Then Morad went to find him a clean gandoura and some babouches, which didn't take long in the bazaar. He led him to a cramped room at the back of the shop where a mountain of carpets rose up to the ceiling.

"Stay here," he said. "We'll talk it over in the morning."

He came back with a sandwich, closed and double-locked the door behind him, and was gone.

We stayed there for several days, in the shadowy half-darkness, not speaking a word to each other, like a surly old couple. Kamal went from bad to worse. He began to cry, playing the film of his imaginary accident over and over again in his mind, filling gaps in the scenes with hallucinatory details. Sometimes snakes would coil themselves around his body to keep him from escaping, or scorpions would form a blockade like a fakir's bed of nails. Sometimes there was a blinding light and ghosts surged toward him, grasping at his face. It was very painful for me not to be able to save him from this nightmare. But what could I do? He was ignoring me. I'd become persona non grata, a stranger as dangerous as the menacing beasts that closed in on him.

Morad paid us visits at mealtimes, bringing a basket of food and several cases of beer. He brought news from the outside too, which was quickly becoming frightening. The police were indeed looking for us. Two inspectors were making rounds of the souk, stall by stall, asking for leads about where we might be. I didn't understand any of it. I knew we hadn't killed anyone; I'd been there at the scene of the accident, and much less inebriated than Kamal. As word spread, I felt Morad's anxiety growing. He wouldn't have abandoned us for anything in the world, I was sure of that, but he was afraid. Doubt gradually came over me, piercing me with its cruel venom. I couldn't see the logic in this story. Why in the hell would the police be looking for a drunk who'd fallen off his moped in a deserted alley? Because they're bored to death down there, and to pass the time, the demons were amusing themselves by toying with our fears, our anxieties, our lives. I know something about that, having frequented the likes of them inside Kamal's feverish body. A body I didn't choose, and that was, so to speak, my purgatory.

If only it hadn't been so horribly sad, the end of this story would have seemed right out of a burlesque farce staged at some provincial theater. But no, our end was unjust: we didn't deserve it.

After rallying the entire family to join in her search, Mama Rosalie, worried sick, had finally alerted the police to her son's disappearance. The inspectors were simply doing their job, trying to bring Kamal back to his mother. That's why they were looking for us. Morad would only understand it much later, after we were gone. Even then, the thought of it all still made Morad gnaw at his fingers as if they were ripe dates.

Kamal's visions were becoming more and more frequent, happening now in broad daylight. Morad couldn't take any more of the screaming; even muffled by the carpets, the noises were frightening the tourists, causing them to flee the bazaar. "It can't go on like this," Morad told us one night, when he brought us our dinner.

His pride injured, Kamal decided to take off right away. He thought of Mama Rosalie saying: *I would rather not be there than outstay my welcome!* And so, without anger, he got back on his moped and abandoned his hideout with dignity. He seemed almost normal, his expression serene; I started to feel reassured. He rode out of the Old Medina, along the ramparts, not sure which direction to take. We had missed the fresh air. We were euphoric, flying with the birds that were still awake at this hour of the night. I heard him murmur that he was happy to breathe air free of carpet dust and of the fetid odor of rats. Our gandoura billowed around us in the wind. For a moment, we felt an odd kind of weightlessness. Seeing a child crossing the road in the middle distance, Kamal turned sharply toward a patch of open ground. Instead of braking he accelerated, following in the direction of a flock of birds. Then silence, a silence like that of the sea, at the bottom of a cesspool where we found ourselves with a shattered skull: a bit drunk, a bit dead. We looked at each other for the last time, and I saw him smile. A shiver ran through us when we glimpsed, on the surface of the water, the silhouette of a dancing child.

Translated from French by Katie Shireen Assef

IN SEARCH OF A SON

BY MOHAMED NEDALI

Bab Ghmat

Old Rezzouk and his wife showed up at the police station at eight o'clock in the morning. Their son Abdeljalil hadn't come home in three days. It was true that the young man occasionally stayed out all night, but never twice in a row, and never without first telling his parents.

The cop at the desk, a man in his forties with a cold, severe expression, asked Rezzouk to describe the missing person. "Name, age, address, and occupation?"

The old man swallowed the frog in his throat. "Abdeljalil Rezzouk," he began. "Twenty-six years old, number eleven, Derb el-Boumba, Bab Ghmat."

"Occupation?" the cop grumbled.

Not knowing how to answer, the old man said nothing.

"Well? Spit it out!" snapped the cop.

Confused, Rezzouk started rambling: "Our—our son was . . . he was, for a few years, a . . . a cigarette vendor, first here in Bab Ghmat, then in other parts of town. And then he . . . he—"

"He moved up the chain!" the cop cut in, jeering. "A classic promotion, no doubt."

The old man and his wife looked at each other, perplexed. "What do you mean by chain, *sidi*?" Rezzouk asked.

"You don't know, or you're pretending not to know?" the cop inquired, a suspicious look in his eyes.

"In the name of Allah, the Most High, I don't know!" Rezzouk roared.

The cop stared at him, one eyebrow raised, an incredulous sneer on his lips. "I'm not taking the bait," he muttered under his breath.

"Pardon, *sidi?*" the old man said. "I didn't hear you."

"Come back in an hour!" the cop barked. He reached into his jacket pocket and took out a cell phone—a Samsung touch screen, very sophisticated, with a black leather case, worth three thousand dirhams at least—and started playing with it.

Rezzouk and his wife hobbled out the door and crossed the street. It was eight fifteen a.m., and the sun was already beating down hard; it was going to be another hot day in the Red City. The old man found two large squares of cardboard next to a garbage bin. He handed one to his wife.

"What are we doing?" she asked.

"Waiting!"

The couple sat down in the shade of a giant eucalyptus tree opposite the station. They had forty-five minutes to kill.

"Isn't that a call shop over there, on the corner?" his wife asked, her voice trembling.

"How many times do I have to tell you, he isn't answering his phone!" the old man replied. "Are you deaf, or do you have amnesia?"

Two fat tears formed in the woman's eyes and pooled there for a moment before streaming down her pale cheeks. She wiped them away with the frayed sleeves of her djellaba. The old man watched her out of the corner of his eye. A moment later he stood up again, as if overcome by remorse or pity, and began walking in the direction of the call shop, fiddling with a piece of paper. His wife watched him until he reached the entrance. *May God finally give us a sign of our son's life*, she implored silently, peering up to the sky. *Deliver us from this unbearable agony!* Two minutes later, the old man returned.

"Well?" she asked him, her gaze fixed on his lips.

The old man sat back down on the square of cardboard. "He

isn't answering his phone," he sighed, throwing his hands in the air. "For three days I've been repeating the same thing to you like a broken record."

His wife began silently crying again. Chin in his hands, face crumpled, the old man just stared at a random point on the ground, absorbed in shadowy thoughts. If misery were one day to take a human form, it would find none better than this old couple from the medina, seated here in the shade of a giant eucalyptus wholly indifferent to their plight.

Every five minutes, the old man glanced at his digital watch, a gray Casio with a stainless steel band. At nine o'clock sharp he stood up. His wife joined him and they returned to the station.

"Come along!" said the cop at the desk, still in a foul mood.

They followed him down a long corridor that reeked of stale cigarette smoke. The offices they passed all locked the same, like high school classrooms. People stood, waiting in front of the doors, anxious and silent. A few crouched down, their backs to the wall, and others paced around the doorways; a young woman was crying alone in a corner. At the end of the corridor, the cop led them up a staircase covered in tarnished mosaic tiles, faintly lit by a fluorescent bulb hanging from the ceiling. On the upper level he stopped in front of the first office on the right. *Chief Hamid Zeghloul*, read the nameplate on the door. The officer bent his index finger and gave two light knocks, barely audible. A "*Zid!*" could be heard from the other side. He went in, touching two fingers to the visor of his cap, and closed the door behind him. Two or three minutes later, he came out again.

"Come in!" the cop ordered the old man. "You, *lalla*, wait on the bench over there!"

His wife reluctantly obeyed.

Chief Zeghloul was a solidly built man with a thick forehead, bulging eyes, a Saddam-like mustache, and a prominent jaw—he didn't look a day over fifty.

"Hello, *sidi*!" Rezzouk said as he stepped through the doorway.

"Hello, *cherif*! Please have a seat," the chief said.

The old man sat down in one of the two chairs facing the desk. His deep suspicion of the police force—a sentiment largely shared by his countrymen—only added to his anxiety over his son's sudden disappearance.

"I'm sorry—profoundly sorry—to inform you that your son, Abdeljalil Rezzouk, died yesterday, around two o'clock in the morning, in a traffic accident."

A pallor spread instantly over the old man's face, but he didn't say a word.

"The police found his body on the side of the road," the chief continued. "The criminal had fled the scene—a drunk driver, presumably. An investigation is underway to determine the exact circumstances of the accident . . . You will be kept informed of the results, of course. Once again, I'm deeply sorry, *cherif*."

"May I have the exact location of the murder, *sidi*?" old Rezzouk asked when he'd recovered enough to speak.

"The *accident* took place . . ." the chief began, caught off guard by the question. "The accident took place . . . the accident took place on . . . Excuse me a moment, I'm going to look for it in the report."

The chief opened a drawer, closed it again, opened another, took out a green folder, extracted a sheet of paper, and skimmed it. "The accident took place on the road that runs parallel to the wall of the Menara gardens," he said. "Near the Larmoud District, to be precise. Do you know where that is?"

The old man parted his lips to speak, but nothing came out. He stayed speechless for a long moment.

The chief stood, placing a hand on his shoulder in a gesture of genuine commiseration. "May God have mercy on his soul," he told Rezzouk.

The old man was paralyzed with grief and could hardly move.

"Now, you'll have to go to the district attorney's office with a copy of your national ID card. He'll give you the authorization to collect the body of the deceased at the morgue in Ibn Tofail University Hospital—the civilian hospital, that is. If you don't feel up to the task, you can designate a third party, a member of your family, preferably . . ."

The old man stood, sputtering his thanks. As he turned to leave, the chief called him back. He held out some banknotes, four or five of them, folded in half. The old man politely declined the offering; the chief insisted.

"It's my contribution to the funeral," the chief said. "And I assure you, *sidi*, I'm more than glad to help."

Rezzouk finally accepted the money, less out of conviction than in deference to this chief who was so kind and respectful; the few cops the old man had previously dealt with were all washed-up brutes, totally insensitive to the hardships of ordinary people like himself. *He must be an exceptional policeman,* he said to himself as he left the office.

The funeral service was held the next day at Bab Ghmat Cemetery, one of the oldest in the medina. The coffin was trailed by a great procession. Practically all the men of Derb el-Boumba were there, women being prohibited from attending burials on Islamic soil. In addition to the imam and his chosen readers of the sacred text, dressed all in white, there were many strangers who had come out of this sense of Muslim solidarity—or maybe pure idleness. Rezzouk believed that the crowd was proof that his departed son had been greatly respected in the neighborhood.

Once the burial was over, the crowd dispersed. The old man remained at the foot of the grave: hunched over, eyes closed, palms held to the sky, he murmured a long prayer for his lost child, imploring Allah, the most merciful and compassionate, to forgive the boy his sins—those committed in words, in deeds, and in thought—to spare him the terrible trials of the last judgment, and to reserve a place for him in paradise, alongside His chosen prophet, His loyal companions, and His blessed faithful.

As soon as the old man had pronounced the final *amine*, a young man approached him.

"My sincere condolences, *s'di* Rezzouk!" the young man said, clutching his shoulder in a formal embrace. "I am so very saddened by this painful event!"

The young man was tall and dark with gray, sparkling eyes and hair cropped close—so close that you could see his scalp. A long diagonal scar ran across his right cheek. The old man looked at him, trying in vain to put a name to his face. He was sure that he'd seen him before, two or three times, maybe more. But where? When? He had no idea.

"You probably don't remember me, *s'di* Rezzouk," the young man went on. "My name is Noureddine, Noureddine L'Guebbas. Abdeljalil and I were good friends a few years ago."

"He was a good man, wasn't he?" the old man replied, his voice choked by tears.

"A very good man," Noureddine said. "And a loyal friend too!" After a silence, he added: "May his murderers be condemned to eternal Gehenna!"

The old man's eyes widened as he looked up, suddenly alert.

"God knows I warned him," Noureddine continued, "and many times over! But Abdeljalil wouldn't listen to me."

"Warned him?" the old man repeated, taken aback. "Of what?"

"Of the fact that he'd been—for some time already—in the crosshairs of the drug squad!"

"What? Why?"

"Abdeljalil refused to pay the current fee for the dealers in our category, a few hundred dirhams per week. And he tried to persuade those who paid it to stop."

"Then my son didn't die in a traffic accident?" the old man asked, stunned.

"No, *s'di* Rezzouk."

"Do you know how he died?"

"I don't know, *s'di* Rezzouk, but . . . but I heard that they smashed his skull against a beam in a jail cell."

The old man's heart tightened, his legs grew weak, and the world went dark around him; everything had taken on a look of sinister unfamiliarity. He collapsed at the edge of an old grave, his head in his hands, devastated.

"Are you all right, *s'di* Rezzouk?" the young man asked.

The old man raised his head with a sorrowful expression, his forehead creased with two deep lines. "Remind me of your name, young man?"

"Noureddine."

"Would you like to help me, Noureddine?"

"Of course, *s'di* Rezzouk!" he answered, vaguely anxious, wondering what the old man was going to ask of him.

"I'll surely need your help to uncover the circumstances of my son's murder."

"What can I do for you, *s'di* Rezzouk?"

The old man reached into his pocket and took out a Bic pen and a small notepad with yellowing pages. "For now, I'll need your phone number."

"What do you plan on doing, *s'di* Rezzouk?"

"I'll bring charges. I'll alert the press, the human rights organizations in Morocco and abroad. I'll write to the governor, to the *wali*, the minister of justice, the prime minister! I'll even write to the king! Yes, I'll write to the king! Is he not our nation's commander in chief?"

Noureddine suddenly became aware of the danger he might face if he got mixed up in this thorny affair. A real danger, perhaps even with fatal consequences. Resting a finger on his temple, he was silent for a moment, growing pensive. The risk was great, certainly, but that shouldn't stop him doing something for the man who'd been his best friend in the underworld. So he gave his phone number to the old man and, just before leaving him, reiterated his condolences.

Now that's what you call a true friend! Rezzouk thought to himself, following Noureddine with his eyes all the way to the cemetery gates. *You don't meet a brave man like that every day.*

That night was a sleepless and cruel one for the old man. In the morning, he returned to the police station.

"What can I do for you, *cherif*?" Chief Zeghloul asked politely.

"I want to know the truth about my son's death!" Rezzouk blurted out in a rage. "The whole truth!"

The chief just stared at the old man.

"My son didn't die in a traffic accident!"

"Just what are you saying, *cherif*?" the cop asked.

"The truth, chief! My son was killed by members of the drug squad."

"What you're saying is serious," the chief replied, his tone suddenly menacing. "Very serious. Do you have proof?"

"Proof, no. But I have a witness."

"Who's this witness?"

"A friend of my late son's."

"His name and address?" the chief requested. "I want to question him as soon as possible."

"His name is Noureddine . . . Noureddine . . ." The old man was silent for a few seconds, searching his memory for a surname. "It will come to me later . . . I have his phone number, though." He took the notepad out of his pocket and flipped through its yellowed pages. "Here it is."

The chief pushed the desk phone toward Rezzouk and pressed the speakerphone button. "Go on," he ordered. "Call him and tell him to meet you somewhere. In a park, for example."

The old man dialed the number and heard a woman's voice at the other end of the line: "*Maroc Telecom, bonjour! The number you have dialed is not in service.*" He tried again, got the same message, and hung up, stupefied.

"Tell me, *cherif*," the chief said after a silence.

"Yes?"

"Where did you meet this Noureddine?"

"At Bab Ghmat Cemetery, near my son's grave."

"There were others around, I imagine?" the chief asked.

"No, no one."

"No one came to the ceremony?"

"Oh, yes. Lots of people," Rezzouk told him. "But after the burial, they all left."

"And you stayed there alone?"

"Yes."

"What were you doing alone by the grave?"

"I was praying for my son's soul," the old man shared, sorrow filling his voice again.

"And how were you praying? Standing up? Kneeling? Describe it to me as carefully as possible," the chief pressed.

Confused and suspicious, the old man stared at the chief. "Those are pointless details."

The chief stared back with a faint, sneering smile. "You must know, *cherif*, that in our work, the truth is like the devil: it hides in details that the average person finds unimportant. A gesture, a look, a trifle, a mere nothing—yes, sometimes the truth hides in nothing at all! Believe me: if I told you all the crimes we've solved thanks to an insignificant detail, I'd be here all day."

Though unconvinced by the chief's argument, the old man relented: "I was there, standing at the foot of the grave, my hands raised to the sky, eyes closed—"

"You had your eyes closed?" the chief interrupted.

"Yes, to better concentrate on the prayer."

"And it was *then* that this Noureddine approached you?"

"Yes."

The chief swiftly pushed his swivel chair back from the desk, nodding his head up and down as if he'd found the key to the mystery. "Go home, *cherif*!" he urged the old man. "You're very tired."

Rezzouk got up and, without saying a word, began walking toward the door.

"Some advice, *cherif*!" the chief called after him with the self-satisfied air of a man who understood life better than most. "The next time you visit the cemetery, be careful not to pray with your eyes closed."

Translated from French by Katie Shireen Assef

MAMA AICHA

BY HALIMA ZINE EL ABIDINE

Jemaa el-Fnaa

As I was getting ready to leave the furnished apartment that I'd rented in the heart of Casablanca, I realized that I had forgotten the most important thing: the organdy. This length of purple silk from Kawamata that I'd spent half my scholarship money to buy during my first year of university in Japan was part of a memory that had been boxed away for twenty years. When I'd arrived there as a teenager, I could think of nothing but the disappointment of it all, the crushing defeat. In my hand I carried a small satchel of clothing, and from my shoulder hung a wallet containing my passport, my registration certificate for the university, and postcards showing scenes from the city I loved more than anything: Marrakech. Marrakech opens her gates to the world, but she had driven me—her own son—out.

My father insisted that I seek refuge in the most remote corner of the earth, where the hurricane winds sweeping our country could not reach. "This is a time of fear and death. I can bear your distance, my son, as long as you're safe," he told me. "I could not keep you here knowing you might be taken at any time by the secret police and the men with whips—seized by treachery or coercion. Though Japan, where your uncle Salim lives, may be far away in the east, it's still closer than the corridors of the commissariat in Jemaa el-Fnaa. Leave your glorious dreams of revolution behind, son, and do something with your youth, and when you are a grown man, you will realize that no revolution in the world was ever led by inexperienced students."

That is what my father said as he bid me goodbye at Marrakech Menara Airport one day in the late seventies. The stern headmaster who terrified everyone in the high school, teachers and students alike, seemed sad, diminished. When he gave me a final parting look, his eyes were full of tears.

Alone with my thoughts as I sat in the window seat on the plane, I let my own tears flow. All of the words that had died on my tongue repeated themselves in my head. Everything I hadn't said to my father. What had we done that we should be either sent to prison or driven out of the country?

My phone rang, and I ignored it as I attempted to find my way out of a garage that was like a maze. Maybe it was my mother, although I'd told her—when I had dinner at her house last night—that I was going to Marrakech today to see Aziz and his mother Aicha.

I'd been gone from Marrakech for twenty years. For twenty years I'd been the cause of my mother's tears. Distracting myself, immersing myself in books and theories. It was true that I had done very well and had become an instructor at a Japanese university. But these were successes without savor. I had no one to celebrate with, no one to whom I could speak in my native tongue about the black misery that blotted out my name from the diplomas I had earned with such distinction. Regret gnawed at every part of me. If only I had not obeyed my father and emigrated to this much larger prison, allowed myself to be torn out by my roots. I had no friends or companions except the postcards that I'd brought with me. I kept them close to my heart, and with them the piece of organdy silk. I saw the faces from my country in them. I talked to them and they spoke back to me. I passed the nights in their company.

As for my uncle Salim, our only connection was through the

money my father sent him to support me during the early years of my exile. Family is not a matter of blood, it is a matter of birth and upbringing—I would console myself with this thought when it became clear that my uncle wasn't going to worry himself about me in a country where sons became adults and took responsibility for themselves as soon as they started university. In Marrakech, where I had come from, sons could have gray hair and they would still be children in the eyes of their parents.

The phone rang again. *Be patient, Mother, I can't answer right now, I'm looking for a way out of this lousy garage that you directed me to.* My poor mother. Perhaps she had wanted to come with me to Marrakech. Maybe that was what she'd been hinting at when we spoke yesterday, revealing a sadness that had spread and taken root like a tree in the depths of her eyes. "While you were gone I might as well have been dead," she'd said. "Aicha was the bosom in which I sought comfort, but in the end, I left her to her tragedies and came to Casablanca to drink from my cup of sorrow alone."

"But you used to spend school vacations at our house in Marrakech, and the majority of the time you were with her," I replied.

She looked long and hard at my face, as though trying to find in it remnants of her seventeen-year-old son who had existed once, before he was torn away from the safety of her lap and flung into the dark spaces of a strange country. "That's right. I couldn't get used to living here in Casablanca. If the secret police hadn't made our life miserable after you went abroad, we would never have left our house and relatives and neighbors. Your father wouldn't have made us move to this noise-infested city."

The phone continued to ring. I picked it up in one hand while the other kept a grip on the steering wheel. It was Aziz. I pulled over next to the curb. His voice sounded weak but animated, as though he were eager to talk. "Why didn't you pick up? Were you still asleep? Or is your phone still set to Japanese time?"

"I'm already on the road. I'll be in Marrakech in three hours," I told him.

"I'll be waiting for you at the Argana Café. From there, we'll go to my mother's house. We're having lunch there, as we agreed."

"I'll drive as fast as I can so I'm on time for Mama Aicha," I promised.

"How she cried when you left the country. Your being there by her side during the year before you left lightened the pain of my absence for her."

How I, too, had cried . . .

We had promised each other that if either of us were arrested, we would die before we confessed the other's involvement, so that one of us would remain to take care of our two mothers. Aziz kept his side of the bargain, but I didn't. He stayed strong and never implicated me, even under torture. I abandoned them both and went abroad.

We were teenagers. My father's bookshelves had taught me to love literature. Aziz and I would devour the novels that I filched from my father's library without his permission. Then, at the Arset el-Hamd youth center, we met some other young men our age or a little older who were training themselves to dream—to look ahead to a more just future. They exchanged forbidden Red Books with us. We even joined the leftists in the March 23 movement. It was a secret organization, and we were part of the cell at the high school. There, we began training to dream collectively. This dream had started to grow inside of us when the police raids caught us by surprise.

"You have to leave. You have to give up on your dreams. You have no other choice," my father had warned me the day he accompanied me to the airport. I'd been aghast. So I would set out alone on a journey into the unknown. A journey without meaning. I endured it as one endures torture. Deep inside me there was a howling, like trapped wolves. I felt like a traitor. I wanted my mother's hand, wanted her to pass it over my chest, to thaw this cold. I had only this still-bleeding wound to remind me, and the fragrance of a city whose soil I smelled in the color of my own skin. That soil from land reclining upon the foothills of the Atlas Mountains, palm trees held in its embrace. When I was a child, the world as far as I was concerned began and ended there. After I grew up a little, I discovered that Jemaa el-Fnaa Square was the beating heart of the city, and Marrakech was the beating heart of the world. Don't tourists flock to it from all over the globe, to dance to its songs and sing along under its glittering lights? Don't they say that Marrakech lavishes a noisy tumult of joy and ecstasy on strangers, while for its sons and daughters it offers only a silent sadness? What is the good humor for which the people of Marrakech are known if not a proud mask concealing the bitterness of their days and the misery of their lives?

Marrakech was slipping away from me. I kept searching in vain for her radiant face in the postcards scattered across my desk and pillow, so that I wouldn't lose my memory of her, so that I wouldn't lose the colors of the city, which had begun to fade from my heart and mind. Words flared up inside of me whenever I thought about the organdy, that piece of fine silk cloth I had rushed to buy as a gift for Mama Aicha. The cloth had remained stored away in my cupboard all these years. I'd made a promise to myself and I hadn't kept it. Marrakech was far away, and the freedom I had dreamed of had gotten tripped up along the way, arriving with its body parts damaged and mutilated.

Aziz and I were born the same year. Mama Aicha had nursed me along with Aziz. We drank the same milk, we studied at the same schools, and we read the same books. Together we dreamed of a cultural revolution that would bring prosperity to our humble families. A revolution that would stay its course until it had granted dignity to all the children of this nation. Mama Aicha's home was next to ours, at the entrance of el-Rahba el-Kadima alley, only a few steps from Jemaa el-Fnaa. It was a beautiful house, overflowing with life. Pots of chrysanthemums, narcissus, jasmine, and crocus clustered along the walls of its interior courtyard, and basil and lavender spilled from trellises across the tiled floors.

In the middle of the courtyard was a large planter box that held a towering mulberry tree whose branches shaded the entire area. Toward the end of winter, the tree filled with magnificently colored migratory moths whose wings made a rustling sound like the ethereal music of sacred temples. As small children, Aziz and I would watch them for hours on end, and we were tempted to try to catch them so that we could keep listening to the music of their wings in private, while we read or studied our lessons. But Mama Aicha was always there to stop us from getting too close to them.

"These moths are going to lay eggs, and from their eggs hundreds of larvae will come out, and they will make cocoons," she'd tell us.

Every time she repeated this our jaws would drop in amazement. She would laugh and explain to us each time how the larva was the silkworm and the cocoon was the ball of silk.

We would ask her: "Why won't you let us play with the balls of silk?"

And every time she would answer: "Because I'm going to turn them into thread, and from this thread I'll weave a purple cloth called organdy, to make a kaftan so fine that only a princess or a queen would wear one like it."

"Why?" we'd ask again.

"Because no one in the whole world knows how to make this kind of silk cloth from a worm except a queen in far-off China. Since she's a queen, she won't sell her cloth to anyone but other queens, and for a very high price. Though I'm not a queen or a princess, I want to wear it too. I've promised myself that one day I'll have my own kaftan of organdy silk."

Every year Mama Aicha gathered the cocoons. And every year she told us about the Chinese queen who owned fields of white mulberry trees. In their branches lived millions of moths, and their cocoons became the silk thread used to make the organdy.

The years passed, and Aziz and I were no longer children. Maybe because we ceased to ask her about the organdy kaftan, Mama Aicha whispered to us once with deep sadness: "I have only a single mulberry tree from which a few larvae feed, and it gives me just a little thread each year. How many years will I have to wait? It won't suit me to wear this kaftan when I'm old." She was silent for a moment, and then her face brightened again and she went on: "But anyway, I'll keep taking care of the mulberry tree and my larvae. If I don't wear the cloth myself, your wife will wear it, Aziz; and yours, Yusuf."

She continued to sit on the edge of the planter. She drank her midday tea there once she had finished the housework and fed her son and her husband, after the first had gone to school and the other to his shop in Souk Semmarine. She hummed along with whatever was playing on the radio fastened on a hook above the window grate in her bedroom: the songs of Umm Kulthum, Fairuz, Abdelwahab Doukkali, and Naima Samih. She had an angelic voice that poured sweetly from her throat like the breeze in Marrakech at the beginning of spring. Yet no one heard her except the mulberry tree and the birds that came seasonally to hunt the moths or their larvae, and Aziz and I on our days off from school. When the songs on the radio stopped, she would tell us captivating stories about her childhood in her Amazigh village. Stories with which our imaginations would roam to strange and wonderful worlds. When we left her to go study our lessons, she would converse with the mulberry tree instead, talk to it, ask it questions, confess her secrets to it. She told it of her kaftan, which was still not finished. She raised her eyes to the sky, wandering in her thoughts far from the orbit of her domestic space. The sky was closer to her than Jemaa el-Fnaa, which she had never seen. Only its sounds reached her. She listened to them furtively and with a great deal of curiosity, trying to find connections between them and what Aziz and I told her about the square. We were children. We told her about our adventures and our small acts of mischief, about the storytelling circles there, about the singers whose voices were not as fine as Mama Aicha's, about the fortune-tellers surrounded by sad women, about the famous street performers Bakchich and Tabib el-Hasharat, and the spectacle of the donkey who could read.

We would take a detour from el-Rahba el-Kadima alley toward Derb Dabachi in order to cut through Jemaa el-Fnaa. Then we would take Prince Avenue until we reached the Hotel Tazi, then veer left in the direction of Arset el-Maach. We spent our day at the Ibn el-Banna Middle School. When we returned home in the evening, we always paused for a few minutes at the edge of a storytelling circle that had just formed so that we could bring back fresh tales from the square, embellished by our own imaginations, for Mama Aicha. Our accounts of the square made her happy. She listened to us with bright eyes and asked for more. Once we moved from the middle school in Arset el-Maach to the Mohammed V High School in Bab Ghmat, Jemaa el-Fnaa was no longer the only wellspring of stories for us. Other sources erupted between our adolescent feet, their stories drawn from the sufferings of the Moroccan people and from accounts of popular revolutions. Our new stories were only for us and our comrades at the high school, and at the Arset el-Hamd youth center. For this reason, we hid them from our mothers.

Mama Aicha knew nothing of the world around her beyond her husband, Si Mohammed el-Blaighi, her only son, Aziz, my mother, who was her friend and neighbor, and me. Only a single wall separated our two houses, and even if this wall prevented my mother from going over to her friend's house to drink a cup of tea with her in the shade of the mulberry tree, it did not stop the two young mothers from communicating. As for Mama Aicha, her feet never crossed the threshold of her own front door. She had not left the house since her husband brought her there as a bride from Souss, a girl of only fifteen.

"A graceful posture and a shapely body like none other. God must have been in a state of the highest pleasure with creation when He made it. I've never seen such blue eyes and such long eyelashes in all of Marrakech. Her gaze is soft, suited to a world of refinement and happiness. When I looked at her face for the first time, I thought it was the round disk of the sun itself," my mother had said when she told my grandmother about her.

Si Mohammed was infatuated with her. He feared the least gust of wind might carry her away. When he left the house, he locked the door with an iron key as thick as the arm of a small child. To keep her from suffering from loneliness in his absence, he brought her first a radio and then the seedling of a tree. As he planted it, he told her about the emperor's wife who discovered a white worm eating the leaves of her mulberry tree, secreting luminous threads in which to wrap itself as it did so. From them, the emperor's wife wove an enchanted silk fabric fit only for queens: organdy.

The seedling became a tree. She was pregnant, and the movements of the fetus filled her with dreams and love and wonderment. One spring morning she gave birth to Aziz. When they celebrated the *aqiqah* afterward, joy radiated from Si Mohammed's eyes as he served food and drink to the well-wishers. He didn't lock the door when he went back to his shop afterward. He handed over the key to Aicha. She believed that she was finally free. She was happy because her husband had entrusted her with the key to the house.

Despite all of this, she was content with the warm, calm monotony of her small space. Content with hearing our stories about what happened outside. She never thought about going out.

Her days passed happily, her mind filled with thoughts of her son, her husband, and the mulberry tree. There was nothing to trouble her. She watched as Aziz grew up, and her dreams grew with him. He was a diligent student, and his success in school made her heart brim with pleasure.

One winter night there was a windstorm. It snapped branches off the mulberry tree and ripped flowers from their beds. The earth dissolved into muddy pools beneath the downpour of rain. The family members huddled in their beds, trying to sleep.

Aicha heard the rapping of claws on the door and voices like the howling of wolves in the mountains where she'd spent her childhood. She reached out to her husband sleeping beside her and cried out with all her might: "The wolves are coming for us, Sidi Mohammed!"

Si Mohammed slept on and did not hear her strangled cry.

An apparition of her son appeared before her, trembling as he ran. Behind him, a wolf bared its fangs. She awoke terrified and dripping with sweat. Her husband finally opened his eyes and asked: "Who's knocking on our door in the middle of the night, and in this storm?"

"Don't answer them!" Aziz shouted, coming into their room dressed in his winter clothes and sneakers.

"Weren't you sleeping?" his father asked him in surprise.

"The knocking woke me up. Don't open the door for them, Father, it's the police."

"What?"

"It's the police. They've come to take me away," Aziz moaned.

"But what did you do? What crime did you commit? They don't show up in the middle of the night like this except to catch the most dangerous criminals. Tell me, son, what crime are you guilty of? When? Where? Answer me, I beg you." His questions tumbled over one another while his son remained silent. He got out of bed and took him by the hand. "Tell me what happened, child, so I know what I should do."

"I've committed no crime, Father," Aziz whispered.

"So what did you do?"

"I dreamed, Father. I only dreamed. I dreamed of clean bread, and a new suit of clothes for everyone on Eid, and notebooks and pens for all the children."

Bewildered, Mama Aicha was blotting at the tears streaming from her eyes with the hem of her nightgown. She tried to speak, but her words were choked. Aziz pressed his palms to her face, brushed away her tears, and kissed her cheek.

The pounding at the door continued, becoming more violent. Aziz loosened her arms from around his neck. "Don't be afraid, Mother . . . Don't be afraid, Father. I won't let them get me, I'll run away."

The door couldn't hold out long against their powerful fists. It soon gave way. Four men in black suits stomped across the threshold. Their chief led the way. To Mama Aicha, he looked like a wolf baring its fangs.

He bellowed in a voice like thunder: "Where's Aziz?"

No answer.

He repeated the question.

No answer.

He made a sign to the others behind him. In the blink of an eye, they spread out through the house, throwing wardrobes to the floor. Clothing scattered everywhere. They dug their claws into the furniture, ripping it open and sending the stuffing flying into the air. Aicha's tears mixed with the rain pouring down into the open courtyard of the house. She asked herself, *What can my son Aziz have hidden in the furniture? How could he hide a weapon when a moth's death makes him cry?*

One of the men returned from Aziz's room. "We found notebooks decorated with a rising sun, and these are the colored pens that were used to draw them."

His mother returned to asking questions no one heard: "Drawings . . . since when is this a crime? And colored pens as well?"

The skinny, mean-faced man who seemed to be their leader ordered them to handcuff the father. They would hold him hostage until the fugitive son surrendered himself. They blindfolded him and threw him into a black car that took off like an arrow.

Mama Aicha tried to leave the house, but the agent who had been left behind to watch her blocked her way.

Time passed slowly. A terrible desperation arose in her chest. The seconds seemed like months, and the hands on the clock did not move. Who would hear the sound of her voice? Was there another mother anywhere on this earth afflicted by such a calamity? Who would bring her news of her son? Of her husband?

She sobbed and sobbed. She wandered aimlessly through the house. She pounded on the walls with both hands and shouted. Perhaps her friend Zahra would hear her. She could shout! This was the first positive thing to come from this ordeal. She had discovered that she possessed a mouth that could raise its voice.

Si Mohammed returned after a two-day absence, which felt like an eternity. He wept bitterly. He didn't hide his tears from his wife. Mama Aicha cried out when she saw him, and a wail escaped her: "No! No, don't tell me they got him!"

"Aziz couldn't escape," he told her. "They had security forces and spies on every road. I watched as they hauled him out of an old car. They dragged him across the ground as blood streamed from his mouth, leaving lines on the pavement. He opened his eyes. He saw me struggling desperately to get to him and embrace him, and the guards restraining me as I tried to throw myself on him and take him in my arms, to erase the whip marks on his chest."

"Did he speak? What did he say to you?"

"He said in a strong voice, *Don't cry, Father. Don't be sad. I won't die. I'll return . . . I'll return.*"

* * *

Mama Aicha waited for the return of her son. The first month passed, then a second and a third. There was no news. She decided to leave the house and track him down on her own.

Her friend Zahra asked her: "Where will you look for him, Aicha, my dear? Neither you nor I know the streets and alleys of Marrakech. Who will help us pick up his trail?"

"I'll go to the fortune-tellers in Jemaa el-Fnaa. Will you come with me, Zahra? Perhaps one of them can tell us of Aziz's fate, or point us in the right direction."

Each woman put on a djellaba and pulled a veil over her face. They headed for Jemaa el-Fnaa Square. Mama Aicha's steps faltered and she stopped, amazed and confused, in the middle of the square. Loud voices. Music. Singing. Prayers. Curses. Brazen laughter. Dirty words. Bodies pressing against each other in the throng. A male body attached itself to her from behind. My mother pulled her firmly away by the hand and turned toward the tall figure wrapped in an old winter djellaba. Like all the rest of them, he was hiding his face beneath the djellaba's hood. They came to Jemaa el-Fnaa to rub up against the behinds of women in the crowd. "Goddamn you," my mother said, uncertainty in her tone. Mama Aicha, for her part, although she was so worried about her son that she could scarcely think about what was happening to her body, was on the verge of collapse from the excessively crowded space and the feelings of shame and humiliation.

They sat down in front of the first fortune-teller they saw. She asked Mama Aicha: "Am I reading your fortune or is there a man in your life whose secrets you need me to tell you?"

"Neither. I only want to know where my son is."

The fortune-teller looked at her cards for a long time, and then said: "Your son was bewitched by a woman and is lost to you."

Mama Aicha went to another fortune-teller and the same exchange was repeated with only slight differences. It seemed to the two women that the fortune-tellers of Jemaa el-Fnaa were all programmed to say that women were a source of temptation and evil, and therefore that they would not find the solution they sought here. A woman who had been watching them instructed them to go to a fortune-teller who appealed to a higher power. Her hut was near the shrine of Moul el-Ksour, one of the seven saints of Marrakech. She was famous throughout the city and beyond for the accuracy of her visions. When the woman realized that the two friends did not know where the shrine was, she offered to accompany them.

The fortune-teller was very thin and tall. Her bug-like eyes squinted toward each other, with the pupil on the right swiveling left and the pupil on the left looking right. Were it not for the nose protruding between them, they would have run together to become a single horrible eye. Mama Aicha prayed to God to protect her when she beheld this ugly creature. The woman who had guided them told them that the fortune-teller had once been beautiful and charming, until one day the prince of the jinn noticed her and fell in love with her. He made her deformed so that no other being would desire her. To compensate her for the loss of her womanly beauty, the cost of his selfish love for her, he revealed to her all the secrets of the world beyond, and lifted the veils from her sight.

The fortune-teller asked Mama Aicha why she had come.

"My son has disappeared, ma'am, and I want you to show me the way to him."

The fortune-teller lit incense and sprinkled the room with rose water. She invoked the names of the kings of the jinn and the righteous among men and uttered other words that they didn't understand. She reached inside a small cupboard covered with a fine green shawl, and she took from it a wooden box painted with a lustrous yellow coating. Inside it were sand and seashells and agate-colored grains of coral. She placed it in front of her and put her hand in the sand. She moved her lips as though she were reciting something to herself, and her eyes flicked rapidly in opposite directions. A terrible fear crept into the hearts of the two friends when they heard sounds like the echo of cannons emerge from the belly of the fortune-teller, who suddenly opened her cavernous mouth wide and said in a harsh voice: "The cards . . . the cards. Yes, My Lord, the cards . . ." She scattered the playing cards in front of her but did nothing to halt the unsettling sound emanating from her abdomen. "Is your son wearing a state uniform?" she asked.

Mama Aicha rejoiced and answered immediately, "Yes," because she knew that a prisoner had his regular clothes taken from him and exchanged for a special prison suit.

"Was your son riding in a vehicle?"

Mama Aicha's heart began to beat faster, as Si Mohammed's voice rang in her ear once more: *I watched as they hauled him out of an old car. They dragged him across the ground as blood streamed from his mouth.* She answered, "Yes."

"Is he with a group of others like him?"

"There's no doubt about that." In every alley of the city there was a bereaved mother—this she had heard from Yusuf, who had not stopped visiting her since those evil hands stretched out to snatch away her own flesh and blood from his very bed.

Then the fortune-teller said something that could scarcely be believed, after the accuracy of everything she had said before: "Give me a piece of his underwear. I will write a charm on it and you must burn a part of it each day for three days. After a time that is neither long nor short, you will find him returning to you, once he has tired of the nightlife and grown to hate the fornicator who seduced him."

Mama Aicha stood up, all of her hope having drained away. "Is this what the jinn who possesses you told you? Tell him to go back to his cards," she snapped. "My son is not seduced by the nightlife or taking shelter in the arms of women. My son, my love . . . I'll look for him myself. Let's go, Zahra, these women are nothing but frauds."

"I knew that. I just wanted to bring you here because I thought it would do you good to get out of the house."

"Don't worry, Zahra. I'll set him free myself." She said this with a strange earnestness and determination, as if another voice, stronger than her own, were emerging from inside of her. The voice of a different woman, not the Aicha we knew.

Her husband didn't forbid her to leave the house, but instead pointed the way himself to the secret cave in which all of the city's most distinguished students, and the best of its high school teachers, were packed away.

When she arrived at the detention center, she saw that it wasn't invisible, as she had previously believed. It was an imposing building with colonial architecture squatting at the northern corner of Jemaa el-Fnaa, not far from the circles of singers and the dancers and acrobats and magicians and food carts. Neither the singers' melodies nor the voices of the storytellers—nor even the clamor of the monkey tamers—could capture Mama Aicha's attention that day. She had always dreamed about the vast possibilities of this freewheeling square, but now that she found herself in the middle of it, she was scarcely aware of the entertainment and diversions that filled it. Her eyes were fixed on the dreaded building. She paused to look at the police station that had swallowed up her son, and she examined the faces of the officers and state security guards who surrounded it.

She approached the terrifying building with hesitant steps. Whom should she ask? And how? What had her son been accused of doing? Why had they taken him? Did they know Aziz? *Do you know Aziz?* Aziz, the handsome young man with the enchanting smile. He was a good boy, did well at school, drew suns with his colored pens. Was it simply because he had drawn a rising sun that he deserved to be punished?

The questions crowded together inside her head. She imagined herself making her way around the building and asking the policemen who surrounded it one by one. But when a stout, cruel-looking officer came over and ordered her to move along, she realized that she was all but rooted in place in front of the building. Her eyes began to overflow with tears, soaking her veil.

The policeman repeated his order. "Can't you hear? I told you to get going. You're not allowed to stand here. There's nothing to see—the show's over there, behind you, you crazy woman. So move along, scram."

"I'm not looking for a show, sir. I want my boy, my son . . ." she said, stumbling over her words in fear.

"Your son? Is he a policeman? Does he work here?"

"My son is only a student, sir, a young man in the baccalaureate division. Ever since he started school he's always been the first in his class. He's seventeen and his name is Aziz."

"I thought you were asking about an employee here. This building is not a school or a youth center. Go look for your son somewhere else."

"But my son is here, sir. Locked up here three months ago."

The policeman was confused. He was only a lowly patrol officer. He had nothing to do with what happened inside. He didn't know what to do. He tried to hide his confusion behind curses and shouts: "I told you to get out of my sight, you bitch! Get on your way or I'll break your teeth! This isn't a high school. If your son is a criminal, go look for him in Boulmharez Prison. This isn't a school or a jail. So get lost!"

No one in her whole life had ever cursed at Mama Aicha. *Bitch*. That was the first time another person had flung this hurtful word in her face. She who knew nothing of the world. She who had left her small Amazigh village to come to her husband's house in Marrakech without ever having had her ears polluted by a dirty word. In Jemaa el-Fnaa, as she moved among the fortune-tellers holding court in the square, she had heard obscenities that embarrassed her. But this foul word now exploded like a bomb in her own face. It was directed at *her*.

"A bitch? I'm a bitch?"

She hurried to get away from the policeman who had broken her resolve and wounded her deeply. As she rushed on, the face of her husband appeared before her tear-filled eyes. How could she confront him after today? How could she look him in the eye now that her modesty had been defiled by a stranger with a word that had never even crossed her mind before? She ran as though she were trying to escape herself and escape the word *bitch* that pursued her. She came to a halt in the middle of a circle of Abidat Rma. They were singing their nomadic songs and dancing. If only she could disappear. To hide from what she was accused of, she slipped in among the audience. Her feet betrayed her and she collapsed into a seated position on the ground in the first row. Her veil hid her face. She stared at the dancers without seeing them, as silent tears soaked her veil and traced rivulets down her cheeks. The roar of the blood in her veins drowned out the voices of the singers and the music they were making. The dance kept going energetically in front of her, but she couldn't see it. She couldn't hear. She couldn't feel.

As she made her way home, crushed with disappointment, she noticed a gathering of people not far from the commissariat, near the taxi stand. Her heart alone steered her toward them. She heard somebody wail in anguish: "Let me talk to the person in charge of the jail so I can ask him about my son! The baccalaureate exam is around the corner and he's being prevented from going to school!"

Aziz was just one of many. She found on every pair of lips her very own questions. They were fathers and mothers, wives and sons, worn out with watching and waiting. Chance had brought them all together in the same place. They came as individuals and convened without having known each other before. Each mother told her story. Each father condemned the brutality with which his son had been treated during his arrest. The police chased them away, but they returned. For Mama Aicha, there was something about finding herself united with those who shared her pain that made her forget the ugly word and feel that at least she was not alone.

The news of the secret jail spread throughout the city, and eventually it was no longer secret. It was the commissariat of Jemaa el-Fnaa. The arrests didn't stop, so the number of guards in the vicinity of the commissariat doubled. The mothers began to gather in the middle of the square. They rested in the chairs belonging to the food vendors. Jemaa el-Fnaa gradually became an area for protests. Tourists and visitors to the square, Moroccan and foreign, wandered through without paying attention to the intermittent clashes between the families of those imprisoned and the security forces, the families forming into lines and moving en masse toward the building, and the police, always vigilant, driving them back among the circles of storytellers.

Suddenly, with no warning, the process of releasing the prisoners began, without a trial. Each day a few would leave, bringing with them news of who would come out next.

The number of families shrank. The remaining ones kept up their vigil near the jail. Their initial worry transformed into a real hope that the confinement might be lifted for all of the city's young men who had disappeared.

Early one morning in January, with rain sweeping across the desolate square as it usually did on cold mornings, the families were surprised to see, through the filaments of falling water, lights shining at the door of the jail. They hurried over to find out what was going on. The lights were from a jeep that was transporting the remaining prisoners. Mama Aicha saw her son as he was being pushed roughly to climb into the vehicle. His head was shaved and a band of black cloth covered his eyes. She slapped her cheeks and cried: "Aziz! It's my son, Aziz! Where are you going, my boy?"

Aziz heard her cry. He raised his shackled hand and clenched his fist. Cries and cheers filled the air. The names of the prisoners were repeated in every corner of Jemaa el-Fnaa that day. Mama Aicha steeled her heart. She banished the tears from her eyes. They were forbidden from betraying her devastation.

It was an agonizing moment for Mama Aicha, who was torn between fear of the cold and the dark, and fear of the wolves that were looking for scapegoats.

The cars began to move and the families trembled with worry. Rumors spread through the city, confirming that the prisoners who had been charged with conspiracy and plotting to overthrow the regime had been transferred directly to the execution wing at Kenitra Central Prison outside of Rabat. They would execute them after a quick trial. The most important work of proving them guilty had already been carried out by the police in the Jemaa el-Fnaa commissariat. Other sources, however, maintained that they were still in Marrakech. That they were being held inside a secret vault in el-Badi Palace, an old prison where the Saadi kings used to entomb their Portuguese prisoners alive. Aziz's mother tried to discover the way to this vault but she could find no one to guide her. She continued meeting regularly with the other mothers and fathers and wives. They met up near the Jemaa el-Fnaa commissariat and then congregated in the shade of the giant trees in Arset el-Bilk just beside the square. The security officers watched them and counted their very breaths, but the families didn't care. They supported each other and fortified themselves against despair by nurturing their dreams and pursuing hope, however false it might be.

Three years they waited, weaving together strands of hope.

Their initial hesitant search efforts transformed into a full-scale protest and then into an understanding that more action was needed to find out the fate of their imprisoned relatives. The first mission that the families undertook, with Mama Aicha among them, was to see the governor of the city.

At first, the governor was the epitome of politeness. He explained to them that they lived, thanks be to God, in a nation of laws. Even the most violent criminals were punished according to the law. If they thought that their relatives, whom they claimed had been locked up by the state, were not guilty, then they should look for them away from the centers of power, because the state did not detain people without trial, and apart from the civil prison at Boulmharez, it had no other place dedicated to this function. "Therefore I advise you," the governor concluded sternly, "to look for your sons far away from us here. Each one of you must do so on his or her own. It's strictly forbidden to gather like this without authorization. This country has laws, and we can't permit you to keep spreading misinformation and disorder like this."

The governor's answer stripped away all remnants of fear from inside Mama Aicha, and she felt a strange power coursing through her body and in her soul. She immediately snapped back at him in a tone that was at once strident and aggressive: "That's why we came to you, sir, because you're the governor for His Majesty in Marrakech. You're the representative of the king here. You're the chief of this city and its protector. If our sons have died, in God's name give us their bodies so we can bury them, and if they're still alive, issue the orders to release them from prison so we can see them. It's been more than three years now since they disappeared."

"That's enough! Go home or I'll have you and everyone with you thrown in jail. I was clear with you. I won't tolerate this kind of disrespect against the state."

They left the governor's building. When they paused outside the door to collect themselves, Mama Aicha addressed the group: "Worse than the jail they threaten us with is what we put up with every moment. Isn't our running frantically through the streets like lost dogs worse than jail? Isn't their kicking us out in this way a punishment no different than torture? Isn't the agony of waiting a kind of death that is slowly creeping up on us? As for me, neither jail nor death frightens me. I will go look for my son, either to get him out of prison or to enter it myself."

"Wherever you go, Aicha, we go with you," said one of the other mothers, "to give credibility to these calls for change."

"In that case, let's go back to Jemaa el-Fnaa. We'll stage a sit-in in front of the commissariat. We'll demand that they tell us where they took our sons."

They occupied the area and were dispersed right away. They returned the following day, the following week, the following month. They always returned. Sometimes the police weren't enough to break up the protest. They arrested them. They arrested Mama Aicha and the other mothers more than once, and then they let them go after a day or two. Mama Aicha always came out even fiercer, more determined. She no longer cared about dying, and she was no longer afraid of being arrested.

When she returned home one evening, she noticed under the door a piece of green paper folded into the shape of an envelope. On the back was a circular seal. She opened it and saw that there was writing on it. A shudder went through her in spite of the August heat. Her feelings swung between happiness and sadness—she didn't know how to read, yet she knew that the letter was from her son. She couldn't wait for her husband to return. She tucked the letter into her bosom and hurried off toward his store in Souk Semmarine. She didn't answer him when he asked, surprised, why she had come, as she had never visited him in his shop before. Out of breath, she handed the letter to him.

"It's from Aziz."

"How do you know? Who told you it's from him?" he asked.

"I felt it with my heart."

"Oh, Aicha, it *is* from him. They've transferred him and all his comrades from the secret underground cell to the Ghbila Prison in Casablanca. It's now possible to visit him. He says that we can go on Saturday morning."

"That's tomorrow!" she exclaimed.

They didn't sleep that night. They went into the kitchen together and prepared Aziz's favorite dish: *tharid* with chicken, onion, and raisins. They went to the wardrobe and selected some of his favorite clothes: his light summer shirt, a new pair of jeans which he'd worn only once or twice before his arrest, clean underwear, and his Adidas sneakers. Before dawn they were at the train station.

They arrived at the prison early in the morning and stood in the line of families which stretched along the whole length of the massive wall, waiting to be called to enter the visiting room. As the hours passed, Mama Aicha counted each second. She kept her eyes fixed on the mouth of the guard, following the movement of his lips with rapt attention, afraid that he would speak their names and they wouldn't hear him. She was assailed by anxiety that the workday would end before they would be allowed to visit. Finally they reached the visiting room. She stuck her head between the bars on the outer window to search with her own eyes for the face of her son among the nearly identical heads behind the second window. Shaved heads, sallow faces that showed their bones, bulging eyes. Before she was able to speak to her son, the screen was lowered and the visit came to an end. She pounded her fist against the window and shouted with all her might: "I'm not leaving this room! I didn't see my son and I didn't speak to him!"

Her anger was contagious, spreading to the other remaining families so that they, too, refused to leave in protest of the shortness of the visiting time. Ten minutes was barely enough time to raise the screen and lower it again. The whole prison mobilized to deal with this emergency. The administrators bargained with the families, but they would not accept; they threatened the families, to no avail. A SWAT team surrounded the visiting room to force the families out at gunpoint. They arrested some of the fathers and forbade the rest of those waiting in line from visiting again. Immediately after that, the prisoners announced an indefinite hunger strike, demanding that the conditions of the prison be improved and the date for a trial be set.

The women resolved that the men should stay out of any active confrontations. They could watch from afar and help with communications. Mama Aicha went out into the streets, joining hands with mothers and wives advocating for the improvement of prison conditions and the acceleration of the announcement of a court date. They staged a sit-in at the Ministry of Justice. They forced their way into the meetings of political parties. They pressured their leaders to end their silence. They brought petitions and proclamations to the newspapers. They went to the colleges and universities to inform the students about the plight of their imprisoned sons.

A few of the prisoners were released to ease some of the tension. Then the trial came. The sentences ranged from five years to life. Aziz's lot was twenty years in jail. After this, the prisoners launched another hunger strike, protesting the even worse conditions of the prison to which they were moved after the trial.

Mama Aicha's house in el-Rahba el-Kadima alley became a regular meeting place for the mothers and wives of those imprisoned, where they strategized and planned counterattacks that would expose jails and jailers alike. In her small house in the heart of ancient Marrakech, a plan was formed to occupy Assounna Mosque, the largest mosque in the capital of Rabat. They staged a sit-in there one Friday immediately after prayers.

They made another plan to go to the Faculty of Literature in Rabat, and so they went. The students there joined forces with them in a demonstration the likes of which Mohammed V University had not seen since the Moroccan Student Union was banned. In Aicha's house, they made signs to carry during the May Day marches. They raised their voices high to expose the truth about the prisoners of conscience who were denied the right to education and medical care. They camped out at the

Ministry of Justice and the minister met with them. He made them promises that the demands of the prisoners would be met, and a committee traveled from his ministry to the prison to negotiate with the inmates to end the strike. The demands were met, but the sacrifices were great. All of them emerged from the forty-day strike as thin as skeletons. A young man from Marrakech named Selim el-Mnabhi had died during the strike. Mama Aicha was right there alongside her comrade Umm Fkhita, the mother of the martyred Selim, as she prepared to receive the corpse and carry out the burial according to custom. They held a martyr's funeral—Selim's funeral—a funeral in which old and young marched together, men and women. Leftist activists from every Moroccan city were in attendance, walking beside the two mothers, Fkhita and Mama Aicha, in a funeral that was unique in all the history of Marrakech.

The phone rang. It was Aziz.

"Hi, Aziz. I've arrived, my friend. I'm in Jemaa el-Fnaa now. I just parked my car. I'll be there in five minutes."

I wandered around the café looking for Aziz, but I didn't see him. I stopped in the middle of the room and dialed his number, only to have his voice speak to me from a table right beside me. I saw an old man with haggard features and white hair searching my face as he tried to smile. But I didn't know him. I approached him to ask him about Aziz. Maybe this was a friend of his. Maybe Aziz was in the bathroom and he would return in a moment. Instead, the old man raised his cloudy eyes to my face and addressed me by name: "At long last, Josef." As he said this, he attempted to rise to embrace me. "At last."

Damn! It was him. He used to address me as *Comrade Josef*, and I would call him *Azizovitch*.

"You didn't recognize me, Yusuf? I've changed that much?"

What? Changed? You're a completely different person, my friend. A person I don't know. A different face. Features I don't recognize.

Only the voice still resembles the old Aziz, I thought. "What did they do to you, my friend, during all those years you spent in prison?"

"I don't remember anymore, Yusuf," he whispered. "I don't remember anything. I don't like to remember. Nothing makes me suffer now except the pain that my condition causes my mother and father when they see death creeping slowly over my body. If you only knew how hard Mama Aicha fought to get me out alive, Josef. Yes, if only you knew."

"I do know, my friend. My mother told me all about Mama Aicha's determination, alongside the mothers and wives of the other political prisoners. How they pressured the regime and embarrassed it in front of the international community before they were able to wring out a blanket pardon for their sons and husbands. Mama Aicha and her companions were behind many changes that this country has seen. When I was in Japan, I used to follow the news from here almost daily, before the Internet—and after. The justice-and-reconciliation initiative that brought about your release, along with the adoption of guidelines for making financial reparations to former detainees—this is what opened the airports and the borders to us." I was proud that something good had come out of the tragedy. "But I didn't come back right away. It was as though I was afraid of seeing you—all of you. I dreaded the moment when my eyes would meet yours. You especially, comrade."

"Oh, my friend . . . whatever was in my eyes has been extinguished forever. You have nothing to fear from them. Forget your friend Aziz. He's only a ghost now. Let's go see your second mother, Aicha. She's waiting for us with a seven-vegetable couscous she made in your honor."

Mama Aicha greeted me with a warm hug. She kissed me and kept kissing me as though I were a sweet child. Her eyes were shining. The house was just as it had been when I left it. Flowerpots still surrounded the courtyard. The mulberry tree was still ripening. Mama Aicha seemed younger than her son. She must have been around fifty-four by now. Were it not for the traces of sadness that lingered in the depths of her eyes, I would have said that she had not changed. She was as radiant and pure as she had been when I last saw her twenty years before.

I handed her my gift, wrapped in rose-colored cellophane paper. She removed the paper with a huge smile. "Cloth made from the purple silkworm. Organdy. My first dream. This is wonderful, Yusuf, my son. How fine and beautiful it is. This is cloth for a sultaness, Aziz. I'll take it to the tailor tomorrow, and within a month at most he'll make me a dress from it. When will you get married, Aziz? When will you get married, my son? I want to wear it in your honor."

Translated from Arabic by Anna Ziajka Stanton

PART III

Outside the City's Walls

FRANKENSTEIN'S MONSTER

BY MY SEDDIK RABBAJ
Sidi Youssef Ben Ali

Marrakech is known for its seven patrons; we call it the city of the Seven Saints. Devout visitors all make the same pilgrimage from one mausoleum to the next, exploring the most intimate corners of the medina. This peregrination begins with the shrine to Sidi Youssef Ben Ali, born Abou Yacoub Senhaji, the revered sage who chose to live outside the walls of the Red City until his death in the year of the hegira 593—more than a century after the capital of the Almoravids was built. It was because he had leprosy that he secluded himself, even digging a deep cellar where he could pray in isolation. Little did the holy man know that a community would form around this place in his honor, growing with the centuries to become Sidi Youssef Ben Ali, a neighborhood defined not only by its borders—it's situated in the zone between the city and its suburbs—but also by the character of its inhabitants. Anywhere in Marrakech, when you introduce yourself as a son of Sidi Youssef Ben Ali, people react with an odd mixture of admiration and suspicion. These "sons" are known for their street smarts: they are cunning almost to the point of crookedness.

Long after his death, the saint continued to watch over his children, preparing them for life by instilling in them a certain self-sufficiency. Here, especially to the north, near the sanctuary, we start to earn our keep at an early age. Several businesses have sprouted up around the marabout's tomb and we all take part in them, we children of the neighborhood. We begin by selling candles in front of the sanctuary, around the age of nine. Poor women who can't afford to buy a full packet as an offering to the saint are content to bargain for a few of the singles that M'kadma, the sanctuary guard, collects and gives us to resell. This business allows us kids—and our supplier—to go home at night with a bit of cash in our pockets. And just as in ancient Rome, when slaves gradually accumulated wages to put toward their emancipation, this modest savings lets us buy our freedom. Our parents leave us to our own devices. We look after ourselves from childhood—or, rather, the saint looks after us.

As we grow up we take on new responsibilities. We become porters, not of luggage but of children—two- and three-year-olds, usually—who we carry down to a sort of underground hovel. We lock the child in there alone for a long while, listening with satisfaction as their screams pierce the darkness. Our saint is known all over the city for his power to cure fitful babies. Mothers bring their little ones who suffer from this particular curse—toddlers who cry for no reason, to the point of seeming possessed—and leave them with one of us. Our task is to place the ailing child in the hands of the saint before bolting up the stairs like a cat, leaving him or her lost in the blackness of the narrow cellar as if at the bottom of a well. The child wails and wails with all its might, and soon rids itself of its affliction.

In the summer we sell jujubes to the tourists visiting the shrine. It's the same fruit we give to children instead of candy, and we also use it to treat coughs. In almost all our families we make it into a jelly that we store for the winter. Summertime is the season we love the most. There's the school vacation, and we also earn good money. We pick the fruit in the Bab Ghmat Cemetery and sell it near the sanctuary in the afternoon.

Our mornings aren't without fun. The cemetery becomes our playground, the ideal setting for our favorite game: hide-and-seek. An endless number of hiding places offer themselves to the connoisseur of this place. There are wild plants and jujube trees sometimes as tall as men, graves exposed by erosion and deep craters of mysterious origin. You would think meteorites had carved them out.

We have a tacit agreement never to let pieces of the dead lie around outside their graves. As soon as we find a shoulder blade, a tibia, a fibula, a phalanx, a rib, a skull, or any bone of the human body, we bring it to a designated hole in the ground that must be either an emptied grave or one of those craters of the necropolis. We have no idea who left the first bone in this place, but we continue to repeat the gesture as if it were our duty, a religious act or a ludicrous rite of passage for frequenters of the cemetery.

Here, in the summer, we become freer than in any other place. We roam the cemetery's overgrown pathways, doing things we can't do anywhere else: chasing stray dogs, talking to birds, masturbating in groups. We indulge in secret eccentricities, no longer inhibited by traditions and rules we don't understand.

This is also the time of the year when we go to el-Hilal cinema. After the mausoleum closes we return home for dinner, bringing a watermelon, a cantaloupe, some peaches, or any other seasonal fruit, or simply a few dirhams to slip into our mothers' hands. This contribution is obligatory as soon as we start to earn money. What we give to the household is always proportional to what we've made. After dinner we're free to come and go as we please. When you're a son of Sidi Youssef Ben Ali, you can revel in your freedom day and night. Usually we go in groups to see the double feature—most often kung fu and Bollywood movies—but if we're short on cash we can resell our ticket to some other penniless filmgoer after the first show, and go out and buy a snack.

Once I went with some friends to the late-night screening and, bizarrely, a different sort of film was showing that night. It was *Frankenstein; or, The Modern Prometheus* by Stefano Massini, based on the Mary Shelley novel. The story tells of Dr. Frankenstein, who creates a grotesque monster without a name or a family, a being built from the parts of several corpses, one who revolts against his maker and becomes capable of terrible crimes.

We didn't need much French in order to understand the film; the images were eloquent enough on their own. We watched the events unfold before us, hunching forward in our seats. At the moment when the monster runs straight toward the camera and seems to want to jump through the screen, the electricity cut out. Voices rang out from all around the room—cries of protest at first, but then of fear and panic. We had no idea what was happening. Had the monster in fact come out from behind the screen to spread all this chaos and confusion, or was it the terror the film had awoken in us that made it seem so? We were used to these prolonged blackouts in Sidi Youssef Ben Ali—they often happened at wedding ceremonies and other important occasions, but never had a blackout seemed as strange to me as at that moment. I clung to a friend and tried to follow the line of spectators weaving their way through the crowd to the exit. I jumped at the slightest contact with other people, and could sense that my friend did too.

The next morning, as usual, we started the day by picking jujubes. We were hard at work when a friend came by to tell us that the bones we'd recently collected in the crater had disappeared. We stared at each other in silence. Cinema el-Hilal was directly opposite the Bab Ghmat Cemetery. We of course assumed the film must somehow be connected to the disappearance of the bones. Had they been cobbled together, like Dr. Frankenstein's body parts, to form a single being? Or was it the monster who had climbed the wall to seek shelter in the necropolis? Did he feed on human bones? A thousand questions flashed through our minds, distracting us from the work we'd begun.

"Look! Look!" a fearful voice cried out. An arm pointed to a large creature, seemingly human, but of exaggerated proportions. He was tall and very thin, with a tuft of hair at the top of his head, and dressed all in rags—mostly old djellabas whose tattered ends flapped behind him like wings. Slowly but surely the heavy footsteps approached us. At this hour, the cemetery was usually empty. Neither gravediggers nor the *tolba*—the Koranic scholars who come to recite verses to soothe the souls of the dead—ever show any sign of life before nine o'clock. We knew them all, for that matter, and by their first names. And so the creature there among the dead, on that morning, was a stranger. The moment we realized this, we ran out from the shade of the jujube trees like a flock of wild birds chased by a predator. We took off toward the exit, paying no attention to the graves we trampled over, nor to the thorny plants that scratched our ankles. We left our harvest behind us, abandoning the only place where we felt truly at ease.

We described what we'd witnessed to all the children in the neighborhood, connecting it to *Frankenstein*. A few of them who hadn't yet seen the film climbed the cemetery wall to get a look for themselves before returning glassy-eyed, pale, barely able to nod to confirm the existence of this bizarre creature who resembled a human yet wasn't quite one.

Over the next few days, the news quickly spread throughout Sidi Youssef Ben Ali. Our parents were the first to voice their concerns. They were afraid for us, yes, but also worried that they might be deprived of our necessary help. We'd been out of work since the incident: the cemetery, our training ground in the jujube business, was now off-limits. We no longer dared set foot in that earthly paradise, not at any time of day or night. Not one of us was capable of facing the terror that took hold as soon as we thought of it. We kept visiting the saint every day, we prayed for him to set us free from the monster, but we would return home with empty pockets. We weren't yet old enough to sell candles, or to bring little children down to the cellar near the saint's tomb; at our age, selling jujubes was the only job we could do.

The adults in the neighborhood were growing increasingly

concerned about the monster's presence. One of the gravediggers claimed to have seen a bizarre creature in the cemetery that spoke to no one and hid there all day long. We wondered what he ate, how he survived, how he spent all those hours in this place of absolute rest.

"We can't keep our children away from there forever," the parents agreed. And so they went to the district's police chief to report the existence of a creature in the neighborhood, an inhuman creature—*Frankenstein's monster*. They didn't dare say the name, even if some were sure of it, for fear of being mocked.

The police chief reassured our parents, promising them to put Inspector Chaloula on the case. Everyone in the neighborhood feared Chaloula. He knew all of us, right down to the ants that circulated in his territory, and even then he could tell the males from the females. When Chaloula was in charge of a case, he refused to sleep until it was solved. Our parents were satisfied, for they knew very well what Chaloula was capable of. The inspector was glad too, as he sensed this case would bring his reputation up another notch. But no one could have predicted what happened next.

Once he'd been briefed on his new mission, Chaloula went home to lunch. His plan was to have his squad burst into the cemetery early the next morning; this way, they would surprise the creature in his sleep. But around two o'clock, as he was walking along the cemetery wall on his way back to work, Chaloula doubled over as if he'd been shot. A few people saw and ran to help him, trying to pry his hands from his stomach and wipe away the foam coming out of his mouth as if he were a rabid dog, but their efforts were in vain. His soul had left his body to join the others behind the wall, his bulging eyes fixed on the necropolis.

The mysterious death of Chaloula terrorized the entire neighborhood, not to mention the police chief, who felt his own end approaching. He spent the whole night awake, tossing and turning, horrible images flashing through his mind. He no longer feared for himself but for his children; he was tormented by the thought that some harm would come to them.

The next day, before Chaloula's burial, the chief brought his entire unit together, including the sentinel, and, like a swarm of bees, they invaded the cemetery. They looked behind every gravestone and up every tree, left no crater unexplored, no bush undisturbed, but it was no use—the monster had vanished.

One by one the chief called us into his office, all of us kids who'd seen the strange creature, and asked us to tell him about it. We all related the same story and described the creature in the same manner. He was able to accept that our monster was more than two meters tall—but that he'd escaped from behind the screen at el-Hilal cinema to go live in the Bab Ghmat Cemetery, or that he was somehow made from the bones we'd collected in the crater, seemed highly improbable to him. And yet, something in him began turning toward a supernatural explanation. He was Moroccan, after all, and he couldn't shake off what he'd been taught from a young age: that the magical and the rational can and do coexist in our world.

While he was investigating Chaloula's death, the chief got word that a strange creature had been seen in Bab er-Robb, the cemetery where Imam Abderahim Souhaili, one of the seven saints of the city, is buried. The description of this creature was nearly identical to the one we had given. And so the chief, escorted by two of his most trusted officers, rushed over to Bab er-Robb to arrest Frankenstein's monster.

This wasn't an easy affair. The demon resisted, kicking and throwing punches in all directions. He was so agile that, for a moment, the chief thought he might actually have a supernatural being on his hands. But the men were finally able to corner him, get him into the car and drive him to the Sidi Youssef Ben Ali station.

As it turned out, this so-called monster was only a poor vagabond. A man who'd been so disappointed by the living that he now preferred the company of the dead.

"What's your name?" the chief asked, his tone forceful.

"I forgot my name and I don't want to remember it," the creature replied, staring at an invisible point on the station's wall.

"Why do you live in cemeteries?"

"No one bothers you in the kingdom of the dead," the creature said.

The policemen soon learned that the monster survived on plants and the few animals he managed to catch in the necropolis. To him, all animals were good to eat: dogs, cats, birds. When asked why he'd left the Bab Ghmat Cemetery, he replied after a long silence—a silence that clearly irritated his listeners—that the living had come there to disturb the dead, and he didn't like that. He thought the living should mind their own business.

The chief felt his blood boiling in his veins. He wanted to give this fool a good hard smack for daring to mock them, but managed to restrain himself for fear of losing precious ground in his investigation. "Explain to us what you've just said," he demanded.

A silence fell over the creature again. None of the policemen dared to prod him, for they knew that the man before them was searching for his words, grasping for the power of speech he'd nearly lost after keeping his silence for so long.

Finally he spoke: "A woman and two men came to the cemetery in the middle of the night. Twice. They dug up a dead body and put it back in its rightful place. Then, the next night, they came back to the same grave, and under the full moon they exhumed the body and buried it again."

His interrogators froze. They were certain that what they'd just heard was true: experience had taught them to read the truth in the faces of witnesses. But they couldn't see the connection between this story and the death of their colleague.

"Let's suppose that what you say is true. But what about Inspector Chaloula? You haven't told us about that yet," the chief said abruptly, hoping to catch the vagabond by surprise.

"Who's Inspector Chaloula? I don't know him, I've never even heard of him."

"Chaloula is the man you killed before you disappeared."

"I didn't kill anyone, I've never killed anyone, it's the others who've killed me many times over," the vagabond asserted.

"And the bones that disappeared from the cemetery?"

"I buried them. Those who are in the ground should stay there," the man added before retreating back into his silence and refusing to answer any more questions.

The chief gave the order to put the poor devil in preventive detention. He called in several other eyewitnesses to the inspector's death, all of whom claimed that they'd never seen the vagabond, and that Chaloula had been walking alone when he'd suffered his fatal attack.

The results of the autopsy put the chief to a new test; it seemed his colleague had been poisoned.

After he'd briefed the squad, they decided it would be wise to go back and trace Chaloula's movements on that fateful day. They learned that he'd had breakfast and lunch at home and a black coffee at work. And so they procured some of the coffee beans from his office and sent them to a lab that confirmed they were of good quality and contained no harmful chemicals. Then they called in Chaloula's wife, who was still in mourning and barely able to respond to the interrogators' questions. Although they knew her well, they didn't spare her the discomfort of testifying. She described the meals she'd prepared for her husband that day, which the whole family had eaten. But the chief noticed that each time the word *poisoned* was spoken, the widow's face went ashen and her lips trembled uncontrollably. He decided to risk everything and ask his next question with utter conviction.

"Why did you kill your husband?"

Those few words were all it took to make Chaloula's wife burst into tears. She explained between sobs that an old woman, a charlatan, had sold her a fruit jelly that had spent the night in the mouth of a dead man. It was supposed to make her husband docile, incapable of raising his voice. She could then do with him as she pleased—that was how the old woman had explained it.

They brought in this charlatan who, seeing the widow's tears, confessed her crime.

It turned out that the dead man in whose mouth the jelly had spent the night was a snake charmer. He'd forgotten to remove the pit viper's venom gland after capturing it, and as he was putting it into a basket he carried on his back, the serpent took advantage of a moment's distraction to sink its fangs into the man's neck.

Translated from French by Katie Shireen Assef

AN E-MAIL FROM THE SKY

BY YASSIN ADNAN

Hay el-Massira

Ashbal al-Atlas Cybercafé: the name is so beautiful—the Atlas Lion Cubs. An extremely successful name. It is true there are no more lions or tigers in the Atlas Mountains near Marrakech, but there are still monkeys. Monkey and boars, as well as some wolves. It's all right. The name is only a metaphor. A metaphorical name for a virtual space. The café is very spacious, Rahal. Not like the other narrow téléboutiques where you buried dozens of years of your life. Since you obtained your BA in Arabic literature from Cadi Ayyad University in 1994 you have tried, in vain, to join L'Ecole Normale Supérieure for teachers. The results are announced at the beginning of October and your name is never among the successful. And, like a mouse, you retreat to your corner in the téléboutique to eavesdrop on the lives of others from behind your old wooden desk.

"Hello, Fatima."

"Hello, Lhaj."

"Hello, Lhajjah."

"Hello, cutie."

"Hi, love."

"Hello. Hello. Hello? You hung up on me, you bitch. Wait until I get my hands on you! Wait and see."

Endless conversations. You provide coins for the customers, as you enjoy spying on their conversations and lives. But things began to change. With cell phones, the customers waned and the téléboutique income deteriorated, and life in this small place became boring. Things have gotten better now. The space has more potential than what you had been dreaming about. The screens now spread all around this place you have built, Rahal. The new mission you have been engaged in is to open doors for your customers on their midnight journeys to a refuge, toward morning lights and ports of virtual blue ether—a mission filling your heart with great pride.

Congratulations! Computers crammed deep to allow the customers to navigate, spellbound, to the screens anchored to the walls. Rahal, you're able to spy on them all from your own computer. You are the only one with your back to the wall, so you can control the room and watch what goes on. And whenever you get tired of spying on the screens of others, you find your private computer in front of you. You can open your Hotmail account and up pops your happy virtual life, just like those of your customers. Life is better on the Internet, Rahal. Life is more beautiful and bright.

New cybercafés have proliferated along Dakhla Avenue and all over the streets of Hay el-Massira, an area that the government launched as a huge residential project in the mideighties. In the beginning, they were intended as houses for the middle class. Later, more economical apartment buildings spread like mushrooms—instead of the green spaces that were planned—bringing a great number of low-level employees before el-Massira was able to assimilate people from the neighboring villages. Provincial villages whose inhabitants practiced agriculture and shepherding in the lands west of Marrakech alongside the road to Essaouira. The lands that were turned into subdivisions and housing developments. Restructuring projects will eventually succeed in integrating these small villages whose children have mixed with those of the middle-class employees at Lycée Zerktouni to become, in turn, the "kids of the sector." These kids are so proud of belonging to Hay el-Massira and patronizing the cybercafés on Dakhla Avenue.

Customers come and go. But a small group slowly begins to form around Rahal. Salim, a high school student spellbound by the new virtual world, has two e-mail accounts so far: a Hotmail and a Yahoo. He sometimes comes with his father and at other times with his little sister Lamya. Salim was the first to point out to Rahal that he should have a printer. He always looks for new sources of information on the Internet and needs to print his findings daily, which he uses to brag to his friends at school.

Samira and Fadoua always arrive, sit, and leave together. Their specialty: chat rooms. Together they merge into one virtual personality. They love to chat with young men in Arabic, French, and English. Their handle: *Marrakech Star*. Two in one: like shampoo and conditioner. Qamar ad-Dine al-Sayouti picks on them whenever they show up at the café. Qamar ad-Dine, the son of Shihab ad-Dine al-Sayouti, the most famous of Islamic education teachers at Lycée Zerktouni, and the one the students tell the most jokes about.

"Which of us is the shampoo? And which is the conditioner?" Fadoua asks him.

"To be honest, I am still not sure. When I decide you're the shampoo, I'll let you know."

Qamar ad-Dine knows all the stories of Marrakech Star because Fadoua and Samira always bring their correspondence in English to him so he can explain to them what they don't understand, and correct their answers so that their messages are sent with fewer mistakes.

Qamar ad-Dine's English is good and so is his French. But he always says that his Arabic is unfortunately not so good. He doesn't show any regret as he repeats this confession; on the contrary, a wicked pride appears on his face. Does he say this to spite his father, Shihab ad-Dine, the teacher of Arabic who switched to teaching Islamic education not for love of religion, but out of laziness and a desire to rid himself of grammar and syntax? Islamic education class is for both students of science and those in the humanities. Two hours a week for each group. Many students consider the session a break to be spent on the playing fields in front of the school, or at Rahal's, for those who can afford it, especially because al-Sayouti does not take attendance.

In reality, Qamar ad-Dine doesn't hate his father, but he does hate talking about him. He prefers the company of students not from Lycée Zerktouni, those who know nothing about al-Sayouti, who have never heard the jokes at his father's expense. Fadoua and Samira are exceptions. Despite the fact that they are his father's students, their relationship with Qamar ad-Dine is predicated upon the café and has nothing to do with the institution. He is a handsome young man who speaks different languages well. Therefore their relationship has been a real advantage for Marrakech Star.

Qamar ad-Dine is always available in the café, to the point that Rahal leaves him in charge when he has some errands to run. In exchange Rahal is lenient with him when it comes to payment. Qamar ad-Dine will sometimes pay for three hours and get five. Rahal makes him an unofficial assistant, even though Qamar ad-Dine is not aware of his secret promotion.

Qamar ad-Dine has begun to enjoy the adventures of Marrakech Star and their international e-conquests. This one is serious, that one chaste, and the other shows promise. This one wants to come to Marrakech to visit an eye doctor, and inquires about the best hotel and airlines. The other suggests that she come visit London; he would take care of the flight and she is welcome to stay in his apartment for a week, or even a month—if she can, of course. Another suggests, with suspicious reverence, that she come for a minor pilgrimage to holy Mecca.

When Amelia the Nigerian arrives at the cybercafé, Marrakech Star fades away. Fadoua notices that Qamar ad-Dine is totally distracted whenever she shows up. Sometimes Amelia comes alone. Other times her friend Flora accompanies her. Yakabo always joins them later. Maybe it's a trick so that Rahal won't tell them not to share one computer. The cybercafé's regulations are clear: two people maximum per computer.

No one knows how Yakabo is related to Amelia and Flora. Is he a brother? Some other relative? A lover? With Africans it can be difficult to guess. In any case, they are lucky: apartment owners don't ask them about their documents. They don't scrutinize them as they would Moroccans. Young Moroccan men find it hard to live with their female friends without marriage documents. But with the Africans no one cares. Even if they are Muslims from Mali or Senegal. That's why they live together. They can pile between five and ten people into a small two-bedroom apartment. Qamar ad-Dine doesn't pay attention to these details. He is not in love with Amelia. He is just glad to see her. She makes him happy and her smile delights him, and that's all he can ask for. It is also a chance for him to practice English with her. However, there is another dynamic at play—a somewhat sensitive one. And it is better to keep it to himself, especially in front of Fadoua and Samira.

Qamar ad-Dine wants to leave the country in any way possible. He is tired of Shihab ad-Dine and the boring life he has at home and at school. And even this damned cybercafé he seems to be addicted to. He is fed up with Rahal's snooping. Whenever he looks up he finds him staring at his screen. He is tired of the small talk of history teachers at school. They come in groups to the café, as if they're going to the mosque. They hog the computers and instead of surfing the net they begin to talk as if they're in the teachers' lounge. They say that life under Hassan II was abominable and that the country's conditions have improved a lot with the coming of the new king.

Expanded freedom, new vitality, and initiatives for change. Qamar ad-Dine does not pay attention to the tales of his father's friends. He doesn't see any change at all. Who cares what they think about life under Hassan II? He was a young kid back then. And now he feels he has grown up and that he doesn't want to regress. He doesn't have any time to waste on such conversations.

Qamar ad-Dine longs for another life, the life he sees in movies and on TV. Life as lived by God's chosen people in the north. Qamar ad-Dine wants to escape from here. Emigration is a sacred right. He doesn't want to stay in a place that chokes him with creatures he doesn't like. He doesn't understand why he doesn't have the right to eject this entire boring world from his days and nights, from his life, from his future, and move on.

"Of course I'm Christian. Why do you want to know?" Amelia asks.

"Just an innocent question. Can we talk outside?"

She leaves Flora staring at the screen alone. She apologizes to her in a Nigerian dialect; Qamar ad-Dine only picks up the name Yakabo, which was repeated three times. Outside he invites her to Milano, a café across the street. He discovers she smokes. As soon as Asma the server puts a cup of coffee in front of her, she takes out a pack of cigarettes: Marquise. She lights one and hands the pack to Qamar ad-Dine.

"Thanks, but I don't smoke. I'll be quick. I want to learn about Christianity from you. I mean: I want to know more. I read online about the Holy Trinity and Unitarianism. About Christ's humanity. About the differences between the Eastern Orthodox Church and Catholicism and also between Lutheranism and Anglicanism. I also read the Sermon on the Mount ten times and I learned part of it in Arabic, French, and English," Qamar rambles. "Want proof? Here's a quote: *You have heard that it was said, an eye for an eye and a tooth for a tooth. But I say to you, do not resist an evil person; but whoever slaps you on your right cheek, turn the other to him also . . . and whoever wants to . . . whoever wants to . . .* Wait, I forget. Here's another quote: *You have heard that it was said, you shall love your neighbor and hate your enemy. But I say to you, love your enemies and pray for those who persecute you, that you may be children of your Father in heaven. He causes His sun to rise on the evil and the good, and sends rain on the righteous and the unrighteous.* There is also, *Ask and it will be given to you.* I memorized them. Listen—"

"No! You listen, Qamar—" she interrupts.

"Abd al-Massih, the Servant of Christ . . . My new name is Abd al-Massih . . . You're the first person I've confessed this to. You must keep it between us."

"Listen, Abd al-Massih, there seems to be some confusion here. When I told you I was Christian, I was talking about the family religion. Believe me, I am not as Christian as you imagine. I don't go to church, I don't read the Bible, and I don't know the Sermon on the Mount. I'm Christian and that's all. Take it as it is. Let's get back to the cybercafé, please. Flora is waiting for me."

Qamar ad-Dine is disappointed. His discovery of Christianity is new. He had started with porn sites. And because this son of a bitch who runs the cybercafé was whipping him with his obtrusive looks, Qamar ad-Dine changed gears toward emigration sites. Then he switched to random groups on the Net. Then one day he found himself on the other side following Jesus Christ: *I will follow you wherever you go, and Jesus said to him, the foxes have holes and the birds of the air have nests, but the Son of Man has nowhere to lay his head.*

You're right, teacher, but the Son of Man has nowhere to lay his head.

Qamar ad-Dine was shocked to receive Amelia's cold answer. He is in dire need of someone to support him in these sensitive times of his Internet searches for the truth. Amelia is his angel, his mother in the cybercafé. His mother. His sister. No difference. He finds in her smile the good-heartedness of the saints. But she has disappointed him and that hurts him a lot. Imagine: she doesn't read the holy book and does not know the Sermon on the Mount!

As for Amelia, she was quite shocked as well. Flora and Yakabo had pointed out to her that Qamar ad-Dine is fond of her. Or at least he is very interested in her. Since then she has been watching him too. She finds him handsome and she likes his teasing, joyfulness, and politeness; his good English; his polite way of speaking. Why not? A sweet young man who deserves her attention. Amelia was ready for anything with Qamar ad-Dine. From fervid passion to passing adventure. When he invited her to the café, she joined him without hesitation, happy and enthusiastic. But the silly man had dragged her into a heavy conversation about the Holy Trinity and the Sermon on the Mount. Amelia knows about Qamar ad-Dine's obsession with emigration, but she could not have imagined his craziness would lead him to choose Christianity as an excuse to leave the country.

Besides, her family has been Christian for generations, from grandfathers to fathers and grandmothers to mothers. If following Christ made it possible to emigrate to Europe, she would have done it from Lagos, honored and revered, and would not have had to do it the hard way through the Sahara before she and her companions found themselves stuck in Morocco.

They have succeeded neither in crossing to Spain nor in going back home to face family and friends with their failures after spending their money on a strenuous, long, and senseless journey.

Qamar ad-Dine seems to enjoy playing the role of everybody's friend in the cybercafé. Moving from computer to computer like an e-butterfly: one time with Salim, helping him complete a school report; another time with Fadoua and Samira, translating an e-mail in English they had just received on Hotmail as Marrakech Star. Sometimes he replaces Rahal when he goes out. Other times he whispers with Yakabo after discovering that the Nigerian is more religious than his two friends.

The opposite of Abd al-Massih was Abu Qatadah.

He doesn't speak to anyone. He enters the cybercafé with his right foot, reciting al-Mu'awwidhatayn, the verses of the Koran about refuge. Of course, greeting Muslims is imperative. But Abu Qatadah finds it hard to say assalamu alaikum whenever he enters the cybercafé and finds the two half-naked girls Fadoua and Samira there, and between them that procurer unjustly and falsely named Qamar ad-Dine, *the moon of faith.*

"What Qamar ad-Dine? Qamar of shit, indeed. Qamar of grief, not Qamar ad-Dine. God curse his birth."

As for the Africans, Abu Qatadah is keen on staying away from them.

It is true that there is no preference for Arabs over non-Arabs. Neither is there preference for white people over black people. Preference is only through righteousness. Yet to Abu Qatadah, the faces of the Africans do not convey any prudence or righteousness. Not because they are black, God forbid! Bilal, the prophet's muezzin, was a black man of Ethiopian origin who had been endowed by Islam with a respected status to a point where the Prophet Muhammad called him a *man of paradise* and said about him: *The muezzins will have the longest necks of the people on the Day of Resurrection.* Abu Qatadah noticed Yakabo's neck is long and thin like that of a giraffe. But his dark face is a long way from emanating the light of Islam, and the same is true for the two ugly girls who barely leave his side. They look like a pair of goats. Curse all three of them!

His name is actually Mahjoub Didi. He's an employee at RADEEMA, the electricity and water authority, and married with two children. What disturbs him more is a burdensome colleague singing to him, "*Didi didi didi didi didi.*" His rudeness caused his friends to avoid humming Cheb Khaled's famous song in front of him, but they still joke about it in his absence. As for the nickname Abu Qatadah, it was coined by one of the brothers, God bless him, in a fragrant *dhikr* ceremony. Since then, his name in divine gatherings and on luminous websites has been

Abu Qatadah, as a good omen of the sublime *sahabi* (a companion of the prophet) Abu Qatadah al-Ansari al-Khazraji, may God be pleased with him.

"Big Brother is watching you!"

Qamar ad-Dine repeats this from time to time, mocking Rahal.

"So sorry. I mean *Little* Brother is watching you!"

The entire cybercafé shakes with laughter.

One must acknowledge that Rahal's English is below average. As for his knowledge of English literature, it is no more than Amelia's knowledge of Imam Malik School. In any case, Rahal is a student of Arabic literature, his specialty being ancient poetry—the hanging poetry of the Jahiliyyah, Umayyad, Andalusian, and Moroccan periods. As for novels, he doesn't read them in Arabic, which he is very good at, so how could he read them in other languages?

And because no one ever explained to him the reference to the famous novel by George Orwell, where Big Brother is watching everybody, he has always wondered why Qamar ad-Dine brags about his brothers, the small and the big, despite the fact that he has only one sister, a graduate student in Rabat.

"Little Brother is watching you!"

Qamar ad-Dine's innuendos do not bother Rahal. But Qamar ad-Dine often gripes about the way Rahal violates his customers' privacy, having no shame fixing his mouse-like eyes on their computer screens. In the first stage of Qamar ad-Dine's virtual life, when he was addicted to porn websites, this bothered him a lot. Even today, he hates it when someone snoops on him. So he began to avoid sites with pictures of churches, icons, and other religious imagery. Most often he copies the text and pastes it on a blank page, then he takes his time reading it in Word. And when he finishes, he moves the file to the trash bin and signs out.

But in Rahal's kingdom there are no trash bins. As soon as the last customer leaves the cybercafé after midnight, Rahal takes a few minutes, sometimes even an hour, to clean up the computers. He checks them one by one, rummaging through the hard drives and discovering the secrets of the customers' digital worlds. Many leave their e-mail accounts and forum memberships open. Brother Abu Qatadah, for example, right after he hears the call to prayer, closes the site and leaves, yet the blog remains open, along with any discussions between the brothers. Sometimes it's about the duty to fight and sacrifice the self if an occupier reaches a Muslim land; other times about using electoral fraud to win government office. Often the discussions are heated—and they almost always involve the topic of elections.

The brothers object to the heresy of the candidates' self-promotion and to the idea that all members of society have equal voices no matter what their degree of learning and piety is. As for Abd al-Massih's courses and his chapters of Holy Scripture, Rahal retrieves them from the trash and copies the Arabic versions to his private computer so he can take his time reading them the following day.

Of course, this takes some extra effort on Rahal's part before closing, but he is the one who signed up the customers in the first place. He records all their usernames, real or pseudonymous, and their passwords as well. No secrets. Rahal knows everything about the subjects of his happy cyberkingdom. Even the Nigerian community in Ashbal al-Atlas Cybercafé—their secrets have been revealed to Rahal since they moved to the electronic sphere. Amelia and Flora are lesbians. Amelia is crazy in love with Flora, but they sell themselves to men while they wait to enter the prominent and growing underground gay community in Marrakech. Yakabo works for them as an escort, bodyguard, and pimp. His relationship with Flora is for cover, silly Qamar ad-Dine. Only for cover, you fool.

Indeed, Rahal. You see them move like puppets in front of

your eyes. They do not know how close your hand is to them at all times: their real names and pseudonyms, innocent virtual friendships as well as illicit adventures. You've got them, Rahal, but you have to be smart. Be very cautious and conceal these secrets; keep them to yourself, you little weasel. Otherwise, if Abu Qatadah learns that Qamar ad-Dine has deviated from Islam, converted to Christianity, and changed his name, or that the Nigerian girls are sapphic sex workers, he might declare holy war right now in the middle of your cybercafé. And so Rahal enjoys spying on the members of his new family—and at the same time remains devoted to providing everyone with the illusion of safety. Indeed, here they are at home and in the hands of their happy families here in these virtual jungles of Ashbal al-Atlas Cybercafé.

But Rahal made a critical mistake by entrusting Abu Qatadah with Abd al-Massih.

Whenever Rahal has to run an errand, he reminds Abd al-Massih to take great care with Abu Qatadah: "Your brother Mahjoub Didi is a jackass and is easily confused when it comes to computers. Therefore remember, Qamar ad-Dine, that if you leave him alone he'll become irritated, and then the cybercafé will lose money waiting for me to reconnect him with his brothers in God. So please treat him as a valued customer."

Abd el-Massih has always volunteered to help Abu Qatadah. The last time, after Didi's computer crashed, he willingly gave him his favorite PC in the café. He did not know that he had made the mistake of a lifetime.

Abu Qatadah could not betray his brother in God, Shihab ad-Dine al-Sayouti. They go to el-Massira Mosque together and a strong trust and friendship has grown between them. So how could he learn of such a bad secret and not inform his brother? It would be a big betrayal. And Abu Qatadah would never betray Shihab ad-Dine. And so he informed him of exactly what he saw.

"Your son was having a discussion with Gerges the Copt as if they were, God forbid, of the same religion. Qamar ad-Dine was calling him Brother Gerges, and in return the Egyptian called him Brother Abd al-Massih. Then the enemy of God—the Copt—wrote to him a verse, which seems to be from the book they call holy. We know how falsified it is and full of deviations: *For even as we have many members in one body, and all the members don't have the same function, so we, who are many, are one body in Christ, and individually members one of another.* At this point, my dear friend, the muezzin announced the prayer and I brought the news straight to you. As I ran I repeated the supplication reported by Aisha, God be pleased with her, which the prophet had made: *O Controller of the hearts, make my heart steadfast in your religion.*"

It happens like this: Shihab ad-Dine does not wait for the prayer, believing he has broken his *wudu'*, or ablution. He leaves the mosque and hurries toward the cybercafé. Rahal has returned and Abd al-Massih is going over receipts when Shihab ad-Dine enters in a state no one has ever seen him in before: he's panting and shaking as if he ran all the way there. Abd al-Massih does not understand what is going on when Shihab ad-Dine jumps on him, drops him to the ground, and begins to kick him. No, he is not kicking him—he's trying to, but he doesn't know how. Now he's biting him—tries to bite again, but his teeth fail him. He pulls his son's hair. He pulls it with both hands, then he lets go of it, drags him violently, and smashes his head on the ground, howling like a wounded wolf, the blood boiling in his veins. He slaps his son's face, then screams: "A Christian, you dog! A Christian, you apostate! When you finished high school but decided against college, we thought you had a different way of looking at life and the future, and we let you be. When you quit the mosque we said, *You are inexperienced but you'll wise up*, and we neglected you. Since you've been living in this infected hole, we've thought, *Let him discover the world*, and we did not watch or question you. And the result? Now you are Christian, you dog. If you were gay and the fornicators fiddled around with your ass, we could pray for your protection. If you doubted God, we could say even Abraham became troubled, doubted, questioned, and then his heart became peaceful, so we would pray that you be guided on the right path. But a Christian, you dog, a Nazarene, as if God Almighty did not choose this nation and from it the last prophet!"

Many did not understand what really happened that night.

The ambulance would take Shihab ad-Dine, who had a severe nervous breakdown, to the hospital. Qamar ad-Dine spent the night in the cybercafé since he couldn't face his mother after this shameful news. As for Mahjoub Didi, didn't visit the cybercafé for more than a month. Is he afraid of Qamar ad-Dine or Rahal? But then, when he suddenly returns one evening, no one talks to him, nor does he talk to anyone else.

"You're a good person, Marrakech Star."

Fadoua and Samira insist on visiting Shihab ad-Dine at the clinic. Salim and his sister accompany them. Rahal apologizes. But what the two girls did not expect was that Yakabo, the Nigerian with the giraffe-like neck, would insist on accompanying them to visit al-Sayouti. His insistence seemed strange at first, especially since the group consisted only of the teacher's former students, but with Yakabo, no one is sure of anything. What should have been a quick ten-minute visit for them to check on the teacher and then leave lasts exactly two hours, enough time for them to deplete the stockpile of juices that visitors have left near Shihab ad-Dine's bed over the previous two days.

Fadoua speaks first, saying that she can't believe what was said about Qamar ad-Dine, especially since it came from Mahjoub.

"Everyone in the cybercafé knows that Mahjoub hates Qamar ad-Dine, despite the fact that your son never hesitated for a minute to help him whenever he had an issue. But Mahjoub's heart is full of hatred. He hates everyone in the cybercafé, especially Qamar ad-Dine. I am afraid he has fed you some false information."

Yakabo jumps in. His French is confused, but not his thoughts; they are clear, and his assertion makes al-Sayouti sit up in his bed. "Monsieur al-Sayouti, there is some truth to what Mahjoub said. Your son Qamar ad-Dine is fascinated by the idea of emigration and wants to leave the country at any cost. He stupidly thought that claiming to be Christian would make it easier for him to move to Europe. He asked me many times about this matter. He might have used a Christian pseudonym to get in touch with those he imagined could help him achieve his goal. Later he began to talk about Georgia. I don't know who pointed him in this direction. Maybe because many Egyptian Copts indeed began to emigrate there. This does not mean that Qamar ad-Dine has converted to Christianity. Never . . . this is impossible.

"First of all, for your son to become Christian, he has to first be baptized. Jesus himself was baptized. John the Baptist performed the ceremony on him in the Jordan River. I know that no priest immersed Qamar ad-Dine in water, nor sprinkled him with holy water in the name of the Father, the Son and the Holy Spirit. Before baptism, the church chooses new parents who agree to adopt him. He would take their family name, and they would choose a new first name for him. Nothing of this happened with Qamar ad-Dine. You're his only father before God, the angels, the saints, the mosque, the church, and the whole world. As for the name Abd al-Massih that Mahjoub mentioned, this is just one of the many pseudonyms we all use online. Your son is reckless, sir, but he is not a Christian. To be Christian, one has to practice the ritual of confession, and your son did not confess anything, neither to a priest nor to anyone else. There is no confession, only this misleading defamation from Mahjoub Didi, and it is unfortunate that you blindly believed him. But don't worry: Fadoua, Samira, and I will be back tomorrow to visit, and we'll bring Qamar ad-Dine with us and you'll hug each other. Tomorrow morning. Tomorrow morning, Monsieur Shihab ad-Dine."

Shihab ad-Dine begins to shake, touched to his core. The big cloud hanging over him dissipates in front of his eyes. He doesn't know how to answer this thin, long-necked African. He wishes he were able to hug him—even before hugging his son when he comes to visit tomorrow. Al-Sayouti looks completely baffled. Confused. But deep inside he's very happy. A befuddled happiness he doesn't know how to express. He finds a few extra juice boxes and offers them to the group: "Have some more, friends . . . drink some more juice."

Zou-l3izah@hotmail.com. The e-mail address is strange, a reference to one of God's ninety-nine names. As for the subject line of the message, it appears between ellipses: . . . *the reminder* . . .

"And remind, for indeed, the reminder benefits the believers. Allah the Magnificent is truthful. But go ahead and open the e-mail, Abu Qatadah."

His hand trembles. He doesn't know why or how, but it trembles. And from the first sentence he understands that the affair is significant:

> *My good servant Mahjoub, son of Yamna, known as Abu Qatadah al-Marrakechi, my greetings come to you and my eyes protect you, then . . .*
>
> *Don't wonder about this message to you, and don't regard it as too much that God the Almighty has favored you with an e-mail instead of the others. I have matters the servants don't see; therefore, ask for my forgiveness and seek protection in me from the wicked Satan.*

Oh, good servant, we have sealed the messages with the Holy Koran and a faithful prophet, and made him our clemency to everyone. However, man was the most argumentative. That is why I have chosen you, Mahjoub, among a group of my good servants, to hoist my banner and remind them of my message and seek my pardon, for I am merciful.

Mahjoub's face turns pale. He thinks about the Prophet Muhammad (God's blessing and peace be upon him), the best of mankind, and how panic-stricken he must have felt when he received the revelation.

It is not a revelation, O Abu Qatadah. You are not a prophet to reveal to. Muhammad Ibn Abdallah was the last prophet and messenger. Yet your God has endowed and chosen you instead of the other living creatures for this e-mail. Well, what are you doing here? Leave this right away and go home. Pray and seek forgiveness and wait for the order of the Almighty.

Mahjoub's mind has been abducted. But he holds his head high as he moves deliberately out of the café, as if he were walking on clouds like a somnambulist. He doesn't look toward Rahal, nor does he think about paying him.

Abu Qatadah isn't here. He is fully absorbed and oblivious. He's almost blind.

Abu Qatadah disappears for three whole days. When he returns he doesn't bother to greet or even look at anyone. He rushes to the first available computer he sees and signs on to his e-mail. But when his inbox loads, he's disappointed—as if he hasn't found what he expected. Rahal watches him with amusement. He doesn't understand what's going on with Abu Qatadah. Mahjoub remains fixed in front of the screen for more than ten minutes. He doesn't even try to move the mouse. He's as motionless as an idol. Suddenly his features relax, his face lights up, and he whoops: "Allahu Akbar, Allahu Akbar!"

Amelia, Flora, and Yakabo look at each other. Salim and his sister glance from him to Rahal, who remains surprised. As for Qamar ad-Dine, he's busy with his computer, deep into whatever he's doing. Qamar ad-Dine has completely avoided Mahjoub since he snitched on him to his father.

The message doesn't come directly from the Almighty this time, but rather from an angel who doesn't mention his name. According to the e-mail, his position in the All-Merciful's group of angels is 8,723, and his e-mail address is *Malak8723@hotmail.com*. The orders of the angel are very specific:

> *Go to the nearest carpenter and convince him to make you a wooden sword. Buy new white clothes: a garment, turban, and slippers. Even the socks and underwear should be white. Purify yourself with reading the Koran, fasting, and praying. Start your fasting tomorrow and keep it up until God realizes something is taking effect. Stop by the cybercafé every three days to check your e-mail. We will let you know the next step in due time. May God protect you and guide your steps. Amen.*

Every three days, Abu Qatadah visits the cybercafé, but in vain, only spending a few minutes there each time. At the café, the rumor is that he has stopped going to work. Rahal confirms to the other patrons that he has lost his mind.

Mahjoub dissociates himself from the maddening crowd, fully devoting himself to fasting, praying, and reciting the Koran in preparation for the holy e-mail. After more than a full month has passed, exclamations of "God is great!" can be loudly heard in Ashbal al-Atlas for a second time. Mahjoub is transfixed in front of the computer when the prophesied message pops up. Angel 8,723 finally appears, once again with extremely detailed instructions:

First, thank God for what He has predicted for us. Abu Qatadah, go to Jemaa el-Fnaa next Friday afternoon. Wear your new white clothes and unsheathe your wooden sword and carry your Koran under your arm. Once you are in the center, good servant, take out your Koran and pull out your sword and start shouting, "Allahu Akbar, Allahu Akbar!" Then the miracle shall happen, God willing. Your wooden sword will be sharp and will cut ten heads; your Koran pages will turn into wings of light and will carry you slowly and become one of the winged horses of paradise. The blessed horse will fly high in the square and you will begin to reap the heads left and right. Your sword will harm only the indecent infidels and their careless hypocritical followers, but the righteous believers will not be hurt, God willing. This is your mission, message, and miracle, you good servant. Get to the holy war. See you Friday afternoon.

"Allahu Akbar, Allahu Akbar!" Mahjoub exclaims as he leaves the cybercafé.

Rahal laughs his head off. "It's really happening: angels are calling the prayer up his ass! Check on Mahjoub, people. He's really lost it."

We can divide the youth of Hay el-Massira into two types: the locals and the newcomers. The latter are the ones who came to live in the neighborhood from the Old Medina, and who retain deep links to their original neighborhoods. Their families and childhood friends still live there, and it is normal that they stay in touch with them. As for the locals, they are the true neighborhood people, born and raised there in the late eighties and nineties. They only know Hay el-Massira. Some of the locals may leave their neighborhood for Daoudiate, where Cadi Ayyad University is, or Gueliz, where the cafes, restaurants, hotels, bars, and cinemas are, but they always return to the warm bosom of Hay el-Massira, while their experience of al-Moravid, al-Mohad, and al-Saadi Marrakech remains quite limited. They are not the crazy tourists who go to Jemaa el-Fnaa to take pictures of monkeys and snakes.

This time you have no choice, Qamar ad-Dine. You have to go. You need to be on-site to follow the last episode of the series. You have to be in the heart of the event.

Qamar ad-Dine arrives before ten. He crosses the huge Arset el-Bilk. The barouches are lined up next to the garden in perfect order, even the horses are well disciplined, calm, and barely moving. Maybe they anticipated a long day of wandering the streets of Marrakech, so they are saving their energy. The barouches' owners are crowded in small groups around teapots and small plates of *bissara*, dried fava bean soup with olive oil. Qamar ad-Dine crosses the square, which is still empty of visitors and entertainers. He orders orange juice from one of the carts spread around its perimeter. The juice refreshes him. He walks around for a while, then goes up to the Argana Café. He orders a cup of coffee and he lingers upstairs, surveying the square from above. White clothes are not strange on Fridays. That is why Qamar ad-Dine doesn't notice Abu Qatadah at first. But when hysterical screaming breaks out in the heart of the square, as people crowd around a crazy person brandishing the Koran and a wooden sword while shouting, "Allahu Akbar, Allahu Akbar!" and threatening the enemies of God as infidels and hypocrites, Qamar ad-Dine rises to his feet as if he has been stung by a snake. He forgets to pay for his coffee. He runs downstairs and into the square to take a photo of his hero—no, Qamar ad-Dine, this is not the Mahjoub Didi you know. He has lost a lot of weight and his face looks stressed and pale, as if he hasn't slept in days. The man is truly crazy, his eyes cloudy and distant, staring at the people in front of him without seeing them. "God is great!"

he repeats, before continuing to rant and rave. Qamar ad-Dine distinguishes the words *God the Almighty*, *Gabriel*, *Michael*, and *angel 8,723*. Mahjoub announces the angel's number in French as if he were talking to his colleagues at work about an electricity or water meter. No, Qamar ad-Dine, the man has gone far beyond the role you laid out for him.

Qamar ad-Dine panics. He wants to punish Mahjoub for his defamation with this trick. Perhaps pull his ear—no more and no less—but the man has lost it, Qamar ad-Dine. The man has lost it.

The police surround the square. It's difficult to disperse the crowd. Visitors are enjoying the show, entertainment being the reason they come here in the morning and evening in the first place. And this is exceptional entertainment, unmatched by any of the *halqas* of dancers and storytellers. Fresh like the orange juice one gets from the carts around the square. Two journalists show up and begin to take pictures of the crazy man as he is arrested.

When Qamar ad-Dine walks past el-Massira Mosque on his way to the cybercafé, he hears Mr. Belafqih deliver the sermon. His brain is frazzled and he doesn't pay it any attention. He thinks, *They are all there listening in reverence: al-Sayouti, the teachers of Lycée Zerktouni, and Salim, who goes to the mosque only on Fridays. But Mahjoub Didi was not among them. For the first time Abu Qatadah has missed Friday prayer in the neighborhood mosque.*

A tear runs down Qamar ad-Dine's cheek. He thinks about going into the mosque to pray and seek forgiveness from God, but he can't. So he proceeds toward the cybercafé. His face is pale and he feels weary. He tries to ignore everyone inside and bury himself in the first available PC. But the entire gang is there, crowded around one computer. Even the three Africans are among them.

"Come here, Qamar ad-Dine," Samira calls out. "Come see the scandal!"

They are gathered around Rahal, watching a live video on *Marrakech Press*: a crazy Salafi is assaulting Jemaa el-Fnaa and terrorizing the tourists.

Translated from Arabic by Mbarek Sryfi

A TWISTED SOUL

BY KARIMA NADIR

Amerchich

I don't really know if I discovered life's pleasures early on. Certainly I found the route to death ahead of time. I smoked my first cigarette on the roof of my friend Latifa's house. We used to call her M'kirita, after the small cake glazed in honey, because she was so tiny for her age, with her pale chestnut hair and her hazelnut eyes. She lived in Mellah and was three years older than me; I was fourteen then. We bought five Marlboros, glancing around the whole time to make sure we hadn't been spotted, and went up to the roof. It was autumn. We hid ourselves in an isolated corner and smoked, keeping keen eyes on the front door from above, so that we'd see when Latifa's mother came home. The first drag of that first cigarette tasted like victory; of whom, over whom, I don't know.

A year later, in the same corner, we smoked a joint I'd been given by my comrade Fattah. He was an undergraduate and I was a freshman in high school. After smoking half of it we stretched out on our backs, Latifa and I on the roof, laughing at anything and everything—until the laughter broke its hold over us a little and we let it go. We were writhing and squirming as though the very rays of the sun were tickling us. I didn't become a true smoker until after I gave birth, but from the first time I tried hash I experienced a profound kind of pleasure. Later I would smoke what Fattah gave me in installments: making, for every two drags, an attempt at poetry.

My son Selim, who is now seven years old, lives in Marrakech.

I had him out of wedlock and in, so I thought, love. His father was a leftist—I adored his idealism: dreams of revolution, the cares of the proletariat, the Palestinian question, Guevara. I was a law school student back then, and had joined an organization on the far left. And since I loved poetry and literature and music, I turned easily into a dense bundle of romantic revolutionary attitudes. A year and a half into our relationship, I discovered I was pregnant. That revolutionary romance rendered abortion impossible: if I stole the right of this creature to life, I could never return to all those slogans I had recited so proudly, to myself and others, like sacred texts. I didn't expect my partisan to evade his part of the responsibility—not he, who preached life as unending struggle! I had believed that in accordance with the ethics of the revolutionary, he would take a position of immediate gallantry. Instead he made it clear, over the phone, that this could not happen. He was not sure, indeed—he who mere seconds before had been glorifying my loyalty as his comrade—that he even had anything to do with my pregnancy, and said that I should call the real father. I resolved without hesitation to consider him dead. I would preserve his life for his successor.

One doesn't picture a woman of nineteen carrying a child. She hides it away, after all, in her womb from her powerful mother, her conservative grandmother, in a society governed more by custom than law. All that matters is: *What will the neighbors say? Hashouma!* Shame! Still, I confronted my mother with it, but only after the end of the sixth month of a pregnancy that had been almost invisible. My body had barely changed and there was no sign of that telltale round belly below my breasts. I told my mother, and I convinced my sister, that I was prepared for everything required to raise a child. I made them both understand that if they tried to dissuade me, I would leave home at once and take refuge with a friend.

At that time I was working as a waitress in one of the guesthouses that had sprung up like mushrooms in the alleys of the Old Medina. The pay was low. But I was also giving lessons in French and English at a private school, and the salaries combined were enough to get by on, even with a child. I was determined to do this, as I had never been determined about anything in my life; I even seriously considered ending my studies. My mother only said, *This is God's will, and we'll pay for it.* My sister was silent—a speaking silence.

He visited me once, my partisan comrade, when I was three months pregnant. He called ahead to tell me he was at the Café de France in Jemaa el-Fnaa. I went to meet him still clutching a shred of hope, trying to tell myself he had been rash, that he regretted it. It doesn't matter now. We drank our black coffee in near silence and then I took him to the Koutoubia Mosque. We smoked hash in the garden there and talked about mundane things, each of us evading a direct glance at the other, trying to dodge any mention of the pregnancy. When lunchtime came we went to Babylon Star Bar in Gueliz, not far from the Dawiya Bar. Babylon Star was one of those places that was difficult to comprehend—exactly what the situation required.

While I was on my fourth beer, I asked him drily, and without preamble: "Why did you come?" Later, upon leaving the bar, I realized I was stronger than this faltering comrade, who had stuttered as he searched for reasons to convince me to get rid of it, with, as he called it, a simple procedure. *He'll be biting his nails for years*, I thought. Life would rattle and batter him, and guilt would deprive him of sleep.

During the months before the birth we slipped back into harmony with Marrakech, my fetus and I. I abandoned drinking and hash, and swapped my cafés for walking. Long, pondering walks. I wandered through Mowqaf Alley and Mouassine, Ksour and Riad Zitoun, and the little mass inside me each day came closer to life. I spoke to it a lot, telling it of my childhood and my adolescence, unfolding my dreams and desires. Once, as I passed by Arset el-Houta, memories of a spring day in 2000 came back to me like a dream. I'd snuck away from middle school that day, just for a while, with Yusuf, Ahmed, Fawzi, Hisham, and Said. I had always made friends with boys, they were better company. We took a trip to the Old Medina and ambled through its damp narrow alleys, shirking the sun that had dared to encroach on our spring. The smell of sewage was overpowering on the streets of Mellah, long since abandoned by its Jewish residents. And from Jinan Binshaqra we took the shortcut to Arset el-Houta, passing through Ba Ahmed Middle School and al-Farabi High School and the carpentry shops. In the midst of the vendors who rule the rest of that narrow space, we squeezed into an alley barely wide enough to fit a person. Fawzi pushed the door of one of the houses open and went in without knocking. Said and Hisham and the others followed. I wanted to go too, but Ahmed asked me to wait for them awhile, or to go back. This place was just for men.

They called the place Madam Kabora's house, and would be received there in succession, to put their little pricks between the thighs of prostitutes their mothers' ages in exchange for the dirhams extracted from them beforehand. I grew bored of waiting outside, so I went up. I found myself in a small hallway. There was a dirty table with a radio on it tuned to Radio Rabat, and I was taking in the vulgarity of the place when a voice, more vulgar still, addressed me: "What d'you want?"

I turned to see an obese woman waiting behind me, swathed in a kaftan and scarves. Her fingers were bare aside from a large gold ring. Unnerved, I approached the massive creature. I sat down beside her and told her, in a confused way, that I had come with my friends, and that I had to wait for them because I didn't know the way back. In fact I was burning with curiosity. What was this place? Where were the boys? She said her name was Kabora and poured me a glass of tea. Without further introductions, and as naturally as if she were speaking with a grown woman, she began telling me about the troublesome police and the various other hardships of her life. I didn't understand everything she said and I was baffled by that gruff voice, vibrating on like a tambourine.

After a few minutes the boys came running down. I smiled at Kabora and watched them without a word. They turned to me, perplexed. "What are you doing!?" they asked as one.

Cheerfully, I answered. "I met Kabora!"

Four years later, Hisham, my boyfriend through college, would tell me stories about Kabora, who lived next to his grandfather in Arset el-Houta. His aunt Safia hated her, claiming she brought disgrace to the whole neighborhood. He told me that Kabora housed girls from the Atlas Mountains and from Agadir and Safi, giving them food, shelter, and clothing, and putting them to work as prostitutes. Hisham also said he heard his father once tell his mother that Kabora had inherited the brothel from a glamorous aunt of hers who had, in the 1930s, been a concubine of Pasha el-Glaoui.

There were so many places I missed. As a child my father would take me around the ancient city on the back of his motorbike. I then infiltrated many of these places as a teenager, driven by a passion for discovery. The Sirsar Inn! I had heard my father telling my uncle its history. It had been a garage for cattle and trucks before it was sold by the guard employed by Sirsar's son, Moulay Walid. The guard sold off the inn piece by piece for bottles of red wine and hash. Other times for dinner, or for someone to share his bed. After that, the place was colonized by carpentry workshops, metalworkers, bone carvers. Since most of the workmen were from another district, after using the workshops in the daytime they would often sleep there at night. Some of them married and had children, so the tight space grew even tighter and the inn gained another floor, creating conditions that perfectly defined the word *slum*. Cafés and grocery shops sprung up too. At six years old, I would travel with my father through the winding corridors of its lower level, dug out in all directions like dancing snakes, trailing behind him until we heard the sounds from the workshop growing louder.

Mr. Alal would always sit in a chair in front of his shop, his body draped in brown trousers, hands covered by the sleeves of a woolen robe that reached his knees. Mr. Alal had been a carpentry teacher. But after years of work, piling one rial on top of another, he got together enough to buy two more shops in the building. And then there were his two sons, who worked under his supervision. But his hands stayed perpetually busy, whether filling smoking pipes from a baggie or preparing a *mashmouma*, or bong. My father jokingly nicknamed him *The Machine*. Mr. Alal would greet us from his seat in his hoarse voice and would gesture at one of his sons to bring two chairs. We would sit, my father and I, in front of the shop and pull out a low wooden drum, upon which they would place the requisite teapot, a pack of Pall Mall cigarettes, and spare pipes. My father was always telling me what a healthy weed kif was for adults.

Mr. Alal was a round-faced man, thin, dark-skinned, with a thick beard, shaggy black hair, and bulging eyes. Pouring us tea, he would get up to call for donuts from Café Rubio in the alley. Inside the shop thrummed the harmonious rhythms of sawmill and hammer, along with music from the radio. It remains anchored in my memory like a first love, emerging and living still inside me years later: *The leaf enchants its blowing* or *Tonight wine and desires sing around us / A sail that swims in the light watches over our shade*—how could my young self have known the meaning of such lines? But I loved those songs. I was as used to hearing them as I was to smelling the smoke from that salutary plant.

Long walks were good for long musings. I shared with my fetus these thoughts and memories, as we also shared the smells and sights and rhythms of Marrakech.

Selim turned two. I had nursed him throughout, even though my nipples were flat; I bought artificial rubber tips from the pharmacy. What an invention! Every time I attached them and contemplated the sight, I burst out laughing. And when Selim was teething we stayed up watching television to drown out his cries.

After a long discussion with my sister, I decided to leave my mother's house. I would try to rebuild from the rubble accumulating inside me, to start afresh. To fashion a character and a life that might be suitable for motherhood: I wanted the child to be proud of me one day. But for now he would stay with my sister. She had a job, a tough one, and a house and car; independent and strong, she lived alone. The idea was hers from the beginning. She was wiser than me, and so much more patient. I left my son in her care, and though I did feel cowardly and selfish, I could already taste the breeze of freedom. It wasn't hardness of heart—or was it? I thought I had a reason to live, a reason to challenge the world, to prove to everyone and to myself that I was worthy of respect, to return to give my son a life of pure light. Perhaps that was true. Perhaps these are excuses, attempts to tint the blackness of my memory, or to deny the things I can't bear to face. Perhaps.

My friend Boushra got me a job in the Mamounia Casino and I moved with her into a small flat in Saada, on the road to Casablanca. Those new districts bore little trace of the city aside from the accents of some of their inhabitants, most of whom actually came from other cities or countries. The world took on new colors, as if I were in a city other than the one I grew up in. I worked nights, sometimes both days and nights. And along Red Beach, a kilometer outside of Marrakech, I was introduced to a vampire people. They gambled with their lives. I saw gay men and lesbians walking around unmolested, high-class sex workers on the lookout for dollars, euros, rials, dinars, and winning tickets, fluent in every language. I saw a people driven by desire, pleasure, money, adrenaline. And I saw the dregs upon whom the rich wiped their feet, and their other things. Climbers awaiting their prey, screwing whomever had anything to offer. In that period, I became friends with DJ Anas. From time to time I would go to his club, Theatro Marrakech, heading directly for the sound booth. I'd sit with him and watch from behind the glass while we smoked hash. I looked out upon that world with perfect neutrality as the DJ wrote the fates of its bodies in music.

A year passed and I grew bored, weighed down under a rhythm that stretched without a horizon. I was tired. And I needed to figure out what I wanted to be. In the past I had always imagined for myself another character, creative and distinguished, and yet here I was, locked into a repeating scene, the lights dimmed. I decided to go back to my studies, though my desire for that soon started to suffocate me. Even so, it didn't take too much preparation. I moved to Casablanca after I'd figured out a living situation with Salma, another friend from those days of revolutionary dreaming. Soon after I arrived I found work in a translation agency. Not much pay, but enough to cover rent and food and cigarettes.

It was hard to get used to the new rhythm, and I waited anxiously for the beginning of the semester, when I would register to begin my BA in English literature. One ordinary weeknight I passed by Mohammed V Street and had a beer in a bar called Petit Poucet, in the courtyard of one of those colonial buildings that had always felt strangely familiar to me. It just so happened that a literary group was meeting that night to honor a Moroccan poet, dead of course. I was enchanted by the scene, the atmosphere—especially because they'd brought along an old-timer to sing Umm Kulthum and Mohammed Abdel Wahab in his husky voice, and to play on an oud, worn out from so many nights like these.

And I met him. A dream made real, a love story I will never

be able to write. I knew him before I knew him. Of course this sounds absurdly romantic, but it could not be closer to the truth; it's certainly truer than anything else I've known. I had never thought that I could make a man the focus of my whole world. And Samir was the older brother of my old partisan comrade, unacknowledged by his father. What a world! Love at first sight, or rather the second. That hadn't been the season for love. But this new evening gave us an excuse to begin the tale.

A week later I moved in with him, as if by prior agreement from long ago; as though he'd been waiting for me. We were married with uncanny speed. There was no need to wait, to get to know each other. We soon learned what the other liked and disliked. I was dynamic, eager, quick to yearn and to love. I loved to immerse myself in him. Samir was sober, a lover of life, a rationalist—sometimes more than was necessary. He had a lot of experience with women, as I had with men. We were brought together by something I'd read about in romance novels, and which until I met him I thought was just ink on paper. Perhaps our story was not that surprising. I really don't know.

My name is Sara. I'm thirty-two years old. I'm getting my doctoral degree in social sciences at the University of Chicago on a scholarship. The story above is not my own.

Alice, a friend of mine, was a resident doctor at Amerchich Hospital, an institution that resembled nothing so much as a prison. All patients who were considered a danger to others were taken to Amerchich, to this secret medical facility in what had once been the suburbs, but which had quickly become central once the Cadi Ayyad University was built in the seventies, not far from the building. A dirty and ancient hospital. There was a special wing there for mentally ill patients, and another for skin disease; internal injuries were covered too. And so it wasn't uncommon for the newspapers to report, every now and then, news of the suicide of one of its inhabitants. Alice specialized in mental illnesses, and so she found herself there, at the Amerchich hospital in Daoudite. Her parents were French but she was Marrakechi through and through.

I had made a habit of visiting her there over the last three years, whenever I came to the city. And one day I met Iman for the first time. Alice was making her daily rounds with the patients. She walked among the dried-up trees in the garden, greeting the lost souls there, people who would talk to themselves all night in a fog of questions and names and images. It was winter and there was a light rain. Our Gauloises cigarettes burned out fast; I shared mine with the wind. And that day in the garden I saw Iman. As if she had stepped out of an old film. Everything was bleak. She appeared to me between the trees like some dreadful corpse: body frail, back bent. She was dressed in a long black coat and her movements were slack. I could hear her humming an old Oriental tune, a classic, one of those songs that you think you don't recognize until you realize that of course you know it well. When she turned, I stopped still. Her face was a pirate's map, its length and width scarred in grooves scraped down to the muscle. When she saw me and realized my terror, she turned her face away quickly, groping at it as if reminded of its horrors. Then she hurried away.

I felt guilty, my stomach prickling. I knew this was nothing I hadn't encountered before, and yet I'd been unable to keep myself from feeling fear and disgust. "Wait! Please wait!" She stopped but did not turn around. I paused two paces behind her. "What's your name?" I asked hesitantly.

She was silent a moment. "Iman," she eventually replied, in a whisper. As if she weren't quite sure.

I stepped closer to her. She was hanging her head like she wanted to bury it in her chest.

She asked for a cigarette and I fumbled for the pack in my pocket.

"Gauloises," she muttered. "Taste like burning hay." Then

she smiled. I tried to avoid eye contact, gazing over her head so as not to unsettle her. She smoked her cigarette away from my prying eyes, sitting at the foot of some stairs that led to a door that looked like it hadn't been opened in a while. She took out a handkerchief from her pocket and laid it beside her. I stood in place for a second before I understood that it was for me, an invitation to sit with her. Something in her voice transported me to Tchaikovsky and *Swan Lake*. Something in her silence and her hesitation rendered me numb.

With some urging, Alice would tell me Iman's story. I didn't believe it at first. I thought my friend the doctor was trying to tease me—to titillate me, as a reader of novels, as a social scientist. But it was true. Iman had lost her memory. She didn't know who she was. Her relatives did, but she wouldn't put up with their visits, so her sister seldom came. She'd just sit with her a little while and then be off. They had brought her to the sanatorium seven years ago, when she was in a bad way. She cried all the time and wouldn't speak. The scars on her face had just healed. Often she stayed huddled in her bed, face to the wall. She tried to kill herself several times, but as Alice said: "Death keeps postponing her."

Alice knew Iman well. "She speaks very elegant French," she told me. "But her English is immaculate—you'd think she'd spent years in the UK."

Of all the sanatorium inhabitants, Alice was closest to Iman, to the extent that she almost no longer considered her a patient. "Quite often," she added. "I'll find myself talking to *her* about the things that bother *me*."

As I sat near Iman, she began asking me about who I was and why I had come to the hospital. She knew even the most fleeting of the visitors, from the families of other patients to the transients who came in from time to time to be seen by the doctors. I told her I was a friend of Alice's. "And a friend of mine also," she said, grinning. I must have worn my emotions on my face—I couldn't hide them—lighting one cigarette after another, as Iman was quick to point out.

"Are you smoking like that out of embarrassment? Or is it fear?" It didn't sound like a question. She was making an observation and trying to calm me. Oh, how terribly strange it was!

We were quiet for a little while, but then she began to sing. Within seconds I felt a warmth wash over me, dispelling my unease. But it was a curious thing: Iman sang as if she were trained. Her performance was technically proficient. She kept rhythm with a small stone which she beat against the steps, a delicate movement, almost soundless. It was more curious still that she sang no wrong notes. Perhaps it was her extreme sensitivity that prompted her to explain in French: "Wrong notes avoid me."

Even though I was there on holiday then, I ended up visiting the sanatorium every day. I would spend all afternoon listening to Iman's tales. I was lulled by her voice as if by sweet wine, and her powers of storytelling astonished me. She knew almost every patient in the hospital and sketched their profiles brilliantly. Once she spent a whole afternoon telling me about the Algerian woman Fatima who had owned an art gallery in Tangier. She'd had a French education *par excellence*. "She speaks like a Parisian," Iman said. She had a passion for contemporary pieces and installations. And as I listened to Iman I realized that she had been affected by Fatima, or at least by her knowledge of art. Since I don't have Iman's brilliance for detail, I remember little of Fatima's story, except that her husband declared himself bankrupt and she was left with terrible debts after he fled to Spain. He told no one, not even his wife, his companion of thirty years, about where he was going. After that his possessions were seized, including the house and the gallery, which had been jointly owned. And when she had nothing left, she was forced to sell her stake in the gallery in order to pay rent and for treatment in a private sanatorium for her twenty-seven-year-old son Fahad, who had suffered severe depression after his father's flight. Months passed, and after several failed attempts Fahad succeeded in taking his own life. They found him hanging in the sanatorium bathroom. Fatima, unable to withstand all that had befallen her, decided to follow in her son's footsteps. By her good luck, or bad, her sister was visiting that same day. She arrived before the worst could happen. "Although," Iman said, "I can hardly imagine worse than what Fatima had already lived through up until then." Things went on this way for ten years, and Fatima was still no better. It was her sister in Marrakech who brought her to Amerchich. (Were a sister's words law in this place?)

As the holiday came to its end I felt a strange tightness in my chest. I had quickly gotten used to Iman's companionship; there was much of me in her. Or rather, to be more accurate, I resembled her. I was endlessly surprised that this woman could forget who she was while at the same time remember other people's stories so precisely, and so much of what she had read: poetry, literature, music, history, philosophy. Perhaps she had a reason. Before leaving, I immediately knew what gift I should give her: five novels from Shatir, the bookstore in Gueliz, a beautiful diary with a leather cover, and some pencils. Alice said I'd fallen in love with her. And I think I had fallen, into the snare of her unknowability. Perhaps if I'd heard her story beforehand I wouldn't have been drawn to her. We hugged warmly. I promised to visit her when I came back from America. She, in return, promised me she would write in the diary all the tales she hadn't yet told me so we could read them together on my return.

I spent the full year in America—in the department of social sciences at the University of Chicago, and in libraries. Every time I entered a library I remembered Iman and her passion for reading; I often lay down at night to chase after her voice in the depths of my soul. A whole year passed in which I spoke to Alice on the phone only a couple of times. I was busy with the final draft of my thesis. Alice said that Iman had gotten better. She toured

Amerchich daily with her pen and her diary, even helping the other patients with her "parallel treatment sessions," listening to them for hours, telling them stories and singing to them. At the end of the year I booked my return ticket to Marrakech. I was excited: I had played out a hundred conversations in my head. I imagined dozens of stories. And I waited so eagerly to see Iman.

I arrived at the end of October. And though I was almost overwhelmed with exhaustion, I dreamed of her. Early the next morning I left Hotel Riad Mogador in Gueliz and walked to the Marché Central. I bought a bunch of beautiful roses, thinking Alice and Iman could give them out among the patients. I didn't call Alice that morning to tell her that I was coming. I felt like a child—I wanted to give her and Iman a joyous surprise.

When I arrived at the hospital, I looked around for Iman. I couldn't find her. I reached Alice's office and waited outside while she dealt with the father of a patient. When I opened the door to greet her, she saw me and her face turned white. An odd fear overtook me. I took a step back. At last I went inside, quickly, and shut the door behind me.

Alice was not a demonstrative woman, but she hugged me very warmly that day. More warmth than even a long absence merited. Like someone apologizing for something. Like someone trying to calm an oncoming storm. Iman had killed herself two weeks before my return: death had not postponed her this time. When no one expected it, late at night in bed, she had sliced open the arteries of her wrists. With a marker she had written her last words on her arms. When they found her in the morning the bed was drenched in blood, tears black with makeup weaving tracks across her face, long like the rays of the night. That's how I imagined her face. How had it happened? I couldn't understand. How could she commit suicide when she had begun to recover, to settle down? Why should Iman die when she had such capacity to bring joy?

Questions jumped inside me. Iman was no relation of mine,

and our friendship was not even long—it had been a month, at best, but that had been enough to send me into mourning now for her strange and extraordinary spirit. Perhaps I had needed a character like her in my life. A personality like that, breathtaking, an unknowable thing. Alice handed me Iman's diary with a little note affixed to it: *I hope you find these stories pleasant. I have missed the surprise of your heart, and of our meetings.*

For three days I didn't leave my hotel room. I thanked the chambermaids from behind the door and asked them to come back later. I had armed myself with two bottles of Absolut and some Marlboros from the duty free. And my best weapon was my weakness. Each time I opened the diary and began to read, Iman's voice dragged me to a place where time stopped. It was a painful journey through those events and places. She remembered who she was. She remembered her son Selim, who had turned fourteen this year: *He must be quite a handsome boy now.* She remembered her beloved Samir, who had left her because she betrayed him on a whim. She remembered how she had returned to Marrakech, grieving and defeated, planning to take her son away to spend some time with him. *I was broken. You could almost see the cracks in me. Between guilt and sadness, failure and remorse, all my feelings were struggling inside me. And I was trying to keep them away, forever. Hash was the only thing that put a stop to this bleeding from my soul, and the only thing that made it worse.*

Iman's sister refused to allow her son to accompany her to Casablanca where she rented a room in a friend's apartment. Iman understood her sister's position. There was no evil intent there: she simply thought Iman was in a state in which she could not take care of a child, given that she was constantly smoking hash. That night Iman went out and met a friend. They went to a Tashfin bar close to Colisée Cinema. She drank a lot and smoked until the fog obscured her vision. They hung out in a car until five thirty in the morning. *How could I think of going home at that hour? I wasn't thinking, or I wouldn't have done it.* Her sister confronted her when she got back, accusing her of negligence. Iman was drunk and high, almost broken, and she slapped her sister. *When she slapped me back, I didn't stop to look at what I had done. I just felt that I had inside me some ungovernable anger that was going to tear out of me like a missile. Unfortunately, it hit my sister.*

The following morning, Iman was determined to take Selim away. He began to get his things together to leave, but her sister was even more determined to stop her. When Iman realized it was impossible she grew violent and aggressive: she swore at her sister, and at a cousin who happened to be visiting, and they ended up having to restrain Iman, tying her hands and feet and gagging her to stop her screams. Iman's eyes remained on the child the whole time as he begged his grandmother not to call the psychiatric clinic. "*Wallah,* nothing can help your mother but Amerchich!" Iman's mother screamed.

Amerchich: not just the name of a neighborhood in Daoudiate. Not just a hospital for a particular class of illness. It was a curse. In Marrakech, Amerchich was the kind of insult you hurled at someone to accuse them of both foolishness and insanity, of being unable to live with other people—with well-adjusted, normal people. And it was Iman's bad luck that her mother had been a nurse before she retired. Naturally, she had contacts at Amerchich.

Between the screaming and exhaustion, the alcohol and the hashish, Iman lost her mind and remembered nothing. From that day on, everything that linked her to her past was erased. She forgot everything. She was rid of everything. Only an obscure and heavy ache remained, crouched in her breast, overwhelming her spirit. An ache whose source she did not know; a pain that led her, several times, to attempt suicide. And also to try to erase the features of her face.

On the last page of her diary she had written a short poem about her father. It had no title. She had written only: *My father. Hahahahaha. And the motorcycle.* She had drawn a child's face, smiling. And then the poem:

On the motorcycle
My father branching like bamboo
In trousers (Pat Delphone)
And a fur hat
Dressed for the weekend.

Since he left my mother a year ago
He brings me a kite
That scatters stars.
My eyes store them up
Those holiday days
Of promenade
Of sleep without cost.
The motorcycle prances
The alleys are a serpent
Carving out arcs through the quarters of Marrakech
Kings and lovers abhor them.
He squeezes me to his chest
A windbreak
We sway like wheatsheaves.
It happens on my father's motorbike
It happens that we also fall
We fall
And explode in riotous laughter.

Translated from Arabic by Hannah Scott Deuchar

BLACK LOVE

BY TAHA ADNAN

Hay Saada

With her heart racing, Noura rushed into the house to deliver the good news to her mother, Lalla Ghitha. Her boyfriend Bilal had only just told her—when he was taking her home from college on the back of his motorcycle, down Lalla Aweesh Street in the Aswal neighborhood—that he intended to bring over his mother, Um al-Khayr, to ask for Noura's hand in marriage. He asked Noura to run the idea by her mother to determine the date of the visit. His brother from Belgium would also be coming to spend New Year's in Marrakech. And it would be wonderful if he could be there for the announcement of their engagement.

Noura's face was covered in sweat and beaming with happiness as she entered the kitchen, her words stumbling out of her mouth with the excitement of a child. Lalla Ghitha began slicing eggplant to put in the oven in preparation for the *zaalouk* salad, which her daughter liked. She appeared to be frowning, as she usually was while cooking, looking as if she'd been forced into doing it. Cutting meat and peeling vegetables with a vengeance like someone settling an old score with nature. Noura was aware of her mother's tense temperament and she was at ease with her moods, but she didn't expect this excessive and frightening response after hearing the news.

A look of mourning crossed Lalla Ghitha's face. And as if the announcement signaled some disaster, she let out a cry: "Woe unto me! Woe unto me. Who? Bilal! As if this pitiful nigger was the last man on earth. Sweetie, why do you wanna drive me crazy? You're not crossed-eyed . . . you're not crippled, are you?"

"Mom, Bilal's a good guy—our neighbor's son. We grew up together before he moved out of our neighborhood," Noura reminded her mother. "We know everything about him—big stuff, little stuff. He doesn't smoke or drink. He keeps to himself. His heart's pure. I swear, Mom, he's a humble man. There's nothing black about him other than his skin."

"Oh God! And what about my grandkids? God forbid, you want them to be niggers? God blessed me with one daughter. I devoted my whole life to her, working for good and bad people. She hankered to turn the world into an olive grove where goats graze."

"What'd they tell you? That I was blond and as white as Nicole Kidman? Mother, he's a good guy, he means well," she said.

"Sweetie, the reasonable thing to do is finish your degree. As for marriage—there'll always be time to get married later."

"Please, Mom. What about all these girls around here who earned their degrees and graduated, and all of them just sit around doing nothing—unemployed or unmarried, they've got nothing," Noura said. "No one cares about them, not even dogs. Bilal agrees that I should finish my studies. Anyway, Hay Saada, where he's living now, is close to the college. And his brother in Belgium opened a store for him in the garage beneath their building. He bought it and left Bilal in charge of the business. Thank God, he is quite well off. And now he wants your blessing so that when his brother comes back in the summer he can help him until the wedding."

"It'll be a funeral, not a wedding," Lalla Ghitha rumbled. "You make my blood boil, you good-for-nothing daughter."

"Shame on you, Mom. What did Bilal do to you? He's only shown us that he's good. And anyway, I love him."

"May a scorpion love you and sting that mouth of yours," Lalla Ghitha snarled, turning away from her daughter. "Get outta my face, may God strike you down—and don't mention this nigger to me anymore. Before, I was happy saying to myself that he'd left us for that disaster of a neighborhood."

"That blight is called Hay Saada."

"Not even! Misery Neighborhood, that's what Hay Saada is known as—not Happiness Neighborhood. They were lying when they named it that. The place where every rotten slut feels at home. What's with him, why can't he find a black chick—and this store his brother from Belgium supposedly started? It was that Senegalese woman who did the paperwork for him. She's got a sister she should offer to Bilal—this would make him go away."

"Look, Mom, he didn't come to beg you. He came to ask for *my* hand."

"Not until he's the last man on earth—then I'll toss you aside to the niggers of Misery Neighborhood," Lalla Ghitha said venomously.

"This Misery Neighborhood you hate is no better than the misery we're living in right here. It took a month for them to take out the pipes when they said they were for drilling for oil. There's nothing left in the Old Medina but filth, Mom. I'm always telling you to sell this dump and the Tameslouht property and let us leave and live decently like other people. We'd even have a business to get us out of this utter poverty."

"These sewage pipes don't stink as much as that mouth on you, God help us. You even want me to part with this house where I still smell the scent of your dead father, you slut!" Lalla Ghitha raged. "It looks like you will finish me off to join your father before my time comes. It's either wrath or contentment . . . choose one: me or that Ebola boy of yours."

When Noura heard the engine of the motorcycle, she knew that Bilal hadn't left right after dropping her off at home—he had lingered instead, perhaps expecting to hear cries of joy. The window had been open to let the cooking smells flow out, and with them flowed all the horrible slurs Lalla Ghitha had uttered.

Noura hurried after him, running and screaming like a crazy person: "Bilal, Bilal, Bilal!" But he didn't turn around. That was the last time she would see him. After that day, he didn't even answer her phone calls.

Lalla Ghitha's words had a dramatic impact on Bilal. His head was spinning faster than the tires of his black Swing motorcycle. He stared at the road that shifted before his eyes into a black line until he could hardly see a thing. He didn't know how he'd arrived at his apartment in Hay Saada. He didn't pay any attention to his mother, who was mumbling something he didn't catch. He headed straight to his room, which he often dreamed would be a love nest for him and his beloved Noura. He locked the door and let his mind drift . . .

He reminisced about his childhood infatuation with Noura. She was younger than him by three years. He was like a big brother to her. He'd watched out for her, since she was deprived of a brother in a neighborhood too tough for a fatherless child without male protection. Since their childhood, the other kids would avoid any dispute with Noura because it would immediately blow up into something bigger with her "dark shadow." Bilal became her little man. He started placing himself at the disposal of Lalla Ghitha for every chore she could ask him to do. She would brush off any flattery and would ask him favors directly and spontaneously without burdening herself with thanking him afterward.

But Bilal was just happy to be there. Happy with his familiarity in the house in which he had regular duties, like filling the gas tank and fixing the constantly leaking faucet, or changing the lightbulbs that swiftly burned out, or climbing up to the roof to adjust the satellite dish when the wind would move it. He hadn't wanted reimbursement or thanks. A look from Noura full of pride and appreciation would suffice. In her eyes, he was the man of the house without a doubt. He was ready to do anything for those eyes, which is how he discovered early on that he was in love with her. And, early on as well, she submitted her young heart to him.

Love had flourished between them ever since. Bilal grew accustomed to the nasty words that followed him: *Negro, mutt, slave boy, black-skin, black-ass,* among other slurs. Bilal dealt with this rotten glossary as mere childish insults. But that one unforgivable word from the mouth of Lalla Ghitha, especially while discussing marriage, had left a particularly bitter taste in his mouth.

He remembered his Arabic class in high school. The teacher, Mr. Sheeki, would constantly repeat verses of al-Mutanabbi's lampoon against Kafur al-Ikhsheedi, the ruler of Egypt, with relish:

The slave is not a brother to a freed and righteous man
If in the freed man's clothes he is born.
Do not buy the slave unless he comes with a whip
For surely slaves are the impure ones of scorn.

The last verse itself was like a whip to Bilal and it struck his ears many times. The contempt in it was balanced and rhyming. Moreover, Mr. Sheeki could not resist pointing at Bilal's face whenever he made a blunder, any one of the many small mistakes made by children at that age. He would ask his students: "What did al-Mutanabbi say? *Do not buy the slave . . .*"

"*. . . unless he comes with a whip,*" answered his pupils in a unified voice with villainous enthusiasm.

But why today did he feel as if he were hearing this expression for the first time in his life? Lalla Ghitha's foul word now filled his mind, which overflowed with humiliation.

Noura couldn't understand Bilal's response. He no longer answered her incessant calling nor her quick attempts to ease his mind. She was prepared for anything—to run away with him to the middle of nowhere if he wanted, and live off nothing but bread, water, and love. But when he finally answered her phone call, he requested in a dry tone that she stop calling.

"Enough, we're finished. We've reached the end of our rope. Throw away my number and we'll both go our own ways."

For the first time in her life, Noura—who'd lost her father when she was a child—felt the injustice of Bilal shunning her true love for him. Sleep avoided her. She could no longer stand chatting with her mother as she had before. She started spending more time in her room, which was decorated with pictures of Will Smith, Jamie Foxx, and 50 Cent. She had been infatuated since her earliest days with work by black artists. Her passion for the songs of Whitney Houston, Lionel Richie, Michael Jackson, and Rihanna led her to study English literature in college. She would stand for hours in front of the mirror, putting on makeup and swinging to the rhythm of the music before school, comfortable with her own style and nonconformist tastes. Her mother never understood how she could waste all that time in front of the mirror and leave with hair wild as a bird's nest. Noura loved to toss locks of her hair in every direction. She would put a lot of effort into fixing her unruly hair with gel so it would stay beautifully chaotic throughout the day. She wore baggy clothes in bright colors, very fitting for a twenty-one-year-old. Noura would buy used clothing from the Sidi Maimoun market. She got pleasure in not being ordinary, searching for clothing not from the best brands, but found in secondhand stores that suited her limited university scholarship.

No one knew how Hay Saada, in Gueliz on the road to Casablanca, had turned into a fortress for immigrants from sub-Saharan Africa. This neighborhood was relatively modern, and it developed faster than anyone could have imagined. Within ten years the first apartments were put up for sale for around 200,000 dirhams. They were cheap apartments, despite this surge in development, yet the real estate developers didn't target the vulnerable groups or low-income communities there. The important thing was that they found buyers willing to put up 50,000 dirhams under the table. And with this the door was opened to real estate speculators, as well as smaller local buyers who relied on renting out rooms in their apartments to supplement their incomes and improve their living conditions. This drew admirers of Marrakech—most of them from Casablanca—who looked for ways to spend the weekends and holidays in the Red City.

Perhaps that is what made the neighborhood, first and foremost, a magnet for prostitutes who could find new apartments for reasonable prices. Then, because it was a new neighborhood, no one knew anyone there, and no one was interested in anyone else's business. So it was possible for girls coming from the neighboring cities and villages, claiming that they worked in hotels or for textile companies or plastics factories in the industrial area nearby, to live their illicit lives without question. Other apartments were set up entirely for *faire l'amour*—this was the neighborhood where tourists from around Morocco would go to seek sexual gratification at affordable prices, worlds apart from the exorbitant riads and expensive Gueliz apartments that the Gulf and European tourists monopolized.

Bilal's store, where he sold cell phone accessories, was on the ground floor of his building, directly below his apartment. On the other side of the building's entrance was Afro Beauty, the salon of the sensuous and alluring Fatimata al-Rasta.

Though unlicensed, the salon grew gradually until it extended onto the pavement. Fatimata found female associates, experts in weaving and braiding hair, for her clientele from sub-Saharan Africa. And they weren't shy about flashing their private parts to passersby to generate additional business. For Fatimata, it was a salon and a shelter—two in one. She didn't compete with the other beauty salons that spread like fungus throughout Hay

Saada—salons filled nightly with restless girls who wouldn't leave for a festive night on the town until they had been fully made up. Fatimata decided, after establishing the place, that she would offer her experience in the service of her countrywomen. Not to mention she was the only one on the street who opened her salon first thing in the morning.

Bilal lived with his mother in a corner apartment on the first floor. There were seven other apartments on their floor. Across the hall lived Hafidh, a young employee of the textile company, together with his veiled wife Badia and their two kids, Anis and Nada. He was a quiet and solitary man who didn't interact with the neighbors. Sometimes he climbed up the stairs talking on the phone in fluent French, his voice low like a whisper, as if this embarrassed him. He always walked right alongside the wall. Hafidh had a feeling that his presence in the building was an accident. He treated the apartment like a tomb. With his small family, he would spend the weekends at his mother's in the Sidi Ghanem neighborhood, not far from the grave of Abu al-Abbas al-Sabati, guardian of the city and the most famous of its seven great men. Completely different was Tamou's apartment, a perpetual screaming factory. Her apartment door was always open, and Tamou was never concerned about transforming the building's hallway into an extension of her kitchen. She had five boys, all close in age, as if she had pushed them all out at once. The youngest one traveled to Syria to be an Islamist *mujahid* immediately after his release from prison, where he had spent a full year for an attempted rape. There in the haven of the East, he had all the Christian, Alawi, and Kurdish women he could desire to practice his beastly arts on, while waiting for his dark-eyed virgins in paradise—unless his faith proved unworthy. As for the two oldest brothers, Majid and Chakib, they didn't communicate with anyone in the building except their mother. They worked together selling odds and ends. Only their car, a black Renault Kangoo, announced their presence at home. Meanwhile, Farid and Said would simply loiter all day in front of the building. An idleness that bothered Bilal, who, despite himself, was their friend.

The next apartment was occupied by Igor and Irina, a young married couple from Poland who both worked in a casino. Every night at seven thirty, the company car would pick them up in their elegant work clothes. Irina's skirt was carefully cut to expose her thighs to the gluttonous eyes inside that lustful club, eyes that would later fantasize about the rest of her body. Outside of these brief moments when Irina spread happiness among the misery of Hay Saada, one could hardly find a trace of them. In the wee hours of the morning only the sounds of the car could be heard, in order to sneak the blond Pole into her resting place. When Igor went shopping by himself at Marjan Supermarket just outside Hay Saada, he carried all the goods in a taxi, avoiding contact with the neighborhood grocers and other locals.

To the left of the stairs was an apartment crowded with young men from Mali. It was barely noticeable to someone passing through the building. In front of it was Naima's apartment. She slept all day, and under the cover of darkness she would go out fully made up into the sleepless nights of Marrakech. She had initially come from Safi to work in a massage parlor in Hay Saada. But she quickly discovered that the clients wouldn't relax at the end of a session until their main limb was massaged, in exchange for a generous tip. She soon left the parlor to be free to massage that privileged organ on her own time. Naima the Masseuse—that's what the neighbors starting calling her. Until one day they woke up to her screams. She had allowed a drunken client into her home and he had proceeded to beat her with his shoe. He struck her across the face, drawing blood. He dragged her around cruelly by her hair. A rational person wouldn't have believed how violent he had become given how intimate they had been just moments before. He claimed that she had taken advantage of him and stolen his money while he was in the bathroom. This was when Farid and Said had pulled him away from

Naima. After this, however, she wasn't able to escape her new nickname: Naima the Whore.

Just beyond Naima's place was a residence of a special type, where Issoufou, a thirty-year-old Nigerian lived. He had broad shoulders, a barrel chest, and a medium frame which obscured his full stomach. He was always smiling and elegant. He studied commerce at the international university in Marrakech. Mostly people just saw him leaving in the morning or returning at night. He gave off the impression that he was always busy with some urgent matter. His father, according to his neighbor, doorman, and assistant Aissatou, was a minister in the government of Mamadou Tandja, and he had been arrested after the military coup in February 2010. This coup was led by Colonel Salou Djibo and it forced Issoufou and the rest of his family to disperse across the world. They had money in a number of different countries, but complicated administrative issues prevented them from accessing those funds legally. Issoufou lived in the apartment alone while his fellow countrymen were crammed like sardines in tiny one-room apartments.

Issoufou didn't go out until he was comfortable with how he looked; it seemed as if Georgio Armani himself had outfitted him. His suit was ironed with careful attention, and the collars of his white shirts were starched and pressed—ever since he'd bought a steam iron from Marjan, his neighbor Aissatou had been in charge of ironing his clothes. A gold necklace hung on his chest, his designer shoes were always polished, and he carried an expensive leather bag. Another gold chain on his wrist competed for attention with the gold ring on his finger. He always smelled of the thick Armani cologne called Attitude.

Aissatou, a twenty-five-year-old Senegalese man, lived in the next apartment. He first came as a migrant to Fes, the center of the Tijani Sufi order, which more than half the Senegalese Muslims had joined, and where the shrine of the great Sheikh Ahmed al-Tijani was held. He remained there until he could travel north to Tangier with the intention of crossing the strait to Europe. There, in Tangier, on the bank of the Mediterranean, the paradise of Europe appeared to be close, like a mirage. But without being able to navigate the strait, the dangers were plentiful. The Mediterranean formed the most violent borders in the world. A sea harvest of victims' souls by the thousands—a gigantic graveyard of bloated corpses and sunken dreams. The living conditions in the nearby forests of Ceuta were unbearable. He never even thought of heading east toward Nador, where his countrymen were living in dire conditions in the Kouruku forest, dreaming of slipping into Melilla before finding themselves, at the end of their hopeless adventure, detained at the camp in the coastal village of Arekmane. The Spanish enclaves of Ceuta and Melilla formed the only land border between Africa and Europe. The guards on the Moroccan borders dedicated themselves to this illegal crossing point for African migrants with gusto, in order to gain the favor of their European associates. Racism against black people had been simmering, especially within the lower classes of the Boukhalef neighborhood, which was known as the center of the African community in Tangier. These sentiments made Aissatou completely rethink his idea of settling in Tangier. Instead he headed south in the direction of the Red City. Marrakech was the most African city of all the metropolises in the kingdom. There he sought out Issoufou, whom he'd previously met through a Tijani friend in Fes. The Nigerian advised him to move into the vacant apartment in front of his.

The apartment was owned by a Moroccan who now lived in Sweden. He had abandoned it a year before after a night of *bunga bunga* had been turned upside down. He had run group sex parties until an underage prostitute was murdered there, and the police raided the apartment and arrested the lot of them—with the exception of the owner, who escaped to his Swedish refuge with the help of a fat bribe.

Aissatou didn't find it difficult to adapt to his new environment. He regularly went to the main mosque in Hay Saada, and his strict adherence to prayer allowed him to become well-known in the neighborhood and trusted by its residents, who found his broken classical Arabic and Senegalese accent to be charming. After finishing his prayers he would spread out his goods for sale—cell phones, wristwatches, and women's accessories—in front of the mosque. He was comfortable with this new pace of life. He would frequent the *dhikr* circles at the Tijani group meetings by Bab Doukkala, and also spent time near Bab Aylan, Bab Ahmar, and in Hay Ksour, where he widened his circle of acquaintances as well as his commercial activities.

Sometimes he would stay with a Sudanese friend named Uthman, a tall and slender young man who was almost thirty. Uthman wore round glasses that filled him with a perhaps unwarranted dignity. His great-grandfather had been one of the sheikhs and a spokesman of the Tijani order in the Sudan, during the days of holy jihad against the English and Turks—the time of the Mahdist Revolution. He studied law in Marrakech before joining the doctoral faculty at Mohammed V University in Rabat. But for about two years now he has devoted himself to preparing his travel papers to move to England and to join his brother. Uthman Mustafa Sheikh lived between Marrakech and Rabat, with dreams of London.

Aissatou wasn't shy about poking holes in his friend's fantasy of lying on the banks of the Thames: "There's no reason to hurry, brother. Do you think the British are burning with desire to welcome you? You'll be met with accusations. You have been inflicted with all the curses: first you're Arab, then Muslim, and on top of that you're black!"

Uthman shook with laughter before answering him: "Fear not, clever one . . . It'll be enough for them to know I'm a Tijani, and a friend of a Senegalese devotee named Aissatou who wanders the country where the Almoravids once ruled. Then their opinions of me will change completely."

* * *

Bilal had ambivalent feelings toward his black neighbors. He would get fed up with Fatimata's screaming. She was clearly incapable of speaking softly. Even the noisy presence of the Malians bothered him. He often complained to Farid and Said about the racket they caused.

"They all talk at the same time. It's like they're fighting," Bilal told them.

"Those bastards have megaphones for mouths," replied Farid.

Despite this, Bilal was quick to come to the defense of his black neighbors, proclaiming his disgust whenever people made inappropriate or openly racist comments. Farid and Said were in their midtwenties and both were unemployed. And since there was no way for them to frequent cafés with their empty pockets, they sought shelter with Bilal, sharing a pot of morning tea that his mother Umm al-Khayr prepared for him at ten. They shared loose cigarettes that they would get from the vendor in front of Café Original on the corner. They were envious of Issoufou, who was sometimes accompanied by girls, which they shamefully begrudged. Because of this, every time someone walked in front of them, the two repeated the song of those congregations in Jemaa el-Fnaa Square by the late Omar Meekhi:

Bambara Bamba,
Bambara the one with the balls.
Bambara Bamba,
The one who likes girls.
White or black ones,
For them his soul dies.

One time Issoufou came home accompanied by a blond foreigner, one of those normally encountered in the tourist areas and who was clearly out of place in Hay Saada. She looked pleased as she followed him into the apartment. Farid and Said glanced at her, observing the scene with a disgust and envy that crushed their hearts. Farid spoke slowly while staring at the blonde: "That bitch is beautiful!"

"Too bad that dung beetle has his arms all over her," replied Said, defeated.

"Mark my words, tomorrow her picture will be in the papers. Really, he'll devour her . . . that son of a bitch, black-ass nigger. He's a cannibal."

"Bro, I don't understand, what do they like about these black men?" Said asked.

"They lick it good."

"I bet he won't just lick—he's gonna eat too. He'll even eat her shit."

"Man, I swear only foreigners make it in this country. This Negro was just jumping around with monkeys yesterday and now he easily finds a European girlfriend, son of a bitch."

Bilal couldn't bear this vulgar talk, remembering how hurt he had been when Lalla Ghitha had called him a nigger. His blood starting to boil with rage, he said: "Get your asses the fuck out of here. Seriously, go jerk off someplace else. This is a respectable business. You spend the whole day leaning on the wall like you're keeping it from falling . . . You'll pick up shit, not foreign women."

Farid and Said didn't understand what had suddenly shaken their friend. Regardless, they were filled with hatred for those former slaves whom they blamed for their problems with Bilal. When a group of Malian children walked past Fatimata's salon that morning, Farid shouted at them: "The country's overflowing with you sons of bitches!"

Issoufou was one of the few Africans who frequented the local cafés, as most in the community tended to live isolated among themselves, far from Moroccans and their problems. Many Africans limited their interactions with Moroccans to the essentials, especially since they perceived among the Moroccans feelings of superiority. Even the most humble grocer would approach them with a false sense of nobility.

Issoufou left his apartment in Hay Saada to wander through the main street. He paused in front of the shops, looking scornfully at the cheap goods before heading to Tito's Café at the intersection of Allal el-Fassi Avenue and Abdelkarim el-Khattabi Boulevard, overlooking the large Marjan Market. Allal el-Fassi and Abdelkarim el-Khattabi had been opposition fighters who fought to expel the French and the Spanish during the struggle against colonization. Today their progeny were ready to dance on their graves in order to attract those same foreigners to come here and invest. Meanwhile, others were ready to give up the nation with all its martyrs and resistance fighters in exchange for residency papers for the blond capitals. The paths of history indeed have strange and deceptive points of intersection.

Issoufou entered the coffee shop, swaying as he removed his Armani glasses. Conspicuously dressed in Armani as well, he scanned the tables and TV screens around the room that were broadcasting songs on the Rotana Records channel. He took a seat in a prime corner booth upstairs, so he could look down on the trifling patrons as he drank his coffee. Recently Noura had started to frequent the café. She secluded herself in another corner, studying for upcoming exams far from the noise of her mother and the incessant racket of Lala Aweesh Street, which always prevented her from focusing. But after a while she noticed this elegant dark man, whom she thought resembled Dr. Eric Forman from the show *House*.

Sometimes she observed Issoufou meeting mysterious folks there—most of them Moroccan. Occasionally a French woman in her midthirties would be there with him. Their relationship appeared to be professional, judging from the papers and documents that they'd whisper over. Issoufou soon noticed Noura's attention and they exchanged a smile once or twice. By the third time, he asked the waiter to bring her a cup of juice, which she gratefully accepted, encouraging him to move over to her table.

Issoufou came exactly at the right time. Noura had been yearning for Bilal's arms, his hot breath, his thick lips, which would bring back memories of the Menara and Agdal gardens, where they would make love beneath the olive trees, after Bilal had silenced the garden's attendant with cash. But for Noura, she desired him as much as she loathed him. And she sympathized with him as a victim of her mother's conduct as much as his neglect had wounded her. The affairs of the heart are capable of transforming a victim into an executioner from one beat to the next. And with that, Issoufou's gentleness and courtesy made him appear like a knight, a savior sent from the heavens, especially since Noura's fruit was ripe enough to fall before her desire in the arms of a new lover.

Noura ended up in Issoufou's bed after a series of dates at Tito's Café and dinners at Kanoun, a nearby Lebanese restaurant. Sometimes he would take her to Café Mama Afrika or the club and restaurant African Chic on the Umm al-Rabi alleyway in Gueliz, behind Hotel Marrakech. There, at African Chic, her heart danced with joy when Issoufou first declared his love for her. He started trusting his feelings for her so that she'd offer him love in return. She found a delicateness and refinement in him. It was true that Bilal had loved her and had wanted to marry her, but he had never made her feel like a princess. With Issoufou she'd become a real princess. He was truly a gentleman. He always complimented her beauty and elegance, and would reveal his feelings to her sincerely and spontaneously. He granted her so much trust and security, even sharing with her many of his deepest secrets. From their first dates he spoke to her about his father, the former minister, who was now a prisoner in Niamey, Niger; about his family scattered across God's vast land; and about their wealth, which he was trying to restore with the help of an international law office in Paris. He told her about the representative in Marrakech, a woman who met with him regularly to discuss the case.

"Is it the Frenchwoman who is sometimes with you in the café?" Noura asked him, as if to reassure her heart.

And he answered her evenly: "Exactly. Her name is Katherine. She's a lawyer. She lives in the Hivernage area of Gueliz and represents her office here. They have a number of French clients residing in Marrakech."

"The case sounds complicated."

"Kind of. But things are moving in a good direction. I've been living here for more than five years now, and I submitted my request for residency to the new bureau for migration and asylum," he explained. "All I have to do is find a worthy partner I can trust. One of the recent administrative measures involves being under the patronage of a local—especially since the new laws ease the paths to residency and work for refugees. We might be able to set up a company and open a joint account for the future funds if I get my legal affairs in order. Because of concerns over terrorist financing, there is growing international surveillance on the movement of capital. However, as soon as I can get ahold of the money to establish the company legally, everything will end up in a good place. The most important part of all this is that I find the right partner."

It hadn't even crossed Noura's mind that she might be this sought-after partner, that a savior had come to rescue her from her miserable life on Lalla Aweesh Street; from her tense relationship with her mother that had become unbearable, especially since the episode with Bilal; from a university that wouldn't grant her a diploma other than to join the ranks of unemployed college graduates. But now she considered selling the Tameslouht land and entering into a professional partnership out of a dream with this dark, handsome gentleman.

Noura learned the meaning of true pleasure with Issoufou. Naked in bed, she experienced an orgasm for the first time. It was real euphoria, not at all like that love stolen between the trees, when Bilal had rubbed up against her body, quickly spilling his semen. Despite the barrier of her virginity, the talented Issoufou did things with his tongue she couldn't believe. After a lengthy session of kissing—just a warm-up—he spread her out on his mattress which was black and white like a zebra. He removed her clothing piece by piece, engrossing himself in suckling at her pear-like breasts with his powerful lips, and then focusing on her nipples, teasing them. With the caution of a mystic, he descended steadily down her chest to her navel, before moving to her inner thighs in a kind of sweet torture. Then he turned toward her small blossom, breathing in deeply before exhaling with his burning breath. He kissed her folds, exciting her clitoris, which he wrestled with his outstretched tongue, until Noura let out a quivering scream—a scream which made Issoufou stroke his loaded rocket, joining her there at the heights of euphoria.

She thought to herself that this feeling, in and of itself, was worth all the risks she took to be alone with Issoufou. She would ask permission from her mother to spend the night at her friend Hayat's house in Daoudiate, claiming they were preparing for exams together, only to go to Issoufou's place instead. He would head upstairs first while she lingered outside, watching Bilal from afar until he was busy with a customer, and then she would sneak through the door. Bilal had been a mere stepping-stone on her road to this new love. She would feel victorious whenever she brushed past him, like a racehorse vaulting over a fence.

Noura was leaving Issoufou's apartment when Bilal suddenly appeared before her with a menacing expression on his face. "Where were you, you slut?"

"How could you call me that? Your sister is the slut . . . and anyway, what business is it of yours? Who are you to ask me?"

"I'm the one who's going to call the cops on you if I keep seeing you run around here with that nigger."

"Nigger! Really? My God. This word just comes out of you smooth and sweet like honeyed butter."

"He's a nigger . . . a cannibal. If I catch you here again, goddamnit, see if I don't get you arrested, the both of you."

Noura didn't know what to say. Bilal glared at her, his eyes burning with anger and hatred. She slunk back to her apartment furious with this bastard who she had once loved. Perhaps she should pick up the pace. She had to find a way to return to Issoufou. She was annoyed with this shit from Bilal, a man who'd abandoned her, fleeing like a coward at the first sign of difficulty, holding her mother's offenses against her. And now he wanted to ruin her newfound love.

Later, Noura told her new knight the whole story with Bilal: about him wanting to get engaged, about her mother's rejection and his fleeing like a coward, even his trying to block her way when she left the apartment. She professed her love for him, saying that she wished to be with him forever. She then offered to sell the Tameslouht land to establish the company's funding—and as soon as Issoufou's money arrived they would move somewhere else, far away from Bilal and this stupid little neighborhood.

Issoufou overflowed with appreciation. Unlike Bilal, Issoufou didn't generally waver in love. And as far as joining the love with business, it couldn't wait. He called Aissatou and asked him to get in touch with his friends in the Sufi order to arrange a marriage contract with Noura. He would later get an officiant to sign the contract, with Aissatou and his Sudanese friend Uthman Mustafa Sheikh serving as witnesses.

Noura didn't resist any of this, wanting to exercise her rights under the new Moroccan family law. Besides, she wasn't going to wager her happiness on seeking her stone-faced mother's approval. Back at home, she told her mother that she had to attend the wedding of Hayat's sister. She dressed in her red and white kaftan, embroidered with gold thread. She draped her white-riveted djellaba over that. She put on her white high-heel shoes patterned with pink flowers. She asked her neighbor's son to get her a taxi to take her to the Tijani Order Center near Bab Doukkala. The taxi driver parked and waited for her at the entrance of the pathway, near the courtyard, because Lalla Aweesh Street was too narrow for a car to pass through. Noura pulled up the edges of her kaftan to avoid the trash and potholes that made the short distance treacherous in heels. She walked without stumbling or twisting her ankle, heading in the direction of her destiny.

Everyone was gathered at the Tijani Order Center when she arrived, waiting for her to ratify the marriage contract. The officiant Moulay al-Ghali, wearing a white djellaba, registered the declarations of the two witnesses who were also dressed in traditional white clothing. Meanwhile, Issoufou remained true to form, sporting a tailored black Armani tuxedo with gray piping and a white shirt with a bow tie, as if he'd just stepped out of a Hollywood film. Next to the others, he resembled a five-star hostage of a terrorist.

After the ceremony, Noura felt like she was floating with happiness, despite some lingering anxiety. The newlyweds celebrated their secret marriage in al-Fassia restaurant on Boulevard Mohamed-Zerktouni in Gueliz, far from all the riffraff. With Andalusian music softly playing in the background, the hostess led them to a private dining room with only two tables. The lights were dim and the table next to them was empty, all of which allowed the necessary intimacy for the most romantic night of Noura's life. Issoufou ordered a bottle of champagne with hors d'oeuvres, and insisted she toast to their eternal happiness; it was the intoxication of love that hindered her ability to refuse.

She hadn't even tried alcohol before, since she had been raised to believe that it inevitably led to debauchery and prostitution.

"But champagne is something else," Issoufou said. "It's the drink of rapture, of honor, of joy."

She felt she had to obey her husband. The server opened the bottle dramatically, causing the golden liquid to bubble over. Her eyes wandered over to the main room of the restaurant: the customers were mostly tourists. She took a sip from her glass, the bubbles tickling her nose. She yielded to another glass soon after and felt the tingling of this wondrous drink in her soul, which started to tremble with elation. They ordered grilled meat with plums—the traditional Moroccan wedding dish. She put aside her knife and fork and used the bread to scoop up her food, as was customary. She found it strange to be eating this dish in a restaurant. Her life had entered a new track from the station of the marriage contract.

When the taxi dropped the couple off at the entrance to their building, Noura was unconcerned about the prospect of encountering Bilal or any of the other rubberneckers standing around the front door. Inside, they only passed Hafidh the textile worker hurrying up the stairs in the company of his wife Badia. They pulled their kids behind them as their eyes remained fixed on the newlyweds. Noura climbed the stairs with the confidence of a queen heading to her promised throne. Aissatou had used his extra key to tidy up Issoufou's apartment in advance. He had started by fixing up the office, then cleaned the bathroom, and finally arranged the bedroom before pumping a half bottle of perfume into it. He had placed candles throughout the room, around which he scattered rose petals. After he paid his respects to the newlyweds, wishing them a joyous night, he left.

The night had started as any virgin would have hoped—passionate gazes were exchanged before they came together in a long, feverish kiss that concluded with them naked in bed. All the familiar intimate opening movements, which delivered Noura into a frenzy, were consummated that evening. Issoufou accomplished this great mission like a professional, as she released an intense scream of ecstasy. A scream that was followed by powerful, hurried knocks on the apartment door: "Open up! Police!"

Terrified, Issoufou's eyes quickly scanned the room while Noura searched in confusion for her underwear and bra which she had thrown someplace in the heat of the moment. Her mind turned to that jackass Bilal—obviously he had gone through with his threat to call the cops. The dog. He didn't even know that Issoufou was now her husband, according to the Holy Book of Allah and the sunna of His Prophet.

Outside, panic and chaos spread across the first floor of the building. Naima the Whore's door opened to allow a frightened man to leave her apartment. He tripped over himself, believing that the police were raiding Naima's place. But he found it difficult to break through the forest of Malians that had sprouted in the middle of the hallway, also heading for the exit. Likewise, Majid and Chakib were seen jumping from their apartment's balcony to escape in their car, the black Kangoo. Irina, who couldn't restrain her curiosity, peeked out to see what was happening. For once, she looked truly disheveled, dressed only in a light nightshirt.

"Irina, what are you doing here at this hour?" asked Umm al-Khayr, who was not used to encountering her Polish neighbor in the evening. She was at her post in front of the door, watching over the scene disinterestedly.

Meanwhile, Lalla Tamou approached in pure mockery, relishing the sight. She was trailed by her other boys Farid and Said, who seemed equally gleeful. Then there was Uthman, the Sudanese man, standing upright like a watchtower monitoring everyone's movements.

The police didn't wait long. They were not forced to break into the apartment because Aissatou had instead used his key to reveal Noura behind the door wrapped in a shawl. In her hand she held her newly minted marriage license—proof of her innocence against the accusation of indecent activities.

Bilal emerged and broke through the rows of onlookers, confused and infuriated. Standing in front of the door, he glimpsed Noura wandering through the apartment, scared, sobbing, traumatized. He tried to move toward her, but a police officer standing by the door turned him away harshly. Bilal's heart filled with pain, and he wished he could tell Noura that he was not responsible for this mess.

Rather, it was Aissatou who stepped resolutely into the apartment to show the security forces several passports, stacks of counterfeit bills in different currencies, as well as other forged documents held in an iron safe hidden in the office closet. A wealth of evidence implicated a man named Mamadou Alseeka, a.k.a. Issoufou, in crimes of establishing and defrauding various businesses in Tangier, Fes, Casablanca, and Marrakech. Further still, they had living proof, scandalously seminude, embodied in the freshly victimized Noura Foukhari. Seizing Issoufou's computer, they would later discover correspondences with other victims he'd conned, as well as with his accomplice—a Frenchwoman named Déborah Lizan, who went by Katherine, and who was illegally residing in the country. They had been forwarding money orders as proof of legal and administrative assets that granted them access to the profits of a fake company which specialized in the production and exportation of uranium.

Issoufou felt dizzy and sick to his stomach, and asked an officer to give him a minute to throw up.

The cop answered sternly: "You'll have plenty of time to puke in prison, you no-good con artist."

Noura didn't understand one bit of what was happening around her. Her face was streaked with tears, her mind was racing, and her strength had collapsed. She looked around as two officers led her knight in shining armor—Issoufou, or rather, Mamadou Alseeka—away in handcuffs and silk Armani pajamas, on their wedding night.

Two other officers dispersed the curious bystanders, including Hafidh and his wife Badia, who were now listening from their front door. Hafidh was quite pleased with his abrupt decision to move from this miserable building in Hay Saada to live in the neighboring Hay Sharaf—the so-called Honor Neighborhood.

Translated from Arabic by Ghayde Ghraowi

[The translator would like to express his enormous gratitude to Nader Uthman, Thouria Benferhat, and Olga Verlato, whose help made this translation possible.]

A PERSON FIT FOR MURDER

BY LAHCEN BAKOUR

L'Hivernage

Whoever said that murder is tricky? It's extremely simple. As trivial as can be and cowardly too. It doesn't have to involve someone with a heart of stone, a dead body, or a rapid-fire weapon to take the place of a shaking hand. All you need is someone fit for murder, a bit of weaponry to store the desire for the first drop of spilled blood, and, once in a while, a bit of uncertainty and some crazy coincidences. That's all that's needed when it comes to having someone give up the ghost, and stopping the heart from beating.

I'm not a retired criminal, someone who has grown tired of murder's costs, who wastes time rehashing postponed decisions, or who simply rambles on regardless. No—I know exactly what I'm talking about. I'm a real killer, someone who still has fresh blood on his clothes!

That's right, I'm a killer! At that particular moment, I was squatting alongside the corpse of my victim. It was Guillaume, my enormous and wonderful friend who was lying beside me, totally peaceful, as though he was exhausted after an intense bout of lovemaking—except that this time his face wasn't flushed with the same kind of elation that usually follows total satisfaction. This time, the rigor enveloping his body was far greater than the feeling of lassitude that normally follows such pleasure.

My hand was shaking. It had gone back to being as weak as it usually is. Just a few moments ago a weird, satanic power had pulsed through it. My hand kept a firm grip on the knife handle as I finished off my enormous, gentle friend Guillaume. After that I squatted down beside his body for a bit so I could shed some tears and try to figure out why I had killed him.

We had arranged to meet today; that's why I came. I had no particular grudge against him. I assumed he was waiting for me as usual. There was the same level of excitement and anticipation, as though we were meeting for the very first time. He lingered under the shower before putting on expensive deodorant. Covering himself with a pink silk bathrobe, he took out that box, put it on the table by the bed, and sat there waiting for me. No sooner had I gone through the entrance to Bab el-Jadid and crossed the street in the direction of the Winter Quarter where I was to meet Guillaume than I was struck by that abrupt transformation inside me, the one that my senses accepted so smoothly. I shook off all the remaining vestiges of noise, crowds, and an almost complete absence of individuality—all to be found in the popular quarter where I live—and plunged into another world, one of quiet and space, no noise, space between people, buildings, and things, the kind of vast, scary silence that arouses your curiosity to find out what's going on behind those high walls and double-glazed windows.

As I walked along the sidewalk, all I could hear was the sound of my own footsteps and the swish of passing limousines as their tires rolled across the asphalt. Meanwhile, the fresh faces of people who had spent most of the day working or sleeping were getting ready for nighttime.

But here you will never see young men leaning their backs against the low walls in case they collapse, while they take turns smoking their way through a shared cigarette; or women sharing gossip the way cats do, with a ball of wool; or even narrow, winding passages where bodies unintentionally bump into each other as they pass by.

No, all you'll see around here is an aged gardener carefully tending and watering the flowers at a villa, a maidservant opening the trunk of a car and carrying provisions into the kitchen by a back door, or a house guard alert and ready to perform any tasks demanded by the people living there.

Guillaume had done well for himself by renting an apartment in this particular area. People here do not usually poke their noses into other people's business. Provided that you take precautions and don't go overboard, you can do pretty much anything you want. Even so, every time I'd come to visit Guillaume, I'd feel beset by worry and concern. Experience has taught me to stay on my guard. Sometimes you may get the impression that the police are not interested or ignoring you completely, whereas in reality the noose is gradually tightening. That's why I'm being more and more cautious; I watched every single step I took before following it with the next one.

Upon reaching Guillaume's apartment complex, I texted him to open the door and leave it ajar, a precaution that we had always taken. Pushing the door open, I snuck inside. The whole place had a wonderful quiet about it. A soft aura of music pervaded the lounge, just like the floral scent that filled the space. At that moment I had a prickly sensation, a feeling of regret that I had decided to come. However, it vanished as quickly as it had first manifested itself. I could hear Guillaume humming to himself in the bedroom and realized that he was setting the mood. He was waiting contentedly, just like a baby about to get a present. Once he realized that I was there, he rushed over and gave me a big, nervous kiss that revealed the extent of his passionate love. We sat there in the lounge for a while and drank a cold beer to celebrate our reacquaintance, but then sheer desire pulled us toward the bedroom.

For some reason, I grew tense and fidgety on the bed, but I did my best to put things right and not spoil our reunion, not only because Guillaume was so good, but also because I was completely broke—I urgently needed the hundred euros he had promised me. At the end of our sessions together, Guillaume would always feel jubilant. When he felt that happy he would become incredibly generous as well; that hundred euros could turn into 120 or even a bit more.

Guillaume let out a long sigh and bellowed like a slaughtered ox. His huge body was taking up most of the bed, and he looked totally satisfied as he let it cool off. For a while we both lay spread-eagle side by side on the bed. He rested his head on my chest and I started using my fingers to play with the abundant hair on his chest, the way he liked me to do. Then I went back to the lounge while he stayed in the bedroom.

After making love, Guillaume liked to be left on his own; at that point he felt a kind of momentary depression. He spread his body out on the space between the bed and the large wardrobe that occupied the entire wall.

Guillaume was an extremely stylish man; he kept an impeccable collection of suits and shoes. Extending his back to the edge of the bed and stretching his feet to the front of the wardrobe, he leaned back and slowly smoked a cigarette before heading for the bathroom and surrendering his body once again to the seductive temptation of water.

I lay out on one of the benches in the lounge, listening to the hiss of the water from the bathroom. If I were in a better mood, Guillaume would invite me to share the shower with him. We would repeat the same game there, relishing the feel of the water as we had done several times before. But today he had noticed that I was a bit on edge, so he made do on his own.

Guillaume was a good person who worshipped money because it could make all roads lead somewhere; as he often told me with a wink, he could open all doors, and windows as well. But he worshipped the body even more, especially if it was male, hairy, and of a light-brown color.

My acquaintance with Guillaume was a genuine gift. When I first met him I was just emerging from a grim and rough experience with another Frenchman—old and skinny, a real miser. Every time I thought back to him, I couldn't help laughing and feeling sorry for him. It took him forever to emerge from the airport that first day. Just as I was about to leave, the arrival gate spat out yet another traveler, walking slowly and dragging a ridiculous antique suitcase behind him. He looked totally oblivious to his surroundings, like someone who had lost his way. I was the only person still waiting and he moved in my direction, staring hard at the sign I was holding and audibly sounding out the name written on it. With that, his features relaxed a bit, and he came rushing over like an aged penguin that had fallen behind its colony. In the photograph that he had sent beforehand, he still possessed a vestige of his youthful glow, but the man now standing in front of me extended a leathery hand, veined and marked with blotches.

After swallowing this bitter pill, I decided to exploit this old man and fleece him for all he was worth. But he proved to be an intolerable skinflint, only ever putting his hand inside his wallet under duress. For three whole days I put up with him, like a sack of garbage that weighed me down, but eventually I got rid of him with no regrets.

He was really ugly. When he was naked, he resembled a snail without its shell. He tried long and hard to arouse in that old body of his a desire that had died ages ago. Eventually, I discovered that what he really needed was someone of the same sex to sit with him, stay with him at the dinner table, and sleep alongside him in the same bed, only touching each other occasionally. In the best of circumstances all we did was exchange frantic kisses which tasted like dust.

You poor old man, dragging your feeble body and sallow spirit around and traveling so far to get here; and then only to strip naked in front of me! He was shivering from old age more than he was from passion, uttering fake, pleading sighs, and then going back the way he had come.

"Till next time!" he told me as he waved goodbye at the airport. He was smiling happily, as though he had successfully completed an important project. And with that he went on his way, dragging his silly suitcase behind him. As I watched him disappear slowly into the distance, I could only think again of the lost penguin. I laughed.

Guillaume emerged from the shower a totally different person, revived and smiling as though his soul had taken a shower with him. Rubbing his thick gray hair around the temples with a towel, he came toward me and stretched out his neck to give me a kiss. Once again, I was struck by how disgusted I was by his eyes; their green coloring made me nauseous. It was only with difficulty that I stopped myself from pushing him away. After he kissed me, I closed my eyes, not because I was thrilled, but because I could not stand having that same glance so close to me.

Ever since I first glimpsed those eyes, I had loathed their soft, limpid green. For ages, I've had an overwhelming desire to plunge into their depths, fathom their secret, and then relax. But I could never look at them for very long. More than once I found myself staring at him intently, but without even meaning to do so. On one occasion, Guillaume snapped, "Stop staring at me like that. You're making me nervous!"

I watched as he went into the bedroom. At precisely that moment, and without any prior intention or clear motive, I found myself heading for the kitchen. My right hand was shaking as I went over to the drawer to take out a large knife with a wooden handle. No sooner had I clasped the knife and taken a look at its sharp blade than my hand stopped shaking. As my feet guided me toward the bedroom, my outstretched hands went ahead of me. I didn't even see Guillaume in front of me, only those hateful green eyes with their sleazy look.

He was standing by the table, rummaging through a box. I approached him cautiously. When I drew close, he became aware of my presence and turned toward me. It was then that I stabbed him with a violent thrust—it was both treacherous and utterly unexpected. Guillaume reeled, let out a loud cry of pain, and put his hand over the gushing wound. After that, I couldn't remember the details exactly. All I came up with were a few fragmentary images—pictures and sounds intermingled, as though I were dreaming or delirious with fever.

Once I recovered consciousness and found myself squatting over Guillaume's motionless body, I wept bitterly, scarcely believing that I had actually killed him, and wondering to myself how I had managed to do it—me, the feeble coward! My hands were stained with his blood and shaking wildly, while the bloodied knife lay close to the body, its task complete.

Blood everywhere—on my hands and shirt, on the floor, on the pajamas that were almost completely off Guillaume's body. Once I realized exactly what had happened, I nearly died as well. For a moment my heart stopped beating. My mind packed up, and all my senses went numb, but then a flood of images and sounds came surging back to the surface of my consciousness like a roaring river. I heard Guillaume screaming in pain; I saw him collide with the wardrobe and stagger around after that first treacherous thrust. He tried to fight back, falling down, then staggering to his feet again. Eventually he collapsed, and his hulking body lay still in the space between the bed and wardrobe. On his pursed lips was the burning question: *Why?* All at once I felt a terrible pain over my entire body. Not knowing which of my limbs to check to see if I was hurt, I found it extremely difficult to bend over. At least two ribs must be broken, and I could not see out of my left eye; the whole thing was completely swollen, and it felt as huge as a zucchini. Guillaume had obviously put up a fierce fight, but his efforts had come too late.

The bedsheets had fallen to the floor and were spattered with dark-red blood, our moments of pleasure now a distant memory. The small suitcase was open, having fallen near the table; its contents were scattered at the foot of the bed: a plastic dildo, lube, and bottles of oils. Guillaume had had no time to arrange them all carefully as he usually did before putting them back in the suitcase and shoving it all deep inside the wardrobe like hidden treasure.

Oh, my dear Guillaume, how I'm going to miss you! In fact, I was only a hundred extra euros away, or slightly more, from actually loving you. That's why I really can't answer that burning question which you yourself were unable to put into words, and which stayed on your lips like an extra Adam's apple: *Why?* Yes indeed, I too don't know why I killed you. I have no idea where I got the power and courage to pick up that dreadful knife and thrust it into your hulking body, still fresh from the shower.

True enough, my dear, you're dead now. There's no way I can bring you back to life. But I owe it to you to at least respond to that last unanswered question of yours. I have the feeling that your spirit is going to linger around here, refusing to leave until it knows what particular curse made me pierce your body. Maybe then it will be able to relax a little before turning away to meet its maker.

I'll not conceal from you, my dear, that, like anyone who finds himself suddenly involved in a murder, I thought of getting away and leaving the place as quickly as possible; either that or throwing myself out the window as a means of escape. But I couldn't do it. My entire body was shattered; it was covered in welts and bruises. The very thought of moving was extremely painful. At the same time, I decided not to leave this place because I needed to understand.

What do you say, my dear, to us having a chat while we're waiting?

I'm well aware that you disliked delving into personal matters; you always kept a veil of secrecy over your personal life. I realize that and understand your motives. I also admit that you never tried to get me to reveal any details about my own life. But who were you really, Guillaume?

Were you a sexual idealist, someone who subsumed all life's pleasures in those of the body? Or maybe you were married and lived a perfectly pleasant life on the other side of the Mediterranean. Once in a while you managed to smuggle out a small part of your family budget and come over here or to other spots across the globe. There you could spend lavishly on your passion before returning to your life as a straight man who loved women, someone who worked hard and waited for the weekend so that he could relax a bit and enjoy a drink with friends.

What harm will it do, Guillaume, if we talk frankly about this final encounter of ours?

Personally, I suddenly have a burning desire to tell you a bit about myself. So, will you listen to me, my dear? You are under no obligation to reciprocate. I won't take long because the police will arrive at any moment; that will terminate all possibilities of such frankness and put an end to all this suffering. By now the stench of death has probably permeated the entire building through the gaps in the doors and windows; it has probably reached all the public spaces. At this point, I can almost see the crowds gathered by the entrance and in the interior courtyard, all of them struck by the electric lightning of curiosity and indulging in all kinds of gossip until the police get here.

Long ago, when I was just a child, I had no interest in rolling a soccer ball around in the dust or clambering up palm trees in the wilderness outside the city to pick dates. My feet much preferred to play hopscotch or jump rope with the girls in the humid alleyways. When I got involved in typical boy fights, with a good deal of insults and even punching, my voice always let me down. When I yelled at my enemy and really needed to sound vicious and harsh to compensate for my puny stature, it always came out lame and meek; it was as though I wanted to flirt with my enemy, not beat him up!

My father sold cigarettes and was permanently drunk. He only emerged from prison in order to bash in someone's head or get arrested for selling his foul hashish to other poor addicts. Then he would return to his favorite spot outside the city walls. My mother made good use of his absences to liberate herself from his violent behavior. She even managed to forget the pain that his cowardly fist would inflict when he drunkenly left terrible bruises on her stomach. Forgetting about me was not something that caused her the slightest distress or hardship. That explains how the proprietor of the games hall in our quarter had no trouble gradually bringing me into his open arms. He kept me a prisoner inside the dark hall when he first groped me in the quiet of that afternoon that I have never forgotten. Once he'd had enough, he pointed a knife at me, with the blade shining straight into my eyes. Rubbing the point slowly over my face, he used his other hand to grab my cheek and plant on it the final kiss. Then he invited me to come and play whenever I wanted, and without charge.

He was a bit weird and kept himself apart from the others in the area. He disappeared soon after my childhood was over—a taciturn old man who spent all day in the games hall, which was always packed with unemployed men and children cutting school. He used to sit by the door, smoking and sipping cups of tea. Once in a while he would disappear inside with a group of young men; they would smoke some hashish and get drunk on wine. But I still remember . . . oh, the sheer horror of it, my dear! Can you even begin to imagine? That man, the one from my childhood, who fiddled with my young body to his heart's content. It went on that whole summer inside the hall. And he had green eyes too.

Those eyes were sultry and slimy green. I could hardly bear to look at them. Whenever our gazes met, I immediately looked at the floor and kept my head down; I had a strange feeling, a mixture of shame, surrender, and other feelings I did not understand. My own footsteps led me inexorably toward him because I was mostly on my own and had no idea what to do with my spare time. With just a brief gesture from those green eyes, I would slink inside the hall.

Dear Guillaume, let me adjust your position a bit; I would like to rest your head on my knees. My, my, how heavy you are! I would like to have you as close to me as possible so I can whisper some last words to you.

Please, Guillaume, don't head into the void with that sarcastic look on your face. That's what you always used to do in responding to my stupid questions or justifying your opinions. Don't do that when I tell you that the reason I killed you was those green eyes. Don't scoff like that—I think it's true.

Your eyes! It is only now that I can carefully examine them as much as I like, without bothering you or having you stare at me with that syrupy look. But now their light has gone out. That green color has now turned into something dead. The gleam of life has left them; their pupils have faded away as though they were made of plastic.

Do you realize, dear Guillaume? I was thinking back to the moment of our very first meeting near the Cinema Mabrouka. I could see your huge hairy fingers reaching up to your sunglasses and preparing to take them off. A smiling acknowledgment of our agreement was lighting up your face, but then you changed your mind and kept them on. At this point, I was telling myself that if you had actually taken them off, your misty eyes with their nasty green color would have repelled me, and I would have refused to be with you. I would not have assumed this heavy burden that will keep weighing me down like an ugly hump for as long as I live.

Just imagine, dear Guillaume, a normal, trivial movement, repeated thousands of times a day. You could have made my fate completely different. I could still be trawling on the edges of Jemaa el-Fnaa and walking the streets in Gueliz, picking up customers rather than simply getting old and letting my bones freeze inside the walls of the Boulmharez Prison. And most likely you would still be enjoying life, pursuing your hankering for hairy brown bodies. Eventually somebody else would kill you, but this time for an obvious and unambiguous reason; either that, or the police would surprise you and put an end to your passions.

My dear, I can fully understand the panic you must have felt when we met for the first time. There you were, with your powerful, athletic figure chasing after my own puny brown body that was strutting along, putting everything on display. You were walking along like any normal tourist who had come to expose his body to the Marrakech sun and his spirits to its delights, but I was exposing you and making your inclinations public. At the time you must have thought people were watching you, and that made you anxious. When we entered a dark alley opposite the post office and I spoke to you, I could tell how worried you really were; beads of sweat were glistening on your forehead. You had heard the comments hurled at us like invisible rocks from passersby, beggars, and shopkeepers standing by the doors of their stores. Those things no longer bother me, but you did not understand a word they were saying.

As soon as I spotted you that very first time, walking along the side of the square with a huge camera over your shoulder, I could easily guess what kind of pleasure you had in mind. There was no need for us to even look at each other—the smile you gave me managed to combine lust with something like fear. No, as soon as I saw you sauntering around, anxious, alone, and without a woman, hiding behind your huge sunglasses, I knew exactly what you wanted. I was certain that women did not interest you. With that, I hurried over to you before someone else snatched you away first.

It looks like I'm getting a Dutch or German customer, I told myself, as I hurried toward you and took in your enormous manicured body. It was then that I realized you were another Frenchman, but different.

Oh my dear! I'm exhausted and sad. I need to rest. If only I could get a bit of sleep, but my eyelids keep resisting and refuse to stay closed. And you, my dear Guillaume, aren't you exhausted as well? There you were from the very start, lying on your back and leaning slightly to the right. Now that you're dead, perhaps you really want me to help change your position, but I too am unable to move.

How long have you stayed like this, my dear Guillaume? An hour or less, a day and night, forever?

Beyond the window, lights are shining in the neighboring apartments, shadows come and go, and television screens gleam and dance. Other bodies might well be making love as though there were no corpse in this apartment, a murdered man and his murderer . . .

I can hear a scary noise in the building. Let's listen for a bit.

At last—the police seem to have arrived. I can hear their voices bouncing off the walls, magnified as though through loudspeakers. There was the sound of their footsteps coming cautiously up the stairs. By now they're clearer and louder. They bang on the door for some time, but I can't get up to open it. They'll knock it down. They'll still find everything in place: the murdered man, his murderer, and the weapon. They'll face an extremely simple problem, one that won't require any real effort to investigate.

They're right by the door now. At first, they knock quite normally, just like any guest or neighbor. But after some tense moments of silence, the knocks get louder and more insistent. Then they start fiddling with the lock; it looks as though it won't hold out for long.

Now here they are, pushing the door down. That causes a

ringing in my ears. I've gradually gotten used to it, and now it goes on and on, like the music of finality.

As though on a bright, flickering television screen, I picture myself as an old man, back bent over, gray hairs invading my temples, walking along the wall of the Boulmharez Prison on a steaming-hot Marrakech day. An ailing spirit lingers inside this man, and he drags an exhausted body around, no longer recalling how to walk on ground that was not bounded by walls or stifled by roofs.

Cautiously, the cops move toward the bedroom. Their highly trained senses tense at the stench of murder that pervades the entire apartment. And now they are using their bodies to block the entrance to the room.

My dear Guillaume, if only your eyes hadn't been green—if only they hadn't been green!

Translated from Arabic by Roger Allen

ABOUT THE CONTRIBUTORS

Halima Zine El Abidine was born in Marrakech in 1954 and has published five novels: *Obsession of the Return* (1999), *Citadels of Silence* (2005), *On the Wall* (2012), *The Dream Is Mine* (2013), and *It Wasn't a Desert* (2017). She has also written three plays: *Who Is in Charge* (1987), *The History of Women* (2003), and *Hnia* (2004).

Mohamed Achaari was born in 1951 in Moulay Driss Zerhoun. He has published a collection of short stories, eleven poetry books, and three novels. After being jailed for his political activities, he went on to serve in a variety of government posts, including as Minister of Culture between 1998–2007. He has twice been elected president of the Union of Moroccan Writers, serving from 1989–1996. He was the joint winner of the 2011 Arabic Booker Prize for his second novel, *The Arch and the Butterfly*.

Ahmed Ben Ismail

Taha Adnan grew up in Marrakech and has lived in Brussels since 1996. He works at the Ministry for Francophone Education. A poet and writer, he directed the Brussels Arabic Literary Salon in Belgium. His poetry collections and plays have been translated into French, Spanish, and Italian, and published internationally. Two anthologies he edited, *Brussels the Moroccan* (2015) and *This Is Not a Suitcase* (2017), were published in French in Casablanca.

Ahmed Ben Ismail

Yassin Adnan was born in 1970 in Safi and grew up in Marrakech, where he still lives. He is best known today for his weekly cultural program *Macharif* on Moroccan television. He has published ten works—including four books of poetry, three short story collections, and two books about Marrakech: *Marrakech: Open Secrets* and *Marrakech: Vanishing Places*. His novel *Hot Maroc*, which also takes place in Marrakech, was nominated for the International Prize for Arabic Fiction.

Lahcen Bakour was born in Mtougga in the countryside near Marrakech in 1977. He works as a civil servant, and is a short story writer and novelist. He has published three works: a collection of short stories, *Man of Chairs*, in 2008, and the novels *Isthmus* (2012) and *The Last Dance* (2017). He has received two literary prizes in Dubai and Sharjah in the United Arab Emirates.

C. Toala

ABDELKADER BENALI is a Moroccan-Dutch writer who was born in 1975 in Morocco and moved to Rotterdam when he was four years old. Benali published his first novel, *Wedding by the Sea*, in 1996; it received the Geertjan Lubberhuizen Prize. For his second novel, *The Long-Awaited* (2002), Benali was awarded the Libris Literature Prize. He has since published the novels *Let Tomorrow Be Fine* (2005) and *Feldman and I* (2006).

Ahmed Ben Ismail

MAHI BINEBINE was born in 1959 in Marrakech and moved to Paris in 1980 to continue his studies in mathematics, which he later taught for eight years. He then devoted himself to writing and painting. His novels, which have been translated into a dozen languages, include *Le Sommeil de l'esclave, Les Funérailles du lait, L'Ombre du poète, Welcome to Paradise, Pollens, Terre d'ombre brûlée, Le Griot de Marrakech*, and *Horses of God*. His paintings are a part of the permanent collection at the Guggenheim Museum.

ALLAL BOURQIA was born in Tangier in 1963 and lives in Brussels. His first novel, *Pure Eternity*, was published by Dar Elain in Cairo in 2010. His second novel, *Death of the Flamenco Dancer*, will be released soon with the same publisher. He contributed to *Brussels the Moroccan* (2015) and *This Is Not a Suitcase* (2017), two anthologies that were published in French in Casablanca.

HANANE DERKAOUI was born in 1971 and has degrees in the history of philosophy and philosophy. She taught philosophy in Marrakech, and she currently lives in the south of France. She has published several novels and collections of short stories, including *White Birds, A Girl from Rabat, A Bad Life*, and *The Beautiful Ladies' Bridge*.

P. Matsas

FOUAD LAROUI was born in Oujda in 1958. An engineer and economist, he now teaches French literature in Amsterdam. He is the author of ten novels, including *Les Tribulations du dernier Sijilmassi*, which was awarded the 2014 Prix Jean Giono. He has also published several collections of short stories, including *L'Étrange affaire du pantalon de Dassoukine*, which won the Prix Goncourt in 2013. Laroui received the Great Medal of the Francophonie of the Académie française in 2014.

Zolikha Arif

Fatiha Morchid is a poet and novelist. She is a pediatrician by profession and presented a health care education program on the Moroccan TV channel 2M, along with a poetry show on the same station. She has published eight books of poetry. The latest is *Unspoken*, which received the Morocco Poetry Prize. Her novels include *Just a Few Moments*, *Fun's Claws*, *The Muses*, *The Right to Leave*, and, most recently, *The Twins*. *As Love Is Not Enough* is her first collection of short stories.

Karima Nadir was born in Marrakech in 1987 and began writing poetry at the age of fourteen. She studied French literature at Hassan II University and translates poetry in addition to writing her own. She works as a freelance journalist. For the last two years, she has lived between Tunis and Casablanca, working as a consultant for international NGOs and projects to fund development and democracy-building.

Ahmed Ben Ismail

Mohamed Nedali was born in Tahannaout, near Marrakech, in 1962. He was educated in Marrakech and at Nancy 2 University in France. From 1985 to 2016, he taught high school French before devoting himself to writing. The author of seven novels, his debut, *Morceaux de choix: les amours d'un apprenti boucher,* won the 2005 Grand Atlas Prize, and in 2009 the International Prize of the Novel of Diversity at the Festival of Cartagena in Spain. In 2012, his novel *Triste jeunesse* won the Mamounia Literary Prize.

Ahmed Ben Ismail

My Seddik Rabbaj was born in Marrakech in 1967; he still lives there and teaches French at a high school. Rabbaj writes in French and has published his novels in Paris, including: *Inch'Allah* (2006), *L'École des sables* (2008), *Le lutteur*, (2015), and *Nos parents nous blessent avant de mourir* (2018). His novel *Siucidaire en sursis* appeared in Morocco in 2013. Rabbaj's forthcoming book is a collection of short stories about his neighborhood: *Une Petite vie à Sidi Youssef Ben Ali.*

Said Gougaz

Mohamed Zouhair was born in Marrakech in 1951. He teaches modern literature and is a member of the Union of Moroccan Writers. His stories and essays have been published both in Morocco and internationally. Zouhair is also a playwright and a theater critic. His plays include *The Call*, which was published in 2013. His collection of short stories, *Voices That I Haven't Heard*, received the Morocco Fiction Prize in 2011.